IMPERIUM

KEITH LAUMER
Edited by ERIC FLINT

IMPERIUM

Copyright © 2005 estate of Keith Laumer. *Worlds of the Imperium* copyright © 1961 by Keith Laumer, first serialized in *Fantastic Stories*, February–April 1961, then released as a novel in an Ace Double Book edition in 1962. *The Other Side of Time* copyright © 1965 by Keith Laumer, first serialized in *Fantastic*, April–June 1965, then released as a novel by Berkley in 1965. *Assignment in Nowhere* copyright © 1968 by Keith Laumer, first published by Berkley.

A Baen Book

Baen Publishing Enterprises
P.O. Box 1403
Riverdale, NY 10471
www.baen.com

ISBN: 978-1-4516-3795-3

Cover art by David Mattingly

First paperback printing, August 2012

Library of Congress Control Number: 2005001011

Distributed by Simon & Schuster
1230 Avenue of the Americas
New York, NY 10020

Pages by Joy Freeman (www.pagesbyjoy.com)
Printed in the United States of America

CONTENTS

IMPERIUM

"This Is Where I Came In"
Preface by Harry Turtledove

Worlds of the Imperium and its first sequel, *The Other Side of Time,* were some of the alternate history I read in the early 1960s—along with *Lest Darkness Fall* and *The Man in the High Castle*—that helped me discover the subgenre. *Assignment in Nowhere,* set in the same multiverse, came along a little later, and isn't a direct sequel to the first two: their protagonist, Brion Bayard, is a bit player in a drama that doesn't center on him.

I think H. Beam Piper, in his Paratime stories, was the first writer to show the vehicle that transported his characters from one timeline to another. Keith Laumer was the first, and I think still the only, writer to show you the Model-T version of a shuttle between timelines. His genius was to make this a nineteenth-century discovery by a pair of Italian scientists, Maxoni and Cocini. Anybody can do it. If you do it close to right, you can go from one alternate world to another on a wing and a prayer. But if you do it wrong...

1

look out! There are uncounted timelines where they did it wrong, and trashed the planet with the energies they unwittingly unleashed. Oops!

In the midst of this Blight of ravaged alternate histories lies *the* world of the Imperium, where they did it right, and which has a tidy little trading empire with worlds far enough removed in probability never to have tried traveling between timelines at all. There is our world, where Maxoni and Cocini apparently never experimented, and there are a couple of others. Brion Bayard is kidnapped from our timeline by the Imperium to help solve a nasty problem stemming from one of those other worlds in the middle of the Blight.

Laumer was clever enough to see that a timeline which discovered a technology for traveling sidewise in time (to steal a title from Murray Leinster) would concentrate on that technology and ignore other possibilities. The traders and officers of the Imperium can scoot across the Blight with, if not the greatest of ease, at least relative safety in *Worlds of the Imperium*—but, even in the 1960s, they've never run into nuclear weapons. That's part of the trouble they're facing. The rest gets a lot more complicated: all kinds of toil and trouble for a double.

If anything, *The Other Side of Time* is even more convoluted than its predecessor. It's also much more audacious, and takes in a much broader swath of the multiverse. Turns out the Imperium isn't the only outfit able to go crosstime after all—and the others who can do it aren't human at all. They're the evolved descendants of the hairy hominids that we *Homo saps* exterminated in this sheaf of timelines—and they look down their (flat) noses at us because we did. To add injury to insult, they've been traveling across the timelines longer than the Imperium has, and their shuttles are considerably more sophisticated than anything mere humans can manufacture. Some of them—the Hagroon—have in mind wiping out the Imperium's timeline altogether, and doing it retroactively so the line was never there at all. Others don't approve of this, which still doesn't mean they have any particular use for people as we know them. Figuring out who's doing what to whom, and why (and staying alive in the process, which ain't easy), is Brion Bayard's task here. He pulls it off with panache, and considerably complicates anthropologists' lives on quite a few timelines.

In *Assignment in Nowhere*, Laumer's headlong narrative drive—always one of the strongest features of his writing—almost gets out of control. Johnny Curlon is a man from our timeline taken by the Imperium to help mend a probability storm heading out of the Blight that threatens all the surviving lines within it. He is also, it turns out, the last surviving scion of the great Plantagenet family, a distant relative of Richard the Lion-Hearted, which was of great importance in the worldlines destroyed by the Blight. He is both aided and opposed by Baron General van Roosevelt, Acting Chief of Imperial Intelligence. How and why did Plantagenets and Roosevelts get to know each other across the timelines? What connection is there between this van Roosevelt and the Roosevelts of our world? The proof is left for the student, as geometry texts used to say; Laumer never explains. But even though the underpinnings may be shaky, the story never flags, and you'll keep turning pages from first to last.

Taken all together, these three novels can't add up to more than 140,000 words: only a medium-sized book by today's standards. But Laumer puts enough interesting ideas in them for not just three but six or eight modern doorstoppers. And he doesn't stint on characterization or dry wit, either. I had an enormous amount of fun rereading these for this introduction. If you've been around a while and run into them before, you'll enjoy them again, too. And if this is your introduction to Keith Laumer's work—well, hold on to your hat, because it's quite a ride.

WORLDS OF THE IMPERIUM

I

I STOPPED IN FRONT of a shop with a small wooden sign which hung from a wrought-iron spear projecting from the weathered stone wall. On it the word ANTIKVARIAT was lettered in spidery gold against dull black, and it creaked as it swung in the night wind. Below it a metal grating covered a dusty window with a display of yellowed etchings, woodcuts, and lithographs, and a faded mezzotint. Some of the buildings in the pictures looked familiar, but here they stood in open fields, or perched on hills overlooking a harbor crowded with sails. The ladies in the pictures wore great bell-like skirts and bonnets with ribbons, and carried tiny parasols, while dainty-footed horses pranced before carriages in the background.

It wasn't the prints that interested me though, or even the heavy gilt frame embracing a tarnished mirror at one side; it was the man whose reflection I studied in the yellowed glass, a dark man wearing a tightly-belted grey trench-coat that was six inches too long. He stood

7

with his hands thrust deep in his pockets and stared into a darkened window fifty feet from me.

He had been following me all day.

At first I thought it was coincidence when I first noticed the man on the bus from Bromma, then studying theatre announcements in the hotel lobby while I registered, and half an hour later sitting three tables away sipping coffee while I ate a hearty dinner.

I had discarded that theory a long time ago. Five hours had passed and he was still with me as I walked through the Old Town, medieval Stockholm still preserved on an island in the middle of the city. I had walked past shabby windows crammed with copper pots, ornate silver, dueling pistols, and worn cavalry sabres; very quaint in the afternoon sun, but grim reminders of a ruder day of violence after midnight. Over the echo of my footsteps in the silent narrow streets the other steps came quietly behind, hurrying when I hurried, stopping when I stopped. Now the man stared into the dark window and waited, the next move was up to me.

I was lost. Twenty years is a long time to remember the tortuous turnings of the streets of the Old Town. I took my guide book from my pocket and turned to the map in the back. My fingers were clumsy.

I craned my neck up at the stone tablet set in the corner of the building; it was barely legible: Köpmangatan. I found the name on the folding map and saw that it ran for three short blocks, ending at Stortorget; a dead end. In the dim light it was difficult to see the fine detail on the map; I twisted the book around and got a clearer view; there appeared to be another tiny street, marked with crosslines, and labeled

Skeppar Olofs gränd. I tried to remember my Swedish; *gränd* meant alley. Skeppar Olof's Alley, running from Köpmangatan to Trädgårdsgatan, another tiny street. It seemed to lead to the lighted area near the palace; it looked like my only route out. I dropped the book back into my pocket and moved off casually toward the Alley of Skeppar Olof. I hoped there was no gate across the entrance.

My shadow waited a moment, then followed. Slowly as I was ambling, I gained a little on him. He seemed in no hurry at all. I passed more tiny shops, with ironbound doors and worn stone sills, and then saw that the next doorway was an open arch. I paused idly, then turned in. Once past the portal, I bounded up the alley at top speed. Six strides, eight, and I was at the end and darting to the left toward a deep doorway. There was just a chance I'd cleared the alley before the dark man had reached the entrance. I stood and listened. I heard the scrape of shoes, then heavy breathing from the direction of the alley a few feet away. I waited, breathing with my mouth wide open, trying not to pant audibly. After a moment the steps moved away. The proper move for my silent companion would be to cast about quickly for my hiding place, on the assumption that I had concealed myself close by. He would be back this way soon.

I risked a glance. He was moving quickly along, looking sharply about, with his back to me. I pulled off my shoes and without taking time to think about it, stepped out. I made it to the alley in three paces, and hurried out of sight as the man stopped to turn back. I was halfway down when my foot hit a loose stone, and I flew the rest of the way.

I hit the cobblestones shoulder first, and followed up with my head. I rolled over and scrambled to my feet, my head ringing. I clung to the wall by the foot of the alley as the pain started. Now I was getting mad, and to hell with strategy. I heard the soft-shod feet coming, and gathered myself to jump him as he came out. The footsteps hesitated just before the arch, then the dark round head with the uncut hair peeped out. I swung a haymaker—and missed. He darted into the street and turned, fumbling in his overcoat. I assumed he was trying to get a gun, and aimed a kick at his mid-section. I had better luck this time; I connected solidly, and had the satisfaction of hearing him gasp in agony. I hoped he hurt as bad as I did. Whatever he was fumbling for came free then, and he backed away, holding the thing to his mouth.

"One-oh-nine, where in bloody blazes are you?" he said in a harsh voice, glaring at me. He had an odd accent. I realized the thing was some sort of microphone. "Come in, one-oh-nine, this job's going to pieces..." He backed away, talking, eyes on me. I leaned against the wall; I hurt too bad to be very aggressive. There was no one else in sight. His soft shoes made whispering sounds on the paving stones. Mine lay in the middle of the street where I had dropped them when I fell.

Then there was a sound behind me. I whirled, and saw the narrow street almost blocked by a huge van. I let my breath out with a sigh of relief. Here was help...

Two men jumped down from the cab, and without hesitation stepped up to me, took my arms and escorted me toward the rear of the van. They wore tight white uniforms, and said nothing.

"I'm all right," I said. "Grab that man..." About that time I realized he was following along, talking excitedly to the man in white, and that the grip on my arms was more of a restraint than a support. I dug in my heels and tried to pull away. I remembered suddenly that the Stockholm police don't wear white uniforms.

I might as well not have bothered. One of them unclipped a thing like a tiny aerosol bomb from his belt and sprayed it in my face. I felt myself go limp. I was still conscious, but my feet dragged as they hauled me around to the back of the van, up a ramp, pushed me into a chair. I was dimly aware of the ramp being pulled in, the doors closing. I was fading but not yet out; I shouted after them, but they didn't answer. I heard more clicks and the sounds of things being moved; then the purr of an engine. There was a sensation of motion, very smooth, nothing more. I tried to yell, gave it up. I gathered my strength and tried to get out of the chair; I couldn't make it. It was too hard to keep my eyes open. My last thought as consciousness left me was that they could have killed me there in the deserted street as easily as they had kidnapped me.

II

THERE WAS A SCRATCHING sound which irritated me. I tried unsuccessfully to weave it into a couple of dreams before my subconscious gave up. I was lying on my back, eyes closed; I couldn't think where I was. I remembered a frightening dream about being followed, and then as I became aware of pain in my shoulder and head, my eyes snapped open. I was lying on a cot at the side of a small office; the scratching came from the desk where a dapper man in a white uniform sat writing. There was a humming sound and a feeling of motion.

I sat up. At once the man behind the desk looked up, rose, and walked over to me. He drew up a chair and sat down.

"Please don't be alarmed," he said in a clipped British accent. "I am Chief Captain Winter. You need merely assist in giving me some routine information, after which you will be assigned comfortable quarters." He said all this in a smooth lifeless way, as though he'd been through it before. Then he looked directly at me for the first time.

"I must apologize for the callousness with which you were handled; it was not my intention.... However," his tone changed, "you must excuse the operative; he was uninformed."

Chief Captain Winter opened a notebook and lolled back in his chair with pencil poised. "Where were you born, Mr. Bayard?"

They must have been through my pockets, I thought; they know my name.

"Who the hell are you?" I said.

The Chief Captain raised an eyebrow. His uniform was immaculate, and brilliantly jeweled decorations sparkled on his chest.

"Of course you are confused at this moment, Mr. Bayard, but everything will be explained to you carefully in due course. I am an Imperial Officer, duly authorized to interrogate subjects under detention." He smiled smoothly. "Now please state your birthplace."

I said nothing. I didn't feel like answering any questions; I had too many of my own to ask first. I couldn't place the fellow's accent; this bothered me because the study of dialects and accents had been a hobby of mine for a long time. He was an Englishman, but I couldn't have said from what part of England. I glanced at the medals. Most of them were strange, but I recognized the scarlet ribbon of the Victoria Cross, with three palms, ornamented with gems. There was something extremely phony about Chief Captain Winter.

"Come along now, old chap," Winter said sharply. "Kindly cooperate. It will save a great deal of unpleasantness."

I looked at him grimly. "I find being chased, grabbed, gassed, stuffed in a cell, and quizzed about my personal life pretty damned unpleasant already, so don't bother trying to keep it all on a high plane. I'm not answering any questions." I reached in my pocket for my passport; it wasn't there.

"Since you've already stolen my passport, you know by now that I'm an American diplomat, and enjoy diplomatic immunity to any form of arrest, detention, interrogation and what have you. So I'm leaving as soon as you return my property, including my shoes."

Winter's face had stiffened up. I could see my act hadn't had much impression on him. He signaled, and two fellows I hadn't seen before moved around into view. They were bigger than he was.

"Mr. Bayard, you must answer my questions; under duress, if necessary. Kindly begin by stating your birthplace."

"You'll find it in my passport," I said. I was looking at the two reinforcements; they were as easy to ignore as a couple of bulldozers in the living room. I decided on a change of tactics. I'd play along in the hope they'd relax a bit, and then make a break for it.

One of the men, at a signal, handed Winter my passport from his desk. He glanced through it, made a number of notes, and passed the booklet back to me.

"Thank you, Mr. Bayard," he said pleasantly. "Now let's get on to particulars. Where did you attend school?"

I tried hard now to give the impression of one eager to please. I regretted my earlier truculence; it made my present pose of cooperativeness a little less plausible. Winter must have been accustomed to the job though, and to subjects who were abject. After a few minutes he waved an arm at the two bouncers, who left the room silently.

Winter had gotten on to the subject of international relations and geopolitics now, and seemed to be fascinated by my commonplace replies. I attempted once or twice to ask why it was necessary to quiz me closely on matters of general information, but was firmly guided back to the answering of questions.

He covered geography and recent history thoroughly with emphasis on the period 1879-1910, and then started in on a biographic list; all I knew about one name after another. Most of them I'd never heard of; a few were minor public figures. He quizzed me in detail on two Italians, Cocini and Maxoni. He could hardly believe I'd never heard of them. He seemed fascinated by many of my replies.

"Niven an *actor*?" he said incredulously. "Never heard of Crane Talbot?" and when I described Churchill's role in recent affairs, he laughed uproariously.

After forty minutes of this one-sided discussion, a buzzer sounded faintly, and another of the uniformed men entered, placed a good-sized box on the corner of the desk, and left. Winter ignored the interruption.

Another twenty minutes of questions went by. Who was the present monarch (of Anglo-Germany, Winter specified); what was the composition of the royal family, the ages of the children, etc, until I had exhausted my knowledge of the subject. What was the status of the Viceroyalty of India; explain the working of the Dominion arrangements of Australia, North America, Cabotsland...I was appalled at the questions; the author of them must have been insane. It was almost impossible to link the garbled references to non-existent political subdivisions and institutions to reality. I answered as matter-of-factly as possible. At least Winter did not seem to be much disturbed by my revision of his distorted version of affairs.

At last Winter rose, moved over to his desk, and motioned me to a chair beside it. As I pulled the chair out, I glanced into the box on the desk. I saw magazines, folded cloth, coins—and the butt of a small automatic protruding from under a copy of the World Almanac. Winter had turned away, reaching into a small cabinet behind the desk. My hand darted out, scooped up the pistol, and dropped it into my pocket as I seated myself.

Winter turned back with a blue glass bottle. "Now let's have a drop and I'll attempt to clear up some of your quite justifiable confusion, Mr. Bayard," he said genially. "What would you like to know?" I ignored the bottle.

"Where am I?" I said.

"In the city of Stockholm, Sweden."

"We seem to be moving; what is this, a moving van with an office in it?"

"This is a vehicle, though not a moving van."

"Why did you pick me up?"

"I'm sorry that I can tell you no more than that you were brought in under specific orders from a very high-ranking officer of the Imperial Service." He looked at me speculatively. "This was most unusual," he added.

"I take it kidnapping inoffensive persons is not in itself unusual."

Winter frowned. "You are the subject of an official operation of Imperial Intelligence. Please rest assured you are not being persecuted."

"What is Imperial Intelligence?"

"Mr. Bayard," Winter said earnestly, leaning forward, "it will be necessary for you to face a number of realizations; the first is that the governments which you are accustomed to regarding as supreme sovereign powers must in fact be considered tributary to the Imperium, the Paramount Government in whose service I am an officer."

"You're a fake," I said.

Winter bristled. "I hold an Imperial Commission as Chief Captain of Intelligence."

"What do you call this vehicle we're in?"

"This is an armed TNL scout based at Stockholm Zero Zero."

"That tells me a lot; what is it, a boat, car, airplane...?"

"None of those, Mr. Bayard."

"All right, I'll be specific; what does it travel on, water, air...?"

Winter hesitated. "Frankly, I don't know."

I saw it was time to try a new angle of attack. "Where are we going?"

"We are presently operating along coordinates zero-zero-zero, zero-zero-six, zero-ninety-two."

"What is our destination? What place?"

"Stockholm Zero Zero, after which you'll probably be transferred to London Zero Zero for further processing."

"What is this Zero business? Do you mean London, England?"

"The London you refer to is London B-I Three."

"What's the difference?"

"London Zero Zero is the capital of the Imperium,

comprising the major portion of the civilized world; North Europe, West Hemisphere, Australia, etc."

I changed the subject. "Why did you kidnap me?"

"A routine interrogational arrest, insofar as I know."

"Do you intend to release me?"

"Yes."

"At home?"

"No."

"Where?"

"I can't say; at one of several concentration points."

"One more question," I said, easing the automatic from my pocket and pointing it at the third medal from the left. "Do you know what this is?"

Winter shrank back in his chair. "Yes," he said. "Where the devil did you get that?"

"Keep your hands in sight; better get up and stand over there."

Winter rose and moved over to the spot indicated. I'd never aimed a pistol at a man point-blank before, but I felt no hesitation now.

"Tell me all about it," I said.

"I've answered every question," Winter said nervously.

"And told me nothing." Winter stood staring at me.

I slipped the safety off with a click. "You have five seconds to start," I said. "One . . . Two . . ."

"Very well," Winter said. "No need for all this; I'll try." He hesitated. "You were selected from higher up. We went to a great deal of trouble to get you in particular. As I've explained, that's rather irregular. However," Winter seemed to be warming to his subject, "all sampling in this region has been extremely restricted in the past; you see, your continuum occupies an island, one of a very few isolated lines in a vast blighted region. The entire configuration is abnormal, and an extremely dangerous area in which to maneuver. We lost many good men in the early years before we learned how to handle the problems involved."

"I suppose you know this is all nonsense to me," I said. "What do you mean by sampling?"

"Do you mind if I smoke?" Winter said. I took a long brown cigarette from a box on the desk, lit it, and handed it to him. "Sampling refers to the collection of individuals or artifacts from representative B-I lines," he said, blowing out smoke. "We in Intelligence are engaged now in mapping operations. It's fascinating work, old boy, picking up the trend lines, coordinating findings with theoretical work, developing accurate calibrating devices, instruments, et cetera. We're just beginning to discover the potentialities of working the Net. In order to gather the maximum of information in a short time, we've found it expedient to collect individuals for interrogation. In this way we quickly gain a general picture of the configuration of the Net in various 'directions.' In your case, I was directed under sealed orders to enter the Blight, proceed to Blight-Insular Three, and take over custody of Mr. Brion Bayard, a diplomat representing, of all things, an American Republic." Winter spoke enthusiastically now. As he relaxed, he seemed younger.

"It was quite a feather in my cap, old chap, to be selected to conduct an operation in the Blight, and I've found it fascinating. Always in the past, of course, I've operated at such a distance from the Imperium that little or no analogy existed. But B-I Three! Why it's practically the Imperium, with just enough variation to stir the imagination. Close as the two lines are, there's a desert of Blight around and between them that indicates how frightfully close to the rim we've trodden in times past."

"All right, Winter. I've heard enough," I said. "You're just a harmless nut, maybe. But I'll be going now."

"That's quite impossible," Winter said. "We're in the midst of the Blight."

"What's the Blight?" I asked, making conversation as I looked around the room, trying to pick out the best door to leave by. There were three. I decided on the one no one had come through yet. I moved toward it.

"The Blight is a region of utter desolation, radiation, chaos," Winter was saying. "There are whole ranges of A-lines where the very planet no longer exists, where automatic cameras have recorded nothing but a vast ring of debris in orbit; then there are the cinder-worlds, and here and there dismal groups of cancerous jungles, alive with radiation-poisoned mutation. It's frightful, old chap. You can wave the pistol at me all night, but it will get you nothing. In a few hours we'll arrive at Zero Zero; you may as well relax till then."

I tried the door; it was locked. "Where's the key?" I said.

"There's no key. It will open automatically at Base."

I went to one of the other doors, the one the man with the box had entered through. I pulled it open and glanced out. The humming sound was louder and down a short and narrow corridor I saw what appeared to be a pilot's compartment. A man's back was visible.

"Come on, Winter," I said. "Go ahead of me."

"Don't be a complete ass, old boy," Winter said, looking irritated. He turned toward his desk. I raised the pistol, sighted, and fired. The shot boomed inside the walls of the room, and Winter leaped back from the desk holding a ripped hand. He whirled on me, for the first time looking really scared. "You're insane!" he shouted. "I've told you we're in the midst of the Blight."

I was keeping one eye on the man up front, who was looking over his shoulder while frantically doing something with his other hand.

"You're leaking all over that nice rug," I said. "I'm going to kill you with the next one. Stop this machine."

Winter was pale; he swallowed convulsively. "I swear, Mr. Bayard, that's utterly impossible. I'd rather you'd shoot me. You have no conception of what you're suggesting."

I saw now that I was in the hands of a dangerous lunatic. I believed Winter when he said he'd rather die than stop this bus—or whatever it was. In spite of my threat, I couldn't shoot him in cold blood. I turned and took three steps up the passage and poked the automatic into the small of the back that showed there.

"Cut the switch," I said. The man, who was one of the two who had been standing by when I awoke in the office, continued to twist frantically at a knob on the panel before him. He glanced up at me, but kept on twiddling. I raised the pistol and fired a shot into the instrument panel. The man jumped convulsively, and threw himself forward, protecting the panel with his body.

"Stop, you bloody fool," he shouted. "Let us explain..."

"I tried that," I said. "It didn't work. Get out of my way. I'm bringing this wagon to a halt one way or another."

I stood so that I could see both men. Winter half crouched in the doorway, face white. "Are we all right, Doyle?" he called in a strained voice. Doyle eased away from the panel, turned his back to me, and glanced over the instruments. He flipped a toggle, cursed, and turned back to face Winter.

"Communicator dead," he said. "But we're still in operation."

I hesitated now. These two were genuinely terrified of the idea of stopping; they had paid as little attention to me and my noisy gun as one would to a kid with a water pistol. Compared to stopping, a bullet was apparently a trifling irritation.

It was also obvious that this was no moving van. The pilots' compartment had more instruments than an airliner, and no windows. Elaborate ideas began to run through my mind. Space ship? Time machine? What the devil had I gotten into?

"All right, Winter," I said. "Let's call a truce. I'll give you five minutes to give me a satisfactory explanation, prove you're not an escapee from the violent ward, and tell me how you're going to go about setting me down right back where you found me. If you can't or won't cooperate, I'll fill that panel full of holes—including anybody who happens to be standing in front of it."

"Yes," Winter said. "I swear I'll do all I can. Just come away from the control compartment."

"I'll stay right here," I said. "I won't jump the gun unless you give me a reason, like holding your mouth wrong."

Winter was sweating. "This is a scouting machine, operating in the Net. By the Net, I mean the complex of Alternative lines which constitute the matrix of all simultaneous reality. Our drive is the Maxoni-Cocini field generator, which creates a force operating at what one might call a perpendicular to normal entropy. Actually, I know little about the physics of the mechanism; I am not a technician."

I looked at my watch. Winter got the idea. "The Imperium is the government of the Zero Zero A-line in which this discovery was made. The device is an extremely complex one, and there are a thousand ways in which it can cause disaster to its operators if a mistake is made. Judging from the fact that every A-line within thousands of parameters of Zero Zero is a scene of the most fearful carnage, we surmise that our line alone was successful in controlling the force. We conduct our operations in all of that volume of A-space lying outside the Blight, as we term this area of destruction. The Blight itself we ordinarily avoid completely."

Winter wrapped a handkerchief around his bleeding hand as he talked.

"Your line, known as Blight-Insular Three, or B-I Three, is one of two exceptions we know to the general destruction. These two lines lie at some 'distance' from Zero Zero, yours a bit closer than B-I Two. B-I Three was discovered only a month or so ago, and just recently confirmed as a safe line. All this exploratory work in the Blight was done by drone scouts, unmanned.

"Why I was directed to pick you up, I don't know. But believe me when I say that if you succeed in crippling this scout, you'll precipitate us into identity with an A-line which might be nothing more than a ring of radioactive dust around the sun, or a great mass of mutated fungus. We cannot stop now for any reason until we reach a safe area."

I looked at my watch again. "Four minutes," I said. "Prove what you've been telling me."

Winter licked his lips. "Doyle, get the recon photos of this sector, the ones we made on the way in."

Doyle reached across to a compartment under the panel and brought out a large red envelope. He handed it to me. I passed it to Winter.

"Open it," I said. "Let's see what you've got."

Winter fumbled a moment, then slipped a stack of glossy prints out. He handed me the first one. "All these photos were made from precisely the same spatial and temporal coordinates as those occupied by the scout. The only difference is the Web coordinates."

The print showed an array of ragged fragments of rock hanging against a backdrop of foggy grey, with a few bright points gleaming through. I didn't know what it was intended to represent.

He handed me another; it was similar. So was a third, with the added detail that one rock fragment had a smooth side, with tiny lines across it. Winter spoke up. "The scale is not what it appears; that odd bit is a portion of the earth's crust, about twenty miles from the camera; the lines are roads." I stared, fascinated. Beyond the strangely scribed fragment, other jagged pieces ranged away to the limit of sight, and beyond. My imagination reeled at the idea that perhaps Winter was telling me the literal truth.

Winter passed over another shot. This one showed a lumpy black expanse, visible only by the murky gleam of light reflected by the irregularities in the surface in the direction of the moon, which showed as a brilliant disc in the black sky.

The next was half obscured by a mass which loomed across the lens, too close for focus. Beyond, a huge sprawling bulk, shapeless, gross, immense, lay half buried in tangled vines. I stared horrified at the tiny cow-like head which lolled uselessly on the slope of the mountainous creature. Some distance away a distended leg-like appendage projected, the hoof dangling.

"Yes," Winter said. "It's a cow. A mutated cow which no longer has any limitation on its growth. It's a vast tissue culture, absorbing nourishment direct from the vines. They grow all through the mass of flesh. The rudimentary head and occasional limbs are quite useless." I pushed the pictures back at him. I was sick. "I've seen enough," I said. "You've sold me. Let's get out of this." I pushed the pistol into my pocket. I thought of the bullet hole in the panel and shuddered.

Back in the office, I sat down at the desk. Winter took the chair. If he had any gimmicks wired up he couldn't reach them from there. He examined his hand distastefully and tightened the handkerchief. I didn't offer to help. He offered me the blue flask again. This time I took a healthy belt from it.

Winter spoke up again. "It's a very unnerving thing, old chap, to have it shown to you all at once that way, I know. I was actually trying to ease the shock, but you must admit you were insistent."

"I can still shoot the pair of you, and anybody else you've got aboard, if it looks like it will help," I said. "I don't like being shanghaied. I don't know what your bosses have in store for me, but I'll bet I won't like it. So what are you going to do about it?"

"I have to bring you in, or give my life in the attempt," Winter said calmly. "I am an Imperial Officer. Inasmuch as you now realize that you can't leave the vessel until we are clear of the Blight, and in view of the fact that in a few hours automatic controls will bring us into phase on the operations ramp at Stockholm Zero Zero, where an escort will be awaiting your arrival, I can't see what advantage you'd derive from killing me. Therefore, we may as well relax and accept the situation." He smiled pleasantly.

I thought about it. I understood on an intellectual level the general idea of what Winter had been telling me, without even beginning to be able to conceive of it as actual physical fact. I thought about it while Winter went on talking, explaining.

I tried to assemble his fragmentary information into a coherent picture: a vast spider web of lines, each one a complete universe, each minutely different from all the others; somewhere, a line, or world, in which a device had been developed that enabled a man to move across the lines. Well, why not, I thought. With all those lines to work with, everything was bound to happen in one of them; or was it?

"How about all the other A-lines, Winter," I said at the thought, "where this same discovery must have been made, where there was only some unimportant difference. Why aren't you swarming all over each other, bumping into yourself?"

"That's been a big question to our scientists, old chap, and they haven't yet come up with any definitive answers. However, there are a few established points. First, the thing is a fantastically delicate device, as I've explained. The tiniest slip in the initial experimentation, and we'd have ended like some of those other lines you've seen photos of. Apparently the odds were quite fantastically against our escaping the consequences of the discovery; still, we did, and now we know how to control it.

"As to the very close lines, theory now seems to indicate that there is no actual physical separation between lines; those microscopically close to one another actually merge, blend...it's difficult to explain. One actually wanders from one to another, at random, you know. In fact, such is the curious nature of infinity, that there seem to be an infinite number of infinitely close lines we're constantly shifting about in. Usually this makes no difference; we don't notice it, any more than we're aware of hopping along from one temporal point to the next as normal entropy progresses."

At my puzzled frown he added, "The lines run both ways, you know; in an infinite number of directions. If we could run straight back along the normal E-line, we'd be traveling into the past. This won't work, for practical reasons involving two bodies occupying the same space, and all that sort of thing. The Maxoni principle enables us to move in a manner which we think of as being at right angles to the normal drift. With it, we can operate through 360 degrees, but always at the same E-level at which we start. Thus, we will arrive at Stockholm Zero Zero at the same moment we departed from B-I Three." Winter laughed. "This detail caused no end of misunderstanding and counter-accusation on the first trials."

"So we're all shifting from one universe to another all the time without knowing it," I said skeptically.

"Not necessarily all of us, not all the time," Winter said. "But emotional stress seems to have the effect of displacing one; of course with the relative positions of two grains of sand, or even of two atoms within a grain of sand being the only difference between two adjacent lines, you'd not be likely to notice; but at times greater slips occur with most individuals. Perhaps you yourself have noticed some tiny discrepancy at one time or another; some article apparently moved or lost; some sudden change in the character of someone you know; false recollections of past events. The universe isn't all as rigid as one might like to believe."

"You're being awfully plausible, Winter," I said. "Let's pretend I accept your story. Now tell me about this vehicle."

"Just a small mobile M C station, mounted on an autopropelled chassis. It can move about on level ground or paved areas, and also in calm water. It enables us to do most of our spatial maneuvering on our own ground, so to speak, and avoid exposing ourselves to the hazards of attempting to conduct ground operations in strange areas."

"Where are the rest of the men in your party," I asked. "There are at least three more of you."

"They're all at their assigned posts," Winter said. "There's another small room containing the drive mechanism forward of the control compartment."

"If the controls are set for an automatic return to your base, why do you need all the technicians on the job?" I asked.

Winter stared. "You don't appreciate the complexity and delicacy of controlling this unit," he said. "Constant attention is required."

"What's this stuff for?" I indicated the box on the desk from which I'd gotten the gun.

Winter looked at it, then said ruefully, "So that's where you acquired the weapon. I knew you'd been searched. Damned careless of Doyle; bloody souvenir hunter! I told him to submit everything to me for

approval before we returned, so I guess it's my fault."
He touched his aching hand tenderly.

"Don't feel too bad about it; I'm just a clever guy,"
I said. "However, I'm not very brave. As a matter of
fact I'm scared to death of what's in store for me
when we arrive at our destination."

"You'll be well treated, Mr. Bayard," Winter assured
me. I let that one pass. Maybe when we arrived, I
could come out shooting, make an escape . . . That line
of thought didn't seem very encouraging either. What
would I do next, loose in this Imperium of Winter's?
What I needed was a return ticket home. I found
myself thinking of it as B-I Three, and realized I
was beginning to accept Winter's story. I took another
drink from the blue bottle.

Except for the hum, it was quiet in the room. The
old man up front stayed hunched over his instruments.
Winter shifted in his chair, cleared his throat, and
said nothing. There was an odd sensation of motion,
in spite of the fact that the room was steady.

"Why don't we explode when we pass through one
of those empty-space lines, or burn in the hot ones,"
I asked suddenly. "Suppose we found ourselves peek-
ing out from inside one of those hunks of rock you
were photographing?"

"We don't linger about long enough, old boy," Winter
said. "We remain in any one line for no finite length of
time, therefore there's no time for us to react physically
to our surroundings."

"How can you take pictures, and use communicators?"

"The camera remains inside the field. The photo is
actually a composite exposure of all the lines we cross
during the instant of the exposure. The lines differ

hardly at all, of course, and the prints are quite clear. Light, of course, is a condition, not an event. Our communicators employ a sort of grating which spreads the transmission."

"I don't get it," I said. I was feeling confused, but a little more at ease. The blue bottle was all right. I had another sample.

"I'm making a special study of what I term 'A-entropy,'" Winter said. "I've taken several rather fascinating sequences using a cine-camera, which seem to indicate that there are other 'streams of consciousness' than those with which we're familiar, those we sense as our own personalities. If one focuses a camera on an individual subject, the progressive changes in the subject, all of course occurring at the same instant of normal time, seem to be almost as purposeful as our progressive spatial changes as we proceed along an E-line." Winter warmed to his subject, ignoring my lack of response.

"Now consider a normal cine sequence. Each frame shows the subject in a slightly different position, spatially and temporally. As we proceed along from one frame to the next, we see the action develop. The man walks, the wave breaks, the horse gallops, etc. Well, the same sort of thing can be seen in my films. I've one fascinating sequence. Here, let me show you," he said.

I leaned forward with the gun in my hand and watched Winter intently as he rose and pulled a small projector from a wall cabinet. He placed it on a table, made a few adjustments, and a scene flashed clearly on the white wall opposite me. A man stood alone in a field.

Winter continued with his running commentary.

"We were progressing directly away from Base; notice the increasing alienness of the scene..."

The man changed, the scene behind him changed, drifting and oddly flowing, though he stood unmoving. The sun was visible in the sky. A leaf falling through the air hung, suspended. The man held a hoe, with which he was in the act of rooting out a small green weed. On the screen, the weed grew visibly, putting out leaves. The leaves grew larger, became splotched with red. The man seemed to shrink back, without moving his feet. The hoe shortened, the metal twisting and writhing into a new shape. The man's arms grew shorter, thicker, his back more stooped.

All around, the other plants drew back, apparently drifting through the soil, some fading down to nothing, others gathering together into gnarled clumps. The weed burgeoned enormously. Fleshy leaves waved out toward the man, now hardly a man. Horny armor spread like a carapace across his shoulders, and great clamp-like hands gripped a glittering scythe. Now teeth were appearing along the edge of each leaf, as the scythe merged with their fat stems. The roots of the plant twisted into view above the ground, entailing the legs of the no longer human creature attacking it. He too gained height now, the head enlarging to accommodate great jaws.

All around, the field lay barren, the remaining plants grouped in tight impregnable mounds here and there. The figure of the monstrous animal now reared high above the plant, locked in its leafy embrace. The scythe, buried among the stems, twisted, and tendrils withered and leaves wilted back to shriveled brown husks as new shoots appeared, raw and pink. Plant teeth grated on flaring armor. It was a grim and silent battle, waged without movement under a changeless sky.

Now the plant shrank back, blackening, drooping. The sharp steel blade was visible once more; the armor plates melted gradually back into the shoulders, as the victorious creature gave up his monstrous defensive form. The great jaws dwindled, the hands and legs changed. In the distance, the mounds opened and plants flowed out across the soil. Another minute and the man, or almost a man if you overlooked the green skin and short horns, stood with upraised hoe before a small crimson weed.

The projector blinked off.

"What did you think of that, old chap?" Winter said.

"A nightmare," I said.

"There's a sequence of cause and effect, of attack and defense, in a completely different fashion from anything we know of course, but quite obvious, I think."

"I think I'd better lay off that little old blue bottle," I said. But I didn't feel as flippant as I sounded. I was shaken all the way through, and for the first time I really believed in what was happening.

"The last of that sequence was made at a tremendous distance from Zero Zero," Winter said. "The frames were actually shot at a rate of one per second of subjective time. No way of telling, of course, just what the normal rate of progression, if any, might be, along that line; what appeared to us to be a brief battle might have been a life-long struggle, or even an age of evolution. The most remote lines we saw, there at the end, represent a divergence point nearly a million years in the past."

"Winter," I said, "this is all extremely interesting, but I'd enjoy it a lot more if I had some idea of what you people have in mind for me. I get the impression that you have small regard for a man's comfort. I think you might be planning to use me in some sort of colorful experiment, and then throw me away; toss me out into one of those cosmic junk-heaps you showed me. And that stuff in the blue bottle isn't quite soothing enough to drive the idea out of my mind."

"Great heavens, old boy!" Winter sat bolt upright. "Nothing of that sort, I can assure you. Why, we're not blasted barbarians! Since you are an object of official interest of the Imperium, you can be assured of humane and honorable treatment."

"I didn't like what you said about 'concentration points' a while back. That sounds like jail to me."

"Not at all," Winter expostulated. "There are a vast number of very pleasant A-lines well outside the Blight which are either completely uninhabited, or are occupied by backward or underdeveloped peoples. One can well nigh select the technological and cultural level in which one would like to live. All interrogation subjects are most scrupulously provided for; they're supplied with everything necessary to live in comfort for the remainder of their normal lives."

"Marooned on a desert island, or parked in a native village? That doesn't sound too jolly to me," I said. "I'd rather be at home."

Winter smiled speculatively. "What would you say to being set up with a fortune in gold, and placed in a society closely resembling that of, say, England in the 17th Century; with the added advantage that you'd have electricity, plenty of modern literature, supplies for a lifetime, whatever you wish. You must remember that we have the resources of all the universe to draw upon."

"I'd like it better if I had a little more choice," I said. It was all very cozy here in this room at the moment, but I was still the victim of a rather crude kidnapping, and I couldn't think of anything practical I could do about it at the moment.

"Suppose we keep right on going, once we're clear of the Blight," I said. "That reception committee wouldn't be waiting then. You could run this buggy back to B-I Three. I could force you."

"See here, Bayard," Winter said impatiently. "You have a gun; very well, shoot me; shoot all of us. What would that gain you? The operation of this machine requires a very high technical skill. The controls are set for automatic return to the starting point. It is absolutely against Imperium policy to return a subject to the line from which he was taken. The only thing for you to do is cooperate with us, and you have my assurance as an Imperial officer that you will be treated honorably."

I looked at the gun. "According to the movies," I said, "the fellow with the gun always gets his own way. But you don't seem to care whether I shoot you or not."

Winter smiled. "Aside from the fact that you've had quite a few draughts from my brandy flask and probably couldn't hit the wall with that weapon you're holding, I assure you—"

"You're always assuring me," I said. I tossed the pistol onto the desk. I put my feet up on the polished top, and leaned back in the chair. "Wake me up when we get there. I'll want to fix my face."

Winter laughed. "Now you're being reasonable, old boy. It would be damned embarrassing for me to have to warn the personnel at base that you were waving a pistol about."

III

I WOKE UP WITH a start. My neck ached abominably; so did the rest of me, as soon as I moved. I groaned, dragged my feet down off the desk, and sat up. There was something wrong. Winter was gone; and the humming had stopped. I jumped up.

"Winter," I shouted. I had a vivid picture of myself marooned in one of those hell-worlds. At that moment I realized I wasn't half as afraid of arriving at Zero Zero as I was of not getting there.

Winter pushed the door open and glanced in. "I'll be with you in a moment, Mr. Bayard," he said. "We've arrived on schedule."

I was nervous. The gun was gone. I walked up and down the room thinking. I wondered where my briefcase was, but it seemed less important now. I was into something bigger. I told myself it was no worse than going to one of the Ambassador's receptions. I would try to take it lightly; there wasn't any doubt that I'd have to take it. My best bet was to walk in as though I'd thought of it myself.

The two bouncers came in, followed by Winter. They all had their uniform caps on now, and were acting very formal. Winter turned to face the others, and they both threw him a British salute, only more so. He returned it with a casual wave, and turned to me as they stepped to the side door.

"Shall we disembark, Mr. Bayard?" he said. One of the two men pushed the door open, and stood at attention beside it. Beyond the opening I could see muted sunshine on a level paved surface, and a group of men in white uniforms, looking in our direction.

Winter was waiting. I might as well take the plunge, I thought. I stepped down through the door and looked around. We were in a large shed, looking something like a railroad station. One of the men in the waiting group turned to another, eyes on me, and said something. The other nodded. They stepped forward.

Winter spoke up from beside me, "Gentlemen, Mr. Brion Bayard."

They looked at me and I looked back. They all wore tight white uniforms, lots of medals, and elaborate brass on their shoulders.

"By jove, Winter," one of them said. "You've brought it off. Congratulations, old man." They gathered around Winter, asking questions, turning to stare at me. None of them said anything to me. I tried to catch Winter's eye. He was standing with one arm behind him, looking smug and modest.

To hell with them, I thought. I turned and started strolling toward the front of the shed. There was one door with a sentry box arrangement beside it. I gave the man on duty a cool glance and started past.

"'Ere, Sir, may I see your i-den-ti-fi-cation," the sentry said as I walked by him.

I turned. I was in a careless mood. "You'd better memorize this face," I said coolly. "You'll be seeing a great deal of it from now on. I'm your new commander." I looked him up and down. "Your uniform is in need of attention." I turned and went on. Behind me the sentry was saying, "'Ere, I say." I ignored him.

Winter appeared at that point, putting an end to what would have been a very neat escape, I thought. But where the hell would I go?

"Here, old man," he said. "Don't go wandering about. I'm to take you direct to Royal Intelligence, where you'll doubtless find out a bit more about the reasons for you, ah," Winter cleared his throat, "visit."

"I thought it was Imperial Intelligence," I said. "And for the high-level operation this is supposed to be, this is a remarkably modest reception. I thought there would be a band, or at least a couple of cops with handcuffs."

"Royal Swedish Intelligence," Winter explained briskly. "Sweden being tributary to the Emperor, of course; Imperial Intelligence chaps will be on hand. As for your reception, we don't believe in making much of a fuss, you know." Winter waved me into a boxy black staff car which waited at the curb. It swung out at once into light traffic which pulled out of our way as we opened up down the center of the broad avenue.

"I thought your scout just traveled cross-ways," I said, "and stayed in the same spot on the map. This doesn't look like the hilly area of the Old Town."

"You have a suspicious mind and an eye for detail,"

Winter said. "We maneuvered the scout through the streets to the position of the ramps before going into Drive. We're on the north side of the city now."

"Who am I going to meet?" I asked. "And will they talk to me, or just talk past my head like that last bunch?"

"You mustn't mind those chaps," Winter said. "They've seen these missions returning a thousand times, and I suppose they've become a bit blasé. They were actually impressed."

Our giant car roared across a bridge, and swirled into a long graveled drive leading to a wrought-iron gate before a massive grey granite building. The people I saw looked perfectly ordinary, with the exception of a few oddities of dress and an unusually large number of gaudy uniforms. The guard at the iron gate was wearing a cherry-colored tunic, white trousers, and a black steel helmet surmounted by a gold spike and a deep purple plume. He presented arms, (a short and wicked looking nickleplated machine gun), and as the gate swung wide we eased past him and stopped before broad doors of polished iron-bound oak. A brass plate beside the entrance said kungliga svenska spionaget.

I said nothing as we walked down a spotless white marble-floored hall, entered a spacious elevator, and rode up to the top floor. We walked along another hall, this one paved with red granite, and paused before a large door at the end. There was no one else around.

"Just be relaxed, Mr. Bayard, answer all questions fully, and use the same forms of address as I."

"I'll try not to fall down," I said. Winter looked as nervous as I felt as he opened the door after a polite tap.

The room was an office, large and handsomely

furnished. Across a wide expanse of grey rug three men sat around a broad desk, behind which sat a fourth. Winter closed the door, walked across the room with me trailing behind him, and came to a rigid position of attention ten feet from the desk. His arm swung up in a real elbow-buster of a salute, and held it.

"Sir, Chief Captain Winter reports as ordered," he said in a strained voice.

"Very good, Winter," said the man behind the desk, sketching a salute casually. Winter brought his arm down with a snap. He rotated rigidly toward the others.

"*Kaiserliche Hochheit*," he said, bowing stiffly from the waist at one of the seated figures. "Chief Inspector," he greeted the second, while the third, a rather paunchy fellow with a jolly expression and a somehow familiar face rated just "sir."

"'*Hochwelgeboren*' will do," murmured the lean aristocratic-looking one whom Winter had addressed first. Apparently instead of an 'imperial highness' he was only a 'high-well-born.' Winter turned bright pink. "I beg Your Excellency's pardon," he said in a choked voice. The round-faced man grinned broadly.

The man behind the desk had been studying me intently during this exchange. "Please be seated, Mr. Bayard," he said pleasantly, indicating an empty chair directly in front of the desk. Winter was still standing rigidly. The man glanced at him. "Stand at ease, Chief Captain," he said in a dry tone, turning back to me.

"I hope that your being brought here has not prejudiced you against us unduly, Mr. Bayard," he said. He had a long gaunt face with a heavy jaw. From pictures I had seen of King Gustav of Sweden, I suspected he was a relative. He confirmed my guess.

"I am General Bernadotte," he said. "These gentlemen are the Friherr von Richthofen, Chief Inspector Bale, and Mr. Goering." I nodded at them. Bale was a thin broadshouldered man with a small bald head. He wore an expression of disapproval.

Bernadotte went on. "I would like first to assure you that our decision to bring you here was not made lightly. I know that you have many questions, and all will be answered fully. For the present, I shall tell you frankly that we have called you here to ask for your help."

I hadn't been prepared for this. I didn't know what I expected, but to have this panel of high-powered brass asking for my puny assistance left me opening and closing my mouth without managing to say anything.

"It's remarkable," commented the paunchy civilian. I looked at him. Winter had called him Mr. Goering. I thought of pictures of Hitler's gross Air Chief.

"Not *Hermann* Goering?" I said.

The fat man looked surprised, and a smile spread across his face.

"Yes, my name is Hermann," he said. "How did you know this?" He had a fairly heavy German accent.

I found it hard to explain. This was something I hadn't thought of; actual doubles, or analogs of figures in my own world. Now I knew beyond a doubt that Winter had not been lying to me. "Back where I came from, everyone knows your name," I said. "Reichmarshall Goering..."

"Reichmarshall!" Goering repeated. "What an intriguing title!" He looked around at the others. "Is this not a most interesting and magnificent information?" He beamed. "I, poor fat Hermann, a Reichmarshall, and known to all." He was delighted.

"I am certain," the general said, "that Mr. Bayard will have many extremely interesting things to tell us. I think we owe it to him to give a full explanation first."

"Thank you, General," I said. "I'd appreciate that."

"How much have you been told of the nature of our governmental structure, Mr. Bayard, and of our operations in the Net?"

"I think I have a fair grasp of the general concept," I said, "and I understand that your Imperial government claims sovereignty over all other governments. That's about all."

"Insofar as we know at present, only this government, with perhaps one exception which I'll mention in a moment, has the technique of Net operation. We therefore exercise a natural influence of wider scope than other governing bodies. This is not to imply that the Imperium seeks to interfere with or to exploit others. Our relations with all lines are based on honorable treaties, negotiated as soon after contact as practicable. In the case of the Blight Insular lines, there are of course difficulties . . ."

Bernadotte hesitated, then added, "The Imperium limits its exercise of sovereignty; it is invoked as an ultimate resort, in case of anti-civil activity."

"Multi-phased reality is of course rather a shocking thing to encounter suddenly," the General went on, "after a lifetime of living in one's own narrow world. To those of us who have grown up with it, it seems only natural, in keeping with the principles of multiplicity and the continuum. The idea of a monolinear causal sequence is seen to be an artificially restrictive conception, an oversimplification of reality growing out of human egotism."

The other three men listened as attentively as I. It was very quiet, with only the occasional faint sounds of traffic from the street below.

"Insofar as we have been able to determine thus far from our studies of the B-I Three line, from which you come, our two lines share a common history up to about the year 1790. They remain parallel in many ways for about another century; thereafter they diverge rather sharply.

"Here in our world, two Italian scientists, Giulio Maxoni and Carlo Cocini, in the year 1893, made a basic discovery, which, after several years of study, they embodied in a device which enabled them to move about at will through a wide range of what we now term Alternate lines, or A-lines.

"Cocini lost his life in an early exploratory test, and Maxoni determined to offer the machine to the Italian government. He was rudely rebuffed.

"After several years of harassment by the Italian press, which ridiculed him unmercifully, Maxoni went to England, and offered his invention to the British government. There was a long and very cautious period of negotiation, but eventually a bargain was struck. Maxoni received a title, estates, and one million pounds in gold. He died a year later.

"The British government now had sole control of the most important basic human discovery since the wheel. The wheel gave man the power to move easily across the surface of his world; the Maxoni principle gave him all the worlds to move about in."

Leather creaked faintly as I moved in my chair. The general leaned back and drew a deep breath. He smiled.

"I hope that I am not overwhelming you with an excess of historical detail, Mr. Bayard."

"Not at all," I replied. "I'm very much interested."

He went on. "At that time the British Government was negotiating with the Imperial Germanic government in an effort to establish workable trade agreements, and avoid a fratricidal war, which then appeared to be an inevitable eventuality if appropriate spheres of influence were not agreed upon.

"The acquisition of the Maxoni papers placed a different complexion on the situation. Rightfully feeling that they now had a considerably more favorable position from which to negotiate, the British suggested an amalgamation of the two empires into the present Anglo-Germanic Imperium, with the House of Hanover-Windsor occupying the Imperial throne. Sweden signed the Concord shortly thereafter, and after resolution of a number of differences in detail, the Imperium came into being on January 1, 1900."

I had the feeling the general was over-simplifying things. I wondered how many people had been killed in the process of resolving the minor details. I kept the thought to myself.

"Since its inception," the general continued, "the Imperium has conducted a program of exploration, charting, and study of the A-continuum. It was quickly determined that for a vast distance on all sides of the Home line, utter desolation existed; outside that blighted region, however, were the infinite resources of countless lines. Those lines lying just outside the Blight seem uniformly to represent a divergence point at about four hundred years in the past; that is to say, our common histories differentiate about the year 1550.

As one travels farther out, the divergence date recedes. At the limits of our explorations to date, the C. H. date is about 1,000,000 B.C."

I didn't know what to say, so I said nothing. This seemed to be all right with Bernadotte.

"Then, in 1947, examination of photos made by automatic camera scouts revealed an anomaly; an apparently normal, inhabited world, lying well within the Blight. It took weeks of careful searching to pin-point the line. For the first time, we were visiting a world closely analogous to our own, in which many of the institutions of our own world should be duplicated.

"We had hopes of a fruitful liaison between the two worlds, but in this we were bitterly disappointed."

The general turned to the bald man whom he had introduced as Chief Inspector Bale.

"Chief Inspector," he said, "will you take up the account at this point?"

Bale sat up in his chair, folded his hands, and began.

"In September, 1948, two senior agents of Imperial Intelligence were dispatched with temporary rank of Career Minister and full diplomatic accreditization, to negotiate an agreement with the leaders of the National People's State. This political unit actually embraces most of the habitable world of the B-I Two line. A series of frightful wars, employing some sort of radioactive explosives, had destroyed the better part of civilization. Europe was a shambles. We found that the NPS headquarters was in North Africa, and had as its nucleus the former French colonial government there. The top man was a ruthless ex-soldier who had established himself as uncontested dictator of what remained of things. His army was made up of units of all the previous combatants, held together by the promise of free looting and top position in a new society based on raw force."

Bale spoke calmly, but with obvious distaste. "There was no semblance whatever of respect for institutions, position, common decency. The fighting man owned everything, subject only to the Dictator's prior claim; women were property to be used as slaves and concubines, and bought and sold freely. No one else counted. And at the top, living off the fat of the land, the Dictator.

"Our agents approached a military sub-chief, calling himself Colonel-General Yang in charge of a rag-tag mob of ruffians in motley uniforms, and asked to be conducted to the headquarters of the Dictator. Yang had them clapped into a cell and beaten insensible, in spite of their presentation of diplomatic passports and identity cards.

"He did however send them along to the Dictator, who gave them an interview. During the talk, the fellow drew a pistol and shot one of my two chaps through the head, killing him instantly. When this failed to make the other volunteer anything further than that he was an accredited envoy of the Imperial government requesting an exequatur and appropriate treatment, prior to negotiating an international agreement, he was turned over to experienced torturers.

"Under torture, the agent gave out just enough to convince his interrogators that he was insane; he was released to starve or die of wounds. We managed to spot him and pick him up in time to get the story before he died."

I still had no comment to make. It didn't sound

pretty, but then I wasn't too enthusiastic about the methods employed by the Imperium either. The general resumed the story.

"We resolved to make no attempt at punitive action, but simply to leave this unfortunate line in isolation.

"About a year ago, an event occurred which rendered this policy no longer tenable." The general turned to the lean faced man.

"Manfred, I will ask you to cover this portion of the briefing."

"Units of our Net Surveillance Service detected activity at a point some distance within the area called Sector 92," Richthofen began. "This was a contingency against which we had been on guard from the first. It was, however, only the second time within the almost 60 years of constant alertness that unauthorized activation of an M-C field had been observed. On the first occasion, nearly fifty years ago, a minor conspiracy among disgruntled officials was responsible, and no harm was done.

"This time it was not so simple. A heavily armed M-C unit of unknown origin had dropped into identity with one of our most prized industrial lines, one of a group with which we conduct a multi-billion-pound trade. The intruder materialized in a population center, and released virulent poisonous gasses, killing hundreds. Masked troops then emerged, only a platoon or two of them, and proceeded to strip bodies, loot shops ... an orgy of wanton destruction. Our NSS scout arrived some hours after the attackers had departed. The scout was subjected to a heavy attack in its turn by the justifiably aroused inhabitants of the area before it was able to properly identify itself as an Imperium vessel."

Richthofen had a disdainful frown on his face. "I personally conducted the rescue and salvage operation; over four hundred innocent civilians dead, valuable manufacturing facilities destroyed by fire, production lines disrupted, the population entirely demoralized. A bitter spectacle for us."

"You see, Mr. Bayard," Bernadotte said, "we are well nigh helpless to protect our friends against such forays. Although we have developed extremely effective M-C field detection devices, the difficulty of reaching the scene of an attack in time is practically insurmountable. The actual transit takes no time, but locating the precise line among numberless others is an extremely delicate operation. Our homing devices make it possible, but only after we have made a very close approximation manually."

"In quick succession thereafter," Richthofen continued, "we suffered seven similar raids. Then the pattern changed. The raiders began appearing in numbers, with large cargo carrying units. They also set about rounding up all the young women at each raid, and taking them along into captivity. It became obvious that a major threat to the Imperium had come into existence.

"At last we had the good fortune to detect a raider's field in the close vicinity of one of our armed scouts. It quickly dropped in on a converging course, and located the pirate about twenty minutes after it had launched its attack. The commander of the scout quite properly opened up at once with high explosive cannon and blew the enemy to rubble. Its crew, demoralized by the loss of their vessel, nevertheless resisted capture almost to the last man. We were able to secure only two prisoners for interrogation."

I wondered how the Imperium's methods of interrogation compared with those of the dictator of B-I Two, but I didn't ask. I might find out soon enough.

"We learned a great deal more than we expected from our prisoners. They were talkative and boastful types. The raiding parties depend for their effectiveness on striking unexpectedly and departing quickly. The number of pirate vessels we placed at no more than four, each manned by about fifty men. They boasted of a great weapon which was held in reserve, and which would undoubtedly be used to avenge them. It was apparent from the remarks of the prisoners that they had not had the M-C drive long, and that they knew nothing of the configuration of the Net, or of the endless ramifications of simultaneous reality. They seemed to think their fellows would find our base and destroy it with ease. They also had only a vague idea of the extent and nature of the Blight. They mentioned that several of their ships had disappeared, doubtless into that region. It appears also, happily for us, that they have only the most elementary detection devices and that their controls are erratic in the extreme. But the information of real importance we learned was the identity of the raiders."

Richthofen paused for dramatic effect. "It was our unhappy sister world, B-I Two."

"Somehow," Bernadotte took up the story, "in spite of their condition of chaotic social disorder and their destructive wars, they had succeeded in harnessing the M-C principle. Their apparatus is even more primitive than that with which we began almost sixty years ago, yet they have escaped disaster.

"The next move came with startling suddenness.

Whether by virtue of an astonishingly rapid scientific development, or by sheer persistence and blind luck, one of their scouts succeeded last month in locating the Zero Zero line of the Imperium itself. The vessel dropped into identity with our continuum on the outskirts of the city of Berlin, one of the royal capitals. The crew had apparently been prepared for their visit. They planted a strange device atop a flimsy tower in a field, and embarked instantly. Within a matter of three minutes, as well as we have been able to determine, the device detonated with unbelievable force. Over a square mile was absolutely desolated; casualties ran into the thousands. And the entire area still remains poisoned with some form of radiation-producing debris which renders the region uninhabitable."

I nodded. "I think I understand," I said.

"Yes," the general said, "you have something of this sort in your B-I Three world also, do you not?"

I assumed the question was rhetorical and said nothing.

Bernadotte continued. "Crude though their methods are, they have succeeded already in flaunting the Imperium. It is only a matter of time, we feel, before they develop adequate controls and detection devices. We will then be faced with the prospect of hordes of ragged but efficient soldiers, armed with the frightful radium bombs with which they destroyed their own culture, descending on the mother world of the Imperium.

"This eventuality is one for which it has been necessary to make preparation. There seemed to be two possibilities, both equally undesirable. We could await further attack, meanwhile readying our defenses, of doubtful value against the fantastic explosives of the enemy; or we could ourselves mount an offensive, launching a massive invasion force against B-I Two. The logistics problems involved in either plan would be unbelievably complex."

I was learning a few things about the Imperium. In the first place, they did not have the atomic bomb, and had no conception of its power. To consider war against an organized military force armed with atomics was proof of that. Also, not having had the harsh lessons of two major wars to assist them, they were naïve, almost backward, in some ways. They thought more like Europeans of the 19th Century than modern westerners.

"About one month ago, Mr. Bayard," the general continued, "a new factor was introduced, giving us a third possibility. In the heart of the Blight, at only a very little distance from B-I Two, and even closer to us than it, we found a second surviving line. That line was of course your home world, designated Blight-Insular Three by us."

Bernadotte nodded at Bale, who took up the account:

"Within 72 hours, 150 special agents of Imperial Intelligence, and selected men from the British, Swedish and German Royal Intelligence services had been placed at carefully scouted positions in B-I Three. Our first preliminary survey, which was carried out under Imminent Calamity priority, had given us the rough picture in less than six hours. We found we were dealing with a line having the same type radium bomb as B-I Two, but which had succeeded in averting general destructive war. We had the broad outlines of the past hundred years' developments, and the approximate present political situation. Our men were stationed at points of maximum activity, and spread thin though they were, they immediately began filling in the outline.

"It was important that we not make the same mistake which we had in B-I Two, of beginning contact on the basis of false assumptions as to the conduct one might expect from civilized men. We had an opportunity with the new B-I Three line to establish a close surveillance point from which to carry on scouting operations aimed at giving us a clearer picture of B-I Two. There was also the possibility of enlisting an ally against B-I Two, but only of course in the event the new line had or was about to achieve the M-C field. Unfortunately, the latter was not the case. Still, we felt there must be some way in which we could turn this find to good advantage."

Bale paused and looked at me sharply. "If this seems overly opportunistic or cynical to you, Mr. Bayard, please recall that we were fighting for our existence. And still are," he added.

I had a distinct feeling that Bale didn't like me. All of them were treating me pretty strangely, I thought, in some subtle way. It was almost as if they were afraid of me.

Winter was still standing, in a rather awkward parade rest position. I got the impression most of this was news to him, too.

"We were determined to make no blunders with regard to B-I Three," Bale continued. "Too much was at stake. As the information flowed in from our men, all of whom, being our top agents, had succeeded in establishing their cover identities without difficulty, it was immediately passed to the General Staff and to the Imperial Emergency Cabinet for study. The two bodies remained in constant session for over a week without developing any adequate scheme for handling the new factor.

"One committee of the Emergency Cabinet was assigned the important task of determining as closely as possible the precise C. H. relationship of B-I Three with both B-I Two and the Imperium. This is an extremely tricky chore, as it is quite possible for an amazing parallelism to exist in one phase of an A-line while the most fantastic variants crop up in another.

"One week ago today the committee reported findings they considered to be 98% reliable. Your B-I Three line shared the history of the B-I Two until the date 1911, probably early in the year. At that point, my colleague, Mr. Goering, of German Intelligence, who had been sitting in on the meeting, made a brilliant contribution. His suggestion was immediately adopted. All agents were alerted at once to drop all other lines of inquiry and concentrate on picking up a trace of—" Bale looked at me. "Mr. Brion Bayard."

They knew I was on the verge of exploding from pure curiosity, so I just sat and looked back at Bale. He pursed his lips. He sure as hell didn't like me.

"We picked you up from records at your University, ah," Bale frowned at me. "Something like aluminum alloy..." Bale must be an Oxford man, I thought.

"Illinois," I said.

"Oh yes, that's it," Bale said.

I looked at him without expression.

"At any rate," Bale went on, "it was a relatively simple matter to follow you up then through your military service and into your Diplomatic Service. Our man just missed you at your Legation at Viat-Kai..."

"Consulate General," I corrected

It annoyed Bale. I was glad; I didn't like him much either.

"You had left the post the preceding day and were proceeding to your headquarters via Stockholm. We had a man on the spot; he kept tabs on you until the shuttle could arrive. The rest you know."

There was a lengthening silence. I shifted in my chair, looking from one expressionless face to another.

"All right," I said. "It seems I'm supposed to ask, so I'll oblige, just to speed things along. Why me?"

Almost hesitantly General Bernadotte opened a drawer of the desk and drew out a flat object wrapped in brown paper. He removed the paper very deliberately as he spoke.

"I have here an official portrait of the Dictator of the world of Blight-Insular Two," he said. "One of the few artifacts we have been able to bring along from that unhappy region. Copies of this picture are posted everywhere there."

He passed it over to me. It was a crude lithograph, in color, showing a man in uniform, the chest as far down as the picture extended covered with medals. Beneath the portrait was the legend: "His Martial Excellency, Duke Of Algiers, Warlord of the Combined Forces, Marshall General of the State, Brion the First, Bayard, Dictator."

The picture was of me.

IV

I STARED AT THE garish portrait for a long time. It wasn't registering; I had a feeling of disorientation. There was too much to absorb.

"Now you will understand, Mr. Bayard, why we have brought you here," the general said, as I silently handed the picture back to him. "You represent our hidden ace. But only if you consent to help us of your own free will." He turned to Richthofen again.

"Manfred, will you outline our plan to Mr. Bayard?"

Richthofen cleared his throat. "Quite possibly," he said, "we could succeed in disposing of the Dictator Bayard by bombing his headquarters. This, however, would merely create a temporary diversion until a new leader emerged. The organization of the enemy seems to be such that no more than a very brief respite would be gained, if any at all, before the attacks would be resumed; and we are not prepared to sustain such onslaughts as these.

"No, it is far better for our purpose that Bayard

remain the leader of the National People's State—and that we control him." Here he looked intently at me.

"A specially equipped TNL scout, operated by our best pilot-technician could plant a man within the private apartment which occupies the top floor of the Dictator's palace at Algiers. We believe that a resolute man introduced into the palace in this manner, armed with the most effective hand weapons at our disposal, could succeed in locating and entering the dictator's sleeping chamber, assassinating him, and disposing of the body.

"If that man were you, Mr. Bayard, fortified by ten days' intensive briefing, and carrying a small net-communicator, we believe that you could assume the identity of the dead man and rule as absolute dictator over Bayard's twenty million fighting men."

"Do I have another double here?" I said, "in your Imperium?"

Bernadotte shook his head. "No, you have remote cousins here; nothing closer."

They were going a little too fast for me. Richthofen had leaned back in his chair and was looking at me in a satisfied way, as though everything was settled now. Goering was plainly waiting in suspense for my reaction, while General Bernadotte, with apparent unconcern, shuffled some papers before him.

I could see that all three of them expected me to act solemn and modest at the honor, and set out to do or die for the Fatherland. They were overlooking a few things, though. This wasn't my Fatherland; I'd been kidnapped here. And oddly enough, maybe, I could not see myself murdering anybody—especially, I had the grotesque thought—myself. I didn't even like the idea of being dropped down in the midst of a pack of torturers.

I was facing facts; I was 42 years old, a disillusioned middle-aged diplomat, accustomed to the stodgy routines of Embassy life and the administration of the cynical and colorless policies of an ineffectual State Department. True, among my colleagues of the Foreign Service, I had been rather less ossified physically and mentally than the average, something of a rebel, even; but this kind of hair-raising escapade was not in my line at all.

I was ready to tell them so in very definite terms, when my eye fell on Bale. He was wearing a supercilious half-smile, and I could see that this was just what he expected. His contempt for me was plain. I sensed that he thought of me—almost—as the man who had killed his best agent in cold blood, a cowardly blackguard. My mouth was open to speak; but under that sneering expression, different words came out; temporizing words. I wouldn't give Bale the satisfaction of being right.

"And after I'm in charge of B-I Two, what then?" I said.

"You will be in constant touch with Imperial Intelligence via communicator." Richthofen spoke eagerly. "You'll receive detailed instructions as to each move you'll make. We should be able to immobilize B-I Two within six months. You'll then be returned here."

"I won't be returned home?"

"Mr. Bayard," Bernadotte said seriously, "you will never be able to return to B-I Three. The Imperium will offer you any reward you wish to name, except that. The consequences of revealing the existence of the Imperium to your line at this time are far too serious to permit consideration of the idea."

"That's not giving me much of a break," I said. "You people seem to take a lot of pride in your high ethical standards. How does this fit in?"

There was a note of anger in Richthofen's tone as he spoke up. "The continued well-being of the Imperium is at stake, Mr. Bayard," he said. "Perhaps even its continued existence. We consider the Imperium to be an institution worth preserving, at whatever cost of individual discomfort or inconvenience. We regret having to infringe your personal rights; but in the cause of Humanity, it is necessary."

Bernadotte spoke in a more conciliatory tone. "There is another, more personal consideration which we can offer to you, Mr. Bayard," he said. "You do not of course know that same devotion to the cause of the Imperium as do we, who have in our lifetimes seen the change it has brought to a petty, brawling, narrow world. We do not expect that you would be eager to risk your life in the service of what perhaps seems to you simply another foreign state. We are prepared to go to great lengths to provide an adequate incentive to you to help us, in the one way in which only you can serve.

"According to the dossier which we compiled, we noted that both of your parents were so unfortunate as to lose their lives in the wreck of an airship in 1953." He paused and looked at me for confirmation.

I nodded. What was this all about? I didn't like being reminded of that bitter night when the airliner on which they had been bound for Europe for a holiday and a visit with me had gone down into the Atlantic.

"We have made an investigation in B-I Two; in that line both of your parents are alive and well."

Bernadotte waited for the effect, then continued. "Since they did not approve of the conduct of their son, the Dictator Bayard, they were not incorporated into the official household, but were established in comfort on an estate in the south of France. They had previously been North African *Colons*, you understand."

I was dumbfounded. I remembered hearing many times as a boy the story of how my father had flipped a great silver 5-franc piece to decide whether to emigrate to North Africa or to North America. In the world I knew, America had been the decision. But in this other strange universe, they had become North Africans; and they still lived!

There was too much that was new, undreamed of, coming at me all at once. I couldn't assimilate it. I'd been very fond of my parents. All I could think of was that perhaps once again I'd meet them, my mother and father, beyond all expectation...

Bernadotte was still talking. "...will of course place them together with you, in whatever setting you elect."

Bernadotte addressed Bale. "Do you have the information on Mr. Bayard's military service?"

Bale spoke from memory. "Mr. Bayard served for two years with the rank of Captain, later Major, in the Army of the United State of America..."

"United *States*," I said; "plural." I enjoyed correcting Bale; he thought he was pretty good at this memory bit. He glared, but continued.

"...during a world-wide war, from 1942-1944. He received a slight wound, and was invalided out just prior to the cessation of hostilities."

Bale annoyed me. Slight wound, hell. I had a scar on my chest and a bigger one on my back, just to the left of the spine; machine gun slugs make a bigger hole leaving than they do going in.

All eyes were on Bernadotte. He looked as though what he was about to say was important.

"I have been authorized by the Emergency Cabinet," he said with gravity, "to offer you an Imperial commission in the rank of Major General, Mr. Bayard. If you accept this commission, your first assignment will be as we have outlined." Bernadotte handed a heavy piece of parchment across the table to me. "You should know, Mr. Bayard, that the Imperium does not award commissions, particularly as General Officer, lightly."

"It will be a most unusual rank," Goering said, smiling. "Normally there is no such rank in the Imperium Service; Lieutenant General, Colonel General, Major General. You will be unique."

"We adopted the rank from your own armed forces, as a special mark of esteem, Mr. Bayard," Bernadotte said. "It is no less authentic for being unusual."

It was a fancy sheet of paper. The Imperium was prepared to pay off well for this job they needed done. Anything I wanted, even things I hadn't conceived of... I think they thought the strange look on my face was greed at the thought of a general's two stars. Well, let them think it. I didn't want to give them any more information which might be used against me.

"I'll think about it," I said. Bale looked disconcerted now. After expecting me to back out, he had apparently then expected me to be dazzled by all the rewards I was being offered. I'd let him worry about it. Suddenly Bale bored me.

Bernadotte hesitated. "I'm going to take an unprecedented step, Mr. Bayard," he said. "For the present, on my personal initiative as head of State, I'm confirming you as Colonel in the Royal Army of Sweden without condition. I do this to show my personal confidence in you, as well as for more practical reasons." He rose and smiled ruefully, as though unsure of my reaction. "Congratulations, Colonel," he said, holding out his hand.

I stood up too. I noticed everyone had.

It was my turn to hesitate. I looked him in the eye. Chief of State he'd said. No wonder he'd looked like the King of Sweden; he *was* the king. And he'd introduced himself simply as General Bernadotte. I liked him. I took his hand.

"Thank you, sir," I said. On impulse, I stepped back a pace and threw him a snappy US-type salute. He returned it with a wide smile.

"You may have twenty-four hours to consider your decision, Colonel," he said. "I'll leave you in the excellent care of Graf von Richthofen and Mr. Goering until then."

Richthofen turned to Winter, still standing silently by. "Won't you join us, Chief Captain," he said.

"Delighted," Winter said.

"Congratulations, old boy, er, Sir," Winter said as soon as we were in the hall. "You made quite a hit with the general." He seemed quite his jaunty self again.

I eyed him. "You mean King Gustav?" I said.

Winter blinked. "But how did you know," he said. "I mean, dash it, how the devil did you know?"

"I have my methods," I said. It was my turn to be mysterious.

"But it must be," Goering said with enthusiasm, "that also he in your home world is known, not so?"

"That's right, Mr. Goering," I said, "now you've dispelled my aura of mystery."

Goering chuckled. "Please, Mr. Bayard, you must call me Hermann." He gripped me on the bicep in friendly fashion as we moved down the hall. "Now you must tell us more about this intriguing world of yours."

I found myself liking Goering. After all, he was no more the brutal cynic of the Luftwaffe than I was the dictator of a ruined world.

Richthofen spoke up. "I suggest we go along to my summer villa at Drottningholm and enjoy a dinner and a couple of good vintages while we hear all about your home, Mr. Bayard; and we shall tell you of ours."

He smiled and added, "We're not often so solemn," he nodded toward the room we had just left. "I'm afraid the spirit of our colleague Bale dominated the meeting."

"Just so," Hermann said. "This has been always the failing of the English; everything is taken with such gravity, just because of a little threat to our existence; no real German battle-joy, you see." He winked at Winter to show it was not ill-meant.

"Now about Chief Captain Winter," he went on. "What is his place in the B-I Three? We should all make a guess. I say a hairdresser, such delicate hands."

"Now, I say, Reichsmarshall," Winter began with mock asperity, then burst out laughing. "I say, actually, Bayard," he said, "what kind of troops did Mr. Goering command back there in B-I Three? Swiss Navy, that sort of thing?"

"Yes," Hermann said. "You don't mind if I call you

Brion? Now, was I a brave commander, or did I show my heels to the enemy?"

"You were a fighter pilot, Hermann," I said. "You were an ace; you shot down over twenty planes in aerial battle in World War One."

I added nothing about Goering's later, less savory career. This fellow had nothing in common with the gross Goering of Nazi Germany.

"Better and better, Brion," Hermann said gleefully. "You see, Manfred, I am a bold fellow after all."

"I say," Winter put in. "World War One, you said. You chaps have had to resort to numbering to keep them straight? How does anyone survive?" He sounded genuinely shocked.

"When did it occur, this war in which our Hermann played such a part?" Richthofen asked, as we entered the elevator.

"From 1914 to 1918," I said. I had a thought. I realized why his name was familiar to me. Manfred Rittmeister, Friherr von Richthofen, Germany's leading ace. Hadn't Bernadotte called him Manfred? I glanced at him. He looked about the right age. A coincidence, or had the Imperium set out to dazzle me with luminaries?

"You were another famous fighter pilot, Graf von Richthofen," I said. "You scored seventy victories; they called you the Red Knight."

Hermann shouted out with laughter. "Hermann and Manfred, the Terrible Two," he said. "What a pair of fighters we are, not so?"

Richthofen smiled a slight smile. "What you tell us sounds remarkably like our boyhood dreams of martial glory, Mr. Bayard," he said. "Quite foreign to our actual selves. We are fortunate that we live in a world where such ferocious ambitions are outgrown and we can mature to more productive endeavor." He glanced fondly at Hermann. "Our friend Goering here plays the clown, and is in fact a fellow of boundless good nature; but he is also one of the most astute planners on the staff of our German Intelligence Service."

"And the modest von Richthofen," Hermann said, "is the chief of that same service; a position of great importance in this age of the Maxoni device."

We emerged from the building and entered another of the immense black cars, which awaited us with engine idling.

"It's astonishing," Winter said, "how many figures you have encountered already who are eminent in your own world."

"Not so astonishing," I said. "They're eminent here, too; ability counts in any world, I see."

"I say," Winter said, "that's a bit of a blow to my ego, old boy; I should like to have been a big-wig in some environment; by your rule, I'm condemned to monotonous anonymity."

The car took the center of a broad tree-lined avenue, sweeping along at fifty, then sixty. Through the window, Stockholm looked gayer in color than the city I knew. We crossed a bridge, for which we slowed slightly, then whirled up a steep street, down another, and followed a wide straight highway out of town into parklike countryside. My companions, or escort, chatted gaily, and I joined in, feeing a quickening of interest in this alien world of the Imperium. There was a vitality here, a *spirit* to which I couldn't help responding.

V

I STOOD BEFORE A long mirror and eyed myself, not without approval. Two tailors and a valet had been buzzing around me like bees for half an hour, putting the finishing touches on their handiwork. I had to admit they had done all right.

It had been a long time since I had taken much interest in the clothes I wore. Every two years, between assignments, I had dutifully re-equipped myself for the next tour with the standard wardrobe of drab business suits, nothing which might attract possibly unfavorable attention to a diplomatic member of an Embassy staff.

Now I wore narrow-cut riding breeches of fine grey whipcord; short black boots of meticulously stitched and polished black leather; a white linen shirt without collar or cuffs beneath a mess jacket of Royal Blue, buttoned to the chin. A gold bordered blue stripe ran down the side of the trousers and heavy loops of gold braid ringed the sleeves from wrist to elbow. A black leather belt with a large square buckle bearing the Royal Swedish crest supported a jeweled scabbard containing a slender rapier with an ornate hilt. In the proper position on the left side of my chest were, to my astonishment, a perfectly accurate set of my World War II service medals and the Silver Star. On the shoulder straps, the bright silver eagles of a U. S. Colonel gleamed. I was wearing the full dress uniform of my new position in the Imperium society.

The valet squatted on the floor, adjusting a pair of silver spurs, while the tailors mouthed pins and conferred over the details of the gold-lined blue cape. I looked at the mirror and readied the usual disparaging comments that the sight of this regalia would require at home; then I checked myself. Damn it, I thought, I might as well be honest with myself; I look great! This is the way a man ought to dress when he goes to a party.

I was glad now I hadn't let myself deteriorate into the flabby ill-health of the average Foreign Service Officer, soft and pale from long hours in offices and late hours of heavy drinking at the interminable diplomatic functions. My shoulders were reasonably broad, my back reasonably straight; no paunch marred the lines of my new finery. This outfit made a man look like a man; how the devil had we gotten into the habit of draping ourselves in shapeless double-breasted suits, in mousy colors, of identical cut?

Goering was sitting in a brocaded armchair in the luxurious suite to which Richthofen had shown me in his 'little villa.'

"You cut a martial figure, Brion," he said. "It is plain to see you have for this new job a natural aptitude."

"I wouldn't count on it, Hermann," I said. His comment had reminded me of the other side of the coin; the deadly plans the Imperium had in mind for me. Well, I could settle that later. Tonight I was going to enjoy myself.

Over a dinner of pheasant served on a sunny terrace in the long Swedish summer evening, Richthofen had explained to me that, in Swedish society, to be without a title was an extremely awkward social encumbrance. It was not that one needed an exalted position, he assured me; merely that there be something for others to call one; Herr Doctor, Herr Professor, Ingenjör, Redaktör; my military status would ease my entry into the world of the Imperium.

It had sounded like a silly masquerade at first, but by the time we finished off the third bottle of Chateau Neuf du Pape, 1953, it was all settled. Tonight was the night of the Empire Day Ball, and we'd all go. I might as well; I was here, and what the hell, I thought. As for the uniform, the King had said no strings attached; and I was over-due for a good time.

Winter came in then, carrying what looked at first like a crystal ball.

"Your topper, sir," he said with a flourish. What he had was a chrome-plated steel helmet, with a rib running along the top, and a gold dyed plume growing out of it.

"Good God," I said. "Isn't that overdoing it a little?" I took the helmet; it was feather light, I discovered. The tailor took over, placed the helmet just so, handed me a pair of white leather gloves, and faded out.

"You have to have it, old boy," Winter said. "Dragoons, you know."

"You are complete," Hermann said. "A masterpiece."

He was wearing a dark grey uniform with black trim and white insignia. He had a respectable but not excessive display of ribbons and orders.

"Hermann," I said expansively, "you should have seen yourself when you were all rigged out in your medals back home. They came down to here," I indicated my knees. He laughed.

Together we left the suite and went down to the study on the ground floor. Winter, I noted, had changed from his whites to a pale yellow mess jacket with heavy silver braid and a nickel-plated Luger.

Richthofen showed up moments later; his outfit consisted of what looked like a set of tails, circa 1880, with silver buttons and a white beret.

"We're a cool bunch of cats," I said. I was feeling swell. I caught another glimpse of myself in a mirror. "Sharp, daddy-o," I murmured.

A liveried butler swung the glass door open for us and we descended the steps to a waiting car. This one was a vast yellow phaeton, with the top down. We slid into our places on the smooth yellow leather seats and it eased off down the drive.

It was a magnificent night, with high clouds and a brilliant moon. In the distance, the lights of the city glittered. We rolled smoothly along, the engine so silent that the sound of the wind in the tall trees along the way was clearly audible.

I had had a good general briefing at dinner on the current state of world affairs, and on the people I might expect to meet tonight. It appeared that the Imperium was not the only important state in this new world after all. A New Roman Empire had inherited much of the domain of its remote predecessor, and now competed in the far corners of the globe for mastery of what still remained uncommitted of Africa, Asia, the Polynesian Isles; the traditionally colonial, backward areas of the world. The rivalry, however, was of a new kind. The great powers competed in the speed and efficiency with which they developed these ancient pestholes of famine, disease, and ignorance into members of modern society. There were a few little wars going on, but I got the impression they were conducted under rules as rigid as any cricket match.

"Civilized man," Richthofen had said, "has a responsibility. His is not the privilege of abdicating the position he holds as leader in the world. His culture represents the best achievements so far made by man in his long climb up from primordial beginnings. We have inherited the fruits of the struggle to master hostile nature, to conquer disease, to harness natural forces; we are less than true men if we allow these achievements to be lost, to leave vast areas to the ancient enemy, ignorance, or worst of all, to lose by default our hard-won position, to retreat before the savage, the backward in the name of enlightened social ideas. We have a duty to perform; not to narrow nationalistic policies, not to false ideas of superiority based on religions, social position, untenable racial theories, skin color; but to mankind, that all shall benefit from the real superiority of our western culture, which is bringing man up off his knees into the light of his glorious future."

"Hear, hear," said Winter.

It sounded like a campaign speech, I thought, but I couldn't argue with it. I'd seen enough starving babies during my duty in the Orient to feel no patience with the policy of letting backward peoples suffer under the rule of local bosses, just because they were local. "Self determination of peoples" they'd called it. A lot like self-determination of kindergarten kids dominated by a bully. I preferred a world in which every human born had a chance at the best humanity had learned, rather than being sacrificed to the neuroses, hatreds, manias and over-compensations for inferiority of petty provincial leaders.

What we lacked, back in my world, I thought, was a sense of responsibility, and the courage to assume the burden of leadership. Here they hadn't hung back; right or wrong, they couldn't be accused of vacillation.

"Boys," I said, "I like you, even if you are a bunch of kidnappers."

Manfred looked at me. "I think the day will come, my friend," he said, "when you will forgive us for that crime."

Goering had thought to bring along a small flask, and by the time we had each tapped it twice we were passing through the iron gates of the Summer Palace. Colored floodlights bathed the gardens and people already filled the terraces on the south and west sides of the building. The car dropped us before the gigantic entry and moved off, as we made our way through the crowd, and into the reception hall.

Light from massive crystal chandeliers glittered on gowns and uniforms, polished boots and jewels, silks, brocades, velvet. A straight-backed man in rose-pink bowed over the hand of a lovely blonde in white. A slender black-clad fellow with a gold and white sash escorted a lady in green gold toward the ballroom. The din of laughter and conversation almost drowned out the strains of the waltz in the background.

"All right, boys," I said. "Where's the punchbowl?"

I don't often set out to get stewed, but when I do, I don't believe in half measures. I was feeling great, and wanted to keep it that way. At the moment I couldn't feel the bruises from my fall, my indignation over being grabbed was forgotten, and as for tomorrow, I couldn't care less. I was having a wonderful time. I hoped I wouldn't see Bale's sour face.

Everybody talked, asked me eager questions, made introductions. I found myself talking to someone I finally recognized as Douglas Fairbanks, Sr.; he was a tough-looking old fellow in a naval uniform. I met counts, dukes, officers of a dozen ranks I'd never heard of, several princes, and finally a short broad-shouldered man with a heavy sun tan and a go-to-hell smile whom I finally realized was the son of the Emperor.

I was still walking and talking like a million dollars, but somewhere along the line I'd lost what little tact I normally had.

"Well, Prince William," I said, maybe weaving just a little, "I understood the House of Hanover-Windsor was the ruling line here. Where I come from the Hanovers and Windsors are all tall, skinny, and glum-looking."

The Prince smiled. "Here, Colonel," he said, "a policy was established which put an end to that unfortunate situation. The Constitution requires that the male heir marry a commoner. This not only makes life more pleasant for the heir, with so many beautiful commoners to choose from, but maintains the vigor of the line. And it incidentally produces short men with happy faces occasionally."

I moved on, meeting people, eating little sandwiches, drinking everything from aquavit to beer, and dancing with one heavenly-looking girl after another. For the first time in my life my ten years of Embassy elbow-bending were standing me in good stead; from the grim experience gained through seven evenings a week of holding a drink in my hand from sundown till midnight while pumping other members of the Diplomatic Corps who thought they were pumping me, I had emerged with a skill; I could hold my liquor.

Somewhere along the line I felt the need for a breath of fresh air and stepped out through the tall French door onto a dark balustraded gallery overlooking gardens. I leaned on the heavy stone rail, looked up at stars visible through tall tree-tops, and waited for the buzzing in my head to die down a little.

The night air moved in a cool torrent over the dark lawn, carrying the scent of flowers. Behind me the orchestra played a tune that was almost, but not quite, a Strauss waltz.

I pulled off the white gloves that Richthofen had told me I should keep on when I left my helmet at the checkroom. I unbuttoned the top button of the tight-fitting jacket.

I'm getting old, I thought; or maybe just tired.

"And why are you tired, Colonel?" a cool feminine voice inquired from behind me.

I turned around. "Ah, there you are," I said. "I'm glad. I'd rather be guilty of talking out loud than of imagining voices."

I worked on focusing my eyes a little better. She had red hair, and wore a pale pink gown that started low and stayed with the subject.

"I'm *very* glad, as a matter of fact," I added. "I like beautiful redheads who appear out of nowhere."

"Not out of nowhere, Colonel," she said. "From in there, where it is so warm and crowded."

She spoke excellent English in a low voice, with just enough Swedish accent to render her tritest speech charming.

"Precisely," I said. "All those people were making me just a little bit drunk, so I came out here to recover." I was wearing a silly smile, and having a thoroughly good time being so eloquent and clever with this delightful young lady.

"My father has told me that you are not born to the Imperium, Colonel," she said. "And that you come from a world where all is the same, yet different. It should be so interesting to hear about it."

"Why talk about that place?" I said. "We've forgotten how to have fun back there. We take ourselves very seriously, and we figure out the most elaborate excuses for doing the rottenest things to each other..."

I shook my head. I didn't like that train of thought. "See," I said, "I always talk like that with my gloves off." I pulled them on again. "And now," I said grandly, "may I have the pleasure of this dance?"

She smiled and held out her hand, and we danced. We moved along closer to the music—or away from the light from the French doors. We talked and laughed while one waltz followed another.

Suddenly I paused. "Don't those boys know anything but waltzes?" I asked.

"You don't like waltzes?" she said.

"Sure, they're great, but wait a minute, I've got an idea." I took her hand and led her back through the French doors, across the floor, around behind a row of giant tropical plants to the concealed orchestra.

I signaled the leader as the musicians paused for a brief break. He came over.

"Yes, Colonel?" he smiled.

"How good are you?" I asked. "I mean..." I tried to figure out how to get it across. "If I hum a tune," I said, "can you play it?"

"That depends on how well you hum, Colonel," he said.

"OK, assuming I hum all right, can you get the tune and play it, with all the trimmings?"

"I think so," he said.

"What about in a different tempo?"

He frowned. "Could you give me an example?"

I was holding my girl's hand. "Listen," I said. I tried a few bars of 'Night and Day.' He looked interested. I cleared my throat and said. "Now get this. It's a great number."

I hummed 'Night and Day' all the way through for him twice. The members of the orchestra gathered around and listened.

"All right, Colonel," he said. "I have it, I think." He hummed it back to me. He had the tempo.

"All right, Gentlemen," he said to the others, "let's try it."

The players returned to their places. The leader turned to me and nodded, with a wink, and raised his arms. "Watch the tempo!" he cautioned the musicians.

"Come on," I said. I grabbed my girl's hand and we headed back for the floor.

The music started, softly at first, but smooth and sure. The beat was heavy, but good; the melody clear and true as only experts can make it.

Couples about to begin a waltz paused, and looked

toward the source of the music. The band was warming to its work now. Like the masters they were, they slid easily into orchestration effects that brought out the best of the old tune.

"Just follow me," I said. She came into my arms. "Closer," I said. "This is no waltz."

The other dancers faded back as if by signal, and an excited murmur ran around the room. My partner was a natural. Without faltering, she followed me through first the simplest and then the more complex of the infinite variations on the basic fox-trot theme that I had practiced as one of the standard diplomatic skills at a thousand dull affairs.

Her eyes were shining as she looked at me. "A strange song," she said. "A strange man."

The orchestra finished a third refrain of the old tune and without a pause eased into one of their old numbers, but rearranged to the new tempo. They were good.

People began tentatively trying out the new music on the floor, watching us, and laughing excitedly as they caught on. In a few minutes the floor was crowded again.

As the music stopped, they crowded around. "What is it called?" they asked. "Wonderful!" "The first really new music in years. Show us another."

We went back, amid a crowd, and congratulated the orchestra. They beamed.

"Want to try another?" I asked the smiling leader. He was eager to go, so I hummed 'Stardust,' 'I'll Get By,' more Cole Porter, whatever I could think of. The leader was like a miner panning out egg-sized nuggets. They played them all, the old familiar tunes, with an odd other-world flavor.

"I love your music," my girl said. "In a few days it will be heard in every town in the Empire."

They wanted more, and more. I gave them 'All the Things You Are,' 'Moon Love,' and finally 'Begin the Beguine.' The crowd went crazy when they finished, clapping and cheering and demanding more.

The orchestra had just begun the encore when a shattering blast rocked the floor, and the tall glass doors along the east side of the ballroom blew in. Through the cloud of dust which followed up the explosion, a swarm of men in motley remnants of uniforms leaped into the room. The leader, a black-bearded giant wearing a faded and patched U. S. Army-type forest green battle jacket and baggy Wehrmacht trousers, jacked the lever on the side of a short drum-fed machine gun, and squeezed a long burst into the thick of the crowd.

While I stood frozen, a tall man with blood on his face, wearing the deep purple of the Imperial Guards Regiment, leaped forward from the front rank of the crowd which had recoiled from the explosion, whipping out his sabre. The gunner whirled toward him, and fired two rounds before the gun jammed. I heard them smack into the man in purple, knocking him backwards. He rolled over, rose to his knees, still gripping the sabre, eyes fixed on the bearded man who cursed and jerked at the operating lever. The officer rose to his feet and lunged, arm and sabre one rigid line aimed at the other's chest. The sabre slammed against the forest green, as the man in purple collapsed amid rubble from the smashed windows. The curtains flapped around the bearded man as he dropped the gun, and gripped with both hands the hilt which protruded from his chest. I watched as he strained at it, and it moved. He was still on his feet, his back arched, biceps bursting through the rotted fabric of the ancient uniform. The blade came sliding out bright and clean. I stared, fascinated. He had it almost clear when his legs folded and he crashed to the floor.

While I had watched this violent exchange, men had poured through the broached wall, firing into the crowd. Men and women alike fell under the murdering attack, but every man who remained on his feet rushed the nearest attacker without hesitation. Standing in the rubble, a bristle-faced redhead wearing an undersized British sergeant's blouse pumped eight shots from the hip, knocking down an oncoming officer of the Imperium with every shot; when he stepped back to jam a new clip into the M-1, the ninth man ran him through the throat with a jewel-encrusted rapier.

I still stood frozen, holding my girl's hand. I whirled, started to shout to her to get back, to run; but the calm look I saw in her eyes stopped me. She'd rather be decently dead than flee this rabble.

I jerked my toy sword from its scabbard, dashed to the wall, and moved along it to the edge of the gaping opening. As the next man pushed through the cloud of dust and smoke, peering ahead, gripping a shotgun, I jammed the point of my sword into his neck, hard, and jerked it back before it was wrenched from my hands. He stumbled on, choking, the shotgun falling with a clatter. I reached out, raked it in, as another man appeared. He carried a Colt .45 in his left hand, and he saw me as I saw him. He swiveled to fire, and as he did I brought the poised blade down on his arm. The shot went into the floor and the pistol bounced out of the loose hand. He fell back into the trampling crowd.

There was the stamp and grating of feet, the cursing and shouting of the attackers, the insistent ragged close range firing, groans from wounded on the floor; and behind, the orchestra calmly struck up the Imperial Anthem. There were no screams from the women, no yells for mercy from a man of the Imperium. They came on silently, dying ten to one, but never pausing.

Another fellow lunged out of the dust, cutting across the room, and saw me. He leveled a heavy rifle on its side across his left forearm. He moved slowly and clumsily. I saw that his left hand was hanging by a thread. I grabbed up the shotgun and blew his face off. It had been about two minutes since the explosion.

I waited a moment, but no more came through the blasted window. I saw a wiry ruffian with long yellow hair falling back toward me as he pushed another magazine into a Browning automatic rifle. I jumped two steps, set the point of the sword just about where the kidneys should be, and rammed with both hands. Not very elegant style, I thought, but I'm just a beginner.

I saw Goering then, arms around a tall fellow who cursed and struggled to raise his battered sub-machine gun. A gun roared in my ear and the back of my neck burned. I realized my jump had literally saved my neck. I ran around to the side of the grappling pair, and shoved the blade into the thin man's ribs. It grated and stuck, but he wilted. I'm not much of a sport, I thought, but I guess guns against pig-stickers makes it even.

Hermann stepped back, spat disgustedly, and leaped on the nearest bandit. I wrenched at my sword, but it was wedged tight. I left it and grabbed up the tommy gun. A long-legged villain was just closing the chamber of his revolver as I pumped a burst into his stomach. I saw dust fly from the shabby cloth of his coat as the slugs smacked home.

I glanced around. Several of the men of the Imperium were firing captured guns now, and the remnant of the invading mob had fallen back toward the shattered wall. Bullets cut them down as they stood at bay, still pouring out a ragged fire. None of them tried to flee.

I ran forward, sensing something wrong. I raised my gun and cut down a bloody-faced man as he stood firing two .45 automatics. My last round nicked a heavy-set carbine man, and the drum was empty. I picked up another weapon from the floor, as one lone thug still standing pounded the bolt of his rifle with his palm.

"Take him alive," someone shouted. The firing stopped and a dozen men seized the struggling man. The crowd milled, women bending over those who lay on the floor, men staggering from their exertions. I ran toward the billowing drapes.

"Come on," I shouted. "Outside . . ." I didn't have time or breath to say more, or to see if anyone came. I leaped across the rubble, out onto the blasted terrace, leaped the rail, and landed in the garden, sprawled a little, but still moving. In the light of the colored floods a grey-painted van, ponderously bulky, sat askew across flower beds. Beside it, three tattered crewmen struggled with a bulky load. A small tripod stood on the lawn, awaiting the mounting of their burden. I had time for one momentary mental vision of what a fission bomb would do to the Summer Palace and its occupants, before I dashed at them with a yell. I fired the pistol I had grabbed, as fast as I could pull the trigger, and the three men hesitated, pulled against each other, cursed, and started back toward the open door of their van with the bomb. One of them fell, and I realized someone behind me was firing accurately. Another of the men yelped and ran off a few yards to crumple on the grass. The third jumped for the open door, and a moment later a rush of air threw dust against my face as the van flicked out of existence. The sound was like a pool of gasoline igniting.

The bulky package lay on the ground now, ominous. I felt sure it was not yet armed. I turned to the others. "Don't touch this thing," I called. "I'm sure it's some kind of atomic bomb."

"Nice work, old boy," a familiar voice said. It was Winter, blood spattered on the pale yellow of his tunic. "Might have known those chaps were fighting a delaying action for a reason. Are you all right?"

"Yeah," I said, breathless. "Let's get back inside. They'll need tourniquets and men to twist them."

We picked our way through the broken glass, fragments of flagstone, and splinters of framing, past the flapping drapes, into the brightly lit dust-rolled ballroom.

Dead and wounded lay in a rough semi-circle around the broken wall. I recognized a pretty brunette in a blue dress whom I had danced with earlier, lying on the floor, face waxen. Everyone was splattered with crimson. I looked around frantically for my redhead, and saw her kneeling beside a wounded man, binding his head.

There was a shout. Winter and I whirled. One of the wounded intruders moved, threw something, then collapsed as shots struck him. I heard the thump and rattle as the object fell, and as in a dream I watched the grenade roll over and over, clattering, stop ten feet away and spin a half a turn. I stood, frozen. Finished, I thought. And I never even learned her name.

From behind me I heard a gasp as Winter leaped past me and threw himself forward. He landed spread-eagled over the grenade as it exploded with a muffled thump, throwing Winter two feet into the air.

I staggered, and turned away, dizzy. Poor Winter. Poor damned Winter.

I felt myself passing out, and went to my knees. The floor was tilting...

She was bending over me, face pale, but still steady. I reached up and touched her hand. "What's your name?" I said.

"My name?" she said. "Barbro Lundin; I thought you knew my name..." She seemed a bit dazed. I sat up. "Better lend a hand to someone who's worse off than I am, Barbro," I said. "I just have a weak constitution."

"No," she said. "You've bled much."

Richthofen appeared, looking grim. He helped me up. My neck and head ached. "Thank God you are alive," he said.

"Thank Winter I'm alive," I replied. "I don't suppose there's a chance...?"

"Killed instantly," Richthofen said. "He knew his duty."

"Poor guy," I said. "It should have been me."

"We're fortunate it wasn't you," Richthofen said. "It was close. As it is, you've lost considerable blood. You must come along and rest now."

"I want to stay here," I said. "Maybe I can do something useful."

Goering had appeared from somewhere, and he laid an arm across my shoulders, leading me away.

"Calmly, now, my friend," he said. "There is no

need to feel it so strongly; he died in performance of his duty, as he would have wished."

Hermann knew what was bothering me. I could have blanked out that grenade as easily as Winter, but the thought hadn't even occurred to me. If I hadn't been paralyzed, I'd have run.

I didn't struggle; I felt washed out, suddenly suffering a premature hangover. Manfred joined us at the car, and we drove home in near silence. I asked about the bomb and Goering said that Bale's men had taken it over. "Tell them to dump it at sea," I said.

At the villa, someone waited on the steps as we drove up. I recognized Bale's rangy figure with the undersized head. I ignored him as he collared Hermann.

I went into the dining room, poured a stiff drink at the sideboard, sat down.

The others came behind me, talking. I wondered where Bale had been all evening.

Bale sat down, eyeing me. He wanted to hear all about the attack. He seemed to take the news calmly but sourly.

He looked at me, pursing his lips. "Mr. Goering has told me that you conducted yourself quite well, Mr. Bayard, during the fight. Perhaps I was hasty in my judgment of you..."

"Who the hell cares what you think, Bale?" I said. "Where were you when the lead was flying? Under the rug? You've got a hell of a lot of gall strutting in here and delivering your pompous opinion." I was getting madder by the second.

Bale turned white, stood up glaring and stalked out of the room. Goering cleared his throat and Manfred cast an odd look at me as he rose to perform his hostly duty of conducting a guest to the door.

"Inspector Bale is not a man easy to associate with," Hermann said. "I understand your feeling." He rose and came around the table.

"I feel you should know," he went on, "that he is among the most skillful with sabre and epee. Make no hasty decision now..."

"What decision?" I asked.

"Already you have a painful wound," he said; "now we must not allow you to be laid up at this critical time. Are you sure of you skill with a pistol?"

"What wound?" I said. "You mean my neck?" I put my hand up to touch it. I winced; there was a deep gouge, caked with blood. Suddenly I was aware that the back of my jacket was soggy. That near-miss was a little nearer than I had thought.

"I hope you will accord Manfred and myself the honor of seconding you," Hermann continued, "and perhaps of advising you..."

"What's this all about, Hermann?" I said. "What do you mean: seconding me?"

"Why," he seemed confused, "we wish to stand with you in your meeting with Bale..."

"Meeting with Bale?" I repeated. I know I didn't sound very bright. I was beginning to realize how lousy I felt.

Goering stopped and looked at me. "Inspector Bale is a man most sensitive of personal dignity," he said. "You have given him a tongue-lashing before witnesses, and a well deserved one it was; however, it remains a certainty that he will demand satisfaction." He saw that I was still groping. "Bale will challenge you, Brion," he said. "You must fight him."

VI

THERE WAS THE SOUND of a car and Manfred rose with a word, went out of the room.

"Doubtless Bale's seconds arrive," Goering said. "I may speak for you?"

"Sure," I said, "but ... yes, thanks, Hermann." Bale hadn't wasted any time.

I heard voices and Manfred came into the room with two strangers. Two blood-spattered officers, fresh from the battle of the ballroom wearing the Grey uniforms of the Imperial Intelligence strolled casually up to us, one young, the other elderly, both slender and tough-looking, both calmly courteous.

"Ah, there you are, Goering," said the older man. He was limping slightly from a wound in the thigh. "You know von Rentz, I believe?" He indicated the younger man.

Goering rose and bowed stiffly from the waist. "I do, your excellency," he said. He turned to me. "Brion, I have the honor to present Count Hallendorf; Captain von Rentz. Gentlemen, Colonel Bayard."

Both officers clicked heels with stiff bows.

"Colonel Bayard," said the count.

"Hiya, boys," I said carelessly. "Bale send you out to do his arguing for him?"

Hermann stepped forward quickly. "Colonel Bayard has done me the honor of permitting me, together with the Friherr von Richthofen, to speak for him, gentlemen," he said smoothly. He took their arms and led them away, talking earnestly. Richthofen came over to me.

"Brion," he said, shaking his head. "I seem to sense that in your country the ritual of the affair of honor is not practiced."

"That's right, Baron," I said. "We insult each other all the time. The guy who can get the other fellow maddest without getting mad himself wins."

"That is not the custom here," Richthofen said. "One substantiates one's opinion with action. This is a most awkward piece of business; we have quite enough to fight in the enemy, I think. But Inspector Bale seems to feel otherwise; the personal affront takes precedence." He stepped over and examined my gouged neck.

"Brion, go and sit down; lie down if you can. You are too important to the Imperium and to us, your friends, to be subjected to this ordeal, but there is nothing for it but to see it through. I'll join you later." He turned away, then back. "What is your choice of weapons, Brion?"

"Water pistols at twenty paces," I said. What with the liquor, the carnage, and the pain in my head, neck, back and assorted other places, I was feeling pretty sardonic.

Richthofen shook his head resignedly and hurried off. There was blood on his boots.

I was cold, chilled to the bone. I was still half asleep, and I carried my head tilted forward and a little to the side in a hopeless attempt to minimize the vast throbbing ache from the furrow across the back of my neck.

Richthofen, Goering and I stood together under spreading linden trees at the lower end of the Royal Game Park. It was a few minutes before dawn. I was taking the "affair of honor" a little more seriously now. I was wondering how a slug in the knee-cap would feel.

There was the faint sound of an engine approaching, and a long car loomed up in the gloom on the road above, lights gleaming through morning mist.

The sound of doors opening and slamming was muffled and indistinct. Three figures were dimly visible, approaching down the gentle slope. My seconds moved away to meet them. One of the three detached itself from the group and stood alone, as I did. That would be Bale.

Another car pulled in behind the first. The doctor, I thought. In the dim glow from the second car's small square cowl lights I saw another figure emerge. I watched; it looked like a woman, wrapped in a cloak. The lights went off, and I looked back to the group of seconds.

I heard the murmur of voices, a low chuckle. They were very pally, I thought. Everything on a very high plane.

I thought over what Goering had told me on the way to the field of honor, as he called it.

Bale had offered his challenge under the Toth convention. This meant that the duelists would not try to kill each other; the object of the game was to inflict painful wounds, to humiliate one's opponent.

This could be a pretty tricky business. In the excitement of the fight, it wasn't easy to inflict wounds that were thoroughly humiliating but definitely not fatal. It was almost as much of a disgrace to kill one's opponent as to fail to meet him, I was told. The latter form of disgrace, however, was not unknown, while the former was unheard of.

I wondered what Bale would try for; possibly he had in mind something more painful even than smashed joints. I didn't know; this was a new sport to me, but Bale was an old-timer. I'd find out in a few minutes, I thought.

It had been explained to me that the most daring choice of weapons was the pistol; one not only ran the risk of inflicting a fatal wound, but one also exposed oneself to greater risk of death. It was commoner to use sabre or epee; first blood was usually satisfaction enough. However, since I was unfamiliar with the latter weapons, Goering and Richthofen had agreed that the pistol was the better choice. Well, I couldn't argue with that; I had carried a .45 for a year or so in Europe during the war, and fired it frequently on the range, as well as at a few moving targets in combat.

I had had about two hours sleep. My seconds had let me go to my suite finally after completing the arrangements, and I had dropped into a coma at once. They had a tough time getting me on my feet again, at five a.m. My morale was always lowest at this hour, even without a slashed neck and the prospect of painful and humiliating wounds. Richthofen had lent me a pair of black trousers and a white shirt for the performance, and a light overcoat against the pre-dawn chill. I wished it had been a heavy one. The only warm part of me was my neck, swathed in bandages.

The little group broke up now. My two backers approached, smiled encouragingly, and in low voices invited me to come alone. Goering took my coat. I missed it.

Bale and his men were walking toward a spot in the clear, where the early light was slightly better. We moved up to join them.

"I think we have light enough now, eh Baron?" said Hallendorf.

Richthofen glanced around. "I think perhaps five minutes more," he said, "for the sake of accuracy."

Goering and von Rentz were discussing the position of the starting line. The doctor stood by silently, bag in hand. Bale stood in the background.

Goering came over to me, muttered a few words of instruction. Bale came forward. Von Rentz handed him something; the seconds stood back. Bale walked over to me, and with a contemptuous gesture tossed a white leather military glove at my feet. I stared at Bale for a moment before stooping over to pick it up and hand it negligently to Goering. I had been briefed on the formal challenge.

Richthofen and Hallendorf were making a little ceremony of opening the heavy box von Rentz had supplied, and looking over the two long-barreled Mausers nestling inside. I thought of the thirty-one people killed in the attack at the palace and the dozens more badly wounded. I would have thought they'd have had their fill of guns for one night.

I could see better now; the light was increasing

rapidly. Long pink streamers flew in the east; the trees were still dark silhouettes.

Hallendorf stepped up to me, and offered the box. I picked up one of the pistols, without looking at it. Bale took the other, methodically worked the action, snapped the trigger, examined the rifling. Richthofen handed each of us a magazine.

"Five rounds," he said. I had no comment.

Bale stepped over to the place indicated by Hallendorf and turned his back. I could see the cars outlined against the sky now. The big one looked like a '30 Packard, I thought. At Goering's gesture, I took my post, back to Bale.

"At the signal, gentlemen," Hallendorf said, "step forward ten paces and pause; at the command, turn and fire. Gentlemen, in the name of the Emperor and of honor!"

The white handkerchief in his hand fluttered to the ground. I started walking. One, two, three...

There was someone standing by the smaller car. I wondered who it was... eight, nine, ten. I stopped, waiting. Hallendorf's voice was calm. "Turn and fire."

I turned, holding the pistol at my side. Bale pumped a cartridge into the chamber, set his feet apart, body sideways to me, left arm behind his back, and raised his pistol. We were a hundred feet apart across the wet field.

I started walking toward him. Nobody had said I had to stay in one spot. Bale lowered the pistol slightly, and I saw his pale face, eyes staring. The pistol came up again, and almost instantly jumped as a flat crack rang out. The spent cartridge popped up over Bale's head and dropped on the wet grass, catching the light. A miss.

I walked on. I had no intention of standing in the

half dark, firing wildly at a half-seen target. I didn't intend to be forced into killing a man by accident, even if it was his idea. And I didn't intend to be pushed into solemnly playing Bale's game with him.

Bale held the automatic at arm's length, following me as I approached. He could have killed me easily, but that was against the code. The weapon wavered; he couldn't decide on a target. My moving was bothering him.

The pistol steadied and jumped again, the shot sounding faint on the foggy air. I realized he was trying for the legs; I was close enough now to see the depressed angle of the barrel.

He stepped back a pace, set himself again, and raised the Mauser higher. He was going to try to break a rib, I guessed. A tricky shot, easy to miss—either way. My stomach muscles tensed with anticipation.

I didn't hear the next one; the sensation was exactly like a baseball bat slammed against my side. I felt that I was stumbling, air knocked from my lungs, but I kept my feet. A great warm ache spread from just above the hip. Only twenty feet away now. I fought to draw a breath.

Bale's expression was visible, a stiff shocked look, mouth squeezed shut. He aimed at my feet and fired twice in rapid succession; I think by error. One shot went through my boot between the toes of my right foot, the other into the dirt. I walked up to him. I sucked in air painfully. I wanted to say something, but couldn't. It was all I could do to keep from gasping. Abruptly, Bale backed a step, aimed the pistol at my chest and pulled the trigger; it clicked. He looked down at the gun.

I dropped the Mauser at his feet, doubled my fist, and hit him hard on the jaw. He reeled back as I turned away.

I walked over to Goering and Richthofen as the doctor hurried up. They came forward to meet me.

"Lieber Gott," Hermann breathed as he seized my hand and pumped it. "This story they will never believe."

"If your object was to make a fool of Inspector Bale," Richthofen said with a gleam in his eye, "you have scored an unqualified success. I think you have taught him respect."

The doctor pressed forward. "Gentlemen, I must take a look at the wound." A stool was produced, and I gratefully sank down on it.

I stuck my foot out. "Better take a look at this too," I said; "it feels a little tender."

The doctor muttered and exclaimed as he began snipping at cloth and leather. He was enjoying every minute of it. The doc, I saw, was a romantic.

A thought was trying to form itself in my mind. I opened my eyes. Barbro was coming toward me across the grass, dawn light gleaming in her red hair. I realized what it was I had to say.

"Hermann," I said; "Manfred; I need a long nap, but before I start I think I ought to tell you: I've had so much fun tonight that I've decided to take the job."

"Easy, Brion," Manfred said. "There's no need to think of it now."

"No trouble at all," I said.

Barbro bent over. "Brion," she said. "You are not badly hurt?" She looked worried.

I smiled at her and reached for her hand. "I'll bet

you think I'm accident prone; but actually I sometimes go for days at a time without so much as a bad fall."

She took my hand in both of hers as she knelt down. "You must be suffering great pain, Brion, to talk so foolishly," she said. "I thought he would lose his head and kill you." She turned to the doctor; "Help him, Dr. Blum."

"You are fortunate, Colonel," the doctor said, sticking a finger into the furrow on my side. "The rib is not fractured. In a few days you will have only a little scar and a big bruise to remind you."

I squeezed Barbro's hand. "Help me up, Barbro," I said.

Goering gave me his shoulder to lean on. "For you now, a long nap," he said. I was ready for it.

I tried to relax in my chair in the cramped shuttle. Just in front of me the operator sat tensed over a tiny illuminated board, peering at instrument faces and tapping the keys of what looked like a miniature calculating machine. A soundless hum filled the air, penetrating my bones.

I twisted, seeking a more comfortable position. My half-healed neck and side were stiffening up again. Bits of fragments of the last ten days' incessant briefing ran through my mind. Imperial Intelligence hadn't been able to gather as much material as they wanted on Marshall of the State Bayard, but it was more than I was able to assimilate consciously. I hoped the hypnotic sessions I had had every night for a week in place of real sleep had taken, at a level where the data would pop up when I needed it.

Bayard was a man of mystery, even to his own

people. He was rarely seen, except via what the puzzled intelligence men said 'seemed to be a sort of electric picture apparatus.' I had tried to explain that TV was commonplace in my world, but they never really understood it.

They had given me a good night's sleep the last three nights, and a tough hour of cleverly planned calisthenics every day. My wounds had healed well, so that now I was physically ready for the adventure; mentally, however, I was fagged. The result was an eagerness to get on with the thing, find out the worst of what I was faced with. I had enough of words; now I wanted the relief of action.

I checked over my equipment. I wore a military tunic duplicating that shown in the official portrait of Bayard. Since there was no information on what he wore below the chest, I had suggested olive drab trousers, matching what I recognized as the French regulation jacket.

At my advice, we'd skipped the ribbons and orders shown in the photo; I didn't think he would wear them around his private apartment in an informal situation. For the same reason, my collar was unbuttoned and my tie loosened.

They had kept me on a diet of lean beefsteak, to try to thin my face a bit. A hair specialist had given me vigorous scalp massages every morning and evening, and insisted that I not wash my head; this was intended to stimulate rapid growth and achieve the unclipped continental look of the dictator's picture.

Snapped to my belt was a small web pouch containing my communication transmitter. We had decided to let it show rather than seek with doubtful success to conceal it. The microphone was woven into the heavy braid on my lapels. I had a thick stack of NPS currency in my wallet.

I moved my right hand carefully, feeling for the pressure of the release spring that would throw the palm-sized slug-gun into my hand with the proper flexing of the wrist.

The little weapon was a marvel of compact deadliness. In shape it resembled a water-washed stone, grey and smooth. It could lie unnoticed on the ground, a feature which might be of great importance to me in an emergency.

Inside the gun a hair-sized channel spiraled down into the grip. A compressed gas, filling the tiny hole, served as both propellant and projectile. At a pressure on the right spot, unmarked, a minute globule of the liquefied gas was fired with tremendous velocity. Once free of the confining walls of the tough alloy barrel, the bead expanded explosively to a volume of a cubic foot. The result was an almost soundless blow, capable of shattering ¼" armor, instantly fatal within a range of ten feet.

It was the kind of weapon I needed; inconspicuous, quiet, and deadly at short range. The spring arrangement made it almost a part of the hand, if the hand were expert.

I had practiced the motion for hours, while listening to lectures, eating, even lying in bed. I was very conscientious about that piece of training; it was my insurance. I tried not to think about my other insurance, set in the hollowed-out bridge replacing a back tooth.

Each evening, after the day's hard routine, I had relaxed with new friends, exploring the Imperial Ballet, theatres, opera and a lively variety show. With Barbro, I had dined sumptuously at half a dozen fabulous restaurants and afterwards we had walked in moonlit gardens, sipped coffee as the sun rose, and talked. When the day came to leave, I had more than a casual desire to return. The sooner I got started, the quicker I would get back.

The first step on my route was the trip to North Africa, so that my shuttle could drop me directly into the palace at Algiers. We had spent a lot of time on pinpointing the exact position of the Dictator's apartment.

Goering and a group of intelligence men had seen me off as I boarded a huge bi-plane with five exposed engines, which looked a little like a Gotha or Handley-Page of World War I. I had made my way up the sloping aisle, and gone to sleep in the wicker seat almost before the plane started moving.

I awoke at dusk as we circled Algiers, and stared down out of the round window at the airport which lay to the east of the old city rather than in its accustomed position. We landed and a small reception committee rushed me along at once to another meeting, for final additions to my instructions.

Afterwards I had a restless night after sleeping all day on the plane and had only started yawning as I sat in the car on the way to the stately manorial house which the Dictator Bayard had enlarged as his personal fortress in the world of B-I Two.

We rode an elevator to the top floor, and climbed a narrow twisting stair to emerge through a door onto the wind-swept roof. I was cold and fuzzy-eyed. I looked up without enthusiasm at the steel scaffold which loomed from the tarred surface of the roof, reaching to the exact height of the floor of the Dictator's apartment—we hoped. I had to climb it to the platform at the top where a miniature version of the M-C scout lay, looking barely big enough for one. I wondered where the Operator would fit.

There was nothing left to say, no reason to wait. The intelligence men shook hands in a brisk no-nonsense way, and I started up. The iron rungs were cold to the touch, and slippery with moisture. Suppose I fell now? Where would the project be then? But one of the things that I admired about these Imperials was that they weren't too damned careful, not so hell-bent for womb-to-tomb security as the scared people at home.

Now, cramped in my seat in the shuttle, waiting for the hours to pass before I should be deposited in the dictator's suite, forty feet above the old roof level, I thought of the Imperial officers and their ladies standing up to the guns barehanded. I thought of the dead, lying in their riddled finery on the polished ballroom floor. I remembered the bearded raider, fighting to withdraw the length of the sabre from his chest, and wondered how many times he had gambled his life, before death called his bet.

He had worn part of an American uniform; perhaps he had been an American, a broken survivor of some hell-bomb war in which another America had not been the victor. I pictured him buying the jacket ten or fifteen years earlier, in some bright American PX, proud of the new gold bar on the shoulder, with his sweetheart at his side. Why wasn't my sympathy with him, and with the desperate courage of his ragged crew? I didn't know; there was a difference.

The Imperials had died with their pride intact. The others had been too much like my own memory of war, vicious and bitter.

I thought of Winter, dying in my place. I had liked Winter. He had been no fanatic, eager to make the grand gesture—but he hadn't hesitated.

Maybe, I said to myself, if a man wants to have something to live for, he's got to have something he'll die for.

The Operator turned. "Colonel," he said, "brace yourself, sir. There's something here I don't understand."

I tensed, but said nothing. I figured he would tell me more as soon as he knew more. I moved my hand tentatively against the slug-gun release. I already had the habit.

"I've detected a moving body in the Net," he said. "It seems to be trying to match our course. My spatial fix on it indicates it's very near."

The Imperium was decades behind my world in nuclear physics, television, aerodynamics, etc., but when it came to the instrumentation of these Maxoni devices, they were fantastic. After all, they had devoted their best scientific efforts to the task for almost sixty years.

Now the Operator hovered over his panel controls like a nervous organist.

"I get a mass of about fifteen hundred kilos," he said. "That's about right for a light scout, but it can't be one of ours..."

There was a tense silence for several minutes.

"He's pacing us, Colonel," the Operator said. "Either they've got better instrumentation than we thought, or this chap has had a stroke of blind luck. He was lying in wait..."

Both of us were assuming the stranger could be nothing but a B-I Two vessel.

"Perhaps they've set up a DEW line to pick up anyone coming in," I said. The Dictator's men were geared to modern war; they wouldn't be likely to ignore such measures. The Imperium didn't yet know the fanatic war-skill of Atomic Man . . . Still, it was strange . . .

"This won't do," the Operator said. "I can't drop out of the Net at our destination with this chap on my back. Not only would there be the devil to pay with this fellow identifying with an occupied space, but there'd be precious little secrecy left about the operation."

"Can't you lose him?" I asked.

He shook his head. "I can't possibly change my course here in the Blight. Correction requires a momentary identification. And, of course, our maximum progression rate is constant, just as his is; he can't help clinging like a leech once he's got us."

I didn't like this at all. The only thing we could do was keep going until we crossed the Blight, then try to shake him off. I didn't want to have this turn into a dry run.

"Can we fire a shot at him?" I asked.

"As soon as the projectile left the M-C field, it would drop into identity," the Operator said. "But, of course, the same thing keeps him from shooting at us."

The Operator tensed up suddenly, hands frozen. "He's coming in on us, Colonel," he said. "He's going to ram. We'll blow sky-high if he crosses our fix."

My thoughts ran like lightning over my slug-gun, the hollow tooth; I wondered what would happen when he hit. Somehow, I hadn't expected it to end here.

The impossible tension lasted only a few seconds; the Operator relaxed.

"Missed," he said. "Apparently his spatial maneuvering isn't as good as his Net mobility. But he'll be back; he's after blood."

I had a thought. "Our maximum rate is controlled by the energy of normal entropy, isn't it?" I asked.

He nodded.

"What about going slower," I said. "Maybe he'll overshoot."

I could see the sweat start on the back of his neck from there.

"A bit risky in the Blight, sir," he said, "but we'll have a go at it."

I knew how hard that was for an Operator to say. This young fellow had had six years of intensive training, and not a day of it had passed without a warning against any unnecessary control changes in the Blight.

The sound of the generators changed, the pitch of the whine descending into the audible range, dropping lower.

"He's still with us, Colonel," the operator said.

The pitch fell, lower, lower. I didn't know when the critical point would be reached when we would lose our artificial orientation and rotate into normal entropy. We sat, rigid, waiting. The sound dropped down, almost baritone now. The Operator tapped again and again at a key, glancing at a dial.

The drive hum was a harsh droning now; we couldn't expect to go much further without disaster. But then neither could the enemy...

"He's right with us, Colonel, only..." Suddenly the Operator shouted.

"We lost him, Colonel! His controls aren't as good as ours in that line, anyway; he dropped into identity."

I sank back, as the whine of our M-C generator built up again. My palms were wet. I wondered into which of the hells of the Blight they had gone. But I had another problem to face in a few minutes. This was not the time for shaken nerves.

"Good work, Operator," I said at last. "How much longer?"

"About—Good God—ten minutes, sir," he answered. "That little business took longer than I thought."

I started a last minute check. My mouth was dry. Everything seemed to be in place. I pressed the button on my communicator.

"Hello, Talisman," I said, "here is Wolfhound Red. How do you hear me? Over."

"Wolfhound Red, Talisman here, you're coming in right and bright, over." The tiny voice spoke almost in my ear from the speaker in a button on my shoulder strap.

I liked the instant response; I felt a little less lonesome.

I looked at the trip mechanism for the escape door. I was to wait for the Operator to say, "Crash out," and hit the lever. I had exactly two seconds then to pull my arm back and kick the slug-gun into my palm before the seat would automatically dump me, standing, out the exit. The shuttle would be gone before my feet hit the floor.

I had been so wrapped up in the business at hand for the past ten days that I had not really thought about the moment of my arrival in the B-I Two world. The smoothly professional handling of my hasty training had given the job an air of practicality and realism. Now, about to be propelled into the innermost midst of the enemy, I began to realize the suicidal aspects of the mission. But it was too late now for second thoughts—and in a way I was glad. I was involved now in this world of the Imperium; it was a part of my life worth risking something for.

I was a card the Imperium held, and it was my turn to be played. I was a valuable property, but that value could only be realized by putting me into the scene in just this way; and the sooner the better. I had no assurance that the Dictator was in residence at the palace now; I might find myself hiding in his quarters awaiting his return, for God knows how long—and maybe lucky at that, to get that far. I hoped our placement of the suite was correct, based on information gotten from the captive taken at the ballroom, under deep narco-hypnosis. Otherwise, I might find myself treading air, 150 feet up...

There was a slamming of switches, and the Operator twisted in his chair.

"Crash out, Wolfhound," he cried, "and good hunting."

Reach out and slam the lever; arm at the side, snap the gun into place in my hand; with a metallic whack and a rush of air the exit popped and a giant hand palmed me out into dimness. One awful instant of vertigo, of a step missed in the dark, and then my feet slammed against carpeted floor. Air whipped about my face, and the echoes of the departing boom of the shuttle still hung in the corridor.

I remembered my instructions; I stood still, turning casually to check behind me. There was no one in sight. The hall was dark except for the faint light from a ceiling fixture at the next intersection. I had arrived OK.

I slipped the gun back into its latch under my cuff. No point in standing here; I started off at a leisurely pace toward the light. The doors lining the hall were identical, unmarked. I paused and tried one. Locked. So was the next. The third opened, and I looked cautiously into a sitting room. I went on. What I wanted was the sleeping room of the Dictator, if possible. If he were in, I knew what to do; if not, presumably he would return if I waited long enough. Meanwhile, I wanted very much not to meet anyone.

There was the sound of an elevator door opening, just around the corner ahead. I stopped; better get out of sight fast. I eased back to the last door I had checked, opened it and stepped inside, closing it almost all the way behind me. My heart was thudding painfully. I didn't feel daring; I felt like a sneak thief. Faintly, I heard steps coming my way. I silently closed the door, taking care not to let the latch click. I stood behind it for a moment before deciding it would be better to conceal myself, just in case. I glanced around, moving into the center of the room. I could barely make out outlines in the gloom. There was a tall shape against the wall; a wardrobe, I thought. I hurried across to it, opened the door, and stepped in among hanging clothes.

I stood for a moment, feeling foolish, then froze as the door to the hall opened and closed again softly. There were footsteps, and then a light went on. My closet door was open just enough to catch a glimpse of a man's back as he turned away from the lamp. I heard the soft sound of a chair being pulled out, and then the tiny jingle of keys. There were faint metallic sounds, a pause, more faint metallic sounds. The man was apparently trying keys in the lock of a table or desk.

I stood absolutely rigid. I breathed shallowly, tried not to think about a sudden itch on my cheek. I could see the shoulder of the coat hanging to my left. I turned my eyes to it. It was almost identical with the one I was wearing. The lapels were adorned with heavy braid. I had a small moment of relief; I had found the right apartment, at least. But my victim must be the man in the room; and I had never felt less like killing anyone in my life.

The little sounds went on. I could hear the man's heavy breathing. All at once I wondered what he would look like, this double of mine. Would he really resemble me, or more to the point, did I look enough like him to take his place?

I wondered why he took so long finding the right key; then another thought struck me. Didn't this sound a little more like someone trying to open someone else's desk? I moved my head a fraction of an inch. The clothes moved silently, and I edged a little farther. Now I could see him. He sat hunched in the chair, working impatiently at the lock. He was short and had thin hair, and resembled me not in the least. It was not the Dictator.

This was a new factor for me to think over, and in a hurry. The Dictator was obviously not around, or this fellow would not be here attempting to rifle his desk. And the dictator had people around him who were not above prying. That fact might be useful to me.

It took him five minutes to find a key that fit. I

stood with muscles aching from the awkward pose, trying not to think of the lint that might cause a sneeze. I could hear the shuffling of papers, faint muttering as the man looked over his finds. At length there was the sound of the drawer closing, the snick of the lock. Now the man was on his feet, the chair pushed back, and then silence for a few moments. Steps came toward me. I froze, my wrist twitching, ready to cover him and fire if necessary the instant he pulled the door open. I wasn't ready to start my imposture just yet, skulking in a closet.

I let out a soundless sigh as he passed the opening and disappeared. More sounds as he ran through the drawers of a bureau or chest.

Suddenly the hall door opened again, and another set of steps entered the room. I heard my man freeze. Then he spoke, in guttural French.

"Oh, it's you, is it, Maurice..."

There was a pause. Maurice's tone was insinuating.

"Yes, I thought I saw a light in the chief's study. I thought that was a bit odd, what with him away tonight."

The first man sauntered back toward the center of the room. "I just thought I'd have a look to see that everything was OK here."

Maurice tittered. "Don't try to rob a thief; I know why you came here—for the same reason as I."

The first man snarled. "You're a fool, Maurice. Come on, let's get out of this."

Maurice didn't sound like a titterer now. "Not so fast and smooth, Flic. Something's coming up and I want in."

"Don't call me Flic," the first man said. "You're crazy."

"You didn't mind being a flic when you threw the weight of the badge around in Marseilles in the Old

Days; see, I know all about you." He laughed, an ugly sound.

"What are you up to," the first man hissed. "What do you want?"

"Sit down, Flic; oh, don't get excited; they all call you that." Maurice was enjoying himself. I listened carefully for half an hour while he goaded and cajoled, and pressured the other. The first man, I learned, was Georges Pinay, the chief of the dictator's security force. The other was a civilian military adviser to the Bureau of Propaganda and Education. Pinay, it seemed had been less clever than he thought in planning a coup that was to unseat Bayard. Maurice knew all about it, and had bided his time; now he was taking over. Pinay didn't like it, but he accepted it after Maurice mentioned a few things nobody was supposed to know about a hidden airplane and a deposit of gold coins buried a few miles outside the city.

I listened carefully, without moving, and after a while even the itch went away. Pinay had been looking for lists of names, he admitted; he planned to enlist a few more supporters by showing them their names in the Dictator's own hand on the purge schedule. He hadn't planned to mention that he himself had nominated them for the list.

I made the mistake of overconfidence; I was just waiting for them to finish up when a sudden silence fell. I didn't know what I had done wrong, but I knew at once what was coming. The steps were very quiet and there was just a moment's pause before the door was flung open. I hoped my make-up was on straight.

I stepped out, casting a cool glance at Pinay.

"Well, Georges," I said, "it's nice to know you

keep yourself occupied when I'm away." I used the same French dialect they had used, and my wrist was against the little lever.

"The Devil," Maurice burst out. He stared at me with wide eyes. For a moment I thought I was going to get away with it. Then Pinay lunged at me. I whirled, side-stepped; and the slug-gun slapped my palm.

"Hold it," I barked.

Pinay ignored the order and charged again. I squeezed the tiny weapon, bracing myself against the recoil. There was a solid thump and Pinay bounced aside, landed on his back, loose limbed, and lay still. Then Maurice hit me from the side. I stumbled across the room, tripped and fell, and he was on top of me. I still had my gun, and tried to bring it into play, but I was dazed, and Maurice was fast and strong as a bull. He flipped me and held me in a one-handed judo hold that pinned both arms behind me. He was astride me, breathing heavily.

"Who are you?" he hissed.

"I thought you'd know me, Maurice," I said. With infinite care I groped, tucked the slug-gun into my cuff. I heard it click home and I relaxed.

"So you thought that, eh?" Maurice laughed. His face was pink and moist. He pulled a heavy blackjack from his pocket as he slid off me.

"Get up," he said. He looked me over.

"My God," he said. "Fantastic. Who sent you?"

I didn't answer. It seemed I wasn't fooling him for a minute. I wondered what was so wrong. Still, he seemed to find my appearance interesting. He stepped forward and slammed the sap against my neck, with a controlled motion. He could have broken my neck with it, but what he did was more painful. I felt the blood start from my half healed neck wound. He saw it, and looked puzzled for a moment. Then his face cleared.

"Excuse me," he said, grinning. "I'll try for a fresh spot next time. And answer when spoken to." There was a viciousness in his voice that reminded me of the attack at the palace. These men had seen hell on earth and they were no longer fully human.

He looked at me appraisingly, slapping his palm with the blackjack. "I think we'll have a little talk downstairs," he said. "Keep the hands in sight." His eyes darted about, apparently looking for my gun. He was very sure of himself; he didn't let it worry him when he didn't see it. He didn't want to take his eyes off me long enough to really make a search.

"Stay close, Baby," he said. "Just like that, come along now, nice and easy."

I kept my hands away from my sides, and followed him over to the phone. He wasn't as good as he thought; I could have taken him anytime. I had a hunch, though, that it might be better to string along a little, try to find out something more.

Maurice picked up the phone, spoke softly into it and dropped it back in the cradle. His eyes stayed on me.

"How long before they get here?" I asked.

Maurice narrowed his eyes, not answering.

"Maybe we have just time enough to make a deal," I said.

His mouth curved in what might have been a smile. "We'll make a deal all right, Baby," he said. "You sing loud and clear, and maybe I'll tell the boys to make it a fast finish."

"You've got an ace up your sleeve here, Maurice," I urged. "Don't let that rabble in on it."

He slapped his palm again. "What have you got in mind, Baby?"

"I'm on my own," I said. I was thinking fast. "I'll bet you never knew Brion had a twin brother. He cut me out, though, so I thought I'd cut myself in."

Maurice was interested. "The devil," he said. "You haven't seen your loving twin in a long time, I see." He grinned. I wondered what the joke was.

"Let's get out of here," I said. "Let's keep it between us two."

Maurice glanced at Pinay.

"Forget him," I said. "He's dead."

"You'd like that, wouldn't you, Baby," Maurice said. "Just the two of us, and maybe then a chance to narrow it back down to one." His sardonic expression turned suddenly to a snarl, with nostrils flaring. "By God," he said, "you, you'd plan to kill me, you little man of straw..." He was leaning toward me now, arm loosening for a swing. I realized he was insane, ready to kill in an instantaneous fury.

"You'll see who is the killer between us," he said. His eyes gleamed as he swung the blackjack loosely in his hand.

I couldn't wait any longer. The gun popped into my hand, aimed at Maurice. I felt myself beginning to respond to his murder-lust. I hated everything he stood for.

"You're stupid, Maurice," I said. "Stupid and slow, and in just a minute, dead. But first you're going to tell me how you knew I wasn't Bayard."

It was a nice try, but wasted.

Maurice leaped and the slug-gun slapped him aside. He hit and lay limp. My arm ached from the recoil. Handling the tiny weapon was tricky. It was good for about fifty shots on a charge; at this rate it wouldn't last a day.

I had to get out fast now. I reached up and smashed the ceiling light, then the table lamp. That might slow them up for a few moments. I eased out into the hall and started for the dark end. Behind me I heard the elevator opening. They were here already. I pushed at the glass door, and it swung open quietly. I didn't wait around to see what their reaction would be when they found Maurice and Georges. I went down the stairs two at a time, as softly as I could. I thought of my communicator and decided against it. I didn't have anything good to report.

I passed three landings before I emerged into a hall. This would be the old roof level. I tried to remember where the stair had come out in the analogous spot back at Zero Zero. I spotted a small door in an alcove; it seemed to be in about the right place.

A man came out of a room across the hall and glanced toward me. I rubbed my mouth thoughtfully, while heading for the little door. The resemblance was more of a hindrance than a help now. He went on, and I tried the door. It was locked, but it didn't look very strong. I put my hip against it and pushed. It gave way with no more than a mild splintering sound. The stairs were there, and I headed down.

I had no plan, other than to get in the clear. It was obvious that the impersonation was a complete flop. All I could do was to get to a safe place and ask for further instructions. I had gone down two flights when I heard the alarm bells start.

I stopped dead. I had to get rid of the fancy uniform.

I pulled off the jacket, then settled for tearing the braid off the wrists, and removing the shoulder tabs. I couldn't ditch the lapel braid; my microphone was woven into it. I couldn't do much else about my appearance.

This unused stair was probably as good a way out as any. I kept going. I checked the door at each floor. They were all locked. That was a good sign, I thought. The stair ended in a damp cul-de-sac filled with barrels and mildewed paper cartons. I went back up to the next landing and listened. Beyond the door there were loud voices and the clatter of feet. I remembered that the entry to the stair was near the main entrance to the old mansion. It looked like I was trapped.

I went down again, pulled one of the barrels aside. By the light of a match I peered behind it at the wall. The edge of a door frame was visible. I maneuvered another barrel out of place and found the knob. It was frozen. I wondered how much noise I could make without being heard; not much, I decided.

I needed something to pry with. The paper cartons looked like a possibility; I tore the flaps loose on one and looked in. It was filled with musty ledger books; no help.

The next was better. Old silverware, pots and pans. I dug out a heavy cleaver and slipped it into the crack. The thing was as solid as a bank vault. I tried again; it couldn't be that strong, but it didn't budge.

I stepped back. Maybe the only thing to do was forget caution and chop through the middle. I leaned over to pick the best spot to swing at—then jumped back flat against the wall, slug-gun in my hand. The door knob was turning.

VII

I WAS CLOSE TO panic; being cornered had that effect on me. I didn't know what to do. I had plenty of instructions on how to handle the job of taking over after I had succeeded in killing the Dictator, but none to cover retreat after failure.

There was a creak, and dust sifted down from the top of the door. I stood as far back as I could get, waiting. I had an impulse to start shooting, but restrained it. Wait and see.

The door edged open a crack. I really didn't like this; I was being looked over, and could see nothing myself. At least I had the appearance of being unarmed; the tiny gun was concealed in my hand. Or was that an advantage? I couldn't decide.

I didn't like the suspense. "All right," I said. "You're making a draft; in or out." I spoke in the gutter Parisian I had heard upstairs.

The door opened farther, and a grimy-faced fellow was visible beyond it. He blinked in the dim light, peered up the stairs. He gestured.

"This way, come on," he said in a hoarse whisper. I didn't see any reason to refuse under the circumstances. I stepped past the barrels and ducked through the low doorway. As the man closed the door, I slipped the gun back into its clip. I was standing in a damp stone-lined tunnel, lit by an electric lantern sitting on the floor. I stood with my back to it. I didn't want him to see my face yet, not in a good light.

"Who are you?" I asked.

The fellow pushed past me and picked up his lantern. He hardly glanced at me.

"I'm just a dumb guy," he said. "I don't ask no questions, I don't answer none. Come on."

I couldn't afford to argue the point; I followed him. We made our way along the hand-hewn corridor, then down a twisting flight of steps, to emerge into a dark windowless chamber. Two men and a dark haired girl sat around a battered table where a candle sputtered.

"Call them in, Miche," my guide said. "Here's the pigeon."

Miche lolled back in his chair and motioned me toward him. He picked up what looked like a letter-knife from the table and probed between two back teeth while he squinted at me. I made it a point not to get too close.

"One of the kennel dogs, by the uniform," he said. "What's the matter, you bite the hand that fed you?" He laughed, not very humorously.

I said nothing. I thought I'd give him a chance to tell me something first if he felt like it.

"A ranker, too, by the braid," he said. "Well, they'll wonder where you got to." His tone changed. "Let's have the story," he said. "Why are you on the run?"

"Don't let the suit bother you," I said. "I borrowed it. But it seemed like the people up there disliked me on sight."

"Come on over here," the other man said. "Into the light."

I couldn't put it off forever. I moved forward, right up to the table. Just to be sure they got the idea, I picked up the candle and held it by my face.

Miche froze, knife point in his teeth. The girl started violently and crossed herself. The other man stared, fascinated. I'd gone over pretty big. I put the candle back on the table and sat down casually in the empty chair.

"Maybe you can tell me," I said, "why they didn't buy it."

The second man spoke. "You just walked in like that, sprung it on them?"

I nodded.

He and Miche looked at each other.

"You got a very valuable property here, my friend," the man said. "But you need a little help. Chica, bring wine for our new friend here."

The girl, still wide-eyed, scuttled to a dingy cupboard and fumbled for a bottle, looking at me over her shoulder.

"Look at him sitting there, Gros," Miche said. "Now that's something."

"You're right that's something," Gros said. "If it isn't already loused up." He leaned across the table. "Now just what happened upstairs," he said. "How long have you been in the palace; how many have seen you?"

I gave them a brief outline, leaving out my mode of arrival. They seemed satisfied.

"Only two seen his face, Gros," Miche said, "and they're out of the picture." He turned to me. "That was a nice bit of work, Mister, knocking off Souvet; and nobody ain't going to miss Pinay neither. By the way, where's the gun? Better let me have it." He held out his hand.

"I had to leave it," I said. "Tripped and dropped it in the dark."

Miche grunted.

"The Boss will be interested in this," Gros said. "He'll want to see him."

Someone else panted up the stairs into the room. "Say, Chief," he began, "we make it trouble in the tower..." He stopped dead as he caught sight of me, and dropped into a crouch, utter startlement on his face. His hand clawed for a gun at his hip, found none, as his eyes darted from face to face. "What—what..."

Gros and Miche burst into raucous laughter, slapping the table and howling. "At ease, Spider," Miche managed. "Bayard's throwed in with us." At this even Chica snickered.

Spider still crouched. "OK, what's the deal," he gasped. "I don't get it." He glared around the room, face white. He was scared stiff. Miche wiped his face, whooped a last time, hawked and spat on the floor.

"OK, Spider, as you were," he said. "This here's a ringer. Now you better go bring in the boys. Beat it."

Spider scuttled away. I was puzzled; why did some of them take one startled look and relax, while this fellow was apparently completely taken in? I had to find out. There was something I was doing wrong.

"Do you mind telling me," I said. "What's wrong with the get-up?" Miche and Gros exchanged glanced again.

"Well, my friend," Gros said, "it's nothing we can't take care of. Just take it easy, and we'll set you right. You wanted to step in and take out the Old Man, and sit in for him, right? Well, with the Organization behind you you're as good as in."

"What's the Organization?" I asked.

Miche broke in, "For now we'll ask the questions," he said. "What's your name? What's your play here?"

I looked from Miche to Gros. I wondered which one was the boss. "My name's Bayard," I said.

Miche narrowed his eyes as he rose and walked around the table. He was a big fellow with small eyes.

"I asked you what's your name, Mister," he said. "I don't usually ask twice."

"Hold it, Miche," Gros said. "He's right. He's got to stay in this part, if he's going to be good; and he better be plenty good. Let's leave it at that; he's Bayard."

Miche looked at me. "Yeah," he said, "you got a point." I had a feeling Miche and I weren't going to get along.

"Who's backing you, uh, Bayard?" Gros said.

"I play a lone hand," I said. "Up to now, anyway. But it seems I missed something. If your Organization can get me in, I'll go along."

"We'll get you in, all right," Miche said.

I didn't like the looks of this pair of hoodlums, but I could hardly expect high-toned company here. As far as I could guess, the Organization was an underground anti-Bayard party. The room seemed to be hollowed out of the walls of the palace. Apparently they ran a spying operation all through the building, using hidden passages.

More men entered the room now, some via the stair,

others through a door in the far corner. Apparently the word had gone out. They gathered around, staring curiously, commenting to each other, but not surprised.

"These are the boys," Gros said, looking around at them. "The rats in the walls."

I looked them over, about a dozen piratical-looking toughs; Gros had described them well. I looked back at him. "All right," I said. "When do we start?" These weren't the kind of companions I would have chosen, but if they could fill in the gaps in my disguise for me, and help me take over in Bayard's place, I could only be grateful for my good luck.

"Not so fast," Miche said. "This thing is going to take time. We got to get you to a layout we got out of town. We got a lot of work ahead of us."

"I'm here now," I said. "Why not go ahead today; why leave here?"

"We got a little work to do on your disguise," Gros said, "and there's plans to make. How do we get the most out of this break and how do we make sure there's no wires on this?"

"And no double-cross," Miche added.

A hairy lout listening in the crowd spoke up.

"I don't like the looks of this stool, Miche. I don't like funny stuff. I say under the floor with him." He wore a worn commando knife in a sheath fixed horizontally to his belt buckle. I was pretty sure he was eager to use it.

Miche looked at me. "Not for now, Gaston," he said.

Gros rubbed his chin. "Don't get worried about Mr. Bayard, boys," he said. "We'll have our eyes on him." He glanced up at Gaston. "You might make a special effort along those lines, Gaston; but don't get ahead of yourself. Let's say if he has any kind of accident, you'll have a worse one."

The feel of the spring under my wrist was comforting. I felt that Gaston wasn't the only one in this crew who didn't like strangers.

"I figure time is important," I said. "Let's get moving."

Miche stepped over to me. He prodded my leg with his boot. "You got a flappy mouth, Mister," he said. "Gros and me gives the orders around here."

"OK," Gros said. "Our friend has got a lot to learn, but he's right about the time. Bayard's due back here sometime tomorrow, so that means we get out today, if we don't want the Ducals all over the place on top of the regulars. Miche, get the boys moving. I want things folded fast and quiet, and good men on the standby crew."

He turned to me as Miche bawled orders to the men.

"Maybe you better have a little food now," he said. "It's going to be a long day."

I was startled; I had been thinking of it as night. I looked at my watch. It had been one hour and ten minutes since I had entered the palace. Doesn't time go fast, I thought to myself, when everyone's having fun.

Chica brought over a loaf of bread and a wedge of brown cheese from the cupboard, and placed them on the table with a knife. I was cautious.

"OK if I pick up the knife?" I asked.

"Sure," Gros said. "Go ahead." He reached under the table and laid a short-nosed revolver before him.

Miche came back to the table as I chewed on a slice of tough bread. It was good bread. I tried the wine. It wasn't bad. The cheese was good, too.

"You eat well," I said. "This is good."

Chica threw me a grateful smile. "We do all right," Gros said.

"Better get Mouth here out of that fancy suit," Miche said, jerking his head at me. "Somebody might just take a shot at that without thinking. The boys have got kind of nervous about them kind of suits."

Gros looked at me. "That's right," he said. "Miche will give you some other clothes. That uniform don't go over so big here."

I didn't like this development at all. My communicator was built into the scrambled eggs on my lapels. I had to say 'no' and make it stick.

"Sorry," I said. "I keep the outfit. It's part of the act. I'll put a coat over it if necessary."

Miche put his foot against my chair and shoved; I saw it coming and managed to scramble to my feet instead of going over with the chair. Miche faced me, skin tight around his eyes.

"Strip, Mister," he said. "You heard the man."

The men still in the room fell silent, watching. I looked at Miche. I hoped Gros would speak up. I couldn't see anything to be gained by this.

Nobody spoke. I glanced over at Gros. He was just looking at us.

Miche reached behind, brought out a knife. The blade snicked out. "Or do I have to cut it off you," he growled.

"Put the knife away, Miche," Gros said mildly. "You don't want to cut up our secret weapon here; and we want the uniform off all in one piece."

"Yeah," Miche said. "You got a point." He dropped the knife on the table and moved in on me. From his practiced crouch and easy shuffling step, I saw that he had been a professional.

I decided not to wait for him. I threw myself forward with my weight behind a straight left to the jaw. It caught Miche by surprise, slammed against his chin and rocked him back. I tried to follow up, catch him again while he was still off balance, but he was a veteran of too many fights. He covered up, back-pedaled, shook his head, and then flicked out with a right that exploded against my temple. I was almost out, staggering. He hit me again, square on the nose. Blood flowed.

I wouldn't last long against this bruiser. The crowd was still bunched at the far end of the room, moving this way, now, watching delightedly, calling encouragement to Miche. Gros still sat, and Chica stared from her place by the wall.

I moved back, dazed, dodging blows. I only had one chance and I needed a dark corner to try it. Miche was right after me. He was mad; he didn't like that smack on the jaw in front of the boys. That helped me; he forgot boxing and threw one haymaker after another. He wanted to floor me with one punch to retrieve his dignity. I dodged and retreated.

I moved back toward the deep shadows at the end of the room, beyond Chica's pantry. I had to get there quickly, before the watching crowd closed up the space.

Miche swung, again, left, right. I heard the air whistle as his hamlike fist grazed me. I backed another step; almost far enough. Now to get between him and the rest of the room. I jumped in behind a wild swing, popped a stinging right off his ear, and kept going. I whirled, snapped the slug-gun into my hand, and as Miche lunged, I shot him in the stomach, faked a wild swinging attack as he bounced off the wall and fell full length at my feet. I slipped the gun back into my cuff and turned.

"I can't see," a man shouted. "Get some light down here." The mob pushed forward, forming a wide ring. They stopped as they saw that only I was on my feet.

"Miche is down," a man called. "The new guy took him."

Gros pushed his way through, hesitated, then walked over to the sprawled body of Miche. He squatted, beckoned to the man with the candle.

He pulled Miche over on his back, then looked closer, feeling for the heartbeat. He looked up abruptly, got to his feet.

"He's dead," he said. "Miche is dead." He looked at me with a strange expression. "It's quite a punch you got, Mister," he said.

"I tried not to use it," I said. "But I'll use it again if I have to."

"Search him, boys," Gros said. They prodded and slapped, everywhere but my wrist. "He's clean, Gros," a man said. Gros looked the body over carefully, searching for signs of a wound. Men crowded around him.

"No marks," he said at last. "Broken ribs, and it feels like something funny inside; all messed up." He looked at me. "He did it bare-handed."

I hoped they would go on believing that. It was my best insurance against a repetition. I wanted them scared of me, and the ethics of it didn't bother me at all.

"All right," Gros called to the men. "Back on the job. Miche asked for it. He called our new man 'Mouth.' I'm naming him 'Hammer-hand.'"

I thought this was as good a time as any to push a little farther.

"You'd better tell them I'm taking over Miche's spot here, Gros," I said. "We'll work together, fifty-fifty."

Gros squinted at me. "Yeah, that figures," he said. I had a feeling he had mental reservations.

"And by the way," I added. "I keep the uniform."

"Yeah," Gros said. "He keeps the uniform." He turned back to the men. "We pull out of here in thirty minutes. Get moving."

I went over to the sink and washed the blood off my face. My nose ached. I peered at it in the broken mirror; it was swelling fast. I went back to the table and finished my bread and cheese while Gros paced up and down, taking reports and giving orders as men came and went. Miche's body was hauled away. I didn't ask where.

Gros came over to the table. "OK, Hammer-hand," he said. "On your feet." He handed me a dingy cape. "Stay right with me and do what I tell you." He hitched his trousers up to be sure I wouldn't miss the revolver stuck in his belt.

I stood up. "I'm ready," I said. I draped the wrap over my shoulders, concealing the insignia.

I followed Gros through the small door opposite the stair by which I had entered. A low-ceilinged passage led downward, twisting around steel pilings occasionally. Gros lit the way ahead with a fading electric lantern. The rest of the men were in nearly total darkness, but they seemed to know the way. Only a curse now and then indicated a collision in the dark.

We arrived at a wooden panel barring the way. Gros called two men forward, and together they drew back half a dozen heavy barrel-bolts. Gros eased the panel aside an inch and peered out. He signaled to the men to set it aside; everyone was silent now.

Gros hissed at me. "Stay close; do what I do. And get ready to run like hell."

I was at Gros's heels as he stepped down into a room dimly illuminated by sunlight filtering through boards covering shattered windows along the far side. Crates, boxes, and lift vans were stacked everywhere. We moved cautiously through them. I wondered why Gros didn't wait until night to make this break.

We stopped by a massive burlap-wrapped bale, and men silently surrounded it, pushing. It slid to one side with only a faint scraping, exposing a trap door. The lid was carefully raised and propped, and Gros motioned me down. I scrambled over the edge and found a wooden ladder with my feet. Gros came behind me, followed by the men.

I reached a dirt floor, wet and slimy with seepage. Gros pushed past me, prowled ahead, neck bent under the wooden beams which reinforced the ceiling. We moved on.

Behind, I heard feet sloshing in the dark, men stumbling and groping. They didn't know this route so well.

There was light ahead now, a faint lessening of darkness. We rounded a curve where a great boulder bulged into the passage, and a ragged line of daylight showed.

Gros beckoned the men closer. They bunched up, filling the cramped passage.

"Most of you never came this way before," he said. "So listen. We push out of here into the Street of

Olive Trees; it's a little side street under the palace wall. There's a dummy stall in front; ignore the old dame in it.

"Ease out one at a time, and move off east; that's to the right. You all got good papers. If the guy on the gate asks for them, show them. Don't get eager and volunteer. If there's any excitement behind, just keep going. We rendezvous at the thieves' market. OK, and duck the hardware."

He motioned the first man out, blinking in the glare as the ragged tarpaulin was pushed aside. After half a minute, the second followed. I moved close to Gros.

"Why bring this whole mob along?" I asked in a low voice. "Wouldn't it be a lot easier for just a few of us?"

Gros shook his head. "I want to keep my eyes on these slobs," he said. "I don't know what ideas they might get if I left them alone a few days; and I can't afford to have this set-up poisoned. And I'm going to need them out at the country place. There's nothing they can do here while I'm not around to tell them."

It sounded fishy to me, but I let it drop. All the men passed by us and disappeared. There was no alarm.

"OK," Gros said. "Stay with me." He slipped under the mouldy hanging and I followed as he stepped past a broken-down table laden with pottery. An old crone huddled on a stool ignored us. Gros glanced out into the narrow dusty street, then pushed off into the crowd. We threaded our way among loud-talking, gesticulating customers, petty merchants crouched over fly-covered displays of food or dog-eared magazines, tottering beggars, grimy urchins. The dirt street was littered with refuse, starving dogs wandered listlessly through the crowd; the heat was baking, early though it was. No one paid the least attention to us. It appeared we'd get through without trouble.

Under the heavy cloak, I was sweating. Flies buzzed about my swollen face. A whining beggar thrust a gaunt hand at me. Gros ducked between two fat men engaged in an argument. As they moved, I had to side-step and push past them. Gros was almost out of sight in the mob.

I saw a uniform suddenly, a hard-faced fellow in yellowish khaki pushing roughly through the press ahead. A chicken fluttered up squawking in my face. There was a shout, people began milling, thrusting against me. I caught a glimpse of Gros, face turned toward the soldier, eyes wide in a pale face. He started to run. In two jumps the uniformed man had him by the shoulder, spun him around, shouting. A dog yelped, banged against my legs, scuttled away. The soldier's arm rose and fell, clubbing at Gros with a heavy riot stick. Far ahead I heard a shot, and almost instantly another, close. Gros was free and running, blood on his head, as the soldier fell among the crowd. I darted along the wall, trying to overtake Gros, or at least keep him in sight. The crowd was opening, making way as he ran, pistol in hand. He fired again, the shot a faint pop in the mob noise.

Another uniform jumped in front of me, club raised; I shied, threw up an arm, as the man jumped back, saluted.

I caught the words, "Pardon, sir," as I went past him at a run. He must have caught a glimpse of the uniform I wore.

Ahead, Gros fell in the dust, scrambled to his knees, head down. A soldier stepped out of an alley, aimed, and shot him through the head. Gros lurched, collapsed, rolled on his back. The dust caked in the blood on his face. The crowd closed in. From the moment they spotted him, he didn't have a chance.

I stopped. I was trying to remember what Gros had told the men. I had made the bad mistake of assuming too much, thinking I would have Gros to lead me out of this. There was something about a gate; everyone had papers, Gros said. All but me. That was why they had had to come out in daylight, I realized suddenly. The gate probably closed at sundown.

I moved on, not wanting to attract attention by standing still. I tried to keep the cloak around me to conceal the uniform. I didn't want any more soldiers noticing it; the next one might not be in such a hurry.

Gros had told the men to rendezvous at the thieves' market. I tried to remember Algiers from a three-day visit years before; all I could recall was the Casbah and the well-lit streets of the European shopping section.

I passed the spot where a jostling throng craned to see the body of the soldier, kept going. Another ring surrounded the spot where Gros lay dead. Now there were soldiers everywhere, swinging their sticks carelessly, breaking up the mob. I shuffled, head down, dodged a backhanded swipe, found myself in the open. The street sloped up, curving to the left. There were still a few cobbles on this part, fewer shops and stalls. Wash hung from railings around tiny balconies above the street.

I saw the gate ahead. A press of people was packed against it, while a soldier examined papers. Three more uniformed men stood by, looking toward the scene of the excitement.

I went on toward the gate. I couldn't turn back

now. There was a new wooden watch tower scabbed onto the side of ancient brick wall where the sewer drained under it. A carbon arc searchlight and a man with a burp gun slung over his shoulder were on top of it. I thought I saw one of The Organization men in the crowd at the gate.

One of the soldiers was staring at me. He straightened, glanced at the man next to him. The other soldier was looking, too, now. I decided a bold front was the only chance. I beckoned to one of the men, allowing the cloak to uncover the front of the uniform briefly. He moved toward me, still in doubt. I hoped my battered face didn't look familiar.

"Snap it up, soldier," I said in my best Ecole Militaire tone; he hove to before me, saluted. I didn't give him a chance to take the initiative.

"The best part of the catch made it through the gate before you fools closed the net," I snapped. "Get me through there fast, and don't call any more attention to me. I'm not wearing this flea-circus for fun." I flipped the cloak.

He turned and pushed through to the gate, said a word to the other soldier, gestured toward me. The other man, wearing sergeant's stripes, looked at me.

I glared at him as I approached. "Ignore me," I hissed. "You foul this up and I'll see you shot."

I brushed past him, thrust through the gate as the first soldier opened it. I walked on, listening for the sound of a round snapping into the chamber of that burp gun on the tower. A goat darted out of an alley, stared at me. Sweat rolled down my cheek. There was a tree ahead, with a black shadow under it. I wondered if I'd ever get that far.

I made it, and breathed a little easier.

I still had problems, plenty of them. Right now I had to find the Thieves' Market. I had a vague memory of such a thing from the past, but I had no idea where it was. I moved on along the road, past a weathered stuccoed building with a slatternly tavern downstairs and sagging rooms above, bombed out at the far end. The gate was out of sight now.

Ahead were more bomb-scarred tenements, ruins, and beyond, open fields. There was a river in sight to the right. A few people were in view, moving listlessly in the morning heat. They seemed to ignore the hub-bub within the walled town. I couldn't risk asking any of them for the place I sought; I didn't know who might be a police informer, or a cop, for that matter. They had been ready for us, I realized. Gros wasn't as well-hidden as he had thought. Probably the police could have cleared his outfit from the palace at any time; I suspected they had tolerated them against such a time as now. The ambush had been neat. I wondered if any of the 'boys' had made it through the gate.

Apparently word had not gone out to be on the alert for a man impersonating an officer; I didn't know how much Maurice had said when he telephoned for his men, but my bluff at the gate indicated no one had been warned of my disguise.

I paused. Maybe my best bet would be to try the tavern, order a drink, try to pick up something. I saw nothing ahead that looked encouraging.

I walked back fifty feet to the doorless entrance to the bistro. There was no one in sight. I walked in, barely able to make out the positions of tables and chairs in the gloom. The glassless windows were shuttered. I blinked, made out the shape of the bar. Outside the door, the dusty road glared white.

A hoarse-breathing fellow loomed up behind the bar. He didn't say anything.

"Red wine," I said.

He put a water glass on the bar and filled it from a tin dipper. I tasted it. It was horrible. I had a feeling good manners would be out of place here, so I turned and spat it on the floor.

I pushed the glass across the bar. "I want wine," I said. "Not what you wring out of the bar-rag." I dropped a worn thousand franc note on the bar.

He muttered as he turned away, and was still muttering when he shuffled back with a sealed bottle and a wine glass. He drew the cork, poured my glass half full, and put the thousand francs in his pocket. He didn't offer me any change.

I tried it; it wasn't too bad. I stood sipping, and waited for my eyes to get used to the dim light. The bartender moved away and began pulling at a pile of boxes, grunting.

I didn't have a clear idea of what to do next if I did find the survivors of the Organization. At best I might find out what was wrong with the imposture, and use their channels to get back into the palace. I could always call for help on my communicator, and have myself set back inside via shuttle, but I didn't like the idea of risking that again. I had almost been caught arriving last time. The scheme couldn't possibly work if any suspicion was aroused.

A man appeared in the doorway, silhouetted against the light. He stepped in and came over to the bar. The bartender ignored him.

Two more came through the door, walked past me and leaned on the bar below me. The bartender continued to shuffle boxes, paying no attention to his customers. I started to wonder why.

The man nearest me moved closer. "Hey, you," he said. He jerked his head toward the gate. "You hear the shooting back there?"

That was a leading question. I wondered if the sound of the shots had been audible outside the walls of the fortified town. I grunted.

"Who they after?" he said.

I tried to see his face, but it was shadowed. He was a thin broad fellow, leaning on one elbow. Here we go again, I thought.

"How would I know?" I said.

"Kind of warm for that burnoose, ain't it?" he said. He stretched out a hand as if to touch the tattered cape. I stepped back, and two pairs of arms wrapped around me in a double bear-hug from behind.

The man facing me twitched the cape open. He looked at me.

"Lousy Ducal," he said, and hit me across the mouth with the back of his hand. I tasted blood.

"Hold on to them arms," another man said, coming around from behind me. This was one I hadn't seen. I wondered how many more men were in the room. The new man took the old military cape in his hands and ripped it off me.

"Look at that," he said. "We got us a lousy general." He dug his finger under the top of the braided lapel of my blouse and yanked. The lapel tore but stayed put. I started to struggle then; that was my communicator they were about to loot for the gold wire in it. I didn't have much hope of getting loose that way, but maybe it would distract them if I kicked a little. I swung a boot and caught the rangy one under the kneecap. He yelped and jumped back, then swung at my face. I twisted away, and the blow grazed my cheek. I threw myself backward, jerking hard, trying to throw someone off balance.

"Hold him," a man hissed. They were trying not to make too much noise. The thin man moved in close, watched his chance, and slammed a fist into my stomach. The pain was agonizing; I cramped up, retching.

The men holding me dragged me to a wall, flung me upright against it, arms outspread. The fellow who wanted the braid stepped up with a knife in his hand. I was trying to breathe, wheezing and twisting. He grabbed my hair, and for a moment I thought he was going to slit my throat. Instead, he sawed away at the lapels, cursing as the blade scraped wire.

"Get the buttons, too, Beau Joe," a husky voice suggested.

The pain was fading a little now, but I sagged, acting weaker than I actually was. The communicator was gone, at least the sending end. All I could try to salvage now was my life.

The buttons took only a moment. The man with the knife stepped back, slipping it into a sheath at his hip. He favored the leg I had kicked. I could see his face now. He had a straight nose, fine features.

"OK, let him go," he said. I slumped to the floor. For the first time my hands were free. Now maybe I had a chance; I still had the gun. I got shakily to hands and knees, watching him. He aimed a kick at my ribs.

"On your feet, General," he said. "I'll teach you to kick your betters."

I rode the kick, rolled to the left, ended on my face a few feet away. I tried to scramble up, still faking a little; but not much. I didn't need to. He followed, fists doubled. A real tough guy.

I made it to my feet, tottered, backed away. I wasn't worried about putting up a front; I just wanted a little room.

The man stepped in fast now, feinted with his left, and punched hard with his right at my face. The only way I could dodge it was to drop. Even so, I took a hard left in the chest. I sat down hard, bounced, as the tall man circled, readying another kick.

The others laughed, called out advice, shuffled around us in a circle. There was an odor of dust and sour wine.

"That General's a real fighter, ain't he?" somebody called. "Fights sittin down." That went over big. Lots of happy laughter.

I grabbed the foot as it came to me, twisted hard, and threw the man to the floor. He swore loudly, lunged at me, but I was up again, backing away. The ring opened and somebody pushed me. I let myself stumble and gained a few more feet toward the shadowed corner. I could see better now, enough to see pistols and knives in every belt. If they had any idea I was armed, they'd use them. I had to wait.

Beau Joe was after me again, throwing a roundhouse left. I ducked it, then caught a couple of short ones. I stepped back two paces, glanced at the audience; they were as far away as I'd get them. It was time to make my play. The man shielded me as the slug-gun popped into my hand, but at that instant he swung a savage kick. It was just luck; he hadn't seen the tiny weapon, but the gun spun into a dark corner. Now I wasn't acting any more.

I went after him, slammed a hard left to his face, followed with a right to the stomach, then straightened him out with another left. He was a lousy boxer.

The others didn't like it; they closed in and grabbed me. Knuckles bounced off my jaw as a fist rammed into my back. Two of them ran me backwards and sent me crashing against the wall. My head rang; I was stunned. I fell down and they let me lie. I needed the rest.

To hell with secrecy, I thought. I got to my knees and started crawling toward the corner. The men laughed and shouted, forgetting about being quiet now.

"Crawl, General," one shouted. "Crawl, you lousy spy."

"Hup, two, soldier," another sallied. "By the numbers, crawl."

That was a good one; they roared, slapped each other. Beau Joe had picked himself up and started for me now. Where the hell was that gun?

He grabbed my jacket, hauled me to my feet as I groped for him. My head spun; I must have a concussion, I thought. He jabbed at me, but I leaned on him, and he couldn't get a good swing. The others laughed at him now, enjoying the farce.

"Watch him, Beau Joe," someone called. "He's liable to wake up, with you shakin' him that away."

Beau Joe stepped back, and aimed a straight right at my chin, but I dropped and headed for the corner again; that was where the gun went. He kicked me again, sent me sprawling into the wall—and my hand fell on the gun.

I rolled over, and Beau Joe yanked me up, spun me around, and stepped back. I stood, slumped, in the corner, watching him. He was enjoying it now. He mouthed words silently, grinning in spite of his bleeding mouth. He intended to keep me propped there in the corner and beat me to death. As he came to me, I raised the gun and shot him in the face.

I wished I hadn't; he did a back-flip, landed head first, but not before I caught a glimpse of the smashed face. Joe was not beau any more.

I held my hand loosely at my side, waiting for the next comer. The same fellow who had grabbed me before rushed up. He jumped the body and twisted to deliver a skull-crusher, face contorted. I raised the gun a few inches as he leaped and fired at his belly. The shot made a hollow whop, as the man's feet left the floor. He smashed into the wall as I side-stepped.

The other three fanned out. It was too dark to see clearly here, and they didn't yet realize what had happened. They thought I had downed the two men with my fists. They were going to jump me together and finish it off.

"Freeze, bunnies!" a voice said from the door. We all looked. A hulking brute stood outlined there, and the gun in his hand was visible.

"I can see you rats," he said. "I'm used to the dark. Don't try nothing." He beckoned a man behind him forward. One of the three in the room edged toward the rear, and the gun coughed, firing through a silencer. The man slammed sideways, and sprawled.

"Come on, Hammer-hand," the big man said. "Let's

get out of here." He spat into the room. "These pigeons don't want to play no more."

I recognized the voice of Gaston, the big fellow who had wanted to bury me under the floor. Gros had appointed him my bodyguard, but he was a little late. I had taken a terrible beating. I tucked the gun away clumsily and lurched forward.

"Cripes, Hammer-hand," Gaston said, stepping forward to steady me. "I didn't know them bunnies had got to you; I thought you was stringing them. I was wondering when you was going to make music with that punch."

He paused to stare down at Beau Joe.

"You pushed his mush right in," he said admiringly. "Hey, Touhey, get Hammer-hand's wrap-around, and let's shove." He glanced once more around the room.

"So long, Bunnies," he said. The other men didn't answer.

VIII

I DON'T REMEMBER MUCH about my trip to the Organization's hide-out in the country. I recall walking endlessly, and later being carried over Gaston's shoulder. I remember terrific heat, and agonizing pain, from my battered face, my half-healed gunshot wounds, and innumerable bruises. And I remember at last a cool room, and a soft bed.

I awoke slowly, dreams blending with memories, none of them pleasant. I lay on my back, propped up on enormous fluffy feather bolsters, with a later afternoon sun lighting the room through partly-drawn drapes over a wide dormer window. For awhile I struggled to decide where I was. Gradually I recalled my last conscious thought.

This was the place in the country Gros had been headed for. Gaston had taken his charge seriously, in spite of his own suggestion that I be disposed of and although he knew Miche and Gros were dead.

I moved tentatively, and caught my breath. That

hurt, too. My chest, ribs, and stomach were one great ache. I pushed the quilt down and tried to examine the damage. Under the edges of a broad tape wrapping, purple bruises showed all around my right side.

Bending my neck had been a mistake; now the bullet wound that Maurice had re-opened with the blackjack began to throb. I was a mess. I didn't risk moving my face; I knew what it must look like.

As a secret-service type, I was a complete bust, I thought. My carefully prepared disguise had fooled no one, except maybe Spider. I had been subjected to more kicks, blows, and threats of death in the few hours I had been abroad in the Dictator's realm than in all my previous 42 years, and I had accomplished exactly nothing. I had lost my communicator, and now my slug-gun, too; the comforting pressure under my wrist was gone. It wouldn't have helped much now anyway; I was dizzy from the little effort I had just expended.

Maybe I had made some progress, though, in a negative way. I knew that walking in and striking a pose wasn't enough to get me by as the Dictator Bayard, in spite of the face. And I had also learned that the Dictator's regime was riddled with subversives and malcontents. Perhaps we could somehow use the latter to our advantage.

If, I thought, I can get back with the information. I thought that over. How would I get back? I had no way of communicating. I was completely on my own.

Always before I had had the knowledge that in the end I could send out a call for help, and count on rescue within an hour. Richthofen had arranged for a 24-hour monitoring of my communications band, alert for my call. Now that was out. If I was to return to the Imperium, I would have to steal one of the crude shuttles of this world, or better, commandeer one as Dictator. I had to get back into the palace, with a correct disguise, or end my days in this nightmare world.

I heard voices approaching outside the room. I closed my eyes as the door opened. I might learn a little by playing possum, if I could get away with it.

The voices were lower now, and I sensed several people coming over to stand by the bed.

"How long has he been asleep?" a new voice asked. Or was it new? It seemed familiar somehow, but I connected it with some other place.

"Doc give him some shots," someone answered. "We brought him in this time yesterday."

There was a pause. Then the half-familiar voice again. "I don't like his being alive. However—perhaps we can make use of him."

"Gros wanted him alive," another voice said. I recognized Gaston. He sounded sullen. "He had big plans for him."

The other voice grunted. There was silence for a few moments.

"He's no good to us until the face is healed. Keep him here until I send along further instructions." The voice spoke in cultivated French, much different than the alley slang of the others. I didn't dare to risk a glimpse; but if I pretended to just be awakening... I groaned and moved, then opened my eyes. I was a little late; the men were already passing through the door.

I hadn't liked what I'd heard, but for the present I had no choice but to lie here and try to regain my strength. At least, I was comfortably set up in this huge bed. I drifted off to sleep again.

I awoke with Gaston sitting by the bed smoking. He sat up when I opened my eyes, crushed out his cigarette in an ash tray on the table, and leaned forward.

"How are you feeling, Hammer-hand?" he said.

"Rested," I said. My voice came out in a faint whisper. I was surprised at its weakness.

"Yeah, them pigeons give you a pretty rough time, Hammer-hand, I don't get why you don't lay the Punch on them sooner."

I tried to speak, croaked instead, shook my head.

"Take it easy," Gaston said. "You lost a lot of blood. Them scalp wounds bleed plenty."

A throb from the back of my head told me where the scalp wound was. I didn't remember getting it.

"I got some chow here for you," Gaston said. He put a tray from the bedside table on his lap and offered me a spoonful of soup. I was hungry; I opened my mouth for it. I never expected to have a gorilla for a nursemaid, I thought.

Gaston was good at his work, though. For the next three days he fed me regularly, changed my bedding, and performed all the duties of a trained nurse with skill, if not with grace. I steadily gained strength, but I was careful to conceal the extent of my progress from Gaston and the others who occasionally came in. I didn't know what might be coming up and I wanted something in reserve.

Gaston told me a lot about the Organization during the next few days. I learned that the group led by Gros and Miche was only one of several such cells; there were hundreds of members, in half a dozen

scattered locations in Algeria, each keeping surveillance over some vital installation of the regime. Their
ultimate objective was the overthrow of Bayard's rule,
enabling them to get a share in the loot.

Each group had two leaders, all of whom reported
to the Big Boss, a stranger about whom Gaston knew
little. He appeared irregularly, and no one knew his
name or where he had his headquarters. I sensed that
Gaston didn't like him.

On the third day I asked Gaston to help me get
up and walk a bit. I faked extreme weakness, but was
pleased to discover that I was feeling better than I had
hoped. After Gaston helped me back into bed and left
the room, I got up again, and practiced walking. It
made me dizzy and nauseated after a few steps, but I
leaned on the bed post and waited for my stomach to
settle down, and went on. I stayed on my feet for fifteen
minutes, and slept soundly afterwards. Thereafter, when-
ever I awoke, day or night, I rose and walked, jumping
back into bed when I heard footsteps approaching.

When Gaston insisted on walking me after that, I
continued to feign all the symptoms I had felt the first
time. The doctor was called back once, but he assured
me that my reactions were quite normal, and that I
could not expect to show much improvement for another
week, considering the amount of blood I had lost. This
suited me perfectly. I needed time to learn more.

I tried to pump Gaston about my disguise, subtly;
I didn't want to put him on his guard, or give any
inkling of what I had in mind. But I was too subtle;
Gaston avoided the subject.

I searched for my clothes, but the closet was locked
and I couldn't risk forcing the door.

A week after my arrival, I allowed myself enough improvement to permit a walk through the house, and down into a pleasant garden behind it. I saw several new faces, men who stared curiously at me, and muttered together as I passed. They seemed neither friendly nor hostile. I caught a glimpse, too, of an elderly female, the housekeeper, I guessed.

The layout of the house was simple. From the garden I had seen no signs of guards. It looked as though I could walk out any time, but I restrained the impulse. I didn't want to get a mile or two, and fall over in a faint; and I needed clothes, papers, information. I wanted my slug-gun, but that was hopeless, I was afraid. I would settle for a pistol, if I could get one. Even that looked impossible. I wondered when I would find out what the Organization planned for me.

One morning Gaston brought me in some clothes to replace the patched bathrobe I had been wearing for my daily exercise. This was a real break for me. I had been assuming that if I decided to leave suddenly, I would have to take the clothes off someone when I left; in my condition, that would be an undertaking in itself.

I still didn't have much in the way of plans. What could I do if I did leave the house? I could try to make my way back into the walled town and re-enter the palace the way I had come out. Once there, I would dispose of the Dictator and, posing as the ruler, order a shuttle placed at my disposal, with an Operator. Then I could return to the Imperium. Very simple, except for a few details.

I walked around the house freely now, using two canes, and resting frequently. There were eight other large bedrooms on the second floor of the house, in addition to mine; only two seemed to be in use. Downstairs, there were two dining rooms, a study, library, large kitchens, and a vast parlor. One room was locked. A wall surrounded the garden. It was a pleasant old place, and I was sure the air of peace and placidity helped in avoiding the attention of the police. It was a clever camouflage, and I thought it would make my departure easy.

By the time ten days had passed, I was getting very restless. I couldn't fake my role of invalid much longer without arousing suspicion. The inactivity was getting on my nerves; I had spent the night lying awake, thinking, and getting up occasionally to walk up and down the room. By dawn, I had succeeded in fatiguing myself, but I hadn't slept at all.

I had to be doing something. I got out my canes, and started to reconnoiter the house after Gaston had taken away my breakfast tray. From the upstairs windows I had a wide view of the surrounding country. The front of the house faced a paved highway, in good repair. I assumed it was a main route into Algiers. Behind the house, tilled fields stretched a quarter of a mile to a row of trees. Perhaps there was a river there. There were no other houses near.

I thought about leaving. It looked to me as though my best bet would be to go over the wall after dark and head for the cover of the trees. I had the impression that the line of trees and the road converged to the west, so perhaps I could regain the road at a distance from the house, and follow it into the city. But first I had to know what the plans of the Organization were; I might be able to turn them to my advantage.

There seemed to be no one stirring in the house as I hobbled along with my two sticks. I wandered up and down the hall, then slowly descended the stair. I was about to go out into the garden, when I heard the sound of a motor approaching. I paused and listened. It pulled up in front of the house and stopped. There was a sound of slamming doors, voices; then the car started up, and headed back the way it had come.

I hurried back into the house, and took the stairs fast. I hoped no one saw me, but I was determined not to call my free wandering to the attention of the man whose voice I had heard. It was the same one I had heard the first day here, and I still couldn't place it; but I was sure that it belonged to the Big Boss Gaston had told me of.

I slowed down at the top of the stairs and picked my way along to my room. I got into bed and waited for something to happen. Surely the Big Boss's return meant an end to suspense.

Hours passed, while I sat on the edge of the bed or paced restlessly but silently up and down, canes in hand in case of sudden interruption. Gaston brought my lunch at noon, but wouldn't stay to answer questions.

Occasionally I heard a raised voice, or the sound of footsteps; otherwise, all was peaceful. About three o'clock, another vehicle approached, a truck this time. From my windows I could see only a part of it, but two men seemed to be unloading something heavy from it. After half an hour it drove away.

It was almost dinner time when I heard them approaching my door. I was lying down, so I stayed where I was and waited. Gaston entered with the doctor. The doctor was pale, and perspiring heavily. He avoided my eyes as he drew out a chair, sat down and started his examination. He said nothing to me, ignoring the questions I asked him. I gave up and lay silently while he prodded and poked. After awhile he rose suddenly, packed up his kit, and walked out.

"What's the matter with the doc, Gaston?" I asked.

"He's got something on his mind," Gaston said. Even Gaston seemed subdued. Something was up; something that worried me.

"Come on, Gaston," I said. "What's going on?"

At first I thought he wasn't going to answer me.

"They're going to do like you wanted," he said. "They're getting ready to put you in for Bayard."

"That's fine," I said. That was what I had come here for. This way was as good as any. But there was something about it...

"Why all the secrecy?" I asked. "Why doesn't the Big Boss show himself? I'd like to talk to him."

Gaston hesitated. I had the feeling he wanted to say more, but couldn't.

"They got a few details to fix yet," he said. He didn't look at me. I let it go at that. At least I knew now things were moving.

After Gaston left the room, I went out into the hall. Through the open back windows I heard the sound of conversation. I moved over to eavesdrop.

There were three men, strolling out into the garden, backs to me. One was the doctor; I didn't recognize the other two. I wished I could see their faces.

"It was not for this I was trained," the doctor was saying. He waved his hands in an agitated way. "I am not a butcher, to cut up a side of mutton for you..."

I couldn't make out the reply, but what I had heard was enough. There was something terrible brewing here in this quiet house. I wanted to get on with the job ahead. I wished the Big Boss would get around to talking to me.

They were all out in the garden now; maybe this would be a good time to take a look around downstairs. I wanted to know what all the gear was. I had seen them bringing in this afternoon. Maybe I could learn something about the coming move.

I went down to the landing and listened. All was quiet. I descended to the hall on the ground floor, listened again. Somewhere a clock was ticking.

I went into the main dining room; the table was set for three, but no food was in sight. I tried the other dining room; nothing. I went across and eased the parlor door open. There was no one there; it looked as unused as ever.

I passed the door I had found locked once before and noticed light under it. I stepped back and tried it. It was probably a broom closet, I thought, as I turned the knob. It opened.

I stood staring. There was a padded white table in the center of the room. At one end stood two flood-lamps on tall tripods. Glittering instruments were laid out on a small table. On a stand beside the operating table lay scalpels, sutures, heavy curved needles. There was a finely made saw, like a big hacksaw, and heavy snippers. On the floor beneath the table was a large galvanized steel wash tub.

The sight of the room frightened me. I didn't like it; it reminded me of a blood-spattered battalion aid station where I had once lain for an hour among the hopeless cases and the dead, while the surgeons worked on the lightly wounded, the ones who might live. They were out of morphine and they had gotten to me after I had lain conscious for more than an hour breathing through a fog of agony, listening to the high wailing screams of the men under the knife.

I didn't understand this; I wished I had stayed upstairs and waited for the Big Boss's proposition. I turned to the door, and heard footsteps approaching.

I looked around, saw a door, jumped to it and jerked it open. When the two men entered the room, I was standing rigid in the darkness of a storeroom, with the door open half an inch.

The flood lights flicked on, then off again. There was a rattle of metal against metal.

"Lay off that," a nasal voice said. "This is all set. I checked it over myself."

"Then it's sure to be loused up," a thin voice answered.

The two bickered and complained as they fussed around the room. They seemed to be medical technicians of some sort.

"They're nuts," Nasal-voice said. "Why don't they wait until morning, when they got plenty sunlight for this? No, they gotta work under the lights."

"I don't get this deal," Thin-voice said. "I didn't get what was supposed to be wrong with this guy's legs, they got to take them off. How come if he's..."

"You ain't clued in, are you, Mac?" Nasal-voice said harshly. "This is a big deal; they're going to ring this mug in when they knock off the Old Man..."

"Yeah, that's what I mean," Thin-voice cut in. "So what's the idea they take off the legs?"

"You don't know much, do you, small-timer?" Nasal-voice said. "Well, listen; I got news for you." There was a pause.

"Bayard's got no pins, from the knees down." Nasal-voice spoke in a hushed tone. "You didn't know that, did you? That's why you never seen him walking around on the video; he's always sitting back of a desk.

"There ain't very many know about that," he added. "Keep it to yourself."

"Cripes," Thin-voice said. His voice was thinner than ever. "Got no legs?"

"That's right. I was with him a year before the landing. I was in his outfit when he got it. Machine gun slug, through both knees. Now forget about it. But maybe now you get the set-up."

"Cripes," Thin-voice said. "Where did they get a guy crazy enough to go into a deal like this?"

"How do I know," the other said. He sounded as though he regretted having told the secret. "These revolutionist types is all nuts anyway."

I stood there feeling sick. My legs tingled. I knew now why nobody mistook me for the Dictator, as I *walked* into a room; and why Spider had been taken in, when he saw me sitting.

The two technicians left the room. I felt weak and nauseated. I looked at the tub under the table, and then down at my legs. I was trembling. I didn't have to think about making a decision any longer; it was made.

I was leaving now. Not tomorrow, not tonight; now. I had no gun, no papers, no map, no plans; but I was leaving.

It was almost dark; I stood in the hall and drew deep

breaths, trying to get hold of myself. My leg muscles twitched and quivered. I pushed the memory of the saw and the tub from my mind. I was getting out.

I thought of food. I didn't want it now, but I knew I would need my strength; I remembered the kitchen, and went to the door. I listened; all was silent. I pushed through the door and in the gloom went to the large refrigerator against the wall. I found a half of a small ham, and a wedge of dry cheese. I took a long pull from a partly used bottle of white wine. It was a little sour, but it helped. I was feeling steadier now.

I dropped my finds into a string bag on the table, and added a round loaf of bread. I selected a sturdy french knife from the drawer, and thrust it in my belt. All set. Let's go.

The kitchen faced the garden, with a back door set just outside the walled portion, a service entrance. That suited me fine; I wouldn't have to climb the wall. Through the window I could see the men in the garden, standing under a small cherry tree in the gloom, still talking. I considered whether to risk opening the door now; the top half of it would be visible to them over the garden wall. I examined it in the failing light. It was a dutch door, the type that opens in two sections. I tried the latches carefully. The upper one was locked, but the bolt holding the halves together opened easily, and the lower part swung silently open—below the line of vision of the men outside. I didn't wait; I bent over and stepped through.

A short path led off to the drive beside the house; I ignored it and crept along beside the wall, through weed-grown flower beds.

I reached the end of the wall, and through the screen of a trellis checked on the three men; they were walking toward the house. They seemed like ordinary men of substance, having a quiet chat and stroll in the garden before dinner. It wasn't dinner they were planning in the old house though; it was my living dismemberment.

I turned to start out across the plowed field and a dark form rose up before me. I recoiled, my wrist twitching in a gesture that had become automatic; but no slug-gun snapped into my hand. I was unarmed, weak, and shaken, and the man loomed over me, hulking. I didn't know what to do.

"Let's go, Hammer-hand," he whispered. It was Gaston.

The thought of running for it flashed through my mind, but it was hopeless; I was trapped here before I had even begun. This was bitter. I backed away, unwilling to accept defeat, but unable to prevent it.

"I'm leaving, Gaston," I said. "Just don't try to stop me." Vague ideas of a bluff were in my mind. After all, he called me Hammer-hand.

He came after me. "Hold it down to a roar," he said. "I wondered when you was going to make your break. You been getting pretty restless these last few days."

"Yeah," I said. "Who wouldn't?" I was just stalling; I had no plan.

"You got more nerve than me, Hammer-hand," Gaston said. "I would of took off a week ago. You must of wanted to get a look at the Big Boss real bad to stick as long as you did."

"I saw enough today," I said. "I don't want to see anymore."

"Did you make him?" Gaston asked. He sounded interested.

"No," I said. "I didn't see his face. But I've lost my curiosity."

Gaston laughed. "OK, chief," he said. He handed me a soiled card, with something scribbled on it. "Maybe this will do you some good. It's the big boss's address out of town. I swiped it; it was all I could find. Now, let's blow out of here."

I stuck the card in my pocket. I was a little confused.

"I'm headed for the river," I said. "I'll kill anyone who gets in my way."

"That's the idea," Gaston said. "We're wasting time."

"You're going with me?" I asked.

"Like the man said, Hammer-hand, I'm with you."

"Wait a minute, Gaston; you mean you're helping me get away?" I couldn't believe it.

"Somebody said I was supposed to keep an eye on you, look out you didn't have no accidents," Gaston said. "I always done all right doing what my brother told me; I don't see no reason to stop now just because they killed him."

"Your brother?" I said.

"Gros was my brother," Gaston said. "I ain't smart like Gros, but he always took care of me. I always done what he said. He told me to look out for you, Hammer-hand."

"What about them?" I asked, nodding toward the house. "They won't like it when they find us both missing."

Gaston spat. "To hell with them monkeys," he said. "They gimme the willies."

I was beginning to feel jolly all of a sudden, by reaction.

"Why the hell didn't you say so a week ago," I said. "You could have saved me some sleepless nights."

"That joint is bugged plenty," Gaston said. "You can't say nothing in there. Besides, in case you didn't make it, I didn't want you to have nothing to conceal, if you know what I mean."

"I wouldn't have talked," I said.

Gaston looked at me. "You would have talked, Hammer-hand. They all do."

"OK," I said. "Never mind that now." I was in a mood to push my luck. "Listen, Gaston; can you go back in there and get the clothes I had on when I got here?"

Gaston fumbled in the dark at a sack slung over his shoulder. "I thought you might want that suit, Hammer-hand," he said. "You was real particular about that with Miche." He handed me a bundle. I knew the feel of it. It was the uniform.

"Gaston," I said, "you're a wonder. I don't suppose you brought along the little gimmick I had on my wrist?"

"I think I stuck it in the pocket," he said. "Somebody swiped the fancy gloves you had in the belt, though. I'm sorry about the gloves."

I fumbled over the blouse, and felt the lump in the pocket. With that slug-gun in my hand I was ready to lick the world.

"That's OK about the gloves, Gaston," I said. I strapped the clip to my wrist and tucked the gun away. I pulled off the old coat I wore and slipped the blouse on. This was more like it.

I looked at the house. All was peaceful. It was dark enough now that we wouldn't be seen crossing the field. It was time to go.

"Come on," I said. I took a sight on a bright star and struck out across the soft ground.

In fifty steps the house was completely lost to view. The wall and high foliage obscured the lights on the first floor; upstairs the house was in darkness. I kept the star before me and stumbled on. I never knew how hard it was to walk in a plowed field in the dark.

Gaston puffed along behind me. I spoke softly every few steps to guide him. Before me there was nothing but darkness.

It was fifteen minutes before I made out a deeper darkness against the faintly lighter sky ahead. That would be the line of trees along the river; I was still assuming there was a river.

Then we were among the trees, feeling our way slowly. The ground sloped and the next moment I was sliding down a muddy bank into shallow water.

"Yes," I said, "it's a river all right." I scrambled out, and stood peering toward the west. I could see nothing. If we had to pick our way through trees all night, without a moon, we wouldn't be a mile away by dawn.

"Which way does this river flow, Gaston?" I asked.

"That way," he said. "To Algiers; into the city."

"Can you swim?" I asked.

"Sure," Gaston replied. "I can swim good."

"OK," I said. "Strip and make a bundle of your clothes. Put whatever you don't want to get wet in the middle; strap the bundle to your shoulders with your belt."

We grunted and fumbled in the darkness.

"What about the shoes?" Gaston said.

"Tie the laces together and hang them around

your neck," I said. "They'll get wet, but that won't matter much."

I finished my packing and stepped down into the water. It was warm weather; that was a break. I still had the slug-gun on my wrist. I wanted it close to me.

"Ready, Gaston," I called softly.

"Right with you, chief."

I stepped out into the stream, pushed off as the bottom shelved. I paddled a few strokes to get clear of the reeds growing near the shore. All around was inky blackness, with only the brilliant stars overhead to relieve the emptiness.

"OK, Gaston?" I called.

I heard him splashing quietly. "Sure," he said.

"Let's get out a little farther and then take it easy," I said. "Let the river do the work."

The current was gentle. Far across the river I saw a tiny light now. We drifted slowly past it. I moved my hands just enough to keep my nose above water. The surface was calm. I yawned; I could have slept tonight, I thought, remembering the sleepless hours of the night before. But it would be a long time between beds for me.

I saw a tiny reflection on a ripple ahead, and glanced back. There were lights on in the second story of the house we had left. It seemed to be about a mile away. That wasn't much of a start, I thought, but maybe they wouldn't look in the middle of the river.

I called to Gaston, pointing out the lights.

"Yeah," he said. "I been watching them. I don't think we got nothing to worry about."

They could follow our trail to the water's edge easily enough I knew, with nothing more than a flashlight. As if in response to my thought, a tiny gleam appeared at ground level, wavering, blinking as trees passed between us. It moved, bobbing toward the river. I watched until it emerged from the trees. I saw the yellow gleam dancing across the water where we had started. Other lights were following now, two, three. The whole household must have joined the chase. They must be expecting to find me huddled on the ground near by, exhausted, ready for the table they had prepared for me in the presence of my enemies.

The lights fanned out, moving along the shore. I saw that we were safely ahead of them.

"Gaston," I said, "have they got a boat back there?"

"Nah," he replied. "We're in the clear."

The little lights were pitiful, bobbing along the shore, falling behind.

We floated along then in silence for an hour or more. It was still, almost restful. Only a gentle fluttering of the hands was required to keep our heads above water.

Suddenly lights flashed ahead, over the river.

"Cripes," Gaston hissed, backing water. "I forgot about the Salan bridge. Them bunnies is out there waitin' for us."

I could see the bridge now, as the lights flashed across the pilings. It was about a hundred yards ahead.

"Head for the far shore, Gaston," I said. "Fast and quiet."

I couldn't risk the splash of a crawl stroke, so I dog-paddled frantically, my hands under the surface. They would have had us neatly, if they hadn't shown the lights when they did, I thought. They couldn't see us without them, though, so it was just a chance they

had to take. They must have estimated the speed of
the river's flow, and tried to pinpoint us. They didn't
miss by much; in fact, they might not have missed at
all. I concentrated on putting every ounce of energy
into my strokes. My knees hit mud, and reeds brushed
my face. I rolled over and sat up, breathing hard.
Gaston floundered a few feet away.

"Here," I hissed; "keep it quiet."

The light on the bridge blinked out suddenly. I wondered what they'd do next. If they headed along the
banks, flashing lights, we'd have to take to the water
again; and if one man stayed on the bridge, and flashed
his light down at just about the right moment...

"Let's get going," I said.

I started up the slope, crouching low. The lights
appeared again, down at the water's edge now, flashing on the tall grass and cat-tails. Another appeared
on the opposite bank. I stopped to listen. Feet made
sloshing sounds in the mud, a hundred feet away.
Good; that would cover our own noise. My wet shoes
dangled by the strings, thumping my chest.

The ground was firmer now, the grass not so tall. I
stopped again, Gaston right behind me, looking back.
They'd find our tracks any minute. We had no time
to waste. The bundle of clothing was a nuisance, but
we couldn't stop now to dress.

"Come on," I whispered, and broke into a run.

Fifty feet from the top we dropped and started
crawling. I didn't want to be seen in silhouette against
the sky as we topped the rise.

We pulled ourselves along, puffing and grunting.
Crawling is hard work for a grown man. Just over the
top we paused to look over the situation. The road

leading to the bridge wound away toward a distant glow in the sky.

"That's an army supply depot out that way," Gaston said. "No town."

I raised up to look back toward the river. Two lights bobbed together, then started slowly away from the water's edge. I heard a faint shout.

"They've spotted the trail," I said. I jumped up and ran down the slope, trying to breathe deep, in for four strides, out for four. A man could run a long time if he didn't get winded. Stones bruised my bare feet.

I angled over toward the highway, with some idea of making better time. Gaston was beside me.

"Nix," he said, puffing hard. "Them bunnies got a machine."

For a moment I didn't know what he meant; then I heard the sound of an engine starting up, and headlights lanced into the darkness, beams aimed at the distant tree-tops as the car headed up the slope of the approach to the bridge from the other side. We had only a few seconds before the car would slant down on this side, and illuminate the road and a wide strip on either side; we'd be spotlighted.

Ahead I saw a fence, just a glint from a wire. That finished it; we were stopped. I slid to a halt. Then I saw that the fence lined a cross road, joining the road we were paralleling twenty feet away. Maybe a culvert... I didn't wait to discuss it; I dived for the only possible shelter.

A corrugated steel pipe eighteen inches in diameter ran beside the main road where the other joined it. I scrambled over pebbles and twigs and into the gaping mouth. The sounds I made echoed hollowly inside. I kept going to the far end, Gaston wheezing behind me. I stopped and looked over my shoulder. Gaston had backed in and lay a few feet inside his end. The glow of the headlights gave me a glimpse of a heavy automatic in his hand.

"Good boy," I hissed. "Don't shoot unless you have to."

The lights of the car flickered over trees, highlighted rocks. Through the open end of the pipe I saw a rabbit sitting up in the glare, a few feet away. He turned and bounded off.

The car came slowly along the road. A sharp stick under my chest poked me, pebbles dug into my knees. I watched the lights; the car passed, moved on down the road. I breathed a little easier.

I was on the point of turning to say something to Gaston when a small stone rolled down into the ditch before me. I stiffened. A faint scuff of shoes on gravel, another stone dislodged—and then a flashlight beam darted across the gully, played on the grass opposite, came to rest on the open end of the drain pipe. I was about two feet inside; the light didn't quite reach me; I held my breath. Then the steps came nearer, and the light probed, found my shoulder. There was a frozen instant of silence, then the sharp slap of the slug-gun hitting my palm. The steps shuffled back, light stabbing into my eyes as I lunged forward, shoulders clear of the pipe. I caught a glimpse of the car a hundred feet away now, still edging along. I heard a sharp intake of breath as the man with the light readied a shout. I pointed the gun to the right of the flash and the recoil slammed my arm back. The flashlight skidded across the rocky bottom of the ditch as the man's body crashed heavily and lay still. The flashlight was still on. I jumped for it, flicked it off, and dropped it on the ground. I groped for the man's feet, hauled him back toward the pipe.

"Gaston," I whispered. The sound was hollow in the dark tunnel. "Give me a hand." He crawled out the far end, turned and reentered head first. The limp body was pulled away into the drain pipe. I pushed at the feet. I couldn't tell who it was. I was glad it wasn't the doctor; he wouldn't have fitted.

I backed out, ran to the far end, and helped Gaston the last two feet. "After the car," I said. I had what I hoped was an idea. I was tired of being chased; the hunted would become the hunter.

I headed up the ditch at a trot, head down, Gaston at my heels. The car had stopped a hundred yards away. I counted three flashlights moving in the edge of the field. I wondered how many there were, whether the driver had remained with the car. We'd soon find out the answer to that.

I stopped. "Close enough," I hissed. "Let's split up now; I'll cross the road and come up the other side. There's only one man over there. You get up in the tall grass and sneak in as close to the car as you can. Watch me and take your cue."

I darted across the road, a grotesque figure, naked, my bundle dangling by its strap from my shoulder. The car's headlights were still on. I was sure no one could see us from beyond them, looking into the glare. I dropped down into the ditch, wincing as sharp sticks jabbed my bare feet. The man on my side was casting about in wide circles, fifty feet from the road. A cricket sawed away insistently.

The car started backing, swung to one side of the road, then went forward; the driver was in the car, all right; he was turning around. They must have come up the road to cut us off, planning to move back to the river, searching foot by foot until they flushed us. No one seemed to have missed the man who now lay quietly in the steel pipe.

The car swung around and moved along at a snail's pace, headlights flooding the road I had just crossed. I hoped Gaston was well concealed on the other side. I couldn't see him. I dropped down to the bottom of the ditch as the lights passed over me. The car came on, and stopped just above me. I could see the driver, staring out through the windshield. He leaned forward, peering. I wondered if he had spotted Gaston. Then I realized he was looking for the man who had been coming along on foot, checking the ditch; he'd be a long time seeing him from here.

He opened the door, stepped out, one foot on the running board. The car was long and top-heavy looking, with flaring fenders. Dust roiled and gnats danced in the beams from the great bowl-shaped headlights. I couldn't just lie here and watch, I thought. I would never have a better chance.

I picked up a heavy stone, rose silently to hands and knees, and crept up out of the ditch. The chauffeur stood with a hand on top of the door, looking over it. He turned his back to me, and ducked his head to re-enter the car. I came up behind him in two steps, and hit him as hard as I could on top of the head. He folded into the seat. I shoved him over, jumped in, and closed the door. It was hard to get the coat off him in the dark, while trying to stay down behind the door, but I managed it. I put it on and sat up. There was no alarm. The three flashlights continued to bob around in the fields. The engine was running quietly. I looked over the controls. The steering wheel was in the center, and there were three pedals on the floor. I pushed at them tentatively. The left hand one caused the engine to race a bit as I touched it; the accelerator. Logically, the one on the right should be the brake. The center one must be the clutch. I pushed it in and the car edged forward. I tried the brake; OK.

I let the center pedal in again, and started off slowly; the car seemed to slip in gear, and the pedal went slack; an automatic transmission. I steered to the right side of the road, crept along the edge. Gaston must be about here, I thought. I stared out into the darkness; I could see practically nothing.

I eased to a stop. The flashlight nearest me swung back and forth, moving toward the bridge. I reached out to the dash, pushed in a lever that projected from it. The headlights died.

I could see better now. The flashlights to my right stopped moving, turned toward me. I waved cheerfully. I didn't think they could make out my face in the dim beam at that distance. One of the lights seemed satisfied, resumed its search; the other hesitated, flashing over the car.

There was a shout then, and I saw Gaston up and running toward me. The flashlights converged on him as he leaped across the ditch ahead, coming into the road. The lights came bounding toward him and someone was yelling. Gaston stopped, whirled toward the nearest light, aiming the pistol. There was a sharp bam, bam. Both lights on his side dropped. Not bad shooting for a .45,

I thought. I jerked open the door and Gaston jumped in beside me. Behind there was a faint shout from the remaining man on the other side of the road, and the crack of a gun. The slug made a solid thunk as it hit the heavy steel of the car. I floorboarded the center and left pedals; the car jumped ahead, then coasted. Another slug starred the glass beside me, scattering glass chips in my hair. I let my foot off, tried again. The car surged forward; the acceleration was excellent. Apparently putting the center pedal all the way in disengaged it. I flipped the lights on. The car shifted up, tires squealing. Ahead, a figure stumbled down into the ditch, scrambled up the other side into the road, waving its arms. I saw the open mouth in the taut white face for an instant in the glare of the lights before it was slammed down out of sight, with a shock that bounced us in our seats.

The bridge loomed ahead, narrow and highly arched. We took it wide open, crushed down in the seat as we mounted the slope, floating as we dropped on the other side. The road curved off to the left, tall trees lining it. The tires howled as we rounded the turn and hit the straightaway.

"This is great, Hammer-hand," Gaston shouted. "I never rode in one of these here machines before."

"Neither did I," I yelled back. I kept moving at top speed for a mile, then slowed to fifty kilometers; I didn't want to get pinched. I followed the road another mile or so, and then turned off down a side road to the right, into the shelter of a clump of trees. I set the brake, but left the engine idling; I didn't know how to start it again.

I leaned back and let out a long breath. "OK, Gaston," I said. "Fall out for a ten-minute break."

IX

I GOT OUT OF the car and opened my bundled clothing on the seat. It was still dry. I felt better when I was dressed again. My feet were cut and bruised; I had to ease the socks and shoes on. Gaston was better off.

We pulled the body of the driver out of the car and laid him out in the grass. It was one of the men I had seen at the house, but not the Big Boss. I wondered if that had been the man who had fired after us. As far as I knew, he was the only one we had left alive.

That was quite a thought. A few weeks ago, I was as mild and inoffensive as any other middle-aged paper-shuffler. Now to get in my way was to die violently. I was learning fast; I had to.

I opened the string bag I had rolled in the middle of my clothing. I was ravenous; I carved slices of ham and bread, and Gaston and I sat in the car and chewed silently.

No cars passed on the road. The night was still black, with no moon. My next problem was to get into the Walled Town. The road led along the river's edge into the heart of the city, according to Gaston. The Dictator's stronghold lay at the edge of the city, north of the highway we were on. He had fortified the area, enclosing shops and houses within an encircling wall like a medieval town, creating a self-sufficient community to support the castle and its occupants, easily patrolled and policed. It was no defense against an army, but practical as a safeguard against assassins and rioters.

"That's us," I said aloud. "Assassins and rioters."

"Sure, chief," Gaston said, swallowing. "Let's go some more."

I backed out, and pulled onto the highway again. There was a glow in the sky ahead. From the road, only a few scattered lights were visible. The countryside seemed almost unpopulated.

Twenty minutes of driving brought us to the bombed-out edge of the city. The rubble stretched ahead, with here and there a shack or a tiny patch of garden. To the right the mass of the castle loomed up, faintly visible in the glow from the streets below it, unseen behind the wall. To the original massive old country house, Bayard had added rambling outbuildings, great mismatched wings, and the squat tower.

I pulled over, cut the headlights. Gaston and I looked silently at the lights in the tower. He lit a cigarette.

"How are we going to get in there, Gaston?" I said. "How do we get over the wall?"

Gaston stared at the walls, thinking. "Listen, Hammerhand," he said. "You wait here, while I check around a little." He flipped the cigarette out the window and fumbled at the door. "How do you open these things," he said. "I don't feel no doorknob."

I opened the door for him.

"I'm pretty good at casing a layout," he said, leaning in the window. "I know this one from the inside; I'll find a spot if there is one. Keep an eye peeled for the street gangs." Then he was gone.

I sat and waited. I rolled up the windows and locked the doors. I couldn't see any signs of life among the broken walls around me. Somewhere a cat yowled.

I checked my clothes over. Both lapels were missing; the tiny set was still clipped to my belt, but without speaker or mike, it was useless. I ran my tongue over the tooth with the cyanide sealed in it. I might need it yet. I thought of the proud face of my red-haired girl, back in Stockholm Zero. I wondered if my failure here would mean the end of her brilliant world of peace and order. Somewhere along the line I dozed off.

The door rattled. I sat up, startled. Gaston's face pressed against the glass. I unlocked it and he slid in beside me.

"OK, Hammer-hand," he said. "Think I got us a spot. We go along the edge of the drainage ditch over there to where it goes under the wall. Then we got to get down inside it and ease under the guard tower. It comes out in the clear on the other side."

I got out and followed Gaston over broken stones to the ditch. It was almost a creek, and the smell of it was terrible.

Gaston led me along its edge for a hundred yards, until the wall hung over us just beyond the circle of light from the guard tower. I could see a fellow with a burp gun leaning against a post on top of the tower, looking down onto the street inside the wall. There were two large floodlights beside him, unlit.

Gaston leaned close to my ear. "It kind of stinks," he said, "but the wall is pretty rough, so I think we can make it OK."

He slid over the edge, found a foothold, and disappeared. I slid down after him, groping with my foot for a ledge. The wall was crudely laid with plenty of cracks and projecting stones, but slimy with moss. I set my foot as well as I could and let myself down, holding onto a knob of rock and feeling for another. Once over the edge, we were out of sight of the guard. I groped along, one precarious foot at a time. We passed the place where the light gleamed on the black water below, hugging the shadow. Then we were under the wall, which arched massively over us. The sound of the trickling water was louder here. I heard Gaston muttering faintly ahead.

I tried to see what was going on. Gaston had stopped and was descending. I could barely make out his figure, knee-deep in the malodorous stream. I moved closer. Then I saw the grating. It was made of iron bars, and completely blocked the passage. I hung on. My arms were beginning to tremble with fatigue.

I climbed over to the grating. It was better there; I leaned against the rusty iron and tired to ease my arms. The defense system didn't have quite the hole in it we thought it had. Gaston moved around below me, reaching under the surface to try to find a bottom edge. Maybe we could duck under the barrier; I didn't like to think about it.

Suddenly I felt myself slipping. I gripped the bars, stifling a cry. Below me, Gaston hissed a curse, scrabbled upward. My grip was firm, I realized in an instant; it was the grating that was slipping. It dropped another eight inches with a muffled scraping and clank, then stopped. The rusty metal must have given under our weight. The corroded ends of the bars had broken off at the left side. There wasn't room to pass, but maybe we could force it a little farther.

Gaston braced himself against the wall and heaved. I got into position beside him and added my weight. The frame shifted a little, then stuck.

"Gaston," I said. "Maybe I can get under it now, and heave from the other side." Gaston moved back, and I let myself down into the reeking water. I worked an arm through, then dropped down waist deep, chest deep, pushing. The rough metal scraped my face, caught at my clothing; but I was through.

I crawled back up, dripping, and rested. From the darkness behind Gaston I heard a meshing of oiled metal parts and then the cavern echoed with the thunder of machine gun fire. In the flashing light I saw Gaston stiffen against the grating and fall. He hung by one hand, caught in the grating. There were shouts, and men dropped onto the stone coping at the culvert mouth. Gaston jerked, fumbled his pistol from his blouse.

"Gaston," I said. "Quick, under the bars..." I was helpless. I knew he was too big.

A man appeared, clinging to the coping with one hand, climbing down to enter the dark opening. He flashed a light at us and Gaston, still dangling by the left hand, fired. The man fell over into the stream with a tremendous splash.

Gaston gasped. "That's...all..." The gun fell from his hand into the black water.

I moved fast now, from one hand-hold to the next,

slipping and clutching, but not quite falling somehow. I managed to get a look back as I reached the open air. Two men were tugging at the body wedged in the opening. Even in death, Gaston guarded my retreat.

I came up over the side, and flattened against the wall, slug-gun in my hand; the street was empty. They must have thought they had us trapped; this side was deserted. I was directly under the tower. I eased out a few feet, and craned my neck; a shadow moved at the top of the tower. There was still one man on duty there. He must have heard the grating fall, and called for reinforcements.

I looked down the street ahead. I recognized the Street of the Olive Trees, the same one I had come through on my way out with Gros, ten days earlier. It slanted down, curving to the right. That was where I had to go, into the naked street, under the guns. I liked it here in the shadow of the tower, but I couldn't stay. I slipped off along the wall, trying to walk quietly. I got about five steps before the searchlight snapped on and swung around. I leaped forward, running for my life. The light found me, burning my leaping shadow against dusty walls and the loose-cobbled street. I tried to guess how many instants it would take the lone man on the tower to leave the light, and get his sights on me. Instinct told me to leap aside. As I did, the gun clattered and slugs whined off the stones to my left. I was out of the light now, and dashing for the protection of the curving wall ahead. The light raked across the street, caught me. Almost instantly the gun broke loose again. I bounded high in the air, twisted, hit and rolled in shadow and was up and running again. The light was still groping as I rounded the turn. Just ahead, a man stepped out of a doorway and spread his arms, crouching. I was moving fast. I stiff-armed him, without breaking my stride. He rolled into the gutter. No lights came on above me; I ran in utter silence. The dwellers in these scarred tenements had learned to sit silent behind barred windows when guns talked in the narrow streets.

I passed the spot where Gros had died, dashed on. In the distance a whistle blew, again and again. A shot ran out, kicking up dust ahead. I kept going.

A newspaper blew along in the gutter. A bristly sewer rat scuttled away ahead. Only the yellow glow of a bare bulb on a tall pole relieved the blackness. My shadow overtook me, leaped ahead.

I heard running feet behind me now. I searched desperately ahead, scanning the shabby stalls, empty and dark, trying to find the one we had used the day we left the palace, where the old woman huddled over her table of clay ware. It had been tiny, with a ragged gray awning sagging over the front, and broken pots scattered before it.

I almost passed it, caught myself, skidded, and dived for the back. I fought the stiff tarpaulin, found the opening, and squeezed through.

I panted in complete darkness now. I tried to remember the trip out. This part was just a narrow tunnel, low ceilinged, leading back to the ladder. I started off, feeling my way. I cracked my head on a low beam, crouched lower. Behind me I heard voices, as the men shouted to each other, searching. I had a moment's relief; they didn't know this entry.

I slipped in the slime on the floor, bumped the walls, felt my way around the boulder, and kept on.

It couldn't be much farther. It had been only a few steps, I thought, on the way out. I came to a turn, and stopped. There had been no turn in this part of the route. I started back, feeling the walls on both sides.

I heard a louder shout and a light flashed in the tunnel, near the entrance; someone had found it. I stopped. The light flashed again, and I saw the ladder, set in a niche at the side. I sprang to it, went up it in two leaps, and crashed against the door overhead. It was solid. I gripped the ladder, remembering the bale that concealed it. It had taken three men to push it aside. I climbed up higher, set my feet at the ends of the rung, put my back under the panel, and surged; it lifted, dropped back. The light lanced out, played over the wall below me. Desperately I put one foot on the next rung and heaved, and heaved again. The lid came up, and flew suddenly open. I crawled out onto the floor, blood pounding in my head. Through a blinding haze of pain in my skull, I saw the empty store-room, the open lid. I gripped my head. It felt as though a spike had been driven into it. I rose to my knees in agony, gasping with each heartbeat. I must have busted something, I thought. That bale weighed five hundred pounds.

A light flickered, casting giant shadows on the wall, then a face appeared in the opening where the lid had fallen back. I lay still, wishing that somehow this nightmare could end now, and let me rest.

The fellow's eyes were not adjusted to the darkness; he peered uncertainly around, throwing the light on looming crates and bales, then stared in my direction. With a sudden twist of his body, he brought up an automatic pistol, and in the same instant I fired the slug-gun once again. I closed my eyes against the sight of the face that tumbled back out of sight. The light went out.

I was tired of killing men; that was the one short-coming of my faithful weapon; it was always fatal.

I got to my feet and groped my way back of a steel lift-van and sank down again. The pain was a little less now, but any movement made it surge up blindingly. I lay there and waited for them to come to me. I couldn't hope to find a better place to make my stand; and I had to have a little time before I could go on.

I could hear the shouts only faintly, rising and falling. After awhile they faded and there was only silence. I raised my head, listening, then rose care-fully and went to the open trap-door. All I heard was a drop of water falling with a soft spat below. I had lost my pursuers.

I felt my confidence returning. I had been dead, trapped there in the fetid tunnel, and yet somehow I lived. The man who had stumbled into the hidden entrance must have done so unobserved, and no one else had looked along that stretch. Probably each man had been assigned a portion of the street to search, and the lucky winner had not been missed in the confusion.

I looked at my watch. Things happened fast in this war world; it was not yet half past nine. I had left the house at seven. I had killed four men in those two hours, and a man had died for me. I thought how easily a man slips back to his ancient role of nature's most deadly hunter.

The pain was washing away from my head now, leaving me shaky and drowsy. I yawned, sat on the floor. I had an impulse to lie back and go to sleep, but instead I got up and began feeling my way toward the panel that concealed the entrance to the passage in the massive walls. I wasn't finished yet; I was in the palace, unwounded, armed. I had all I had a right to hope for: a fighting chance.

I bumped into things in the darkness, trying to stay on course. I wished I had been more observant on the way out, but then I had no thought of coming back alone. I reached the wall, groped along it. I hoped I would be able to identify the panel when I found it. I tapped hopefully, listening for a hollow sound. I wasn't yet ready to start worrying about how I would pass the heavy bolts that held it shut.

The walls sounded solid. I shuffled along, feeling for hinges, cracks, anything to betray the false section of wall. There was nothing. I retraced my steps, wishing for light, found nothing. I came to a corner, started back. The boards lining the wall were heavy slabs, rough surfaced. I felt nail heads and splinters, nothing else.

I had to have light. I thought of the flashlight the man had been carrying; it was lying at the bottom of the ladder now. It was either that or wait until morning when a little sunlight would filter through the boarded windows. I might as well get going.

I moved off in what I hoped was the direction of the trap door, going slowly, feeling with my feet. I didn't want to find the open door by falling through it. I groped, banged my shins, cracked my head, swore. I cast about, working in the dark with no sound but my own breathing and the scrape of my shoes. I found it at last, when the open lid took the skin off a knuckle as I swung my arms ahead of me.

I felt for the ladder with my feet, went down. At the bottom I tried to avoid stepping on the body by putting my foot down wide of the ladder, and jerked it back as I felt the yielding mass. I swung off on the other side.

I didn't like the idea, but I reached down and began running my hands over the wet mud floor. There were shallow pools of gritty water, and round pebbles, a dead rat, and once something alive that wriggled from under my hand. I felt around the body, and finally under it. It seemed immensely heavy as I dragged it aside, and my head throbbed again. I had to be careful; I had a lot to do before I could relax and be an invalid.

After nearly an hour's search, I found it lying against the wall twenty feet from the ladder. I grabbed it up, flicked the switch, and it went on. The lens was cracked, but the thing worked. I was grateful then for the soft mud of the passage floor.

In two minutes I was back at the wooden wall, flashing the light along the joints. I saw the door almost at once; it was easy if you knew what to look for. I pushed against it; it was as unyielding as the rest of the wall. I had to have something to work on it with.

I threw the light over the creates nearby, started off among them. With any luck, there should be a crowbar here somewhere, to pry the lids off the boxes. I prowled up and down the narrow aisles between the looming crates, and among broken boards in the far corner discovered scattered tools; a nail-puller, heavy pliers, rusty tin snips—and a five-foot pry bar. I was still lucky. That suited me just fine.

As I pushed the end of the bar into the crack at the side of the door, I wondered what attention the noise would attract. If anyone heard it, it would probably be one of the Organization's stand-by crew, and they knew me. I wasn't too worried, and I had no choice. I heaved, splintering wood.

The big bar worked fast. In five minutes I had a twelve inch board hanging by a few nails at the top. Carrying the steel bar, I lifted the board and slipped under it into the passage. There were no branching corridors to get lost in, I saw. I quickly covered the distance to the door opening onto the room where I had met Miche and Gros. It stood half open. I looked into the room, flashing my light. It was deserted. I wondered where the Organization's men were. I had expected to find someone here.

I stepped past the door, and a rope dropped over my shoulders pinioning my arms. I was hauled backwards, slammed against a table. I threw myself forward, twisting, the light and the pry bar clattering to the floor. The light cast a dim beam toward a distant corner; I couldn't see my assailant.

The rope twisted around my chest now, tightening, and I was jerked back, falling against the table again. This time I was forced down on it, and the rope creaked as it was cinched up under the table, tying me down.

Other ropes flipped across me, pinioning my legs. I fought, kicked, wrenched a leg loose and had it trapped again. There was a rope around my neck now, and for a moment I thought I was going to be choked; but it held at the last instant, leaving me just breathing space.

"You want it tightened up?" a meaty voice grated in my ear. "Just lay nice and quiet."

I got the idea; I lay still. I didn't know whether I was in the hands of the Organization or the Ducal Guard. Maybe if I waited and said nothing, I would find out.

I couldn't see much, only the cobwebbed ceiling. The light moved, flashed in my face. I couldn't see who was behind it.

"It's the stoolie," the voice said unemotionally. "Lots of gall coming back here. What were you after, stoolie, figure on fingering the rest of the boys?"

"Use your head," I said. "I came back here to finish the job I came for; to..."

A blow rocked my head. There was a long silence while my head rang. The light went off. Feet shuffled. A match scratched, and the candle gave a weak illumination.

"I seen you kill Miche," the voice said softly. "You're a pretty hard boy, but I put you down. You look real nice laid out there. I'm going to cut you up a little and then I'm going to see what I can do with the irons. I ain't as good as Miche was with the irons, but Miche would of liked it this way."

"I was almost killed in the ambush myself," I said. I wanted to talk him into letting me go. I didn't want to kill anymore.

There was the sound of a knife being whetted. A shadow moved rhythmically on the ceiling as he stroked the blade across the stone. This one was really nuts, I thought.

My arms were at my sides, held by a rope across the forearms. I worked at the rope, got it up to the elbow. I felt over the other ropes in reach, but there were no knots that I could feel. I wanted to relieve the pressure on my throat, but I couldn't quite reach that high.

"Cut the ropes," I called. "I'm not an informer. I've just come from the place in the country, with Gaston."

The whetting sound stopped. "Where's Gaston?"

I hesitated. "He was killed," I said. "The sentry..."

The man laughed, a breathy cackle. "Yeah," he said. "It works out like that, don't it?" His voice hardened. "I'll think about Gaston and Miche and the others while I work with the knife."

So be it, I thought. I twitched my wrist, and the slap of the gun was loud in the silence.

"What's that?" the voice snapped, the chair rasped, feet scraped. My hands were relaxed against the table, the tiny gun held by one thumb against my palm. The light came closer, and I saw the man behind it now, in the faint glow of the candle; grey stubble across a hollow cheek, narrowed eyes, bushy hair. I wanted him to come a little closer. I slapped the table with my left hand; it sounded a little like the other slap.

"You can't blame me for trying," I whined.

He seemed to relax a bit, edged closer. "You was a tricky guy..." That was as far as he got. I raised the gun and blew him out like the light in his hand. The thud and clatter echoed and died. I was alone again in silence.

I relaxed then, went limp; all the energy seemed to drain out of me. The temptation to sleep was almost undeniable. But the rope galled my throat, and I had to free myself. I started in, tugging and twisting, working the rope down. I thought of how my reactions had changed in the few weeks since Winter had plucked me from the street in the Old

Town. I had been outraged by the brutality of that kidnapping, had considered myself recklessly daring when I waved the little pistol at my captors.

And now, my strongest reaction when the rope dropped on me in the dark had been the thought that I would have to kill again. Being tied no longer bothered me; I knew I could free myself. The only thought that stirred me was that in a few minutes, with luck, I would face the Dictator in his most inner fortress.

I couldn't understand where the rest of the Organization was. This poor mad fellow I had had to kill talked as though he were the only survivor. Maybe the ambush in the Street of the Olive Trees had been followed up by an extermination of the rats in the walls, too.

I worked one arm free, then quickly loosened the rope from my feet and waist; it fell slack around my neck, and I slid from under it. I yawned, then slapped at my face to try to wake myself up. I hadn't slept for forty hours and I had exerted myself in ways I hadn't even thought of for years; I was exhausted.

I went over to Chica's cupboard, rummaged in it, and found a bit of cheese and a bottle of wine. I was thirsty, but the wine would make me even drowsier. I nibbled at the cheese and wondered where Chica was. I hoped she was safe; she seemed like a shy and hopeful girl.

There was no reason to linger here. I crossed to the stair and made my way up to the corridor. The silence was complete until I reached the door which had caused me such consternation when it opened, as I stood at bay at the foot of the hidden stair. I put my ear to the panel, and caught a faint and distant hum of voices, the tiny clatter of things being rattled together. It was the normal hubbub of an occupied household. I felt an unexpected quickening of my pulse; I was sure somehow that I would find the Dictator in residence this time.

I turned the knob and pushed the door open a crack. It grated against a box outside. I forced it six inches, and peered through. There was only darkness, and the sounds, a little louder now. My heartbeat quickened to match the rise in volume. I was nearing my goal. I was no longer the eager neophyte, I thought, ignorant of the realities; I came now, steeled by necessity, a hardened fighter, a practical killer. I was armed and I was desperate, and I bore the scars of combat. I did not intend to fail.

I went up the stairs, pausing at each landing to listen. There was nothing but the sounds of normal activity. I reached the level of the old roof, and for a moment remembered vividly the other stair that I had climbed in another world, mounting to the tower where my shuttle lay. I didn't linger with the thought. There were no sounds from beyond the door; the latch still hung from splintered wood, just as I had left it when I passed this way coming down. I opened it silently, crossed quickly to the other door from which the private stair led up, and was beyond it, waiting for the sound of any notice I might have attracted. All was quiet; I breathed a sigh, relaxed my tense right wrist. Murdering people is getting to be a chore, I thought.

I yawned, shook my head. I couldn't seem to clear my thoughts fully; I tried to realize that in a matter of minutes, or perhaps even seconds, I might be face to face with my double, my other self, the Dictator of the State. I yawned again.

Forty feet to go, I thought. I went up, passing landings, moving silently. The walls here were smooth and new looking, painted a pale green. The doors were new, of heavy polished wood. Nothing old and shabby would be fitting in the tower apartment of the Dictator.

I reached the top, listened again. I eased the door open and looked down the length of the hall. This was the first sight I had seen when the shuttle had pitched me headlong into this living nightmare. It hadn't changed. I stepped into the hall, tried the first door. It opened, and I saw that it was a bedroom. I went in, and by the faint light shining through the curtains from below, looked over a wide bed, a large desk against the far wall, a closet door, an easy chair, and through a partly open door, a roomy bathroom to the right. There was a closed door in the center of the left wall, probably a communicating door to a sitting room, I thought. I closed the door behind me, and crossed to the windows. There were steel shutters, painted light green to match the walls, folded back behind the draperies. On impulse, I closed them. They fitted well. I went to the desk and found the lamp in the dark, flipped it on. I had had enough of groping through the dark for one night.

The room was very handsome, spacious, with a deep pile grey-green rug and a pair of bold water-colors on the wall. Suddenly I was aware of my own reek. The clothes seemed to crawl on my back. I had lain in mud, waded a sewer, crept through ancient dust.

I was filthy. Without considering further, I pulled the encrusted tunic off, tossed my clothes in a heap by the door, and headed for the bath.

It was finished in grey-green tile, and the tub was long and deep. I turned the tap, and hot water poured forth. I climbed in, adjusted the temperature, and looked around for the soap. The slug-gun was in the way; I laid it on the floor beside me.

I took half an hour soaping myself, and then climbed out and got my uniform. I had nothing else to put on, and I wouldn't wear it as it was. I soaped it up, rinsed it out, and draped it over the side of the tub. There was a vast white bathrobe behind the door, and I wrapped myself in it and went back into the bedroom. I liked the room; it was what I would like to have for myself, some day. And the thought struck me that we must be much alike in some ways, my twin and I.

I remembered the slug-gun, and retrieved it. The thought penetrated to my dulled mind that I was behaving dangerously. I had no idea when my victim might return; he could have come in when I was naked and helpless in the bathtub. I tried again to shake myself alert. But alarm wouldn't come. I felt perfectly safe, secure, comfortable. This won't do, I thought. I'm going to go to sleep on my feet.

I have to keep active, I told myself. I've got to stay alert. I'll hear him coming, and have a moment to hide in the bathroom. I yawned again.

I sat down in the chair opposite the door, and prepared to wait it out. I got up, as an afterthought, and turned the light out. I don't remember sitting down again.

X

I DREAMED I WAS at the seashore, and the sun reflected from the glassy water. It flashed in my eyes, and I turned away. I twisted in the chair, opened my eyes. My head was thick.

I stared at the pale green walls of the room, across the grey-green rug. It was silent in the room and I didn't move. The connecting door stood open.

I remembered turning the light off, nothing more. Someone had turned it on; someone had opened the door. I had come as a killer in the night; and someone had found me here sleeping, betrayed by my own exhaustion.

I sat up, and in that instant realized I was not alone. I turned my head, and looked at the man who sat quietly in the chair on my left, leaning back with his legs thrust out stiffly before him, his hands lightly gripping the arms of a rosewood chair upholstered in black leather. He smiled, and leaned forward. It was like looking into a mirror.

I didn't move. I stared at him. His face was thinner than mine, more lined. The skin was burned dark, the hair bleached lighter by the African sun; but it was me I looked at. Not a twin, not a double, not a clever actor; it was myself, sitting in a chair, looking at me.

"You have been sleeping soundly," he said. I thought of hearing my voice on a tape recorder, except that this voice spoke in flawless French.

I moved my hand slightly; my gun was still there, and the man I had come to kill sat not ten feet away, alone, unprotected. But I didn't move. I wasn't ready, not yet. Maybe not ever.

"Are you rested enough," he said, "or will you sleep longer before we talk?"

"I'm rested," I said.

"I do not know how you came here," he said, "but that you are here is enough. I knew that my destiny would not desert me. I did not know what gift the tide of fortune would bring to me, but there could be no finer thing than this; a brother."

I didn't know what I had expected the Dictator Bayard to be; a sullen ruffian, a wild-eyed megalomaniac, a sly-eyed schemer. But I had not expected a breathing image of myself, with a warm smile, and a poetic manner of speech, a man who called me brother.

He looked at me with an expression of intense interest.

"You speak excellent French, but with an English accent," he said. "Or is it perhaps American?" He smiled. "You must forgive my curiosity; linguistics, accents, they are a hobby of mine; and in your case, I am doubly intrigued."

"American," I said.

"Amazing," he said. "I might have been born an American myself...but that is a long dull tale to tell another time."

No need, I thought. My father told it to me often, when I was a boy...

He went on, his voice intense, but gentle, friendly. "They told me, when I returned to Algiers ten days ago, that a man resembling myself had been seen here in the apartment. There were two men found in my study, quite dead, a great deal of excitement, a garbled report. But I was struck by this talk of a man who looked like me. I wanted to see him, talk to him; I have been so very much alone here. It was a thing that caught my imagination. Of course, I did not know what brought this man here; they even talked of danger..." He spread his hands in a Gallic gesture.

"But when I came into this room and found you here, sleeping, I knew at once that you could not have come but in friendship. I was touched, my friend, to see that you came here as to your own, entrusting yourself to my hands."

I couldn't say anything. I didn't try.

"There are few in this land who have the courage to stand before me as a man, to treat me as a friend. There are legends of my ferocity, my deadliness, which keep all men on guard in my presence, fear blending with hatred. But they are only legends, born out of the same fear and hatred they engender; the two emotions we know most well in these bitter days. Love and trust—those words—we have all but forgotten.

"When I lit the lamp and saw your face, I knew at once that this was more than some shallow impersonation; I saw my own face there, not so worn by war as my own, the lines not so deeply etched; but there was the call of blood to blood; I knew you for my brother."

I licked my lips, swallowed. He leaned forward, placed his hand over mine, gripped it hard.

"Together, my brother, we shall yet redeem a civilization that must not die; you with your whole body, your strong legs, to be everywhere at once; and I with my dream, and the lessons the years have taught me. It is not too late even now to triumph over the petty plotters, the gnawers from within, who seek to bring down the little island of order I have created in the ruins of war; bring it down so that they may loot the ruins, kill the last feeble flower of Western Culture, and give the world over to barbarians."

He fell silent then, abruptly. He smiled, gripped my hand again, and leaned back in his chair with a sigh.

"Forgive me again, brother; I fall easily into oratory, I fear; a habit I should do well to break. There is time enough for plans later. But now, will you tell me of yourself? I know you have in you the blood of the Bayards."

"Yes, my name is Bayard."

"You must have wanted very much to come to me, to have made your way here alone and unarmed. No one has ever passed the wall before, without an escort and many papers."

I couldn't sit here silent, but neither could I tell this man anything of my real purpose in coming. I reminded myself of the treatment the Imperial ambassadors had received at his hands, of all that Bale had told me that first morning in the meeting with Bernadotte; but I saw nothing here of the ruthless tyrant I expected; instead, I found myself responding to his spontaneous welcome.

I had to tell him something. My years of diplomatic experience came to my assistance once again. I found myself lying smoothly, by indirection.

"You're right in thinking I can help you, Brion," I said. I was startled to hear myself calling him by his first name so easily, but it seemed the natural thing to do.

"But you are wrong in assuming that your State is the only surviving center of civilization. There is another, a strong, dynamic, and friendly power, which would like to establish amicable relations with you. I am the emissary of that government."

"Marvelous," he said, "but where?" He leaned forward again, eyes lighting. "There is nothing but silence on the wireless, and reconnaissance as far north as Moscow, east to India, and westward to the sea has discovered to me nothing but ruin and savagery." He sat up. "Of course; America!"

I sought for a neutral replay as he paused, went on.

"I grieved for your country, my brother. It was one of the first and fairest victims of the Age of Madness. You cannot know what gratitude I feel to know that of it something still remains; that the spark was not wholly quenched."

"Humans are tough animals," I hedged. "Not easy to kill."

"But why did you not come to me openly? The course you chose, while daring, was of extreme danger; but it must be that you were aware of the treachery all about me, and feared that my enemies would keep you from me."

He seemed so eager to understand that he supplied most of his own answers. I seemed to be doing pretty well by keeping my comments to a minimum. But this seemed an opportune moment to broach the subject of Bale's two agents who had carried full diplomatic credentials, and who had been subjected to beating, torture, and death. It was a contradiction in the Dictator's character I wanted to shed a little light on.

"I recall that two men sent to you a year ago were not well received," I said. "I was unsure of my reception. I wanted to see you privately, face to face."

Bayard's face tensed. "Two men?" he said. "I have heard nothing of ambassadors."

"They were met first by a Colonel-General Yang," I said, "and afterward were interviewed by you personally."

Bayard's face was white. "There is a dog of a broken officer who leads a crew of cutthroats in raids on what pitiful commerce I have been able to encourage. His name is Yang. If he has molested a legation sent to me from your country, I promise you his head."

"It was said that you yourself shot one of them," I said, pressing the point.

Bayard gripped the arm of the chair, his eyes on my face.

"I swear to you by the honor of the House of Bayard that I have never heard until this moment of your Embassy, and that no harm came to them through any act of mine."

I believed him. I was starting to wonder about a lot of things. He seemed sincere in welcoming the idea of an alliance with a civilized power. And yet, I myself had seen the carnage done by his raiders at the Palace, and the atom bomb they had tried to detonate there.

"Very well," I said. "On behalf of my government, I accept your statement; but if we treat with you now, what assurance will be given to us that there will be no repetition of the bombing raids..."

"Bombing raids!" He stared at me. There was a silence.

"Thank God you came to me by night, in secret," he said. "It is plain to me now that control of affairs has slipped from me farther even than I had feared."

"There have been seven raids, four of them accompanied by atomic bombs, in the past year," I said. "The most recent was less than one month ago."

His voice was deadly now. "By my order, every gram of fissionable material known to me to exist was dumped into the sea on the day that I established this State. That there were traitors in my service, I knew; but that there were madmen who would begin the Horror again, I did not suspect. If it is not now too late, I can only ask that you accept my pledge to you and to your government that I will place every resource of this State at the disposal of a force of my most loyal men, a division known as the Ducal Guard, veterans who have been with me since I led them into battle at Gibraltar, on the last day that I stood with my own feet on this earth. They will go with death orders to seek out and destroy those guilty of this monstrousness."

"It is not too late," I said.

He turned and stared across the room at a painting of sunlight shining through leaves onto a weathered wall. "Many times, brother, in these years, I have prayed that it was not too late. Do not mistake me; I prayed to no hollow God of the priests; I prayed to the manhood within myself that I should be able to do what no one else would pause from looting long enough to try; to save what remained of man's accomplishments in the arts, to keep a little foothold against returning darkness. I fought them when they burned the libraries, melted down the Cellini altar pieces, trampled the Mona Lisa in the ruins of the Louvre.

"There was loot for all, mountains of loot; so many had died and there were whole cities almost intact. Yes, loot is the one thing we do not lack. Destruction seemed to become an end in itself. I could save only a fragment here, a remnant there, always telling myself that it was not too late. But the years passed, and they have brought no change. Instead, it is the people who have changed; they seem to live now only for looting. At first it was a necessity; the survivors of twenty years of war, atomic bombings, disease, starvation, were forced to prowl through the ruins in search of the necessities of life. But there was so much treasure to uncover, so few to divide it among; it became a way of life.

"There was an end to industry, farming, family life. No one has children now. There are no marriages, just casual liaisons; and now they fight over the spoils.

"Even with the plenty that lies about us for the taking, men fight over three things; gold, liquor, and women.

"I have tried to arouse a spirit of rebuilding against the day when even the broken store houses run dry; but it is useless. Only my rigid martial rule holds them in check.

"I will confess, I had lost hope. There was too much

decay all around me; in my own house, among my closest advisors, I heard nothing but talk of armament, expeditionary forces, domination, renewed war against the ruins outside our little island of order. Empty war, meaningless overlordship of dead nations. They hoped to spend our slender resources in stamping out whatever traces might remain of human achievement, unless it bowed to our supremacy."

When he looked at me I thought of the expression, 'blazing eyes.'

"Now, my hope springs up renewed," he said. "With a brother at my side, we will prevail."

I thought about it. The Imperium had given me full powers. I might as well use them.

"I think I can assure you," I said, "that the worst is over. My government has resources; you may ask for whatever you need; men, supplies, equipment. We ask only one thing of you; friendship and justice between us."

He leaned back, closed his eyes. "The long night is over," he said.

There were still major points to be covered, but I felt sure that Bayard had been grossly misrepresented to me, and to the Imperial government. I wondered how Imperial Intelligence had been so completely taken in and why. Bale had spoken of having a team of his best men here, sending a stream of data back to him.

There was also the problem of my transportation back to the Zero Zero world of the Imperium. Bayard hadn't mentioned the M-C shuttles; in fact, thinking over what he had said, he talked as though they didn't exist. Perhaps he was holding out on me, in spite of his apparent candor.

Bayard opened his eyes. "There has been enough of gravity for now," he said. "I think that a little rejoicing between us would be appropriate. I wonder if you share my liking for an impromptu feast on such an occasion?"

"I love to eat in the middle of the night," I said, "especially when I've missed my dinner."

"You are a true Bayard," he said. He reached to the table beside me and pressed a button. He leaned back and placed his finger tips together.

"And so now we must think about the menu." He pursed his lips, looking thoughtful. "Something fitting for the event," he said.

"And with a bottle of wine, I hope," I said. I was feeling more at ease now. I liked the Dictator Bayard, even if I still had reservations.

"But naturally, brother," he said, staring at me with a smile. "I think I shall be able to offer you something quite adequate in wines." He hesitated. "May I not use your given name? I feel that between us there should be no need for formality."

Now it was my turn to hesitate. "My name is also Brion," I said after a moment. "So we can call each other Brion," I added with a smile.

He laughed. "Splendid. And now let me make a suggestion. Tonight permit me to select the dinner; we will see if our tastes are as similar as ourselves."

"Fine," I said.

There was a tap at the door. At Brion's call, it opened and a sourfaced fiftyish little man came in. He saw me, started; then his face blanked. He crossed to The Dictator's chair, drew himself up, and said, "I come as quick as I could, Major."

"Fine, fine, Luc," he said. "At ease. My brother and I are hungry. We have a very special hunger, and I want you, Luc, to see to it that our dinner does the kitchen credit."

Luc glanced at me from the corner of his eye. "I seen the gentleman resembled the Major somewhat," he said.

"An amazing likeness. Now," he stared at the ceiling. "We will begin with a very dry Madeira, I think; Sercial, the 1875. Then we will whet our appetites with Les Huitres de Whitstable, with a white Burgundy; Chablis Vaudesir. I think there is still a bit of the '29."

I leaned forward. This sounded like something special indeed. I had eaten oysters Whitstable before, but the wines were vintages of which I had only heard.

"The soup, Consommé Double aux Cepes; then, Le Supreme de Brochet au Beurre Blanc, and for our first red Burgundy, Romanee-Conti, 1904."

Brion stared with speculative eyes at the far corner of the room. "Next, Les Quenelles de Veau Benedict, with a Bordeaux; the Chateau Lafite-Rothschild, 1890. By then, I think a Grouse d'Ecosse Rotie sur la Canapé would be appropriate, followed by Poireaux Meuniere for a touch of sweet.

"We will have a demi-bouteille of Le Croton '33 then, along with something to nibble; Brie de Meaux, Stilton, and Roquefort will do.

"Crusted Port, 1871, should clear the palate of cheese in readiness for café and Brandy; The Reserve, 1855, Luc. The occasion demands it." He turned to me.

"Among the treasures I was able to rescue from wanton destruction are included what remains in the world of the great vintages. Curiously, the troops usually smashed the wine cellars in disappointment at not having found something stronger. I saved what I could." I was impressed.

"Those old years," I said. "Fabulous!"

"The tragedy is," he said sadly, "that there are no new years. The last authentic vintage year was 1934; a few barrels only. Now the vineyards of France are dead. I am doing what I can here with a few vines, but it is not a thing that interests people today."

Luc went away quietly. If he could carry that in his head, I thought, he was the kind of waiter I'd always wanted to find.

"Luc has been with me for many years," Brion said. "A faithful friend. You noticed that he called me 'Major.' That was the last official rank I held in the Army of France-in-Exile, before the collapse. I was later elected as Colonel over a regiment of survivors of the Battle of Gibraltar, when we had realized that we were on our own. Later still, when I saw what had to be done, and took into my hands the task of rebuilding, other titles were given me by my followers, and I confess I conferred one or two myself; it was a necessary psychological measure, I felt. But to Luc I have always remained 'major.' He himself was a sous-officer, my regimental Sergeant-Major."

"That must have been a terrible time," I said.

"The most terrible part was the realization in recent years that men have changed," he said. "At first, we all seemed to have the same aim; to rebuild. We had to use the only organizing force remaining in our shattered world, military discipline, to make a beginning, to set up some sort of framework within which we could rebuild. I tried, as soon as we had pacified a few hundred square miles, to hold an election. I wished to turn the leadership over to another, so that I could rest and perhaps forget a little; but I almost lost all we had gained in the riots that broke out. I tried twice again in the next ten years, and always the result was the same; bloodshed, a raw struggle for power. So I remain, an unwilling master.

"Now it appears that even that uneasy peace was not long to endure; only your coming will save what we have built."

"I know little about events of the last few years in Europe," I said. "Can you tell me something about them?"

He sat thoughtfully for a moment. "The course was steadily downhill," he said, "from the day of the unhappy Peace of Munich in 1919. Had America come into the war, perhaps it would have ended differently; but of course you know and remember the armed truce of the 20's. America faced the Central Powers alone, and the end was inevitable. When America fell under the massive onslaught in '32, it seemed that the Kaiser's dream of a German-dominated world was at hand. Then came the uprisings. I was only a boy, but I held a second Lieutenant's commission in the Army of France-in-Exile. We spearheaded the organized resistance, and the movement spread like wildfire. Men, it seemed, would not live as slaves. We had high hopes in those days.

"But the years passed, and stalemate wore away at us. At last the Kaiser was overthrown by a palace coup, and we chose that chance to make our last assault. I led my battalion on Gibraltar, and took a steel-jacketed bullet through both knees almost before we were ashore.

"I will never forget the hours of agony while I lay conscious in the surgeon's tent. There was no more morphine, and the medical officers worked over the minor cases, trying to get men back into the fight; I was out of it, and therefore took last priority. It was reasonable, but at the time I did not understand."

I listened, rapt. "When," I asked, "were you hit?"

"That day I will not soon forget," he said. "April 15, 1945."

I stared. I had been hit by a German machine gun slug and had waited in the aid station for the doctors to get to me—on April 15, 1945. There was a strange affinity that linked this other Bayard's life with mine, even across the unimaginable void of the Net.

At my host's suggestion, we moved out to the terraced balcony and deft men in white jackets spread a table there with fine linen, Swedish glass, and old silver.

Luc came back with the Madeira then, poured it silently, left. We talked, exchanged reminiscences. I limited myself to generalities and in return learned a lot about this lonely man. His parents—our parents—lived at a distance from Algiers; not, as I had been told, because they were estranged from their son, but because he had removed them to a place of safety far from the storm center of Algiers. I thought of seeing them soon, but there was a sense suddenly of unreality about it all.

The courses arrived one by one, wheeled onto the terrace by bustling servitors supervised by Luc, each dish surpassing the last in its perfection. I saw that the Dictator was a gourmet of rare distinction; and Luc was as good as he seemed.

We mellowed with each succeeding bottle of great

wine. I hinted, and finally asked Bayard openly about the shuttles, and the M-C drive. He didn't know what I was talking about. Even through the glow I felt the tension begin again inside me; although I had won my way into the palace and the Dictator's friendship, I was still marooned. The raids and the shuttles were under the control of some other hand here. The job of finding that hand still lay ahead.

We were feeling wonderful now. I told Bayard about my escape from the ambush at the bridge and got out my faithful slug-gun to explain to him how it worked. He was enthralled, and asked if they could be supplied to his Ducal Guard. I laid the gun on the table, and showed him the clip on my wrist that flipped the gun into my hand at a motion.

He countered by calling for Luc to bring a heavy walnut gun case containing a beautiful collection of strange automatics, multi-barreled pistols, and miniature revolvers.

We finished the 1855 brandy, and still we sat, talking through the African night. We laid ambitious plans for the rebuilding of civilization. We enjoyed each other's company, and all stiffness had long since gone. I closed my eyes, and I think I must have dozed off. Something awakened me.

Dawn was lightening the sky. Brion sat silent, frowning. He tilted his head.

"Listen."

I listened. I thought I caught a faint shout and something banged in the distance. I looked inquiringly at my host. His face was grim.

"All is not well," he said. He gripped the chair arms, rose, got his canes, started around the table.

I got up and stepped forward through the glass doors into the room. I was dizzy from the wine and brandy. There was a louder shout outside in the hall and a muffled thump. Then the door shook, splintered and crashed inward.

Thin in a tight black uniform, Chief Inspector Bale stood in the opening, his face white with excitement. He carried a long-barreled Mauser automatic pistol in his right hand. He stared at me, stepped back, then with a sudden grimace raised the gun and fired.

In the instant before the gun slammed, I caught a blur of motion from my right, and then Brion was there, half in front of me, falling as the shot echoed. I grabbed for him, caught him by the shoulders as he went down, limp. Blood welled from under his collar, spreading; too much blood, a life's blood.

He was on the floor, on his back, and I crouched over him. His mouth opened, and he tried to say something; I never knew what it was. He was looking in my face as the light died from his eyes.

"Get back, Bayard," Bale snarled. "Rotten luck, that; I need the swine alive for hanging." I stood up slowly, thinking of the gun on the table behind me.

He stared at me, gnawing his lip. "It was you I wanted dead, and this fool's traded lives with you."

He seemed to be talking to himself. I recognized the voice now, a little late. Bale was the Big Boss. It was the fact that he spoke in French here that had fooled me.

"All right," he said in abrupt decision. "He can trade deaths with you, too. You'll do to hang in his place. I'll give the mob their circus. You wanted to take his place, here's your chance."

He stepped farther into the room, motioned others in. Evil-looking thugs came through the door, peering about, glancing at Bale for orders.

"Truss this man up," he said, jerking his head toward me. "Just his arms."

I stepped back, edging toward the table. If I could have just one shot at that thin-lipped face.

Two of them grabbed at me; I dodged back, turned, reached for the gun. My fingers hit it, knocked it spinning to the floor. Then they had me, twisting my arms behind me.

"I want him put where he'll keep for a few hours," Bale said.

"Yeah," one of the men said. "I know a place; he'll keep good down in them cells over the other side of the shelters; OK we dump him there?"

"Very well," Bale said. "But I'm warning you, Cassu; keep your bloody hands off him; I want him strong for the surgeon."

Cassu grunted, twisted my arm until the joint creaked, and pushed me past the dead body of the man I had come in one night to think of as a brother. He had fought for his cause through bitter years; I hoped he had died before he realized that he had fought in vain.

They marched me off down the corridor, pushed me into an elevator, led me out again through a mob of noisy roughs armed to the teeth, down stone stairs, along a damp tunnel in the rock, and at the end of the line, sent me spinning with a kick into the pitch black of a cell. I fell, groped for a wall for support, found a bare wooden shelf which was the bed, and sat down on it. The iron-barred door clanged.

My stunned mind worked, trying to assimilate what had happened. Bale! And not a double; he had known who I was. It was Bale of the Imperium, a traitor. That answered a lot of questions. It explained the perfect timing and placement of the attack at the palace, and why Bale had been too busy to attend the gala affair that night. I realized now why he had sought me out afterward; he was hoping that I'd been killed, of course. That would have simplified matters for him. And the duel; I had never quite been able to understand why the intelligence chief had been willing to risk killing me, when I was essential to the scheme for controlling the dictator. And all the lies about the viciousness of the Bayard of B-I Two; Bale's fabrications, designed to prevent establishment of friendly relations between the Imperium and this unhappy world.

Why? I asked myself. Did Bale plan to rule this hell-world himself, make it his private domain? It seemed so. Here was a world enough like the world of the Imperium that Bale would have at his disposal the same luxuries and conveniences that he knew at home; he could loot this world's duplicates of the treasure troves of the cities; stores, palaces and museums.

And I saw that Bale did not intend to content himself with this world alone; this would be merely a base of operations, a source of fighting men and weapons, including atomic bombs. Bale himself was the author of the raids on the Imperium. He had stolen shuttles, or components thereof, and had manned them here in B-I Two, and set out on a career of piracy. The next step would be the assault on the Imperium itself, a full-scale attack, strewing atomic death. The men of the

Imperium would wear gay uniforms and dress sabres into battle against atomic cannon.

I wondered why I hadn't realized it sooner. The fantastic unlikeliness of the development of the M-C drive independently by the war-ruined world of B-I Two seemed obvious now.

While we had sat in solemn conference, planning moves against the raiders, their prime mover had sat with us. No wonder an enemy scout had lain in wait for me as I came in on my mission. The wonder was that I'd escaped death on that first step of my journey.

When he found me at the hide-out, Bale must have immediately set to work planning how best to make use of the unexpected stroke of luck. And when I had escaped, he had had to move fast.

I could only assume that the State was now in his hands; that a show execution of Bayard in the morning had been scheduled to impress the populace with the reality of the change in regimes.

Now I would hang in the Dictator's place. And I remembered what Bale had said; he wanted me strong for the surgeon. The wash tub would be useful after all. There were enough who knew the Dictator's secret to make a corpse with legs embarrassing.

They would shoot me full of dope, perform the operation, bind up the stumps, dress my unconscious body in a uniform, and hang me. A dead body wouldn't fool the public. They would be able to see the color of life in my face, even if I were still out, as the noose tightened.

I heard someone coming, and saw a bobbing light in the passage through the barred opening in the door. I braced myself. Maybe this was the man with the saws and the heavy snippers already.

Two men stopped at the cell door, opened it, came in. I squinted, at the glare of the flashlight. One of the two dropped something on the floor.

"Put it on," he said. "The boss said he wanted you should wear this here for the hanging."

I saw my old costume, the one I had washed. At least it was clean, I thought. It was strange, I considered, how inconsequentials still had importance.

A foot nudged me. "Put it on, like I said."

"Yeah," I said. I took off the robe and pulled on the light wool jacket and trousers, buckled the belt. There were no shoes; I guessed Bale figured I wouldn't be needing them.

"OK," the man said. "Let's go, Hiem."

I sat and listened as the door clanked again; the light receded. It was very dark.

I wasn't thinking about anything, now. My mind wandered over bits and fragments from the past few weeks; the street where I'd been picked up, the office where Bernadotte had told me about the job, Goering's face as he grappled the raider on the ballroom floor; and Barbro's red hair and level grey eyes.

I fingered the torn lapels of my jacket. The communicator hadn't helped me much. I could feel the broken wires, tiny filaments projecting from the cut edge of the cloth. Beau Joe had cursed as he clashed at them.

I looked down. Tiny blue sparks jumped against the utter black as the wires touched.

I sat perfectly still. Sweat broke out on my forehead. I didn't dare move; the pain of hope awakening against all hope was worse than the blank acceptance of certain death.

My hands shook. I fumbled for the wires, tapped them together. A spark; another.

I tried to think. The communicator was clipped to my belt still; the speaker and mike were gone, but the power source was there. Was there a possibility that touching the wires together would transmit a signal? I didn't know. I could only try.

I didn't know Morse Code, or any other code; but I knew S O S. Three dots, three dashes, three dots; over and over, while I suffered the agony of hope.

A long time passed. I wondered when the surgeon would arrive. Probably Bale had sent to the house in the country for him; it shouldn't take more than an hour and a half, or at most two hours; and surely it had been that long. I had to fight to stay awake now. Fatigue, a heavy dinner, and too much good wine were catching up with me.

My fingers cramped, stiff and aching. It was cold in the cell, and my clothes were still damp. I tapped the wires together and watched the blue spark dance.

I thought of Bayard, holding on alone against the tide of destruction, decay, anarchy, battling to preserve something of civilization out of the ruin of a world; I thought of the gallant men of the Imperium, facing disaster sword in hand; and I thought of blandfaced men in dowdy grey flannel suits, sitting in embassy offices back in my own world, devising petty swindles, engaging in spiteful office intrigues, little greedy selfish men, feathering their nests.

I knew I didn't have much longer to wait. I went over it again in my mind; it would take perhaps thirty minutes for Bale to get a messenger on the way to the hideout; the trip itself might take twenty minutes. Then allow half an hour to load the table, the instruments—and the wash tub. Another twenty minutes for the return, and then maybe another half hour to set up the operating room. That totaled a little over two hours. My sense of time was confused, but surely it had been that long. I tapped the wires, and waited. I almost fell off the bunk as I dozed for an instant. I couldn't stop; I had to try until time ran out for me.

I heard them coming from far off, the first faint grate of leather on dusty stone, a clink of metal. My mouth was dry, and my legs began to tingle. I thought of the hollow tooth, and ran my tongue over it. The time for it had come. I wondered how it would taste, if it would be painful. I wondered if Bale had forgotten it, or if he hadn't known. I took a breath; there was no reason to wait.

There were more sounds in the passage now, sounds of men and loud voices; a clank of something heavy, a ponderous grinding. They must be planning on setting the table up here in the cell, I thought. I went to the tiny opening in the door and looked through. I could see nothing but almost total darkness. Suddenly light flared brilliantly, and I jumped, blinded.

There was more noise, then someone yelled. They must be having a hell of a time getting the stuff through the narrow hall, I thought. My eyeballs ached. I noticed my legs were trembling. My stomach suddenly felt bad. I gagged. I hoped I wouldn't go to pieces. Time for the tooth now. I thought of how disappointed Bale would be when he found me dead in my cell; it helped a little; but still I hesitated. I didn't want to die. I had a lot of living I wanted to do first. I tried to look at the light again and couldn't.

There was a terrible din in the hall now. I thought I heard shots, and I was on my feet again, squinting through the glare. I caught a glimpse of a man backing toward the door, falling. Something was going on out there.

My eyes ached, I shut them, backed up, trying to think. A voice was shouting nearby.

There was nothing I could do; I couldn't even tell what was happening. The voice was louder now.

"Wolfhound!"

My head came up. My code name. I tried to shout, choked. "Yes," I croaked. I jumped to the bars again, yelled.

"Wolfhound, where in hell..."

I had my eyes shut. "Here!" I yelled, "here!"

"Over here," the voice shouted. The racket was terrible now.

"Get back, Colonel," someone said at my head. "Get in the corner and cover up."

I obeyed. I moved back and crouched, arms over my head. There was a sharp hissing sound, and a mighty blast that jarred the floor under me. Tiny particles bit and stung, and grit was in my mouth. There was a chemical reek and my head hummed. With a drawn-out clang, the door fell into the room.

Arms grabbed me, pulled me through the boiling dust, out into the glare. I stumbled, trying to blink, and felt broken things under foot.

"Lower the lights," the voice called. The shouts were less now, and the scuffling. I heard other sounds building in the distance; shouts, running feet.

I opened my eyes again, and now it was almost bearable. Men milled around a mass blocking the passage. Canted against the wall a great box sat with a door hanging wide, light streaming out. Arms helped me through the door, and I saw wires, coils, junction boxes, stapled to bare new wood, with angle iron here and there. White-uniformed men crowded into the tiny space; a limp figure was hauled through the door.

"Full count," someone yelled. "Button up!" Wood splintered as a bullet came through.

The door banged shut, and the box trembled while a rumble built up into a whine, then passed on up out of audibility.

Some one grabbed my arm. "My God, Brion, you must have had a terrible time of it."

It was Richthofen, in a grey uniform, a cut on his face, staring at me.

I tried to smile, I was very weak suddenly. I was too old for this sort of thing.

"No hard feelings," I said. "Your timing...was good."

"We've had a monitor on your band day and night, hoping for something," he said. "We'd given you up, but couldn't bring ourselves to abandon hope; then four hours ago the tapping started coming through. They went after it with locators, and fixed it here in the wine cellars. Word went out to the patrol scouts, but they couldn't get in here; no room. We pitched this box together and came in."

"Fast work," I said. I thought of the trip through the dreaded Blight, in a jury-rig made of pine boards. I felt a certain pride in the men of the Imperium.

"Make a place for Colonel Bayard, men," some-one said. A space was cleared on the floor, jackets laid out on it. Richthofen was holding me up, and I made a mighty effort, got to the pallet and collapsed.

Richthofen said something but I didn't hear it. I wondered what had held the meat-cutters up so long, and then let it go. Thinking was hard work, and now I was going to rest. But I had to say something first, warn them. I couldn't remember...

XI

I WAS LYING IN a clean bed in a sunny room, propped up on pillows. It was a little like another room I had awakened in not so long before, but there was one important difference. Barbro sat beside my bed, knitting a ski stocking from red wool. Her hair was piled high on her head, and the sun shone through it, coppery red. Her eyes were hazel, and her features were perfect, and I liked lying there looking at her. She had come every day since my return to the Imperium, and read to me, talked to me, fed me soup and fluffed my pillows. I was enjoying my convalescence.

They had let me sleep for twelve hours before Richthofen, Goering, and several lesser lights of the various intelligence services had gathered in my room to hear my report.

They had listened when I told them of my meeting with Bale, and when I finished two of Goering's men left the room at a whispered word from him. I told them all that had happened—three times. Details that seemed unimportant, Richthofen cautioned me, might be useful; so I left out nothing.

They took the news calmly, I thought. After the others left, I eyed Richthofen quizzically. "You don't seem very surprised to learn that one of your top intelligence men is a traitor to the Imperium," I said.

Richthofen looked serious. "No, Brion, we had begun to fear something of the sort. Inspector Bale has disappeared. He has not been seen for almost a week. We missed him first a day before your signal. We feared foul play, and began an investigation; a number of interesting facts turned up, including several brief disappearances in the past, which had been unreported. With Bale chief of the shuttle service and the patrol activities, he could move about freely; no one checked on him. In fact, we had most of our information on B-I Two through Bale. He could easily arrange matters to suit himself.

"There were also discrepancies in the supplies of M-C drive components requisitioned and on hand. Your experience is pretty well borne out by our findings. We found several of his top aides also missing and collected a few others who seemed involved in some odd bits of business."

"That's bad," I said. "I was counting on nabbing him here."

"Doubtless he feared to return, after your escape," Richthofen said. "Perhaps that will be the end of his activities here."

I doubted that. I discussed the measures that might be taken to set up some sort of monitor post in the B-I Two world, to help in eventually reestablishing order there. I felt an obligation to Brion to do that.

And I also asked what was being done to bring my parents in. Richthofen reassured me that plans were well under way.

There still remained no solution to the grim threat to the Imperium. Bale was still free to raid at will; only his movement in the ferrying of supplies was impeded by the alerted M-C scouts now under Goering's direction. So far no activity had been reported.

There was nothing more I could do now, Richthofen assured me. Aside from daily visits by him and Goering, one call by the King, whom I still called General, and the soothing and exciting presence of Barbro for several hours each day, I was left alone to recuperate.

If you are good, Brion," Barbro said, "and eat all of your soup today, perhaps by tomorrow evening you will be strong enough to accept the King's invitation to sit in the royal box and listen to the orchestra at the Emperor Ball."

"Did the doctor say that?" I asked. "I thought it was just a sort of rhetorical invitation."

The King wants very much for you to come and the doctor says you are making splendid progress. Wouldn't you like to go?"

"And just sit?" I said.

"But I will be sitting with you, Brion."

"OK," I said. "It's a deal."

"I think it will be even better sitting above looking down on the lovely people," Barbro said. "It is the most brilliant ball of the year; the only time that all the three Kings and the Emperor with their ladies are there together. And it is only once in three years that the Emperor Ball is held at Stockholm. I have already been to several, so I will not mind sitting this time to watch. And we will see more." She had a lovely smile.

I smiled at her; that was the way she made me feel. "What is the occasion?" I asked.

"It is the anniversary of the signing of the Concord which resulted in the creation of the Imperium," she said. "It is a very happy time."

I was thinking. There seemed to be something I wasn't figuring out. I had been leaving all the problems to the intelligence men, but I knew more than they did about Bale.

I thought of the last big affair, and the brutal attack. I suspected that this time every man would wear a slug-gun under his braided cuff. But the fight on the floor had been merely a diversion, designed to allow the crew to set up an atomic bomb.

I sat bolt upright. That bomb had been turned over to Bale. There would be no chance of surprise attack from a shuttle this time, with alert crews watching around the clock for traces of unscheduled M-C activity; but there was no need to bring a bomb in. Bale had one here.

"What is it, Brion?" Barbro asked, leaning forward.

"What did Bale do with that bomb?" I said, staring at her, "the one they tried to set off at the dance? Where is it now?"

"I don't know, Brion," Barbro said. "Shall I call Baron Richthofen and ask him?" I liked the way she didn't flutter and look helpless.

"Yes," I said, "please do."

I waited impatiently while she got through to Imperial Intelligence, spoke to Manfred. She put the trumpet-shaped earpiece back on its brass hook and turned to me.

"He doesn't know, Brion," she said. "Already an attempt has been made to discover what was done with it, but nothing has been learned."

I had to realize that the Imperial officials still didn't fully understand the bomb's power. But I felt certain that the thing was still here in the Imperium, and that Bale would find a way to use it. He could wipe out the city, if the bomb were a big one; and I had an idea it was.

Another thought struck me.

"When do the royal parties arrive for the Emperor Ball?" I asked.

"They are already in the city," Barbro said, "at Drottningholm."

I felt my heart start to beat a little faster. Bale wouldn't let this opportunity pass. With the three kings here in the city, and an atomic bomb hidden somewhere, he had to act. At one stroke he could wipe out the leadership of the Imperium, and follow-up with a full-scale assault; and against his atomic weapons, the fight would be hopeless.

"Call Manfred back, Barbro," I said. "Tell him that bomb's got to be found fast. The kings will have to be evacuated from the city; the ball will have to be canceled."

Barbro spoke into the phone, looked back at me. "He has left the building, Brion," she said. "Shall I try to reach Herr Goering?"

"Yes," I said. I started to tell her to hurry, but she was already speaking rapidly to someone at Goering's office. Barbro was quick to catch on.

"He also is out," Barbro said. "Is there anyone else..."

I thought furiously. Manfred or Hermann would listen to anything I might say, but with their stags it would be a different matter. To call off the day of celebration, disturb the royal parties, alarm the city, were serious measures; no one would act on my vague suspicions alone. I had to find my friends in a hurry; or find Bale...

Imperial Intelligence had made a search, found nothing. His apartment was deserted, as well as his small house at the edge of the city. And the monitors had detected no shuttle not known to be an Imperium vessel moving in the Net recently.

There were several possibilities; one was that Bale had returned almost at the same time as I had, slipping in before the situation was known, while some of his own men still manned the alert stations. A second was that he planned to come in prepared to hold off attackers until he could detonate the bomb. Or possibly an accomplice would act for him.

Somehow I liked the first thought best. It seemed more in keeping with what I knew of Bale, shrewder, less dangerous. If I were right, Bale was here now, somewhere in Stockholm, waiting for the hour to blow the city sky-high.

As for the hour, he would wait for the arrival of the Emperor, not longer.

"Barbro," I said, "when does the Emperor arrive?"

"I'm not sure, Brion," she said. "Possibly tonight, but perhaps this afternoon."

That didn't give me much time. I had to get out of here, do something. I jumped out of bed, and staggered. Barbro stood up quickly and put out her hand to steady me. "Are you sure you are strong enough to get up, Brion?"

"Here I come, ready or not," I said. "I can't just

lie here, Barbro. Maybe I can think better if I get outside. Do you have a car?" I was fumbling at my pajama buttons. I had to have some clothes. I started for the closet.

"Yes, my car is downstairs, Brion. Sit down and let me help you." She went to the closet and I sank down. I seemed always to be recuperating lately. I had been through this shaky-legs business just a few days ago, and here I was starting in again. Barbro turned, holding a brown suit in her hands.

"This is all there is, Brion," she said. "It is the uniform of the Dictator, that you wore when you came here to the hospital."

"It will have to do," I said. I didn't bother to be shy about stripping and pulling on the wrinkled clothes in front of Barbro, and she didn't act coy; she helped me dress, and we left the room as fast as I could walk. A passing nurse stared, but went on. I was dizzy and panting already.

The elevator helped. I sank down on the stool, head spinning. I rubbed my chest; it was still sore from Beau Joe's attentions.

I felt something stiff in the pocket, and suddenly I had a vivid recollection of Gaston giving me a card as we crouched in the dusk behind the hideout near Algiers, telling me that he thought it was the address of the Big Boss's out-of-town headquarters. I grabbed for the card, squinted at it in the dim light of the ceiling lamp as the car jolted to a stop.

"Tegeluddsvägen 71" was scrawled across the card in blurred pencil. I remembered how I had dismissed it from my mind as of no interest when Gaston had handed it to me; I had hoped for something more useful. Now this might be the little key that could save an Empire.

"What is it, Brion," Barbro asked. "Have you found something?"

"I don't know," I said. "Maybe just a dead end, but maybe not." I handed her the card. "Do you know where this is?"

She read the address. "I think I know the street," she said. "It is not far from the docks, in the warehouse district."

"Let's go," I said.

We turned away from the reception desk and headed for a small side entrance at the end of the hall. It was a long trip, but I was getting over the dizziness. I had to pause to rest at the door, then made it to the curb. I sat on a stone bench under a linden tree and waited. In less than a minute Barbro swept around the corner in a low-slung red cabriolet. I got in and we swung east, moving fast.

There were few cars on the streets of the Imperium's Stockholm. Ownership of an automobile had not become a national mania, a caste-mark. We roared across a bridge, continued on into Kungsgatan, cut around an immense green limousine under the bridge, and angled across Stureplan towards Humlegården. An excited policeman blew a whistle, and a trolley jingled a bell indignantly, but we were picking up speed again.

For four days I had idled in bed while somewhere the bomb lay waiting; and now I was forced to leap off on a wild hunch, because there was no time left. If I could have contacted Manfred or Hermann, even checked on the Emperor's arrival time, we could have planned this, prepared for emergency; but now there was only this, a wild dash and a fervent hope that we were right, and not too late.

We squealed around a corner, slowed in a street of gloomy warehouses, blind glass windows in looming brick-red facades, with yard-high letters identifying the shipping lines which owned them.

"This is the street," Barbro said. "And the number was seventy-one?"

"That's right," I said. "This is fifty-three; it must be a block or two farther along."

"Sixty-nine there," Barbro said. "The next one must be it, but I don't see a number." The car eased to a halt.

"Let's get out," I said. I stepped out onto a gritty sidewalk, shaded by the bulk of the buildings, silent. There was a smell of tar and hemp in the air and a hint of sea water.

I stared at the building before me. I couldn't make out any identifying number. Barbro went around the car, walked a few feet farther on, came back.

"That must be the one, Brion," she said. "The next one is seventy-three."

There was a small door set in the front of the building beside the loading platform. I went up to it, tried it; locked. I leaned against it and rested.

"Barbro," I said. "Get me a jack handle or tire tool from your car." I hated to drag Barbro into this, but I had no choice. I couldn't do it alone.

She came back with a flat piece of steel eighteen inches long. I jammed it into the wide crack at the edge of the door and pulled. Something snapped, and with a jerk the door popped open.

It was dark inside. We went in and I pulled the door shut behind us. A stair ran up into gloom above. A side door opened from the short hall onto a vast space piled with crates. What we wanted must be up the stairs. That would be quite a climb for me. Barbro gave me an arm, and we started up.

We went three flights, a few steps at a time. I was soaked with sweat, and thought seriously about losing my dinner. I sat down and breathed hard through my nose. The hard work helped to keep my mind off the second sun that might light the Stockholm sky at any moment. We went on.

Five flights up, we reached a landing. The door we faced was red-stained wood, solid, and with a new lock. It looked like maybe we were on to something.

I tried the steel bar again, with no luck. Then Barbro went to work with a long pin with a large sapphire on the end of it. That was no good either. I looked at the hinge pins. They didn't look as good as the lock.

It took fifteen minutes, every one of which took a year off my life, but after a final wrench with the steel bar, the last pin clattered to the floor. The door pivoted out and fell against the wall.

"Wait here," I said. I started forward, into the papered hall.

"I go with you, Brion," Barbro said. I didn't argue.

We were in a handsome apartment, a little too lavishly furnished. Persian rugs graced the floor, and in the bars of dusty sunlight that slanted through shuttered windows, mellow old teak furniture gleamed, and polished ivory figurines stood on dark shelves under silk scrolls from Japan. An ornate screen stood in the center of the room. I walked around a brocaded ottoman over to the screen and looked behind it. On a light tripod of aluminum rods rested the bomb.

Two heavy castings, bolted together around a central flange, with a few wires running along to a small metal box on the underside. Midway up the curve of the side, four small holes, arranged in a square. That was all there was; but it could make a mighty crater where a city had been.

I had no way of knowing whether it was armed or not. I leaned toward the thing, listening. I could hear no sound of a timing device. I thought of cutting the exposed wires, which looked like some sort of jury-rig, but I couldn't risk it; that might set it off.

Barbro stood behind me. "Brion," she said. "You have found it!"

"Yes," I said. "Here it is; but when does it go up?" I had an odd sensation of intangibility, as though I were already a puff of incandescent gas. I tried to think. We had to get this thing out of here.

"Start searching the place, Barbro," I said. "You might come across something that will give us a hint. I'll phone Manfred's office and get a squad up here to see if we can move the thing without blowing it."

I dialed Imperial Intelligence. Manfred wasn't in, and the fellow on the phone was uncertain what he should do.

"Get a crew here on the double," I yelled. "Somebody who can at least make a guess as to whether this thing can be disturbed."

He said he would confer with General Somebody. I yelled some more, but after all, who was I to this bureaucrat? Even here they had a few.

"When does the Emperor arrive?" I asked him.

He was sorry, but he was not at liberty to discuss the Emperor's movements. I slammed the receiver down.

"Brion," Barbro called. "Look what's here."

I went to the door which opened onto the next room. A two-man shuttle filled the space. Its door stood open. I looked inside. It was fitted out in luxury; Bale provided well for himself even for short trips. This was what he used to travel from the Home line to B-I Two; and the fact that it was here should indicate that Bale was here also; and that he would return to it before the bomb went off.

But then again, perhaps the bomb was even now ticking away its last seconds, and Bale might be far away, safe from the blast. If the latter were true, there was nothing I could do about it; but if he did plan to return here, arm the bomb, set a timer and leave via the shuttle in the bedroom—then maybe I would stop him.

"Barbro," I said, "you've got to find Manfred or Hermann. I'm going to stay here and wait for Bale to come back. If you find them, tell them to get men here fast who can make a try at disarming this thing. I don't dare move it, and it will take at least two to handle it. If we can move it, we can shove it in the shuttle and send it off; I'll keep phoning. I don't know where you should look but do your best."

Barbro looked at me. "I would rather stay here with you, Brion," she said. "But I understand that I must not."

"You're quite a girl, Barbro," I said.

I was alone now, except for the ominous sphere behind the screen. I hoped for a caller, though. I'd better get ready for him. I went to the door which leaned aslant against the rough brick wall outside and unlatched it, maneuvered it into place and dropped the pins back in the hinges, then closed and relatched it.

I went back to the over-stuffed room, started looking through drawers, riffling through papers on the desk. I hoped for something, I didn't know what; something that might give a hint of what Bale planned. I didn't find any hints, but I did find a long-barreled twenty-two pistol, and a tiny thirty-two, tucked away under clothing in a dresser drawer. The twenty-two was a revolver, loaded. That helped. I put it in my pocket and tossed the automatic under the couch. I hadn't given much thought to what I would do when Bale got here; I was in no condition to grapple with him; now I had a reasonable chance.

I picked out a hiding place to duck into when and if I heard him coming, a storeroom in the hall, between the bomb and the door. I found a small liquor cabinet and poured myself two fingers of sherry.

I sat in one of the fancy chairs, and tried to let myself go limp. I was using up too much energy in tension. My stomach was a hard knot. I could see the edge of the bomb behind its screen from where I sat. I wondered if there would be any warning before it detonated. My ears were cocked for a click, or a rumble from the silent grey city-killer.

The sound I heard was not a click; it was the scrape of shoes on wood, beyond the door. I sat paralyzed for a moment, then got to my feet, stepped to the storeroom and eased behind the door. I loosened the revolver in my pocket and waited.

The sounds were closer now, gratingly loud in the dead silence. Then a key scraped in the lock, and a moment later the tall wide figure of Chief Inspector Bale, traitor, shuffled into view. His small bald head was drawn down between his shoulders, and he looked around the room almost furtively. He pulled off his coat, and for one startled instant I thought he would come to my storeroom to hang it up; but he threw it over the back of a chair.

He went to the screen, peered at the bomb. I could easily have shot him, but that wouldn't have helped me. I wanted Bale to let me know whether the bomb was armed, if it could be moved. He was the only man in the Imperium who knew how to handle this device. I thought of holding a gun on him, and forcing him to disarm it; but I had learned that that only works in the movies. He could easily be fanatic enough to set it off instead, if he knew his plot had failed.

I watched him. He leaned over the bomb, took a small box from his pocket, and stared at it. He looked at his watch, went to the phone. I could barely hear his mutter as he exchanged a few words with someone. He went into the next room, and as I was about to follow to prevent his using the shuttle, he came back. He looked at his watch again, sat in a chair, and opened a small tool kit which lay on the table. He started to work on the metal box with a slender screwdriver. This, then, was the arming device. I tried not to breathe too loud, or to think about how my legs ached.

Shocking in the stillness, the phone rang. Bale looked up startled, laid the screwdriver and the box on the table, and went over to the phone. He looked down at it, chewing his lip. After five rings it stopped. I wondered who it was.

Bale went back to his work. Now he was replacing the cover on the box, frowning over the job. He got up, went to the bomb, licked his lips and leaned over it. He was ready now to arm the bomb. I couldn't wait any longer.

I pushed the door open, and Bale leaped upright, grabbing for his chest, then jumped for the coat on the chair.

"Stand where you are, Bale," I said. "I'd get a real kick out of shooting you."

Bale's eyes were almost popping from his head, his head was tilted back, his mouth opened and closed. I got the impression that I had startled him.

"Sit down," I said, "there." I motioned with the pistol as I came out into the room.

"Bayard," Bale said hoarsely. I didn't say anything. I felt sure now that the bomb was safe. All I had to do was wait until the crew arrived, and turn Bale over to them. Then we could carry the bomb to the shuttle, and send it off into the Blight. But I was feeling very bad now.

I went to a chair, and sank down. I tried not to let Bale see how weak I was. I leaned back, and tried breathing deep through my nose again. If I started to pass out I would have to shoot Bale; he couldn't be left free to threaten the Imperium again.

It was a little better now. Bale stood rigid, staring at me.

"Look, Bayard," he said. "I'll bring you in on this with me. I swear I'll give you a full half share. I'll let you keep B-I Two as your own, and I shall take the Home line; there's plenty for all. Just put that gun aside..." He licked his lips, started toward me.

I started to motion with the gun, squeezed the trigger instead. A bullet slapped Bale's shirt sleeve, smacked the wall. He dropped down into the chair behind him. That was close, I thought. That could have killed him. I've got to hold on.

I might as well impress him a little, I thought. "I know how to use this pop gun, you see," I said. "Just a quarter of an inch from the arm, firing from the hip; not bad, don't you agree? Don't try anything else."

"You've got to listen to me, Bayard," Bale said; "Why should you care what happens to these popinjays? They've kidnapped you, sent you off into danger, and offered nothing in return except a scrap of paper. Don't you see they're all using you, making you a tool in their game? They've filled you full of rubbish about the glorious Imperium. Well, I propose to bring it down with raw power; the power of that bomb. I can use power as well as the next man; and I'll share it all with you. We can rule as absolute monarchs..."

Bale went on, but I was thinking. Why indeed should I fight for the Imperium? I wasn't sure I could answer that. I only knew that I believed in its high purpose, and its decency, and the courage and *élan* of its people. I had wanted something that I could give my loyalty to without reservation. I had given years of my life to the service of my own country, back in the sickly twilit world I came from. I had seen the shabbiness, the pettiness, the trivial venality, and I had tried to believe in my service in spite of what I saw. In the end I had resigned rather than go along; and the granite walls of the Embassy chancery could not have looked down on me more coldly than my ex-colleagues on the day I left them. I wondered if

I were merely dramatizing myself; but nothing could change the facts that I remembered; the duty I had tried to do, and the ease with which the little crooked men had prevailed.

Here I found men like Winter, who had died without hesitation when he saw that his duty demanded it; Richthofen and all his crew, who had ridden a hay-wired rig into the horror of the Blight, to keep faith with a man from another world; and Barbro, the incomparable...

You could laugh at them if you wished, a cynical laugh at gaudy uniforms, and hereditary titles, and pomp and ceremony; the laugh of the smugly unillusioned at the bright romantic; but no one could laugh at the officers who had charged with sabres into machine-gun fire at the attack on the palace, or the women who had stood their ground behind them.

I didn't have to explain; I didn't have to apologize. This world of the Imperium had won my loyalty, and I would fight for it to the death against a narrow maniac like Bale.

"...take one moment, and we're off. What about it?"

Bale was looking at me, with a look of naked greed. I didn't know what he had been saying. He must have interpreted my silence as weakness; he got up again, moved toward me. It was darker in the room, I rubbed my eyes. I was feeling very bad now, very weak. My heart thumped in my throat, my stomach quivered. I was in no shape to be trying to hold this situation in check alone.

Bale stopped, and I saw that he suddenly realized that I was blacking out. He crouched, and with a snarl jumped at me. I would have to kill him. I fired the pistol twice, and Bale reeled away, startled, but still standing.

"Hold on, Bayard, for the love of God," he squealed. He saw that I was still alive enough to kill him. I raised the pistol, aimed again and fired. I saw a picture jump on the wall. Bale leaped aside. I didn't know if I had hit him yet or not. I was losing my hold, but I couldn't let him get away. I fired twice more, peering from my chair and I knew it was the light in my mind fading, not in the room. Bale yelled; I saw that he didn't dare to try for the door to the hall or the room where the shuttle waited. He would have to pass me. He screamed as I aimed the pistol with wavering hands, and dived for the other door. I fired and heard the sound echo through a dream of blackness.

I wasn't out for more than a few minutes; I came to myself, sitting in the chair, the pistol lying on my lap. The screen had fallen over, and lay across the bomb. I sat up, panicky; maybe Bale had armed it. And where was Bale? I remembered only that he had dashed for the next room. I got up, grabbed for the chair again, then got my balance, made my way to the door. There was a strange sound, a keening, like a cat in a distant alley. I looked into the room, half expecting to see Bale lying on the floor. There was nothing. The light streamed through an open window, and a curtain flapped. Bale must have panicked and jumped, I thought. I went to the window, and the keening started up again.

Bale hung by his hands from the eave of the building across the alley, fifteen feet away. The sound came from him. The left leg of his trousers had a long stain of blackish red on it, and drops fell from the toe of his shoe, five stories to the brick pavement below.

"Good God, Bale," I said. "What have you done?" I was horrified. I had been ready to shoot him down, but to see him hanging there was something else again.

"Bayard," he croaked, "I can't hold on much longer. For the love of God..."

What could I do? I was far too weak for any heroics. I looked around the room frantically for an inspiration; I needed a plank, or a piece of rope. There was nothing. I pulled a sheet off the bed; it was far too short; even two or three would never make it; and I couldn't hold it even if I could throw it and Bale caught it. I ran to the phone.

"Operator," I called. "There's a man about to fall from a roof. Get the fire department here with ladders, fast; seventy-one Tegeluddsvägen, fifth floor."

I dropped the phone, ran back to the window. "Hold on, Bale," I said. "Help's on the way." He must have tried to leap to the next roof, thinking that I was at his heels; and with that hole in his leg he hadn't quite made it.

I thought of Bale, sending me off on a suicide mission, knowing that my imposture was hopeless as long as I stood on my own legs; of the killer shuttle that had lain in wait to smash us as we went in; of the operating room at the hideout, where Bale had planned to carve me into a shape more suitable for his purpose. I remembered Bale shooting down my new-found friend and brother, and the night I had lain in the cold cell, waiting for the butcher; and I still didn't want to see him die this way.

He started to scream suddenly, kicking desperately.

He got one foot up on the eave beside his white straining hands; it slipped off. Then he was quiet again. I had been standing here now for five minutes. I wondered how long I had been unconscious. Bale had been here longer now than I would have thought possible. He couldn't last much longer.

"Hold on, Bale," I called. "Only a little while. Don't struggle."

He hung, silent. Blood dripped from his shoe. I looked down at the alley below and shuddered.

I heard a distant sound, a siren, howling; whoop, whoop. I dashed to the door, opened it, listened. Heavy footsteps sounded below.

"Here," I shouted, "all the way up."

I turned and ran back to the window. Bale was as I had left him. Then one hand slipped off, and he hung by one arm, swinging slightly.

"They're here, Bale," I said. "A few seconds..."

He didn't try to get a new hold. He made no sound. Feet pounded on the stairs outside, and I yelled again.

I turned back to the window as Bale slipped down, silent, his tie fluttering gaily over his shoulder. I didn't watch. I heard him hit—twice.

I staggered back, and the burly men called, looked out the window, milled about. I made my way back to the chair, slumped down. I was empty of emotion. There was noise all around me, people coming and going. I was hardly conscious of it. After a long time I saw Hermann, and then Barbro was leaning over me. I reached for her hand, hungrily.

"Take me home, Barbro," I said.

I saw Manfred.

"The bomb," I said. "It's safe. Put it in the shuttle and get rid of it."

"My crew is moving it now, Brion," he said.

"You spoke of home, just now," Goering put in. "Speaking for myself, and I am sure also for Manfred, I will make the strongest recommendation that in view of your extraordinary services to the Imperium you be dispatched back to your home as soon as you are well enough to go, if that is your wish. I hope that you will stay with us. But it must be for you to make that decision."

"I don't have to decide," I said. "My choice is made. I like it here, for many reasons. For one thing, I can use all the old clichés from B-I Three, and they sound brand new; and as for home." I looked at Barbro:

"Home is where the heart is."

THE OTHER SIDE OF TIME

CHAPTER ONE

IT WAS ONE OF those tranquil summer evenings when the sunset colors seemed to linger on in the sky even longer than June in Stockholm could explain. I stood by the French windows, looking out at pale rose and tawny gold and electric blue, feeling a sensation near the back of the neck that always before had meant trouble, big trouble, coming my way.

The phone jangled harshly through the room. I beat the track record getting to it, grabbed the old-fashioned Imperium-style, brass-mounted instrument off the hall table, and waited a moment to be sure my voice wouldn't squeak before I said hello.

"Colonel Bayard?" said the voice at the other end. "The Freiherr von Richthofen calling; one moment, please..."

Through the open archway to the dining room I could see the dark gleam of Barbro's red hair as she nodded at the bottle of wine Luc was showing her. Candlelight from the elaborate chandelier over her head cast a soft light on snowy linen, gleaming crystal, rare old porcelain, glittering silver. With Luc as our household major domo, every meal was an occasion, but my appetite had vanished. I didn't know why. Richthofen was an old and valued friend, as well as the head of Imperial Intelligence...

"Brion?" Richthofen's faintly accented voice came from the bell-shaped earpiece of the telephone. "I am glad to have found you at home."

"What's up, Manfred?"

"Ah..." he sounded mildly embarrassed. "You have been at home all evening?"

"We got in about an hour ago. Have you been trying to reach me?"

"Oh, no. But a small matter has arisen..." There was a pause. "I wonder, Brion, if you could find the time to drop down to Imperial Intelligence Headquarters?"

"Certainly. When?"

"Now. Tonight...?" the pause again. Something was bothering him—a strange occurrence in itself. "I'm sorry to disturb you at home, Brion, but—"

"I'll be there in half an hour," I said. "Luc will be unhappy, but I guess he'll survive. Can you tell me what it's about?"

"I think not, Brion; the wires may not be secure. Please make my apologies to Barbro—and to Luc too."

Barbro had risen and come around the table. "Brion—what was the call—" She saw my face. "Is there trouble?"

"Don't know. I'll be back as soon as I can. It must be important or Manfred wouldn't have called."

I went along the hall to my bedroom, changed into street clothes, took a trench coat and hat—the nights were cool in Stockholm—and went out into the front hall. Luc was there, holding a small apparatus of spring wire and leather.

"I won't be needing that, Luc," I said. "Just a routine trip down to HQ."

"Better take it, sir." Luc's sour face was holding its usual expression of grim disapproval—an expression I had learned masked an intense loyalty. I grinned at him, took the slug gun and its special quick-draw holster, pulled back my right sleeve and clipped it in place, checked the action. With a flick of the wrist, the tiny slug gun—the shape and color of a flattened, water-eroded stone—slapped into my palm. I tucked it back in place.

"Just to please you, Luc. I'll be back in an hour. Maybe less."

I stepped out into the gleam of the big, square, thick-lensed carriage lights that shed a nostalgic yellow glow over the granite balustrade, went down the wide steps to the waiting car, and slid in behind the thick oak-rimmed wheel. The engine was already idling. I pulled along the graveled drive, out past the poplars by the open iron gate, into the cobbled city street. Ahead, a car parked at the curb with headlights burning pulled out, took up a position in front of me. In the rearview mirror I saw a second car ease around the corner, fall in behind me. Jeweled headlights glinted from the elaborate star-burst badge of the Imperial Intelligence bolted to the massive grill. It seemed Manfred had sent along an escort to be sure I made it to headquarters.

It was a ten-minute drive through the wide, softly lit streets of the old capital, superficially like the

Stockholm of my native continuum. But here in the Zero-zero world of the Imperium, the center of the vast Net of alternate worlds opened up by the M-C drive, the colors were somehow a little brighter, the evening breeze a little softer, the magic of living a little closer.

Following my escort, I crossed the Norrbro Bridge, made a hard right between red granite pillars into a short drive, swung through a set of massive wrought-iron gates with a wave to the cherry-tunicked sentry as he presented arms. I pulled up before the broad doors of polished ironbound oak and the brass plate that said kungliga svenska spionaget, and the car behind me braked with a squeal and doors slammed open. By the time I had slid from behind the wheel, the four men from the two cars had formed a casual half-circle around me. I recognized one of them—a Net operative who had chauffeured me into a place called Blight-Insular Two, a few years back. He returned my nod with a carefully impersonal look.

"They're waiting for you in General Baron von Richthofen's suite, Colonel," he said. I grunted and went up the steps, with the curious feeling that my escort was behaving more like a squad of plainclothes-men making a dangerous pinch, than an honor guard.

Manfred got to his feet when I came into the office. The look he gave me was an odd one—as though he weren't quite sure just how to put whatever it was he was about to say.

"Brion, I must ask for your indulgence," he said. "Please take a chair. Something of a ... a troublesome nature has arisen." He looked at me with a worried expression. This wasn't the suave, perfectly poised von

Richthofen I was used to seeing daily in the course of my duties as a colonel of the Imperial Intelligence. I sat, noticing the careful placement of the four armed agents in the room, and the foursome who had walked me to the office, standing silently by.

"Go ahead, sir," I said, getting formal just to keep in the spirit of the thing. "I understand this is business. I assume you'll tell me what it's all about, in time."

"I must ask you a number of questions, Brion," Richthofen said unhappily. He sat down, the lines in his face suddenly showing his nearly eighty years, ran a lean hand over smooth iron grey hair, then straightened himself abruptly, leaned back in the chair with the decisive air of a man who has decided something has to be done and it may as well be gotten over with.

"What was your wife's maiden name?" he rapped out.

"Ludane," I answered levelly. Whatever the game was, I'd play along. Manfred had known Barbro longer than I had. Her father had served with Richthofen as an Imperial agent for thirty years.

"When did you meet her?"

"About five years ago—at the Royal Midsummer Ball, the night I arrived here."

"Who else was present that night?"

"You, Hermann Goering, Chief Captain Winter . . ." I named a dozen of the guests at the gay affair that had ended so tragically with an attack by raiders from the nightmare world known as B-I Two. "Winter was killed," I added, "by a hand grenade that was meant for me."

"What was your work—originally?"

"I was a diplomat—a United States diplomat—until your lads kidnapped me and brought me here." The last was just a subtle reminder that whatever it was that required that my oldest friend in this other Stockholm question me as though I were a stranger, my presence here in the world of the Imperium had been all his idea in the first place. He noted the dig a moment before going on to the next question.

"What is your work here in Stockholm Zero-zero?"

"You gave me a nice job in Intelligence as a Net Surveillance officer—"

"What is the Net?"

"The continuum of alternate world lines; the matrix of simultaneous reality—"

"What is the Imperium?" he cut me off. It was one of those rapid-fire interrogations, designed to rattle the subject and make him forget his lines—not the friendliest kind of questioning a man could encounter.

"The overgovernment of the Zero-zero A-line in which the M-C generator was developed."

"What does M-C abbreviate?"

"Maxoni-Cocini—the boys that invented the thing, back in 1893—"

"How is the M-C effect employed?"

"It's the drive used to power the Net shuttles."

"Where are the Net operations carried out?"

"All across the Net—except for the Blight, of course—"

"What is the Blight?"

"Every A-line within thousands of parameters of the Zero-zero line is a hell-world of radiation or—"

"What produced the Blight?"

"The M-C effect, mishandled. You lads here in the Zero-zero line were the only ones who controlled it—"

"What is the Zero-zero line?"

I waved a hand. "This universe we're sitting in right now. The alternate world where the M-C field—"

"Do you have a scar on your right foot?" I smiled—slightly—at the change of pace question.

"Uh-huh. Where Chief Inspector Bale fired a round between my big toe and—"

"Why were you brought here?"

"You needed me to impersonate a dictator—in a place called Blight-Insular Two—"

"Are there other. viable A-lines within the Blight?"

I nodded. "Two. One is a war-blasted place with a Common History date of about 1910; the other is my native clime, called B-I Three—"

"You have a bullet scar on your right side?"

"Nope; the left. I also have—"

"What is a Common History date?"

"The date at which two different A-lines' histories diverge—"

"What was your first assignment as a Colonel of Intelligence?"

I answered the question—and a lot of other ones. For the next hour and a half he covered every facet of my private and public life, digging into those odd corners of casual incident that would be known only to me—and to himself. All the while, eight armed men stood by, silent, ready...

My pretense of casual acceptance of the situation was wearing a little thin by the time he sighed, laid both hands on the table—I had the sudden, startled impression that he had just slipped a gun into a drawer out of my line of vision—and looked at me with a more normal expression.

"Brion, in the curious profession of which we are

both members one encounters the necessity of performing many unpleasant duties. To call you here like this..." he nodded at the waiting gun handlers, who quietly faded away. "Yes, under guard—to question you like a common suspect—has been one of the most unpleasant. Rest assured that it was necessary—and that the question has now been resolved to my complete satisfaction." He rose and extended a hand. I got up, feeling a little suppressed anger trying to bubble up under my collar. I took his hand, shook it once, and dropped it. My reluctance must have showed.

"Later, Brion—perhaps tomorrow—I can explain this farcical affair. For tonight, I ask you to accept my personal apologies for the inconvenience—the embarrassment I have been forced to cause you. It was in the interests of the Imperium."

I made polite but not enthusiastic noises, and left. Whatever it was that was afoot, I knew Richthofen had a reason for what he had done—but that didn't make me like it any better—or reduce my curiosity. But I was damned if I'd ask any questions now.

There was no one in sight as I went along to the elevator, rode down, stepped out into the white marble-paved corridor on the ground floor. Somewhere at the far end of the wide hallway feet were hurrying. A door banged with a curious air of finality. I stood like an animal testing the air before venturing into dangerous new territory. An air of crisis seemed to hang over the silent building.

Then I found myself sniffing in earnest. There was a smell of burning wood and asphalt, a hint of smoke. I turned toward the apparent source, walking rapidly but quietly. I passed the wide foot of the formal staircase that led up to the reception hall one floor above—and halted, swung back, my eyes on a dark smudge against the gleaming white floor tiles. I almost missed the second smudge—a good two yards from the first, and fainter. But the shape of both marks was clear enough: they were footprints. Six feet farther along the corridor there was another faint stain—as though someone had stepped into hot tar, and was tracking it behind him.

The direction of the prints was along the corridor to the left. I looked along the dimly lit way. It all seemed as peaceful as a mortuary after hours—and had that same air of grim business accomplished and more to come.

I went along the hall, paused at the intersection, looking both ways. The odor seemed stronger—a smell like singed paint now. I followed the prints around the corner. Twenty feet along the corridor there was a large burn scar against the floor, with footprints around it—lots of prints. There was also a spatter of blood, and on the wall the bloody print of a hand twice the size of mine. Under a sign that said service stair there was a second hand-print on the edge of a door—a hand-print outlined in blistered, blackened paint. My wrist twitched—a reflex reminder of the slug gun Luc had insisted I bring along.

It was two steps to the door. I reached for the polished brass knob—and jerked my hand back. It was hot to the touch. With my handkerchief wrapped around my hand, I got the door open. Narrow steps went down into shadows and the smell of smouldering wood. I started to reach for the wall switch, then thought better of it, closed the door silently behind me, started down. At the bottom, I waited for a moment, listening, then gingerly poked my head out to look along the dark basement hall—and froze.

Dim shadows danced on the wall opposite—shadows outlined in dull reddish light. I came out, went along to a right-angle turn, risked another look. Fifty feet from me, a glowing figure moved with erratic, jerky speed—a figure that shone in the gloom like a thick-limbed iron statue heated red hot. It darted a few feet, made movements too quick to follow, spun, bobbed across the narrow passage—and disappeared through an open door, like a paper cutout jerked by a string.

My wrist twitched again, and this time the gun was in my hand—a smooth, comforting feeling—nestling against my palm. The odor of smoke was stronger now. I looked down, and in the weak light from behind me made out blackened footprints against the wood plank flooring. The thought occurred to me that I should go back, give an alarm, and then carry on with a few heavily armed guards; but it was just a thought. I was already moving along toward the door, not liking it very well, but on the trail of something that wouldn't wait.

The odor was thick in the air now. The hot cloth smell of a press-'em-while-you-wait shop, mingled with the hot metallic tang of a foundry, and a little autumnal woodsmoke thrown in for balance. I came up smooth and silent to the door, flattened myself against the wall, covered the last few inches like a caterpillar sneaking up on a tender young leaf. I risked a fast look inside. The glow from the phantom intruder threw strange reddish shadows on the walls of an unused storeroom—dusty, dark, scattered with odds and ends of litter that should have been swept up but hadn't.

In the center of the room, the fiery man himself leaned over a sprawled body—a giant figure in a shapeless coverall. The fiery man's hands—strange, glowing hands in clumsy looking gauntlets—plucked at his victim with more-than-human dexterity; then he straightened. I didn't take time to goggle at the spectacle of a three-hundred-degree centigrade murderer. There was a chance that his victim wasn't dead yet—and if I hit him quick enough to capitalize on the tiny advantage of surprise...

I forgot all about the slug gun. I went through the door at a run, launched myself at the figure from whom heat radiated like a tangible wall and saw it turn with unbelievable, split-second speed, throw up a hand—five glowing fingers outspread—take one darting step back—

Long, pink sparks crackled from the outflung hand, leaping toward me. Like a diver hanging suspended in midair, I saw the harsh electric glare, heard the *pop!* as the miniature lightnings closed with me...

Then a silent explosion turned the world to blinding white, hurling me into nothingness.

For a long time I lay, clinging to the dim and formless dream that was my refuge from the hazy memory of smouldering footprints, a deserted room, and a fantastic glowing man crouched over his victim. I groaned, groped for the dream again, found only hard, cold concrete against my face, a roiling nausea in the pit of my stomach, and a taste like copper pennies in my mouth. I found the floor, pushed hard to get my face up out of the grit, blinked gummed eyes...

The room was dark, silent, dusty and vacant as a robbed grave. I used an old tennis shoe someone had left in my mouth as a tongue, grated it across dry lips, made the kind of effort that under other circumstances had won luckier souls the Congressional Medal, and sat up. There was a ringing in my head like the echo of the Liberty Bell just before it cracked.

I maneuvered to hands and knees, and, taking it by easy stages, got to my feet. I sniffed. The burning odor was gone. And my quarry hadn't waited around to see whether I was all right. He—or it—had been gone for some time—and had taken the corpse with him.

The light in the room was too weak to show me any detail. I fumbled, got out a massive flint and steel Imperium-style lighter, made three tries, got a smoky yellow flame and squinted to find the trail of blackened prints that would show me which way the fiery man had gone.

There weren't any.

I went all the way to the door, looking for the scars I had seen earlier, then came back, cast about among empty cardboard cartons and stacked floor wax drums. There were no footprints—not even the old-fashioned kind—except for mine. The dust was thick, undisturbed. There were no marks to show where the body had lain, not a trace of my wild charge across the room. Only the scrabble marks I had made getting to my feet proved that I wasn't dreaming my own existence. I had heard of people who pinched themselves to see if they were dreaming. It had always seemed a little silly to me—you could dream a pinch as well as any other, more soothing, sensation. But I solemnly took a fold of skin on the back of my hand, squeezed hard. I could hardly feel it.

That didn't seem to prove anything one way or another. I made it to the door like a man walking to the undertaker's to save that last cab fare, and went into the hall. The lights were out. Only a dim, phosphorescent glow seemed to emanate from the walls and floor. The sight of the wood planking gave me no comfort at all. The prints burned here had been dark, distinct, charred. Now the dull varnish gleamed at me, unmarked.

The buzzing in my head had diminished to a faint hum, like that of a trapped fly, as I pushed through the door into the ground floor hallway. The milk glass globe hanging from the high ceiling glared at me with an unhealthy electric blue. A blackish haze seemed to hang in the still air of the silent corridor, lending a funereal tinge to the familiar vista of marble floor and varnished doors. Behind me, the door clicked shut with a shockingly loud, metallic clatter. I took a few breaths of the blackish air, failed to detect any hint of smoke. A glance at the door showed me what I had expected—smooth dark brown paint, unmarked by burning handprints.

I crossed the hall, pushed into an empty office. On the desk, a small clay pot sat on a blotter, filled with hard, baked-looking dirt. One dry leaf lay on the desk beside it. The desk clock said twelve-oh-five. I reached past it, picked up the phone, jiggled the hook. The silence at the other end was like a concrete wall. I jiggled some more, failed to evoke so much as a crackle of line static. I left the room, tried the next office with the same result. The phones were as dead as my hopes of living to a ripe old age outside a padded cell.

My footsteps in the corridor had a loud, clattering quality. I made it to the front entrance, pushed out through the heavy door, stood on the top step looking down at my car, still sitting where I had left it. The two escort vehicles were gone. Beyond the car, I noticed that the guard shack at the gate was dark. The street lamps seemed to be off too, and the usual gay pattern of the lights of the city's towers was missing. But a power failure wouldn't affect the carbide pole lights... My glance went on to the sky; it was black, overcast. Even the stars were in on the black out.

I got into the car, turned the switch and pressed the starter button on the floor. Nothing happened. I muttered an impolite suggestion, tried again. No action. The horn didn't work either, and twisting the light switch produced nothing but a dry *snick!*

I got out of the car, stood undecided for a moment, then started around the building for the garages in the rear. I slowed, halted before I got there. They were dark, the heavy doors closed and barred. I fetched up another sigh, and for the first time noticed the dead, stale smell of the air. I walked back along the drive, passed the guard post, unaccountably deserted, emerged onto the street. It stretched into shadows, silent and dark. Predictably, there were no cabs in sight. A few cars stood at the curb. I started off toward the bridge, noticed a dark shape midway in the span. For some reason, the sight shocked me. A small, uneasy feeling began to supplant the irritated frustration that had been gathering strength somewhere down below my third shirt button. I walked along to the car, peered in through the rolled up windows. There was no one inside. I thought of pushing the car to the side of the street, then considered the state of my constitution at the moment and went on.

There were more abandoned cars in Gustav Adolfstorg, all parked incongruously in midstream. One was a boxy, open touring car. The ignition switch was on, and the light switch too. I went on, checked the next one I came to. The switches were on. It appeared that there had been an epidemic of automotive ignition trouble in the city tonight, as well as a breakdown in the power plants—a coincidence that did nothing to improve my spirits.

I walked on across the square with its heroic equestrian statue, past the dark front of the Opera House, crossed Arsenalsgatan, turned up Västra Trädgårdsgatan, walked past shuttered shops, bleak in an eerie light like that of an eclipse. The city was absolutely still. No breeze stirred the lifeless air, no growl of auto engines disturbed the silence, no clatter of feet, no distant chatter of voices. My first faint sense of uneasiness was rapidly developing into a full-scale cold sweat.

I cut across the corner of the park, skirting the glass display cases crowded with provincial handicrafts, and hurried across a stretch of barren clay.

The wrongness of it penetrated my preoccupation. I looked back across the expanse of sterile earth, searching on across the garden—the oddly naked garden. There were the graveled paths, the tile lined pools—their fountaining jets lifeless—the band shell, the green painted benches, the steel lampposts with their attached refuse containers and neatly framed tram schedules. But not one blade of grass, not a tree or flowering shrub—no sign of the magnificent bed of prize rhododendron that had occupied a popular magazine's rotogravure section only a week earlier. I turned and started on, half-running now, the unease turning to an undefined dread that caught at my throat and surged in my stomach like foul water in a foundering galley's bilge.

I pushed through the iron gates of my house, wheezing like a blown boiler from the run. I stared at the blank black windows, feeling the implacable air of abandonment, desolation—of utter vacantness. I went on up the drive, taking in the bare stretch of dirt that had been verdant only hours before. Where the poplars had stood, curious foot-wide pits showed black against the grey soil. Only a scatter of dead leaves was left to remind me that once trees had stood here. The crunch of my feet on the gravel was loud. I stepped off onto the former lawn, felt my feet sink into the dry, crumbling earth. At the steps, I looked back. Only my trail of footmarks showed that life had ever existed here—those, and a scatter of dead insects under the carriage lamps. The door opened. I pushed inside, stood savoring the funereal hush, my heart thudding painfully, high in my chest.

"Barbro!" I called. My voice was a dry croak—a croak of cold fear. I ran along the unlighted hall, went up the stairs four at a time, slammed through the sitting room door, on through into the bedroom. I found only silence, an aching stillness in which the sounds of my passage seemed to echo with a shocked reproach. I stumbled out of the room, yelling for Luc, not really expecting an answer now, yelling to break the awful, ominous stillness, the fear of what I might find in the dark, dead rooms.

I searched room by room, went back and tried the

closets, shouting, slamming doors wide, not fighting the panic that was welling up inside me, but giving it vent in violent action.

There was nothing. Every room was in perfect order, every piece of furniture in its accustomed place, every drape discreetly drawn, every dish and book and garment undisturbed—but on the marble mantelpiece, the brass clock sat silent, its tick stilled. And in the pots where the broad-leafed plants had lent their touch of green, only the dead soil remained. I stood in the center of the dark library, staring out at the grim, metallic glow of the night sky, feeling the silence flow back in like a tangible thing, trying now to regain my control, to accept the truth: Barbro was gone—along with every other living thing in the Imperial capital.

CHAPTER TWO

I DIDN'T NOTICE THE sound at first. I was sitting in the empty drawing room, staring out past the edge of heavy brocaded drapes at the empty street, listening to the thud of my empty heart...

Then it penetrated: a steady thumping, faint, far away—but a sound—in the silent city. I jumped up, made it to the door and was out on the steps before the idea of caution occurred to me. The thumping was clearer now: a rhythmic slap, like the feet of marching troops, coming closer—

I saw them then, a flicker of movement through the iron spears of the fence. I faded back inside, watched from the darkness as they swung past, four abreast, big men in drab, shapeless coveralls. I tried to estimate their number. Perhaps two hundred, some laden with heavy packs, some with rifle-like weapons, one or two being helped by their comrades. They'd seen action somewhere tonight.

The last of them passed, and I ran softly down the

drive. Keeping to the shelter of the buildings along the avenue, I followed a hundred yards behind them.

The first, stunning blow was past now, leaving me with a curious sense of detachment. The detachment of the sole survivor. The troop ahead swung along Nybroviken, grim, high-shouldered marchers a head taller than my six feet, not singing, not talking—just marching, block after block, past empty cars, empty buildings, empty parks—and a dead cat, lying in the gutter. I paused, stared at the ruffled, pathetic cadaver.

They turned right into Birger Jarlsgatan—and I realized then where they were headed—to the Net Terminus Building at Stallmästargården. I was watching from the shelter of a massive oak a hundred yards away as the end of the column turned in at the ornate gate, and disappeared beyond the massive portal that had been smashed from its hinges. One man dropped off, took up a post at the entry.

I crossed the street silently, followed the walk around to the side entrance, wasted a few seconds wishing for the keys in my safe back at the house, then headed for the back of the building. Stumbling through denuded flower beds, I followed the line of the wall, barely visible in the blackish light—a light that seemed, curiously, to shine upward from the ground rather than impinge from the starless sky. A masonry wall barred my way. I jumped, caught the top edge, pulled myself over, dropped into the paved court behind the Terminal. Half a dozen boxy wheeled shuttles were parked here, of the special type used for work in some of the nearer A-lines— world with Common History dates only a few centuries in the past, where other Stockholms existed with streets in which a disguised delivery van could move unnoticed.

One of the vehicles was close to the building wall. I climbed up on its hood, reached, tried to lift the wide, metal frame, double-hung window. It didn't budge. I went back down, fumbled in the dark under the shuttle's dash, brought out the standard tool kit, found a hammer, scrambled back up, and as gently as I could, smashed the glass from the frame. It made a hell of a racket. I stood listening, half expecting to hear indignant voices calling questions, but the only sound was my own breathing, and a creak from the shuttle's springs as I shifted my weight.

The room I clambered into was a maintenance shop, lined with long workbenches littered with disassembled shuttle components, its walls hung with tools and equipment. I went out through the door at the far end of the room, along the corridor of the big double doors leading into the garages. Faint sounds came from within. I eased the door open a foot, slipped inside, into the echoing stillness of the wide, high vaulted depot. A double row of Net shuttles reared up in the gloom—heavy, ten-man machines, smaller three-man scouts, a pair of light new-model single-seaters at the far end of the line.

And beyond them—dwarfing them—a row of dark blocky machines of strange design, massive and ugly as garbage scows, illogically dumped here among the elegantly decorated vehicles of the Imperial TNL service. Dark figures moved around the strange machines, forming up into groups beside each heavy transport, responding to gestures and an occasional grunted command. I walked along behind the parked shuttles, eased forward between two from which I had a clear view of the proceedings.

The doors to the first of the five alien machines were open. As I watched, a suited man clambered in, followed by the next in line. The troops—whoever they were—were reembarking. They were clumsy, slope-shouldered heavyweights, covered from head to toe in baggy, dull grey suits with dark glass face-plates. One of the Imperial machines was impeding the smooth flow of the moving column; two of the intruders stepped to it, gripped it by its near side runner, and, with one heave, tipped it up, dumped it over on its side with a heavy slam and a tinkle of breaking glass. I felt myself edging farther back out of sight; the scout weighed a good two tons.

The first shuttle was loaded now. The line of men shuffled along to the next and continued loading. Time was slipping past. In another ten minutes all the suited men would be aboard their machines, gone—back to whatever world-line they had come from. It was clear that these were invaders from the Net—a race of men, unknown to Imperial authorities, who possessed an M-C drive of their own. Men who were my only link with the vanished inhabitants of desolated Stockholm Zero-zero. Waiting here wouldn't help; I had to follow them, learn what I could . . .

I took a bracing lungful of the stale Terminal air and stepped out of my hiding place, feeling as exposed as a rat between holes as I moved along the wall, putting distance between myself and the strangers. My objective was one of the two-man scouts—a fast, maneuverable machine with adequate armament and the latest in instrumentation. I reached it, got the door open with no more than a rattle of the latch that sent my stomach crowding up under my ribs; but there was no alarm.

Even inside, there was enough of the eerie light to see my way by. I went forward to the control compartment, slid into the operator's seat, and tried the main drive warm-up switch.

Nothing happened. I tried other controls, without response. The M-C drive was as dead as the cars abandoned in the city streets. I got up, went back to the entry and eased it open, stepped silently out. I could hear the invaders working away two hundred feet from me, shielded from view by the ranked shuttles. An idea was taking form—an idea I didn't like very well. The first thing it would require was that I get around to the opposite side of the Terminal. I turned...

He was standing ten feet away, just beyond the rear corner of the shuttle. At close range he looked seven feet tall, wide in proportion, with gloved hands the size of briefcases. He took a step toward me, and I backed away. He followed, almost leisurely. Two more steps and I would be clear of the shelter of the machine, exposed to the view of any of the others who might happen to glance my way. I stopped. The stranger kept on coming, one immense, stubby-fingered hand reaching for me.

My wrist twitched, and the slug gun was in my hand. I aimed for a point just below the center of his chest, and fired. At the muffled *slap!* of the gun, the monster-man jackknifed, went down backward with a slam like a horse falling in harness. I jumped past him to the shelter of the next machine, and crouched there, waiting. It seemed impossible that no one had heard the shot or the fall of the victim, but the sounds from the far end of the vast shed went on, uninterrupted. I let out a breath I just realized I had been holding, feeling my heart thumping in my chest like a trapped rabbit's.

With the gun still in my hand, I stepped out, went back to the man I had shot. He lay on his back, spread-eagled like a bearskin rug—and about the same size. Through his shattered faceplate, I saw a broad, coarse, dead-grey face, with porous skin, and a wide, lipless mouth, half-open now to show square, yellow teeth. Small eyes, pale blue as a winter sky, stared lifelessly under bushy yellow brows that grew in a continuous bar across the forehead. A greasy lock of dull blonde hair fell beside one hollow temple. It was the most appallingly hideous face I had ever seen. I backed off from it, turned and started off into the shadows.

The last in line of the alien shuttles was my target. To get to it, I had to cross an open space of perhaps fifty feet, concealed by nothing but the dimness of the light. I stepped out, started across the exposed stretch as silently as slick leather soles would let me. Every time one of them turned in my direction, I froze until he turned away. I had almost reached shelter when one of the officers tallying men turned to stare toward the other end of the huge shed. Someone had missed the one I had shot. The officer called— a sudden hoarse cry like a bellow of mortal agony. The others paid no attention. The officer snapped an order, started off to investigate.

I had perhaps half a minute before he found his missing crewman. I slipped into the shadow of the supply shuttle, worked my way quickly to the last in line, slid around the end. The coast was clear. I made it to the entry in three quick steps, swung myself up, and stepped inside the empty machine.

There was a sickish animal odor here, a subtle alienness of proportion. I took in the control panels, the operator's chair, the view-screens, and the chart table in a swift glance. All were recognizable—but in size and shape and detail they differed in a hundred ways from the familiar Imperial patterns, or from any normal scheme of convenience. I hitched myself into the high, wide, hard seat, stared at squares and circles of plastic glowing in clashing shades of brown and violet. Curious symbols embossed on metal strips labeled some of the baroquely curved levers which projected from the dull ochre panel. A pair of prominent foot pedals, set awkwardly wide apart, showed signs of heavy wear.

I stared at the array, feeling the sweat begin to pop out on my forehead. I had only a few seconds to decide—and if my guess were wrong—

A simple knife switch set in the center of the panel drew my attention. There were scratches on the panel around it, and worn spots on the mud-colored plastic grip. It was as good a guess as any. I reached out tentatively—

Outside, a horrific shriek ripped through the silence. I jerked, smashing my knee against a sharp corner of the panel. The pain brought a warm flood of instinctive anger and decision. I ground my teeth together, reached again, slammed the lever down.

At once, the lights dimmed. I heard the entry close with an echoing impact. Heavy vibration started up, rattling ill-fitting panel members. Indicator lights began to wink; curious lines danced on a pair of glowing pinkish screens. I felt a ghostly blow against the side of the hull. One of the boys wanted in, but he was a trifle too late. The screens had cleared to show me a view of black desolation under a starless sky—the familiar devastation of the Blight. The M-C field was operating; the stolen shuttle was carrying me out across the Net of alternate worlds—and at terrific speed, to judge from the quicksilver flow of the scene outside as I flashed across the parallel realities of the A-lines. I had made my escape. The next order of business was to determine how to control the strange machine.

Half an hour's study of the panel sufficed to give me a general idea of the meanings of the major instruments. I was ready now to attempt to maneuver the stolen shuttle. I gripped the control lever, tugged at it—it didn't move. I tried again, succeeded only in bending the metal arm. I stood, braced my feet, put my shoulders into it. With a sharp clang, the lever broke off short. I sank back in the chair, tossed the broken handle to the floor. Evidently, the controls were locked. The owners of the strange shuttle had taken precautions against any disgruntled potential deserter who might have an impulse to ride the machine to some idyllic world line of his own choice. Once launched, its course was predetermined, guided by automatic instruments—and I was powerless to stop it.

CHAPTER THREE

TWO HOURS PASSED WHILE the shuttle rushed on into the unexplored and uncharted depths of the Net. I sat watching the fantastic flow of scenes beyond the view screens—the weird phenomenon that Chief Captain Winter of the TNL Service had called A-entropy.

At the speed at which I was traveling—far greater than anything ever managed by Imperial technicians—living creatures would not be detectable; a man would flash across the screen and be gone in a fraction of a microsecond. But the fixed features of the scene—the streets, the buildings, the stone and metal and wood—loomed around me. And as I watched, they changed...

The half-familiar structures seemed to flow, to shrink or expand gradually, sprouting outré new elements. I saw doorways widen, or dwindle and disappear; red granite blocks rippled and flowed, changed by degrees to grey polished slabs. The nearly legible lettering on a nearby shop window writhed, reformed itself, the Roman capitals distorting into forms like Cyrillic letters, then changed again, and again, to become lines of meaningless symbols. I saw sheds and shacks appear and swell, crowding among the older structures, burgeoning mightily into blank, forbidding piles that soared up out of sight. Balconies budded as window ledges grew into great cantilevered terraces, then merged, shutting out the sky—and then they, in turn, drew back, and new facades stood revealed: grim, blackish ribbed columns, rearing up a thousand feet into the unchanging sky, linked by narrow bridges that shifted, twitching like nervous fingers, widening, spreading into a vast network that entangled the spires like a spider's web, then broke, faded back, leaving only a dark bar here and there to join the now ponderous squat towers like chains linking captive monsters. All this in a frozen, eternal instant of time, as the stolen shuttle rushed blindly across the lines of alternate probability toward its unknown destination.

I sat entranced, watching the universe evolve around me. Then I found myself nodding, my eyes aching abominably. I suddenly realized that I hadn't eaten my dinner yet—nor slept—in how many hours? I got out of the chair, made a quick search of the compartment, and found a coarse-woven cloak with a rank odor like attar of locker room blended with essence of stable. I was too weary to be choosy, though. I spread the cloth on the floor in the tiny space between the operator's seat and the power compartment, curled up on it, and let the overwhelming weariness sweep over me...

...and awakened with a start. The steady drone of the drive had changed in tone, dropped to a deep thrumming. My watch said I'd been on the way a little less than three and a half hours—but brief as the trip had been, the ugly but fantastically efficient shuttle had raced across the Net into regions where the Imperial scouts had never penetrated. I scrambled up, got my eyes open far enough to make out the screens.

It was a scene from a drunk's delirium. Strange, crooked towers rose up from dark, empty canyons where footpaths threaded over heaped refuse among crowded stalls, doorless arches, between high-wheeled carts laden with meaningless shapes of wood and metal and leather. From carved stone lintels, cornices, pilasters, grotesque faces peered, goggled, grimaced like devils in an Aztec tomb. As I gaped, the growl of the drive sank to a mutter, died. The oddly shifting scene froze into the immobility of identity. I had arrived—somewhere.

But the street—if I could use that term for this crowded alley—was deserted, and the same odd, fungoid light I had seen in the empty streets of Stockholm glowed faintly from every surface under the dead, opaque blackness of the sky above.

Then without warning a wave of nausea bent me double, retching. The shuttle seemed to rise under me, twist, spin. Forces seized me, stretched me out as thin as copper wire, threaded me through the red-hot eye of a needle, then slammed me into a compacted lump like a metal-baler cubing a junked car. I heard a whistling noise, and it was me, trying to get enough air into my lungs to let out a yell of agony—

And then the pressure was gone. I was sprawled on my back on the hard floor, but still breathing and in my usual shape, watching lights wink out on the panel. I felt the sharp, reassuring pain of an honest cut on my knee, saw a small dark patch of blood through a tear in the cloth. I got to my feet, and the screen caught my eye...

The two-foot rectangle of the view-plate showed me a crowd packing the narrow street that had been deserted a moment ago. A mob of squat, hulking, long-armed creatures surging and milling in an intricate play of dark and light where vivid shafts of sunlight struck down from high above into deep shadow—

Then behind me metal growled. I whirled, saw the entry hatch jump, swing open. The shuttle trembled, lurched—and a vast, wide shape stepped in through the opening—a fanged monstrosity with a bulging, bald head, a wide, thin-lipped, chinless face, huge, strangely elaborate ears, a massive, hulking body buckled into straps and hung with clanking bangles, incongruous against a shaggy pelt like a blonde gorilla's.

The muscles of my right wrist tensed, ready to slap the slug gun into my hand, but I relaxed, let my arms fall to my sides. I could kill this fellow—and the next one who stepped inside. But there was more at stake here than my own personal well-being. A moment before, I had seen the miracle of a deserted street transformed in the wink of an eye into a teeming marketplace packed with sunlight and movement. If these grotesque, golden-haired apes knew the secret of that enchantment then maybe my own Stockholm could also come back from the dead... if I could find the secret.

"All right, big boy," I said aloud. "I'll come along peacefully."

The creature reached, clamped a hand like a power shovel on my shoulder, literally lifted me, hurled me at the door. I struck the jamb, bounced, fell out into an odor like dead meat and broccoli rotting together. A growl ran through the shaggy mob surrounding me. They jumped back, jabbering. I made it to my feet, slapping at the decayed rubbish clinging to my jacket, and my captor came up from behind, grabbed my arm as though he had decided to tear it off, and sent me spinning ahead. I hooked a foot in a loop of melon rind, went down again. Something hit me across the back of the shoulders like a falling tree. I oofed, tried to get to hands and knees to make my white god speech, and felt a kick that slammed me forward, my face ploughing into spongy, reeking garbage. I came up spitting, in time to take a smashing blow full in the face, and saw bright constellations burst above me, like a Fourth of July display long ago in another world.

I was aware of my feet dragging, and worked them to relieve the gouging of hard fingers under my arms. Then I was stumbling, half dragged between two of the hairy men, who shouldered their way through the press of babbling spectators that gave way reluctantly, their eyes like blue marbles staring at me as though I were a victim of a strange and terrible disease.

It seemed like a long way that they hauled me, while I gradually adjusted my thinking to the reality of my captivity by creatures that awakened racial memories of ogres and giants and things that went bump in the night. But here they were, as real as life and twice as smelly, scratching at hairy hides with fingers like bananas, showing great yellowish fighting fangs in grimaces of amazement and disgust, and looming over me like angry goblins over a small boy. I stumbled along through the hubbub of raucous sound and eye-watering stench toward whatever fate trolls kept in store for mortals who fell among them.

We came out from the narrow way into a wider but not cleaner avenue lined with curious, multitiered stalls, where grey-maned merchants squatted, peering down from their high perches, shouting their wares, tossing down purchases to customers, catching thick, square coins on the fly. There were heaped fruits, odd-shaped clay pots of all sizes capped and sealed with purplish tar, drab-colored mats of woven fiber, flimsy-looking contraptions of hammered sheet metal, harnesses, straps of leather with massive brass buckles, strings of brightly polished brass and copper discs like old English horse brasses.

And in this fantastic bazaar a horde of variegated near-humanity milled. A dozen races and colors of shaggy sub-men, half-men, ape-men: man-like giants with great bushes of bluish hair fringing bright red faces; incredibly tall, slim creatures, with sleek, black fur, curiously short legs and long, flat feet; wide, squat individuals with round shoulders and long, drooping noses. Some wore great loops and strings of the polished brasses, others had only one or two baubles pinned to the leather straps that seemed to constitute their only clothing. And others, the more bedraggled members, with strap-worn shoulders and horny bare feet, had no brass at all. And over all, great blue and green flies hovered, droning, like a living canopy.

I saw the crowd part to let a great, slow-moving beast push through, a thing as big as a small Indian elephant, and with the same ponderous tread; but the trunk was no more than an exaggerated pig's snout, and from below it two great shovel tusks of yellow ivory thrust out from the underslung jaw above a drooping pink lower lip, looped with saliva and froth. Wide strips of inch-thick leather harnessed the beast to a heavy cart stacked with hooped barrels, and a shaggy driver atop the load slapped a vast braided whip across the massive back of the animal. Farther on, two of the short, burly man-things—they would weigh in at five hundred pounds apiece, I estimated—toiled in harness beside a mangy mastodon-like animal whose blunt tusks were capped with six-inch wooden knobs.

· We reached the end of the boulevard and after a short delay to kick a few determined spectators back, my bodyguard urged me roughly up a wide, garbage-littered flight of steep, uneven stone steps—on through a gaping, doorless opening where two lowbrowed louts in black straps and enameled brasses rose from crouching positions to intercept us. I leaned on the wall and worked on getting my arms back into their sockets while the boys staged a surly reunion. Other members emerged from the hot, zoo-smelling gloom of the rabbit warren building; they came over to wrinkle brows and grimace at me, prodding and poking with fingers like gun barrels. I backed away, flattened myself against the wall, remembering, for some unfortunate reason, a kitten that Gargantua had been very fond of until it broke...

My guards pushed through, clamped onto my arms again in a proprietary way, hooted for gangway, and dragged me into one of the arched openings off the irregularly-shaped entry hall. I tried to follow the turnings and twisting and dips and rises of the tunnel-like passage with some vague idea of finding my way back later, but I soon lost track. It was almost pitch dark here. Small, yellowish incandescent bulbs glowed at fifty-foot intervals, showing me a puddled floor, and rough-hewn walls with many branching side passages. After a couple of hundred yards, the hall widened into a gloomy thirty-foot chamber. One of my keepers rooted in a heap of rubbish, produced a wide strap of thick blackish leather attached to the wall by a length of rope. He buckled it around my right wrist, gave me a shove, then went and squatted by the wall. The other cop went off along a corridor that curved sharply up and out of sight. I kicked enough of the damp debris aside to make a place to sit, and settled down for a wait. Sooner or later someone in authority would be wanting to interrogate me. For that, communication would have to be established—and as a Net-traveling race, I assumed my captors would have some linguistic capability. After that...

I remember stretching out full length on the filthy floor, having a brief thought that for slimy brick, it was amazingly comfortable; then a big, hard foot was kicking at me. I started to sit up, was hauled to my feet by the rope on my arms, and marched along another dingy passage. My feet were almost too heavy to lift now, and my stomach felt like a raw wound. I tried to calculate how many hours it had been since I had eaten, but lost count. My brain was working sluggishly, like a clock dipped in syrup.

The chamber we arrived at—somewhere high in the squat building, I thought; the walk had been mostly along upward-slanting corridors—was domed, roughly circular, with niches set in the irregularly-surfaced walls. There was a terrible odor of dung and rotting hay. The room seemed more like a den in a zoo than an apartment in a human dwelling. I had an impulse to look around for the opening the bear would emerge from.

There were heaps of grayish rags dumped in some of the niches. One of them moved, and I realized that it was a living creature—an incredibly aged, scruffy specimen of my captors' race. The two escorting me urged me closer to the ancient. They had a subdued air now, as though in the presence of rank. In the poor light that filtered in from an arrangement of openings around the walls, I saw a hand like a grey leather-covered claw come up, rake fitfully at the thin, moth-eaten chest hair of the oldster. I made out his eyes then—dull blue, half-veiled by drooping upper lids, nested in the blood-red crescents of sagging lower lids. They stared at me fixedly, unblinking. Below, great tufts of grey hair sprouted from gaping half-inch nostrils. The mouth was puckered, toothless, as wide as a hip pocket. The rest of the face was a mass of doughy wrinkles, framed between long locks of uncombed white hair from which incredibly long-lobed ears poked, obscenely pink and naked. The chin hair, caked with foreign matter, hung down across the shrunken chest, against which bony, bald knees poked up like grey stones. I accidentally breathed, choked at a stench like a rotting whale, and was jerked back into position.

The patriarch made a hoarse, croaking noise. I waited, breathing through my mouth. One of my jailers shook me, barked something at me.

"Sorry, fellows," I croaked. "No kapoosh."

The bearded elder jumped as though he'd been poked with a hot iron. He squalled something, spraying me in the process. He bounced up and down with surprising energy, still screeching, then stopped abruptly and thrust his face close to mine. One of my guards grabbed my neck with a hard hand, anticipating my reaction. I stared into the blue eyes—eyes as human as mine, set in this ghastly caricature of a face—saw the open pores as big as match heads, watched a trickle of saliva find its way from the loose mouth down into the beard...

He leaned back with a snuffle, waved an arm, made a speech. When he finished, a thin voice piped up from the left. I twisted, saw another mangy bear-skin rug shifting position. My owners propelled me in that direction, held me while the second oldster, even uglier than the first, looked me over. While he stared and drooled, my gaze wandered up to a higher niche. In the shadows, I could barely make out the propped bones of a skeleton, the empty eye sockets gazing down, the massive jaws grinning sardonically, a thick leather strap still circling the neck bones. Apparently promotion to the local Supreme Court was a life appointment.

A jerk at my arm brought me back to more immediate matters. The grandpa before me shrilled. I didn't answer. He curled his lips back, exposing toothless yellowish gums and a tongue like a pink sock full of sand, and screamed. That woke up a couple more wise men; there were answering hoots and squawks from several directions.

My keepers dutifully guided me over to the next judge, an obese old fellow with a bloated, sparsely-haired belly over which large black fleas hurried on erratic paths like bloodhounds looking for a lost trail.

This one had one tooth left—a hooked, yellow-brown canine over an inch long. He showed it to me, made gobbling noises, then leaned out and took a swipe at me with an arm as long as a dock crane. My alert guardians pulled me back as I ducked; I was grateful; even this senile old reprobate packed enough wallop to smash my jaw and break my neck if he had connected.

At a querulous cry from a niche high up in a dark corner, we steered in that direction. A lank hand with two fingers missing groped, pulled a crooked body up into a sitting position. Half a face looked down at me. There were scars, then a ragged edge, then bare, exposed bone where the right cheek had been. The eye socket was still there, but empty, the lid puckered and sunken. The mouth, with one corner missing, failed to close properly—an effect that produced a vacuous, loose-lipped smile—as appropriate to this horror as a poodle shave on a hyena.

I was staggering now, not reacting as promptly as my leaders would have liked. The one on the left—the more vicious of the two, I had already decided—lifted me up by one arm, slammed me down, jerked me back to my feet, then shook me like a dusty blanket. I staggered, got my feet back under me, jerked free, and hit him hard in the belly. It was like punching a sandbag; he twisted me casually back into position. I don't think he even noticed the blow.

We stood in the center of the room for a while then, while the council of elders deliberated. One got mad and spat across the room at the big-bellied one, who replied with a hurled handful of offal. Apparently that was the sign for the closing of the session. My helpers backed off, shoved me out into the corridor, and hustled me off on another trip through the crooked passages, with hoots and snarls ringing from the chamber behind us.

This journey ended in still another room, like the others no more than a wide place in the corridor. There was a stone bench, some crude-looking shelves big enough for coffins in one corner, the usual dim bulb, heaped garbage, and odds and ends of equipment of obscure function. There was a hole in the center of the chamber from which a gurgling sound came. Sanitary facilities, I judged, from the odor. This time I was strapped by one ankle and allowed to sit on the floor. A clay pot with some sort of mush in it was thrust at me. I got a whiff, gagged, pushed it away. I wasn't that hungry—not yet.

An hour passed. I had the feeling I was waiting for something. My two proprietors—or two others, I wasn't sure—sat across the room, hunkered down on their haunches, dipping up their dinner from their food pots, not talking. I could hardly smell the place now—my olfactory nerves were numb. Every so often a newcomer would shamble in, come over to gape at me, then move off.

Then a messenger arrived, barked something peremptory. My escorts got to their feet, licked their fingers carefully with thick, pink tongues as big as shoe soles, came over and unstrapped the ankle bracelet, and started me off again. We went down, this time—taking one branching byway after another, passing through a wide hall where at least fifty hulking louts sat at long benches, holding some sort of meeting, past an entry through which late evening light glowed, then down again, into a narrow passage that ended in a cul-de-sac.

Lefty—my more violent companion—yanked at my

arm, thrust me toward a round, two-foot opening, like an oversized rat-hole, set eighteen inches above the floor. It was just about wide enough for a man to crawl into. I got the idea. For a moment, I hesitated; this looked like the end of the trail. Once inside, there'd be no further opportunities for escape—not that I had had any so far.

A blow on the side of the head slammed me against the wall. I went down, twisted on my back. The one who had hit me was standing over me, reaching for a new grip. I'd had about enough of this fellow. Without pausing to consider the consequences, I bent my knee, smashed a hard, ikedo-type kick to his groin. He doubled over, and my second kick caught him square in mouth. I got a glimpse of pinkish blood welling—

The other man-ape grabbed me, thrust me at the burrow almost casually. I dived for it, scrambled into a damp chill and an odor as solid as well-aged cheese. A crawl of five feet brought me to a drop-off. I felt around over the edge, found the floor two feet below, swung my legs around and stood, facing the entrance with the slug gun in my hand. If Big Boy came in after me, he'd get a surprise.

But I saw the two of them silhouetted against the light from along the corridor. Lefty was leaning on his friend, making plaintive squeaking noises. Then they went off along the corridor together. Apparently whatever their instructions were, they didn't including taking revenge on the new specimen—not yet.

Chapter Four

THE TRADITIONAL FIRST MOVE when imprisoned in the dark was to pace off the dimensions of the cell, a gambit which presumably lends a mystic sense of mastery over one's environment. Of course, I wasn't actually imprisoned. I could crawl back out into the corridor—but since I would undoubtedly meet Lefty before I had gone far, the idea lacked appeal. That left me with the pacing off to do.

I started from the opening, took a step which I estimated at three feet, and slammed against a wall. No help there.

Back at my starting point, I took a more cautious step, then another—

There was a sound from the darkness ahead. I stood, one foot poised, not breathing, listening...

"*Vansi pa' me' zen pa',*" a mellow tenor voice said from the darkness. "*Sta' zi?*"

I backed a step. The gun was still in my hand. The other fellow had the advantage; his eyes would be used to the dark, and I was outlined against the faint glow from the tunnel. At the thought, I dropped flat, felt the cold wetness of the rough floor come through my clothes.

"Bo'jou', ami," the voice said. "E' vou Gallice?"

Whoever he was, he was presumably a fellow prisoner. And the language he had spoken didn't sound much like the grunts and clicks of the ogres outside. Still, I had no impulse to rush over and get acquainted.

"*Kansh' tu dall' Scansk...*" The voice came again. And this time I almost got the meaning. The accent was horrible, but it sounded almost like Swedish...

"Maybe Anglic, you," the voice said.

"Maybe," I answered, hearing my voice come out as a croak. "Who're you?"

"Ah, good! I took a blink from you so you come into." The accent was vaguely Hungarian and the words didn't make much sense. "Why catch they you? Where from commer you?"

I edged a few feet to the side to get farther from the light. The floor slanted up slightly. I thought of using my lighter, but that would only make me a better target if this new chum had any unfriendly ideas—and nothing I had encountered so far in giant-land led me to expect otherwise.

"Don't be shy of you," the voice urged. "I am friend."

"I asked you who you are," I said. My hackles were still on edge. I was tired and hungry and bruised, and talking to a strange voice in the dark wasn't what I needed to soothe my nerves just now.

"Sir, I have honor of to make known myself: Field Agent Dzok, at the service."

"Field agent of what?" My voice had a sharp edge.

"Perhaps better for further confidences to await closer acquaintance," the field agent said. "Please, you will talk again, thus allowing me to place the dialect more closely."

"The dialect is English," I said. I eased back another foot, working my way up-slope. I didn't know whether he could see me or not, but it was an old maxim to take the high ground...

"English? Ah, yes. I think we've triggered the correct mnemonic now. Not a very well-known sub-branch of Anglic, but then I fancy my linguistic indoctrination is one of the more complete for an Agent of Class Four. Am I doing better?"

The voice seemed closer, as well as more grammatical. "You're doing fine," I assured it—and rolled quickly away. Too late, I felt an edge under my back, yelled, went over, and slammed against hard stone three feet below the upper level. I felt my head bounce, heard a loud ringing, while bright lights flashed. Then there was a hand groping over my chest, under my head.

"Sorry, old fellow," the voice said up close. "I should have warned you. Did the same thing myself my first day here..."

I sat up, groped quickly, found the slug gun, tucked it back into my cuff holster.

"I guess I was a little over-cautious," I said. "I hardly expected to run into another human being in this damned place." I worked my jaw, found it still operable, touched a scrape on my elbow.

"I see you've hurt your arm," my cell-mate said. "Let me dab a bit of salve on that..." I heard him moving, heard the snap of some sort of fastener, fumbling noises. I got out my lighter, snapped it. It caught, blazed up blindingly. I held it up—and my jaw dropped.

Agent Dzok crouched a yard from me, his head turned away from the bright light, a small first aid kit in his hands—hands that were tufted with short, silky red-brown hair that ran up under the grimy cuffs of a tattered white uniform. I saw long thick-looking arms, scuffed soft leather boots encasing odd long-heeled feet, a small round head, dark-skinned, long-nosed. Dzok turned his face toward me, blinking deepset yellowish eyes set close together above a wide mouth that opened in a smile to show square, yellow teeth.

"The light's a bit bright," he said in his musical voice. "I've been in the dark for so long now..."

I gulped, flicked off the lighter. "Sorry," I mumbled. "Wha—who did you say you were?"

"You look a trifle startled," Dzok said in an amused tone. "I take it you haven't encountered my branch of the Hominids before?"

"I had a strange idea we Homo sapiens were the only branch of the family that made it into the Cenozoic," I said. "Meeting the boys outside was quite a shock. Now you..."

"Ummm. I think our two families diverged at about your late Pliocene. The Hagroon are a somewhat later offshoot, at about the end of the Pleistocene—say half a million years back." He laughed softly. "So you see, they represent a closer relationship to you sapiens than do we of Xonijeel..."

"That's depressing news."

Dzok's rough-skinned hand fumbled at my arm, then gripped it lightly while he dabbed at the abrasion.

The cool ointment started to take the throb from the wound.

"How did they happen to pick you up?" Dzok asked. "I take it you were one of a group taken on a raid?"

"As far as I know, I'm the only one." I was still being cautious. Dzok seemed like a friendly enough creature, but he had a little too much hair on him for my taste, in view of what I'd seen of the Hagroon. The latter might be closer relatives of mine than of the agent, but I couldn't help lumping them together in my mind—though Dzok was more monkey-like than ape-like.

"Curious," Dzok said. "The pattern usually calls for catches of at least fifty or so. I've theorized that this represents some sort of minimum group size which is worth the bother of the necessary cultural analysis, language indoctrination, and so on."

"Necessary for what?"

"For making use of the captives," Dzok said. "The Hagroon are slave raiders, of course."

"Why 'of course'?"

"I assumed you knew, being a victim..." Dzok paused. "But then perhaps you're in a different category. You say you were the only captive taken?"

"What about you?" I ignored the question. "How did you get here?"

The agent sighed. "I was a trifle incautious, I fear. I had a rather naïve idea that in this congeries of variant hominid strains I'd pass unnoticed, but I was spotted instantly. They knocked me about a bit, dragged me in before a tribunal of nonagenarians for an interrogation, which I pretended not to understand—"

"You mean you speak their language?" I interrupted.

"Naturally, my dear fellow. An agent of Class Four

could hardly be effective without language indoctrination."

I let that pass. "What sort of questions did they ask you?"

"Lot of blooming nonsense, actually. It's extremely difficult for noncosmopolitan races to communicate at a meaningful level; the basic cultural assumptions vary so widely—"

"You and I seem to be doing all right."

"Well, after all, I *am* a Field Agent of the Authority. We're trained in just such communicative ability."

"Maybe you'd better start a little farther back. What authority are you talking about? How'd you get here? Where are you from in the first place? Where did you learn English?"

Dzok had finished with my arm now. He laughed—a good-natured chuckle. Imprisonment in foul conditions seemed not to bother him. "I'll take those questions one at a time. I suggest we move up to my dais now. I've arranged a few scraps of cloth in the one dry corner here. And perhaps you'd like a bit of clean food, after that nauseous pap our friends here issue."

"You've got food?"

"My emergency ration pack. I've been using it sparingly. Not very satisfying, but nourishing enough."

We made our way to a shelf-like flat area high in the right rear corner of the cell, and I stretched out on Dzok's neatly arranged dry rags and accepted a robin's-egg-sized capsule.

"Swallow that down," Dzok said. "A balanced ration for twenty-four hours; arranged concentrically, of course. Takes about nine hours to assimilate. There's water too." He passed me a thick clay cup.

I gulped hard, got the pill down. "Your throat must be bigger than mine," I said. "Now what about my questions?"

"Ah, yes, the Authority; this is the great Web government which exercises jurisdiction over all that region of the Web lying within two million E-units radius of the Home Line..."

I was listening, thinking how this news would sit with the Imperial authorities when I got back—if I got back—if there was anything to go back to. Not one new Net-traveling race but two—each as alien to the other as either was to me. And all three doubtless laying claim to ever-wider territory...

Dzok was still talking, "...our work in the Anglic sector has been limited, for obvious reasons—"

"What obvious reasons?"

"Our chaps could hardly pass unnoticed among you," Dzok said dryly. "So we've left the sector pretty much to its own devices—"

"But you *have* been there?"

"Routine surveillance only, mostly in null time, of course—"

"You use too many 'of courses,' Dzok," I said. "But go on, I'm listening."

"Our maps of the area are sketchy. There's the vast desert area, of C—" he cleared his throat. "A vast desert area known as the Desolation, within which no world lines survive, surrounded by a rather wide spectrum of related lines, all having as their central cultural source the North European technical nucleus—rather a low-grade technology, to be sure, but the first glimmering of enlightenment is coming into being there..."

He went on with his outline of the vast sweep of A-lines that constituted the scope of activities of the Authority. I didn't call attention to his misconceptions regarding the total absence of life in the Blight, or his seeming ignorance of the existence of a line with Net-traveling capabilities. That was information I would keep in reserve.

"...the scope of the Authority has been steadily extended over the last fifteen hundred years," the agent was saying. "Our unique Web-transit abilities naturally carry with them a certain responsibility. The early tendency toward exploitation has long been overcome, and the Authority now merely exercises a police and peace-keeping function, while obtaining useful raw materials and manufactured products from carefully selected loci on a normal commercial basis."

"Uh-huh." I'd heard the speech before. It was a lot like the pitch Bernadotte and Richthofen and the others had given me when I first arrived at Stockholm Zero-zero.

"My mission here," Dzok went on, "was to discover the forces behind the slave raids which had been creating so much misery and unrest along the periphery of the Authority, and to recommend the optimum method of eliminating the nuisance with the minimum of overt interference. As I've told you, I badly underestimated our Hagroon. I was arrested within a quarter-hour of my arrival."

"And you learned English on your visits to the, ah, Anglic Sector?"

"I've never visited the sector personally, but the language libraries naturally have monitored the developing dialects."

"Do your friends know where you are?"

Dzok sighed. "I'm afraid not. I was out to cut a bit of a figure, I realize now—belatedly. I envisioned myself reporting back in to IDMS Headquarters with the solution neatly wrapped and tied with pink ribbon. Instead—well, in time they'll notice my prolonged absence and set to work to find my trail. In the meantime..."

"In the meantime, what?"

"I can only hope they take action before my turn comes."

"Your turn for what?"

"Didn't you know, old chap? But of course not; you don't speak their beastly dialect. It's all because of the food shortage, you see. They're cannibals. Captives that fail to prove their usefulness as slaves are slaughtered and eaten."

"About how long," I asked Dzok, "do you suppose we have?"

"I estimate that I've been here for three weeks," the agent said. "There were two poor sods here when I came—a pair of slaves of a low order of intelligence. As well as I could determine, they'd been here for some two weeks. They were taken away a week ago. Some sort of feast for a high official, I gathered. Judging from the look of the menu, they'd have need of those ferocious teeth of theirs. Tough chewing, I'd say."

I was beginning to see through agent Dzok. His breezy air covered a conviction that he'd be in a Hagroon cooking pot himself before many more days had passed.

"In that case, I suppose we'd better start thinking about a way to get out of here," I suggested.

"I hoped you'd see that," Dzok said. "I have a chance of sorts—but it will require two men. How good are you at climbing?"

"As good as I have to be," I said shortly. "What's the plan?"

"There are two guards posted along the corridor. We'll need to entice one of them inside so as to deal with him separately. That shouldn't be too difficult."

"How do we get past the other one?"

"That part's a bit tricky—but not impossible. I have some materials tucked away here—items from my survival kit as well as a number of things I've salvaged since I arrived. There's also a crude map I sketched from memory. We'll have approximately one hundred meters of corridor to negotiate before we reach the side entry I've marked as our escape route. Our only hope lies in not running into a party of Hagroon before we reach it. Your disguise won't stand close examination."

"Disguise?" I had the feeling I had stumbled into somebody else's drunken dream. "Who are we going as? Dracula and the wolf man?" I was light-headed, dizzy. I lay back on my rags and closed my eyes. Dzok's voice seemed to come from a long way off:

"Get a good rest. I'll make my preparations. As soon as you wake, we'll make our try."

I came awake to the sound of voices—snarling, angry voices. I sat up, blinking through deep gloom. Dzok said something in a mild tone, and the voice snapped back—a booming, animal snort. I could smell him now—even in the fetid air of the cell, the reek of the angry Hagroon cut through. I could see him, a big fellow, standing near the entry. I wondered how he'd gotten through; the opening was barely big enough for me...

"Lie still and make no sound, Anglic," Dzok called in the same soothing tone he had been using to the Hagroon. "This one wants me. My time ran out, it seems..." Then he broke into the strange dialect again.

The Hagroon snarled and spat. I saw his arm reach, saw Dzok duck under it, plant a solid blow in the bigger creature's chest. The Hagroon grunted, crouched a little, reached again. I came to my feet, flicked my wrist, felt the solid slap as the slug gun filled my palm. Dzok moved back and the jailor jumped after him, swung a blow that knocked the agent's guard aside and sent him spinning. I took two quick steps to the Hagroon's side, aimed, and fired at point-blank range. The recoil kicked me halfway across the room as the monsterman reeled back, fell to the floor, kicking, his long arms wrapped around himself. He was making horrible, choked sounds, and I felt myself pitying the brute. He was tough. The blast from the slug at that range would have killed an ox, but he was rolling over now, trying to get up. I followed him, picked out his head against the lesser dark of the background, fired again. Fluid spattered my face. The huge body gave one tremendous leap and lay still. I wiped my face with a forearm, snorted the rusty odor of blood from my nostrils, turned back to Dzok. He was sprawled on the floor, holding one arm.

"You fooled me, Anglic," he panted. "Damned good show...you had a weapon..."

"What about that plan?" I demanded. "Can we try it now?"

"Damned...brute," Dzok got out between his

teeth. "Broke my arm. Damned nuisance. Perhaps you'd better try it alone."

"To hell with that. Let's get started. What do I do?"

Dzok made a choked sound that might have been a laugh. "You're tougher than you look, Anglic, and the gun will help. All right. Here's what we have to do..."

Twenty minutes later I was sweating inside the most fantastic getup ever used in a jail break. Dzok had draped me in a crude harness made from strips of rags—there had been a heap of them in the den when he arrived—luxurious bedding for the inmates. Attached to the straps were tufts of greasy hair arranged so as to hang down, screening my body. The agent had traded his food ration to his former cell-mates in return for the privilege of trimming hair samples from their shaggy bodies, he explained. The dead Hagroon had supplied more. Using adhesives from his kit, he had assembled the grotesque outfit. It hung down below my knees, without even an attempt at a fit.

"This is fantastic," I told him. "It wouldn't fool a newborn idiot at a hundred yards in a bad light!"

Agent Dzok was busy stuffing a bundle inside what was left of his jacket. "You'll look properly bulky and shaggy. That's the best we can do. You won't have to pass close scrutiny—we hope. Now let's be going."

Dzok went first, moving awkwardly with his broken arm bound to his chest, but not complaining. He paused with his head out in the corridor, then scrabbled through.

"Come on, the coast is clear," he called softly. "Our warden is taking a stroll."

I followed, emerged into air that was comparatively cool and clean after the stale stink of the den. The light was on along the passage as usual. There was no way to tell the time of day. A hundred feet along, the corridor turned right and up; there were no openings along the section we could see. The guard was presumably loitering farther along.

Dzok moved silently off, slim-hipped, low-waisted, his odd, thin legs slightly bent at the knee, his once natty uniform a thing of tatters and tears through which his seal-sleek pelt showed. Before we reached the turn, we heard the rumble of Hagroon voices. Dzok stopped and I came up beside him. He stood with his head cocked, listening.

"Two of them," he whispered. "Filthy bit of luck..."

I waited, feeling the sweat trickle down inside my clown suit of stinking rags and dangling locks of hair. There was a sudden sharp itch between my shoulder blades—not the first since I had been introduced to Hagroon hospitality. I grimaced but didn't try to scratch; the flimsy outfit would have fallen to pieces.

"Oh-oh," Dzok breathed. "One of them is leaving. Changing of the guard."

I nodded. Another minute ticked by like a waiting bomb. Dzok turned, gave me a large wink, then said something in a loud, angry snarl—a passable imitation of the Hagroon speech pattern. He waited a moment, then hissed: "Count to ten, slowly—" and started on along the passage at a quick, shambling pace. Just as he moved out of sight around the corner, he looked back, shouted something in a chattering language. Then he was gone.

I started my count, listening hard. I heard the Hagroon guard snort something, heard Dzok reply. Five. Six. Seven. The Hagroon spoke again, sounding closer. Nine. Ten—

I took a deep breath, tried to assume the sort of hunch-shouldered stance the Hagroon displayed, moved on around the turn in a rolling walk. Twenty feet ahead, beyond the light, Dzok stood, waving his good arm, yelling something now, pointing back toward me. A few yards farther on, the guard, a squat, bristly figure like a pile of hay, shot a glance in my direction. Dzok jumped closer to him, still shouting. The Hagroon raised an arm, took a swing that Dzok just managed to avoid. I came on, getting closer to the light bulb now. Dzok dashed in, ducked, got past the guard. The Hagroon had his back to me, fifteen feet away now, almost within range. I flipped the gun into my hand, made another five feet—

The guard whirled, started an angry shout at me— then suddenly got a good look at what must have been only a dim silhouette in the bad light at his first glance. His reflexes were good. He lunged while the startled look was still settling into place on the wide, mud-colored face. I got the shot off just as he crashed into me, and we went down, his four-hundred-pound body smashing me back like a truck hitting a fruit cart. I managed to twist aside just enough to let the bulk of his weight slam past before I hit the pavement and skidded. I got some breath back into my lungs, hauled my gun hand free for another shot. But it wasn't necessary—the huge body lay sprawled half on me, inert as a frozen mammoth.

Dzok was beside me, helping me to my feet with his good hand.

"All right, so far," he said cheerfully rearranging my hair shirt. "Quite a weapon you have there. You sapiens are marvelous at the sort of thing—a natural result of your physical frailty, no doubt."

"Let's analyze me later," I muttered. My shoulders

were hurting like hell where I had raked them across the rough paving. "What next?"

"Nothing else between us and the refuse disposal slot I told you about. It's not far. Come along." He seemed as jaunty as ever, unbothered by the brief, violent encounter.

He led the way down a slanting side branch, then up a steep climb, took another turnoff into a wider passage filled with the smell of burning garbage.

"The kitchens," Dzok hissed. "Just a little farther."

We heard loud voices then—the Hagroons never seemed to talk any other way. Flat against the rough-hewn wall, we waited. Two slope-shouldered bruisers waddled out from the low-arched kitchen entry, and went off in the opposite direction. We went on, following a trail of spilled refuse, ducked under a low doorway and into a bin layered with putrefying food waste. I thought I had graduated from the course in bad smells, but this was a whole new spectrum of stench. We splashed through, looked out a two-yard-wide, foot-high slot crusted with garbage. The view was darkness, and a faint glistening of web cobbles far below. I twisted, looked up. A ragged line of eaves showed above my head.

"I thought so," I said softly. "The low ceilings meant the roof had to be next. I think these people stacked this pile of stone up here and carved the rooms out afterward."

"Precisely," Dzok said. "Not very efficient, perhaps, but in a society where slave labor is plentiful and architectural talent nonexistent, it serves."

"Which way?" I asked. "Up or down?"

Dzok looked doubtfully at me, eyeing my shoulders

and arms like a fight manager looking over a prospective addition to his stable. "Up," he said. "If you think you can manage."

"I guess I'll have to manage," I said. "And what about you, with that arm?"

"Eh? Oh, it may be a bit awkward, but no matter. Shall we go?" And he slipped forward through the opening in the two-foot-thick wall, twisting over on his back; then his feet were through and out of sight, and suddenly I was very much alone. Behind me the growl of voices and an occasional clatter seemed louder than it had before. Someone was coming my way. I turned over on my back as Dzok had done, eased into the slot. The garbage provided adequate lubrication.

My head emerged into the chilly night. Above I saw the cold glitter of stars in a pitch-black sky, the dim outlines of nearby buildings, a few faint lights gleaming from openings cut at random in the crude masonry walls. It was a long reach to the projecting cornice just above me. I stretched, trying not to think about the long drop below—found a handhold, scrambled up and over. Dzok came up, as I rolled and sat up.

"There's a bridge to the next tower a few yards down the far side," he whispered. "What kept you?"

"I just paused to admire the view. Here, help me get rid of the ape suit." I shed the costume, caked and slimy with garbage now, while Dzok slapped ineffectually at the samples adhering to my back. He looked worse than I did, if possible. His sleek fur was damp and clotted with sour-smelling liquid.

"When I get home," he said, "I shall have the longest, hottest bath obtainable in the most luxurious sensorium in the city of Zaj."

"I'll join you there," I offered. "If we make it."

"The sooner we start, the sooner the handmaidens will ply their brushes." He moved away across the slight dome of the roof, crouched at the far edge, turned, and slipped from sight. It appeared that there was a lot more monkey in Dzok than I'd managed to retain. I got down awkwardly on all fours, slid over the edge, groped with a foot, found no support.

"Lower yourself to arm's length," Dzok's voice came softly from the darkness below—how far below I couldn't say. I eased over the edge, scraping new abrasions in my hide. Dangling at full length, I still found nothing under my toes.

"Let go and drop," Dzok called quietly. "Just a meter or so."

That was a proposal I would have liked to mull over in the quiet of my study for a few hours, but it wasn't the time to argue. I tried to relax, then let go. There was a dizzy moment of free fall, a projecting stone ripped my cheek as I slammed against a flat ledge and went down, one hand raking stone, and the other stabbing down into nothingness. Dzok caught me, pulled me back. I sat up, made out the dim strip of dark, railess walk arching off into the night. I started to ask if that was what we had to cross, but Dzok was already on the way.

Forty-five minutes later, after a trip that would have been unexceptional to the average human fly, Dzok and I stood in the deep shadow of an alley carpeted in the usual deposit of rubbish.

"This place would be an archaeologist's paradise," I muttered. "Everything from yesterday's banana peel to the first flint that ever chipped is right here underfoot."

Dzok was busy opening the bundle he had carried inside his jacket. I helped him arrange the straps and brasses taken from the Hagroon I had killed in the cell.

"We'll exchange roles now," he said softly. "I'm the captor, if anyone questions us. I may be able to carry it off. I'm not certain just how alien I may appear to the average monster in the street; I saw a few australopithecine types as they brought me in. Now, it's up to you to guide us to where you left the shuttle. About half a mile, you said?"

"Something like that—if it's still there." We started off along the alley which paralleled the main thoroughfare I had traversed under guard eighteen hours earlier. It twisted and turned, narrowing at times to no more than an air space between crooked walls, widening once to form a marketplace where odd, three-tiered stalls slumped, deserted and drab in the postmidnight stillness. After half an hour's stealthy walk, I called a halt.

"The way these alleys wander, I'm not a damned bit sure where we are," I said. "I think we'll have to risk trying the main street, at least long enough for me to get my bearings."

Dzok nodded, and we took a side alley, emerging in the comparatively wide avenue. A lone Hagroon shambled along the opposite side of the street. Wide-spaced lamps on ten-foot poles shed pools of sad, yellow light on a littered walk that ran under windowless facades adorned only by the crooked lines of haphazard masonry courses, as alien as beehives.

I led the way to the right. A trough of brownish stone slopping over with oil-scummed water looked familiar; just beyond this point I had seen the harnessed mastodon. The alley from which the shuttle had operated was not far ahead. The street curved to the left. I pointed to a dark side way debouching from a widening of the street ahead.

"I think that's it. We'd better try another alley and see if we can't sneak up on it from behind. They probably have guards on the shuttle."

"We'll soon know." A narrow opening just ahead seemed to lead back into the heart of the block of masonry. We followed it, emerged in a dead end, from which an arched opening like a sewage tunnel led off into utter darkness.

"Let's try that route," Dzok suggested. "It seems to lead in the right general direction."

"What if it's somebody's bedroom?" I eyed the looming building; the crudely mortared walls gave no hint of interior function. The Hagroon knew only one style of construction: solid-rock Gothic.

"In that case, we'll beat a hasty retreat."

"Somehow the thought of pounding through these dark alleys with a horde of aroused Hagroon at my heels lacks appeal," I said. "But I guess we can give it a try." I moved to the archway, peered inside, then took the plunge. My shoes seemed loud on the rough floor. Behind me I could hear Dzok's breathing. The last glimmer of light faded behind us. I was feeling my way with a hand against the wall now. We went on for what seemed a long time.

"Hssst!" Dzok's hand touched my shoulder. "I think we've taken a wrong turning somewhere, old boy..."

"Yeah..." I thought it over. "We'd better go back."

For another ten minutes we groped our way back in the dark, as silently as possible. Then Dzok halted. I came up behind him.

"What is it?" I whispered.

"Shhh."

I heard it then: a very faint sound of feet shuffling. Then a glow of light sprang up around a curve ahead, showing a dark doorway across the passage.

"In there," Dzok whispered, and dived for it. I followed, slammed against him. There was a sound of heavy breathing nearby.

"What was that you said about bedrooms?" he murmured in my ear.

The breathing snorted into a resonant snore, followed by gulping sounds. I could hear a heavy body moving, the rustle of disturbed rubbish. Then an eerie silence settled.

Suddenly Dzok moved. I heard something clatter in the far corner of the room. His hand grabbed at me, pulling me along. I stumbled over things, heard his hand rasping on stone, then we were flat against the wall. A big Hagroon body rose up, moved into the light from the open door through which we had entered. Another of the shaggy figures appeared outside; this would be the one we had first heard in the alley. The two exchanged guttural growls. The nearer one turned back into the room—and abruptly the chamber was flooded with wan light. I saw that Dzok and I were in an alcove that partly concealed us from view from the door. The Hagroon squinted against the light, half-turned away—then whirled back as he saw us. Dzok jumped. The gun slapped my hand—but Dzok was past him, diving for another opening. I was behind him, ducking under the Hagroon's belated grab, then pelting along a tunnel toward a faint glow at the far end, Dzok bounding ten yards in the lead.

There were yells behind us, a horrible barking roar, the pound of feet. I hadn't wanted a horde of trolls chasing me through the dark—but here I was anyway.

Ahead, Dzok leaped out into the open, skidded to a halt, looked both ways, then pointed, and was gone. I raced out into the open alley, saw Dzok charging straight at a pair of Hagroon in guards' bangles—and beyond him, the dark rectangular bulk of the shuttle. The agent yelled. I recognized the grunts and croaks of the Hagroon language. The two guards hesitated. One pointed at me, started forward, the other spread his arms, barked something at Dzok. The latter, still coming on full tilt, straight-armed the heavier humanoid, dodged aside as the Hagroon staggered back, and made for the shuttle. I brought the slug gun up, fired at extreme range, saw the Hagroon bounce back, slam against the wall, then reach—but I was past him. Dzok's opponent saw me, dithered for a moment, then whirled toward me. I fired—and missed, tried to twist aside, slipped, went down and skidded under the Hagroon's grasp, leaving a sleeve from my coat dangling in his hands. I scrambled, made it to all fours, dived for the open entry to the shuttle. Dzok's hand shot out, hauled me inside, and the door banged behind me as the sentry hit it like a charging rhino.

Dzok whirled to the operator's seat.

"Great Scott!" he yelled. "The control lever's broken off short!" The shuttle was rocking under blows at the entry port. Dzok gripped the edge of the panel with his one good hand; the muscles of his shoulder bunched, and with one heave, he tore it away, exposing tight-packed electronic components.

"Quick, Anglic!" he snapped. "The leads there—cross

them!" I wedged myself in beside him, grabbed two heavy insulated cables, twisted their ends together. Following the agent's barked instructions, I ripped wires loose, made hasty connections from a massive coil—which I recognized as an M-C field energizer—to a boxed unit like a fifty KW transformer. Dzok reached past me, jammed a frayed cable end against a heavy bus bar. With a shower of blue and yellow sparks, copper welded to steel. A deep hum started up; abruptly the shattering blows at the entry ceased. I felt the familiar tension of the M-C field close in around me. I let out a long sigh, slumped back in the chair.

"Close, Anglic," Dzok sighed, "But we're clear now..." I looked over at him, saw his yellowish eyes waver and half-close; then he fell sideways into my lap.

CHAPTER FIVE

DZOK WAS LYING WHERE I had dragged him, in deep grass under a small, leafy tree, his chest rising and falling in the quick, shallow, almost panting, breathing of his kind.

The shuttle rested fifty feet away, up against a rocky escarpment at the top of which a grey, chimp-sized ape perched, scratching thoughtfully and gazing down at us. My clothes were spread on the grass along with what remained of Dzok's whites. I had given them a scrubbing in the sandy-bedded stream that flowed nearby. I had also inventoried my wounds, found nothing worse than cuts, scrapes and bruises.

The agent rolled over on his side, groaned, winced in his sleep as his weight pressed against his bound arm; then his eyes opened.

"Welcome back," I said. "Feel better?"

He groaned again. His pale tongue came out, touched his thin, blackish lips.

"As soon as I'm home again I shall definitely resign

my commission," he croaked. He moved to ease the arm, lifted it with his good hand and laid it across his chest.

"This member seems to belong to someone else," he groaned. "Someone who died horribly."

"Maybe I'd better try to set it."

He shook his head. "Where are we, Anglic?"

"The name's Bayard. As to where we are, your guess is better than mine, I hope. I piled the scout along full tilt for about five hours, then took a chance and dropped in here to wait for you to come around. You must have been in worse shape than you told me."

"I was close to the end of my resources," the agent admitted. "I'd been beaten pretty badly on three occasions, and my food pellets were running low. I'd been on short rations for about a week."

"How the devil did you manage to stay on your feet—and climb, and fight, and run—and with a broken arm?"

"Small credit to me, old fellow. Merely a matter of triggering certain emergency metabolic stimulators. Hypnotics, you know." His eyes took in the scene. "Pretty place. No sign of our former hosts?"

"Not yet. It's been about four hours since we arrived."

"I think we're safe from intrusion. From what little we'd learned of them, they have very poor Web instrumentation. They won't trail us." He studied the ragged skyline.

"Did you maneuver the shuttle spatially? We seem to be out in the wilds."

I shook my head. "These cliffs here," I indicated the rising pinnacles of warm, reddish-brown stone that ringed the glade. "I watched them evolve from what were buildings back in the inhabited regions. It gives you the feeling that we men and our works are just a force of nature, like any other catastrophe."

"I've seen the same thing," Dzok agreed. "No matter what path you choose to follow across the alternate world-lines, the changes are progressive, developmental. A puddle becomes a pond, then a lake, then a reservoir, then a swimming pool, then a swamp filled with dead trees and twenty-foot snakes; trees stretch, or shrink, grow new branches, new fruits, slide away through the soil to new positions; but always gradually. There are no discontinuities in the entropic grid—excepting, of course, such man-caused anomalies as the Desolation."

"Do you know where we are?" The grey ape on the cliff top watched me suspiciously.

"Give me a moment to gather my forces," Dzok closed his eyes, took deep breaths. "I'll have to drop back on self-hypnotic mnemonic conditioning. I have no conscious recollection of this region."

I waited. His breathing resumed its normal rapid, shallow pattern. His eyes popped open.

"Right," he said briskly. "Not too bad, at all. We're about six hours' run from Authority Central at Zaj, I'd guess." He sat up, got shakily to his feet. "May as well get moving. I'll have a bit of work to do calibrating the instruments; bit awkward navigating with dead screens." He was looking at me thoughtfully. "Which brings me to wonder, Bayard, ah...just how did you manage to control the shuttle?"

I could feel my forehead wrinkling. I couldn't tell yet whether I was going to frown or grin.

"I may as well confide in you, Dzok," I said. "I know a little something about shuttles myself."

He waited, looking alert and interested.

"Your Authority isn't the only power claiming control of the Net. I represent the Paramount Government of the Imperium."

Dzok nodded kindly. "Glad you decided to tell me. Makes things cozier all around. Lends an air of mutual confidence, all that sort of thing."

"You already knew?"

"I must confess I used a simple hypnotic technique on you while you were resting, back in our digs. Dug out some fascinating data. Took the opportunity to plant a number of suggestions, too. Nothing harmful, of course. Just a little dampening of your anxiety syndrome, plus, of course, a command to obey my instructions to the letter."

I looked at him, gazing airily at me. My expression settled into a wide and rather sardonic grin.

"I'm very relieved to hear it. Now I don't feel like such a stinker for working on you while you were out."

For a moment he looked startled, then his complacent expression returned.

"Sorry to disappoint you, old chap, but of course I'm well protected against that sort of thing—" he broke off, looking just a little worried, as though a thought had just struck him.

I nodded. "Me too."

Suddenly he laughed. His cannonball head seemed to split in a grin that showed at least thirty-six teeth. He leaned and slapped his knee with his good hand, doubled over in a paroxysm of hilarity, staggered toward me, still roaring. I took a step back, tensed my wrist.

"You have an infectious laugh, Dzok," I said. "But not infectious enough to let you get me in range of that pile driver arm of yours."

He straightened, grinning rather ruefully now. "Seems to be a bit of an impasse," he conceded.

"I'm sure we can work it out," I said. "Just don't keep trying those beginners' tricks. I've had to learn all about them."

He pursed his wide, thin lips. "I'm wondering why you stopped here. Why didn't you press on, reattain the safety of your own base while I was unconscious?"

"I told you. I don't know where I am. This is unfamiliar territory to me—and there are no maps aboard that tub."

"Ah-hah. And now you expect me to guide you home—and myself into an untenable position?"

"Just rig up the board and calibrate it. I'll do my own steering."

He shook his head. "I'm still considerably stronger than you, old fellow—in spite of my indisposition." He twitched his broken arm. "I fail to see how you can coerce me."

"I still have the gun we sapiens are so clever about making."

"Quite. But shooting me would hardly be to your advantage." He was grinning again. I had the feeling he was enjoying it all. "Better let me run us in to Xonijeel. I'll see to it you're given all possible aid."

"I've had a sample of hairy hospitality," I said. "I'm not yearning for more."

He looked pained. "I hope you don't lump us australopithecines in with the Hagroon, of all people, just on the basis of a little handsome body hair."

"Are you promising me you'll give me a shuttle and turn me loose?"

"Well..." he spread his wide, deeply-grooved hands. "After all, I'm hardly in a position..."

"Think of the position you'd be in if I left you here."

"I'd have to actively resist any such effort, I'm afraid."

"You'd lose."

"Hmmm. Probably. On the other hand, I'd be much too valuable a prisoner in this Imperium of yours, so it's just as well to die fighting." He tensed as though ready to go into action. I didn't want that.

"I'll make another proposal," I said quickly. "You give me your word as an officer of the Authority that I'll be given an opportunity to confer with the appropriate high officials at Zaj—and I'll agree to accompany you there first."

He nodded promptly. "I can assure you of that much. And I'll take it upon myself to personally guarantee you'll receive honorable treatment."

"That's a deal." I stepped forward, put out my hand, trying not to look as worried as I felt. Dzok looked blank, then reached out gingerly, took my hand. His palm felt hot and dry and coarse-skinned, like a dog's paw.

"Empty hand; no weapon," he murmured. "Marvelous symbolism." He grinned widely again. "Glad we worked it out. You seem like a decent sort, Bayard, in spite—" The smile faded slightly. "I have a curious feeling you've done me, in some obscure way..."

"I was wondering how I'd talk you into taking me to Zaj," I said, grinning back at him now. "Thanks for making it easy."

"Ummm. Trouble at home, eh?"

"That's a slight understatement."

He frowned at me. "I'll get to work on the instruments, while you tell me the details."

One hour, two skinned knuckles, and one slight electric shock later, the shuttle was on its way, Dzok in the operator's seat crouched over the jury-rigged panel.

"This curious light you mentioned," he was saying. "You say it seemed to pervade even enclosed spaces, cut off from any normal light source?"

"That's right. A sort of ghostly, bluish glow."

"There are a number of things in your account that I can't explain," Dzok said. "But as for the light effect, it's plain you'd been transposed spontaneously into a null-time level. The Hagroon are fond of operating there. The apparent light is due to certain emanations arising from the oscillation of elementary particles at a vastly reduced level of energy; a portion of this activity elicits a response from the optic nerve. Did you notice that it arose particularly from metal surfaces?"

"Not especially."

Dzok shook his head, frowning. "A fantastic energy input is required to transfer mass across the entropic threshold. Far more than is needed to set up the drift across the A-lines, for example. And you say you found yourself there, without mechanical aid?"

I nodded. "What is this null time?"

"Ah, a very difficult concept." Dzok was busily noting instrument readings, twiddling things, taking more readings. As a shuttle technician, he was way ahead of me. "In normal entropy, of course, we move in a direction which we can conveniently think of as forward; with Web travel, we move perpendicular to this vector—sideways, one might say. Null time . . . well, consider it as offset at right angles to both: a stunted, lifeless continuum, in which energies flow in strange ways."

"Then it wasn't the city that was altered—it was me. I had been ejected from my normal continuum into this null-time state—"

"Quite correct, old fellow," Dzok blinked at me sympathetically. "I can see you've been laboring under a ghastly strain, thinking otherwise."

"I'm beginning to get the picture," I said. "The Hagroon are studying the Imperium from null time—getting set for an attack, I'd guess offhand. They've got techniques that are way beyond anything the Imperium has. We need help. Do you think the Authority will give it to us?"

"I don't know, Bayard," Dzok said. "But I'll do my best for you."

I had a few hours' restless nap on the floor behind the control seat before Dzok called me. I climbed up to lean over his chair, staring into the screen. We were among spidery towers now; minarets of lofty, fragile beauty, soaring up pink, yellow, pale green, into a bright morning sky.

"Nice," I said. "We're close to your home line now, I take it?"

"Ah, the towers of Zaj," Dzok almost sang. "There's nothing to equal them in all the universes!"

"Let's hope I get a reception to match the pretty buildings."

"Look here, Bayard, there's something I feel I ought to ... ah ... tell you," Dzok said hesitantly. "Frankly, there's a certain, well, ill-feeling in the minds of some against the sapiens group. Unreasonable, perhaps—but it's a factor we're going to have to deal with."

"What's this ill-feeling based on?"

"Certain, ah, presumed racial characteristics. You have a reputation for ferocity, ruthless competitiveness, love of violence..."

"I see. We're not nice and mild like the Hagroon, say. And who was it that I saw bounce one of the Hagroon out of the way in order to steal this scout we're riding in?"

"Yes, yes, all of us are prey to a certain degree of combativeness. But perhaps you noticed that even the Hagroon tend to enslave rather than to kill, and though they're cruel, it's the cruelty of indifference, not hate. I saw you kick one of them just as you entered the cell. Did you note that he took no revenge?"

"Anybody will fight back when he's been knocked around enough."

"But only you sapiens have systematically killed off every other form of hominid life in your native continua!" Dzok was getting a little excited now. "You hairless ones—in every line where you exist—you exist alone! Ages ago, in the first confrontation of the bald mutation with normal anthropos—driven, doubtless, by shame at your naked condition—you slaughtered your hairy fellow men! And even today your minds are warped by ancient guilt-and-shame complexes associated with nudity!"

"So you're holding the present generation responsible for what happened—or may have happened—thousand of years ago?"

"In my world sector," Dzok stated, "there are three major races of Man: we australopithecines, to employ your English terms; the Rhodesians—excellent workers, strong and willing, if not overly bright; and the

Pekin derivatives—blue-faced chaps, you know. We live together in perfect harmony, each group with its societal niche, each contributing its special talents to the common culture. While you sapiens—why, you even set upon your own kind, distinguishable only by the most trivial details!"

"What about me, Dzok? Do I seem to you to be a raving maniac? Have I indicated any particular distaste for you, for example?"

"Me?" Dzok looked amazed, then whooped with laugher. "Me!" he choked. "The idea..."

"What's so funny?"

"You...with your poor bald face—your spindly limbs—your degenerate dentition—having to overcome your natural distaste for *me*!" He was almost falling out of his chair now.

"Well, if I had any natural distaste, I at least had the decency to forget it!" I snapped.

Dzok stopped laughing, dabbed at his eyes with a dangling cuff. He looked at me almost apologetically.

"You did, at that," he conceded. "And you bound up my arm, and washed my poor old uniform for me—"

"And your poor old face too, you homely galoot!"

Dzok was smiling embarrassedly now. "I'm sorry, old boy; I got a bit carried away. All those personal remarks—a lot of rot, actually. Judge a chap on what he does, not what he is, eh? None of us can help our natural tendencies—and perhaps overcoming one's instinct is in the end a nobler achievement than not having the impulse in the first place." He put out his hand uncertainly.

"Empty hand, no weapon, eh?" He smiled. I took the hand.

"You're all right, Bayard," Dzok said. "Without you I'd have been rotting in that bloody cell. I'm on your side, old fellow—all the way!"

He whirled as a buzzer went, slapped switches, threw out the main drive, watched needles creep across dials, flipped the transfer switch. The growl of the field generators faded down the scale. Dzok beamed at me.

"We're here." He held a thumb up. "This may be a great day for both our races."

We stepped out into a wide sweep of colorfully tiled plaza dotted with trees, the bright geometric shapes of flower beds, fountains splashing in the sunshine. There were hundreds of australopithecines in sight, strolling leisurely in pairs, or hurrying briskly along with the air of urgency that was apparently as characteristic of Xonijeelian bureaucrats as of their hairless counterparts at home. Some wore flowing robes like Arab djellabas; others were dressed in multicolored pantaloon and jacket outfits; and here and there were the trim white uniforms that indicated the IDMS. Our sudden arrival in the midst of the pack caused a mild stir that became a low murmur as they caught sight of me. I saw noses wrinkle in flat, toothy faces, a few hostile stares, heard snickers from here and there. Someone called something to Dzok. He answered, took a firm grip on my arm.

"Sorry, Bayard," he muttered. "Mustn't appear to be running loose, you know." He waved an arm at a light aircraft cruising overhead. I thought it was a heli until I noticed its lack of rotors. It dropped into a landing and a wide transparent hatch opened like a clamshell. A close relative of Dzok's showed a fine set of teeth and waved, then his gaze settled on me and his grin dropped like a wet bar rag. He fluted something at Dzok, who called an answer back, took my arm, urged me along.

"Ignore him, Bayard. A mere peasant."

"That's easy. I don't know what he's saying."

I climbed into the well-sprung seat. Dzok settled in beside me, gave the driver an address.

"This adventure hasn't turned out too badly after all," he said expansively. "Back safe and sound—more or less—with a captive machine and a most unusual, ah, guest."

"I'm glad you didn't say prisoner," I commented, looking down on a gorgeous pattern of parks and plazas and delicate spires as we swooped over them at dashing speed. "Where are we headed?"

"We're going directly to IDMS Headquarters. My report will require quick action, and of course you're in haste as well."

There didn't seem to be much more to say. I rode along, admiring the city below, watching a massive white tower grow in the distance. We aimed directly for it, circled it once as though waiting for landing instructions, then hovered, dropped down to settle lightly on a small pad centered in a roof garden of tall palms, great banks of yellow and blue blossoms, freeform reflecting pools with caged birds and animals completing the jungle setting.

"Now, just let me do the talking, Bayard," Dzok said, hurrying me toward a stairwell. "I'll present your case to our Council in the most favorable light, and I'm confident there'll be no trouble. You should be on your way home in a matter of hours."

"I hope your Council is a little less race-minded than the yokels down below—" I started, then broke off, staring at a camouflaged cage where a hairless, tailless biped, two-feet tall, with a low forehead, snouted face and sparse beard stared out at me with dull eyes.

"My God!" I said. "That's a man—a midget—"

Dzok turned sharply. "Eh? What?" He gaped, then grinned. "Oh, good Lord, Bayard, it's merely a tonquil! Most amusing little creature, but hardly human—"

The little manikin stirred, made a plaintive noise. I went on then, feeling a mixture of emotions, none of which added to my confidence.

We descended the escalator, went along a wide, cool corridor to a glass door, on into a wide skylighted room with a pool, grass, tables, and a row of lockers at the far side. Dzok went to a wall screen, talked urgently, then turned to me.

"All set," he told me. "Council's in session now, and will review the case."

"That's fast action," I said. "I was afraid I'd have to spend a week filling out forms and then sweat out a spot on the calendar."

"Not here," Dzok said loftily. "It's a matter of pride for local Councils to keep their dockets clear."

"Local Council? I thought we were going to see the big wheels. I need to make my pitch to the top level—"

"This is the top level. They're perfectly capable of evaluating a situation, making a sound decision, and issuing appropriate orders." He glanced at a wall scale which I assumed was a clock.

"We have half an hour. We'll take a few moments to freshen up, change of clothes and all that. I'm afraid we still smell of the Hagroon prison."

There were a few other customers in the room, lanky, sleek Xonijeelians who stroked to the length of the pool or reclined in lounge chairs. They stared curiously as we passed. Dzok spoke to one or two, but didn't linger to chat. At the lockers, he pressed buttons, used an attached tape to measure me, worked a lever. A flat package popped out from a wide slot.

"A clean outfit, Bayard—not exactly what you've been used to, but I think you'll find it comfortable— and frankly, the familiar garments may be a help in overcoming any initial—ah—distaste the Council Members may feel."

"Swell," I muttered. "Too bad I left my ape suit. I could come as a Hagroon."

Dzok tutted and selected clothing for himself, then led me into a shower room where jets of warm, perfumed water came from orifices in the domed ceiling. We stripped and soaped down, Dzok achieving a remarkable lather, then air-dried in the dressing room. My new clothes—a pantaloon and jacket outfit in blue and silver satin with soft leather-like shoes and white silk shirt—fitted me passably. Dzok snickered, watching me comb my hair. I think he considered it hardly worth the effort. He gave the mirror a last glance, settled his new gold-braided white pillbox cap on his round head, fitted the scarlet chin strap under his lower lip, gave the tight-fitting tunic a last tug. "Not often an agent returns from the field with a report he's justified in classifying Class Two Sub-Emergency," he said in a satisfied tone.

"What's the emergency? Me or the Hagroon slave-runners?"

Dzok laughed—a bit uneasily, perhaps. "Now, now,

don't be anxious, Bayard. I'm sure the Councilors will recognize the unusual nature of your case..."

I followed him back into the corridor, thinking that one over.

"Suppose I were a 'usual' case, what then?"

"Well, of course, Authority policy would govern in that instance. But—"

"And what would Authority policy dictate?" I persisted.

"Let's just wait and deal with the situation as it develops, eh?" Dzok hurried ahead, leaving me with an unpleasant feeling that his self-confidence was waning the closer we came to the huge red-gilt doors that blocked the wide corridor ahead.

Two sharp sentries in silver-trimmed white snapped to as we came up. Dzok exchanged a few words with them. Then one thumbed a control and the portals swung open. Dzok took a deep breath, waiting for me to come up. Beyond him I saw a long table behind which sat a row of faces—mostly australopithecines, but with representatives of at least three other types of Man, all with grey or grizzled heads, some in red-ornamented whites, a few in colorful civvies.

"Stiff upper lip, that's the drill," Dzok muttered. "To my left and half a pace back. Follow my lead on protocol..." Then he stepped off toward the waiting elders. I adjusted a nonviolent, uncompetitive look on my face and followed. A dozen pairs of yellow eyes watched me approach; twelve expressions faced me across the polished table of black wood—and none of them were warm smiles of welcome. A narrow-faced grey-beard to the left of center made a smacking noise with his mobile lips, leaned to

mutter something to the councilor on his left. Dzok
halted, executed a half-bow with a bending of the
knees, spoke briefly in his staccato language, then
indicated me.

"I introduce to the Council one Bayard, native to
the Anglic Sector," he said, switching to English. "As
you see, a sapiens—"

"Where did you capture it?" the thin-faced member
rapped out in a high, irritable voice.

"Bayard is not . . . ah . . . precisely a captive, Excellency," Dzok started.

"Are you saying the creature forced its way here?"

"You may ignore that question, Agent," a round-
faced councilor spoke up from the right. "Councilor
Sphogeel is venting his bias in rhetoric. However,
your statement requires clarification."

"You're aware of Authority policy with regard to
bald antropoids, Agent?" another put in.

"The circumstances under which I encountered
Bayard were unusual," Dzok said smoothly. "It was
only with his cooperation and assistance that I escaped
prolonged imprisonment. My report—"

"Imprisonment? An Agent of the Authority?"

"I think we'd better hear the Agent's full report—at
once," the councilor who had interrupted Sphogeel said,
then added a remark in Xonijeelian. Dzok replied in
kind at some length, with considerable waving of his
long arms. I stood silently at his left and a half pace
to the rear as instructed, feeling like a second hand
bargain up for sale, with no takers.

The councilors fired questions then, which Dzok
fielded crisply, sweating all the while. Old Sphogeel's
expression failed to sweeten as the hearing went on.

Finally the round-faced councilor waved a long-fingered greyish hand, fixed his gaze on me.

"Now, Bayard, Agent Dzok has told us of the circumstances under which you placed yourself in his custody—"

"I doubt very much that Dzok told you any such thing," I cut him off abruptly. "I'm here by invitation, as a representative of my government."

"Is the Council to be subjected to impertinence?" Sphogeel demanded shrilly. "You speak when ordered to do so, sapiens—and keep a civil tongue in your head!"

"And I'm also sure," I bored on, "that his report included mention of the fact that I'm in need of immediate transportation back to my home line."

"Your needs are hardly of interest to this body," Sphogeel snapped. "We know quite well how to deal with your kind."

"You don't know anything about my kind!" I came back at him. "There's been no previous contact between our respective governments—"

"There is only one government, sapiens!" Sphogeel cut me off. "As for your kind..." His long, flexible upper lip was curled back, showing shocking pink gums and lots of teeth, in a sneer like that of an annoyed horse. "...we're familiar enough with your record of mayhem—"

"Hold on there, Sphogeel," another member broke in. "I for one would like to hear this fellow's account of his experiences. It appears the activities of the Hagroon may have some significance—"

"I say let the Hagroon do as they like insofar as these fratricidal deviants are concerned!" Sphogeel came back. He seemed to be even more upset than his prejudices warranted. I could see the line he was taking now: he didn't intend even to give me a hearing. It was time for me to get my oar into the water.

"Whether you like it or not, Sphogeel," I cut across the hubbub, "the Imperium is a first-class, Net-traveling power. Our two cultures were bound to meet sooner or later. I'd like to see our relations get off to a good start."

"Net-traveling?" the fat councilor queried. "You failed to mention that, Agent." He was looking at Dzok.

"I was about to reach that portion of the briefing, Excellency," Dzok said smoothly. "Bayard had made the claim that although he was transported to the Hagroon line in a Hagroon shuttle, his people have a Web drive of their own. And, indeed, he seemed to be somewhat familiar with the controls of the primitive Hagroon machine."

"This places a different complexion on matters," the official said. "Gentlemen, I suggest we take no hasty action which might prejudice future relations with a Web power—"

"We'll have no dealings with the scum!" old Sphogeel shrilled, coming to his feet. "Our present policy of expl—"

"Sit down, Councilor!" the fat member roared, jumping up to face the thin one. "I'm well aware of the policies pertaining to this situation! I suggest we refrain from announcing them to the world!"

"Whatever your policy has been in the past," I interjected into the silence, "it should be reevaluated in the light of new data. The Imperium is a Net power, but there's no need of any conflict of interest—"

"The creature lies!" Sphogeel snarled, staring at me

across the table. "We've carried out extensive reconnaissance in the entire Sapient quadrant—including the so-called Anglic Sector—and we've encountered no evidence whatever of native Web-transit capability!"

"The Zero-zero line of the Imperium lies within the region you call the Desolation," I said.

Sphogeel gasped. "You have the audacity to mention that hideous monument to your tribe's lust for destruction? That alone is sufficient grounds for your expulsion for the society of decent Hominoids!"

"How is that possible?" another asked. "Nothing lives within the Desolation..."

"Another of the debased creature's lies," Sphogeel snapped. "I demand that the Council expel this degenerate at once and place a Class Two reprimand in the file of this agent—"

"Nevertheless," I yelled the councilors down, "a number of normal lines exist in the Blight. One of them is the seat of a Net government. As an official of that government, I ask that you listen to what I have to say, and give me the assistance I ask for."

"That seems a modest enough demand," the fat member said. "Sit down, Councilor. As for you, Bayard—go ahead with your story."

Sphogeel glowered, then snapped his fingers. A half-grown youth in unadorned whites stepped forward from an inconspicuous post by the door, listened to the oldster's hissed instructions, then darted away. Sphogeel folded his arms and glowered.

"I submit," he snapped. "Under protest."

Half an hour later I had finished my account. There were questions then—some from reasonable-sounding members like the chubby one whose name was Nikodo, others mere inflammatory remarks of the "Are you still beating your wife" type. I answered them all as clearly as I could.

"We're to understand then," a truculent-looking councilor said, "that you found yourself in a null-time level of your native continuum, having arrived there by means unknown. You then observed persons, presumably Hagroon, boarding transports, preparatory to departure. You killed one of these men, stole one of their crude Web-travelers, only to find yourself trapped. Arriving at the Hagroon world line, you were placed under confinement, from which you escaped by killing a second man. You now present yourself here with the demand that you be given valuable Authority property and released to continue your activities."

"That's not fairly stated, Excellency," Dzok started, but a dirty look cut him off.

"The man is a self-confessed double murderer," Sphogeel snapped. "I think—"

"Let him speak," Nikodo barked.

"The Hagroon are up to something. I'd say an attack on the Imperium from null time would be a likely guess. If you won't give us assistance, then I'm asking that you lend me transportation home in time to give a warning—"

The young messenger slipped back into the room, went to Sphogeel, handed him a strip of paper. He glanced at it, then looked up at me with a fierce glitter in his yellow eyes.

"As I thought! The creature lies!" he rasped. "His entire fantastic story is a fabric of deceit! The Imperium, eh? A Web Power, eh? Ha!" Sphogeel thrust the paper at the next councilor, a sad-looking, pale tan creature with bushy muttonchop whiskers and no chin. He blinked at the paper, looked up at me with a startled expression, frowned, passed the paper along. When it reached Nikodo, he read it, shot me a puzzled look, reread it.

"I'm afraid I don't understand this, Bayard." His look bored into me now. His dark face was getting blackish-purple around the edges. "What did you hope to gain by attempting to delude this body?"

"Maybe if you'll tell me what you're talking about, I could shed some light on it," I said. Silently, the paper was tossed across to me. I looked at the crow tracks on it.

"Sorry. I can't read Xonijeelian."

"That should have been sufficient evidence in itself," Sphogeel growled. "Claims to be a Web operative, but has no language background..."

"Councilor Sphogeel had your statement checked out," Nikodo said coldly. "You stated that this Zero-zero world line lay at approximately our coordinates 875-259 within the area of the Desolation. Our scanners found three normal world lines within the desert—to that extent, your story contained a shred of truth. But as for coordinates 875-259..."

"Yes?" I held my voice steady with an effort.

"No such world exists. The uninterrupted sweep of the destroyed worlds blankets that entire region of the Web."

"You'd better take another look—"

"Look for yourself!" Sphogeel thrust a second paper across the table toward me—a glossy black photogram, far more detailed than the clumsy constructions used by the Imperial Net mapping service. I recognized the familiar oval shape of the Blight at once—and within it the glowing points that represented the worlds known as Blight-Insular Two and Three—and a third A-line within the Blight, unknown to me. But where the Zero-zero line should have been—was nothing.

"I think the Council has wasted sufficient time on this charlatan," someone said. "Take the fellow away."

Dzok was staring at me. "Why?" he said. "Why did you lie, Bayard?"

"The creature's purpose was clear enough," Sphogeel grated. "Ascribing his own base motivations to others, he assumed that to confess himself a citizen of a mere sub-technical race would mean he'd receive scant attention. He therefore attempted to overawe us with talk of a great Web power—a veiled threat of retaliation! Pitiful subterfuge! But nothing other than that would be expected from such a genetic inferior!"

"Your equipment's not working properly," I grated. "Take another scan—"

"Silence, criminal!" Sphogeel was on his feet again. He had no intention of losing the advantage his shock technique had gained him.

"Sphogeel has something he doesn't want known," I yelled. "He faked the shot—"

"That is not possible," Nikodo rapped out. "Wild accusations will gain you nothing, sapiens!"

"All I've asked for is a ride home." I flipped the scan photo across the table. "Take me there, and you'll see soon enough whether I'm lying!"

"Suicidal, he asks that we sacrifice a traveler and crew to play out his folly," someone boomed.

"You talk a lot about my kind's murderous instincts," I barked. "Where are the sapiens types here in this cozy little world of yours? In concentration camps, getting daily lectures on brotherly love?"

"There are no intelligent hairless forms native to Xonijeel," Nikodo snapped.

"Why not?" I rapped back at him. "Don't tell me they died out?"

"Their strain was a weak one," Nikodo said defensively. "Small, naked, ill-equipped to face the rigors of the glacial periods. None survived into the present era—"

"So you killed them off! In my world maybe it worked out the other way around—or maybe it was natural forces in both cases. Either way you slice it, it's ancient history. I suggest we make a new start now—and you can begin by checking out my story—"

"I say we put an end to this farce!" Sphogeel pounded on the table for attention. "I move the Council to a formal vote! At once!"

Nikodo waited until the talk died away. "Councilor Sphogeel has exercised his right of peremptory motion," he said heavily. "The vote will now be taken on the question, in the form proposed by the councilor."

Sphogeel was still standing. "The question takes this form," he said formally. "To grant the demands of this sapiens..." he looked around the table as though gauging the tempers of his fellows.

"He's risking his position on the wording of the Demand Vote," Dzok hissed in my ear. "He'll lose if he goes too far."

"...or, alternatively..." his eyes were on me now "...to order him transported to a sub-technical world line, to live out his natural span in isolation."

Dzok groaned. A sigh went around the table.

Nikodo muttered. "If only you'd come to us honestly, sapiens," he started—

"The vote!" Sphogeel snapped. "Take the creature outside, Agent!"

Dzok took my arm, guided me out in the corridor. The heavy panels clicked behind us.

"I don't understand at all," he said. "Telling them all that rubbish about a Web power. You've prejudiced the Council hopelessly against you—and for what?"

"I'll give you a clue, Dzok," I said. "I don't think they needed any help—they already have their opinion of Homo sapiens."

"Nikodo was strongly inclined to be sympathetic," Dzok said. "He's a powerful member. But your senseless lies—"

"Listen to me, Dzok—" I grabbed his arm. "I wasn't lying! Try to get that through your thick skull! I don't care what your instruments showed. The Imperium exists!"

"The scanner doesn't lie, sapiens," Dzok said coldly. "It would be better for you to admit your mistake and plead for mercy." He pulled his arm free and smoothed the crease in the sleeve.

"Mercy?" I laughed, not very merrily. "From the kindly Councilor Sphogeel? You people make a big thing of your happy family philosophy—but when it gets right down to practical politics, you're as ruthless as the rest of the ape-stock!"

"There's been no talk of killing," Dzok said stiffly. "Relocation will allow you to live out your life in reasonable comfort—"

"It's not my life I'm talking about, Dzok! There are three billion people living in that world you say doesn't exist. A surprise attack by the Hagroon will be a slaughter!"

"Your story makes no sense, Anglic! Your claims have been exposed for the fancies they are! There is no such world line as this Imperium of yours!"

"Your instruments need overhauling. It was there forty-eight hours ago—"

The Council Chamber doors opened. The sentry listened to someone inside, then beckoned Dzok. The agent gave me a worried look, passed inside. The two armed men came to port arms, silently took up positions on either side of me.

"What did they say?" I asked. Nobody answered. Half a minute went by, like an amputee on crutches. Then the door opened again and Dzok came out. Two of the Council Members were behind him.

"An . . . ah . . . decision has been reached, Bayard," he said stiffly. "You'll be escorted to quarters where you'll spend the night. Tomorrow . . ."

Sphogeel shouldered past him. "Hesitant about performing your duty, Agent?" he rasped. "Tell the creature, His plots are vain! The Council has voted relocation—"

It was what I had expected. I stepped back, slapped my gun into my hand—and Dzok's long arm swept down, caught me across the forearm with a blow like an axe, sent the slug gun bouncing off along the carpeted hall. I whirled, went for the short flit gun the nearest sentry was holding. I got a hand on it too—just as steel hooks clamped on me, hauled me back. A grayish-tan hand with black seal's fur on its back was in front of my face, crushing a tiny ampoule. An acrid odor hit my nostrils. I choked, tried not to breathe it in... My legs went slack as wet rope, folded. I hit the floor without feeling it. I was on my back, and Dzok was leaning over me, saying something.

"... regret... my fault, old boy..."

I made the supreme effort, moved my tongue, got out one word—"... Truth..."

Someone pushed Dzok aside. Close-set yellow eyes stared into mine. There were voices:

"... deep mnemonics..."

"... finish the job..."

"... word of honor as an officer..."

"... devil take him. An Anglic's an Anglic..."

Then I was falling, light as an inflated balloon, seeing the scene around me swell, blur, fade into a whirling of lights and darkness that dwindled and was gone.

CHAPTER SIX

I WATCHED THE PLAY of sunlight on the set of gauzy curtains at the open window for a long time before I began to think about who owned them. The recollection came hard, like a lesson learned but not used for a while. I had had a breakdown—a nervous collapse, that was it—while on a delicate mission to Louisiana—the details were vague—and now I was resting at a nursing home in Harrow, run by kindly Mrs. Rogers...

I sat up, felt a dizziness that reminded me of the last time I had spent a week flat on my back after a difficult surveillance job in...in...I had a momentary half-recollection of a strange city, and many faces, and...

It was gone. I shook my head, lay back. I was here for a rest; a nice, long rest; then, with my pension—a sudden, clear picture of my passbook showing a balance of 10,000 gold Napoleons on deposit at the Banque Crédit de Londres flashed across my mind—I could settle somewhere and take up gardening, the way I'd always wanted to...

The picture seemed to lack something, but it was too much trouble to think about it now. I looked around the room. It was small, cheery with sunlight and bright-painted furniture, with hooked rugs on the floor and a bedspread decorated with a hunting scene that suggested long winter nights spent tatting by an open fire. The door was narrow, paneled, brown-painted wood, with a light brass knob. The knob turned and a buxom woman with grey hair, cheeks like apples, a funny little hat made of lace, and a many-colored skirt that brushed the floor came in, gave a jump when she saw me, and beamed as though I'd just said she made apple pie like Mother's.

"Mr. Bayard! Ye're awake!" She had a squeaky voice as jolly as the whistle on a peanut stand, with an accent I couldn't quite place.

"And hungry, too, I'm guessing! Ye'd like a lovely bowl of soup, now would't ye, sir? And maybe a dab of pudding after."

"A nice steak smothered in mushrooms sounds better," I said. "And, ah..." I had meant to ask her who she was, but then I remembered: kindly Mrs. Rogers, of course...

"A glass of wine, if it's available," I finished, and lay back, watching little bright spots dance before me.

"Of course, and a nice hot bath first. That'll be lovely, Mr. Bayard. I'll just call Hilda..." Things were a little hazy then for a few minutes. I was vaguely aware of bustlings and the twitter of feminine voices. Hands plucked at me, tugged gently at my arms. I made an effort, got my eyes open, saw the curve of a colored apron over a girlish hip. Beyond her, the older woman was directing two husky, blonde males in maneuvering something heavy below my line of sight. The girl straightened, and I caught a glimpse of a slim waist, a nicely rounded bosom and arm, a saucy face under straight-cut hair the color of clover honey. The two men finished and left, the motherly type with them. The girl fussed about for a minute, then followed the others, leaving the door open. I got up on one elbow, saw a six-foot-long enameled bathtub half full of water placed neatly on the oval rug, a big fluffy towel, a scrub brush, and a square cake of white soap on a small stool beside it. It looked inviting. I sat up, got my legs over the side of the bed, took deep breaths until the dizziness went away, then pulled off the purple silk pajama bottoms and stood, shakily.

"Oh, ye shouldn't try to walk yet, sir!" a warm contralto voice said from the doorway. Honey-hair was back, coming toward me with a concerned look on her pert features. I made a halfhearted grab for my pants, almost fell, sat down heavily on the bed. She was beside me now, with a strong hand under my arm.

"Gunvor and I've been worried about ye, sir. The doctor said ye'd been very sick, but when ye slept all day yesterday..."

I wasn't following what she said. It's one thing to wake up in a familiar room and have a little trouble getting oriented; it's considerably different to realize that you're among total strangers, and that you have no recollection at all of how you got there...

With her assistance, I made the three steps to the tub, hesitated before tackling the climb in.

"Just put your foot in, that's right," the girl was saying. I followed orders, stepped in and sat down, feeling too weak even to wince at the hot water. The girl perched on the stool beside me, tossed her head to get her hair back, reached for my arm.

"I'm Hilda," she said. "I live just along the road. It was exciting when Gunvor phoned and told me about yer coming, sir. It isn't often we see a Louisianan here—and a diplomat, too. Ye must lead the most exciting life! I suppose ye've been in Egypt and Austria and Spain—and even in the Seminole Nation." She chattered and sudsed me, as unconcernedly as a grandmother bathing a five-year-old, and it felt good to have this lively creature briskly massaging my back with the brush while the sun shone through the window and the breeze flapped the curtain.

"... yer accident, sir?" I realized Hilda had asked a question—an awkward one. I had a powerful reluctance to admit that I had—or appeared to have—some sort of mild amnesia. I hadn't forgotten everything, of course. It was just that the details were hazy...

"Hilda—the man that brought me here—did he tell you anything about me—about the accident?..."

"The letter!" Hilda jumped up, went across to a table decorated with red, yellow, blue, and orange painted flowers, brought back a stiff square envelope.

"The doctor left this for ye, sir. I almost forgot!"

I reached for it with a wet hand, got the flap open, pulled out a single sheet of paper on a fancy letterhead, formally typed:

> Mr. Bayard,
>   It is with deep regret and expressions of the highest personal regard that I confirm herewith your retirement for disability from

the Diplomatic Service of His Imperial
Majesty, Napoleon V...

There was more—all about my faithful service and
devotion to duty, regrets that I hadn't recovered in
time for a personal send-off, and lots of hopes for a
speedy convalescence. Included was the name of the
lawyer in Paris who would answer all my questions,
and if at any time could be of assistance, etc, etc.
The name at the end was unfamiliar—but then, of
course, everybody knew Count Regis de Manin, Deputy
Foreign Minister for Security. Good old Reggie...

I read the letter twice, then folded it and crammed
it back into the envelope. My hands were quivering.

"Who gave you this?" my voice came out harsh.

"T'was the doctor, sir. They brought ye in the carriage, two nights since, and he was most particular
about ye. A pity about yer friends having to hurry to
catch the steam packet for Calais—"

"What did he look like?"

"The doctor?" Hilda resumed her scrubbing. "He
was a tall gentleman, sir, handsomely dressed, and
with a lovely voice. Dark he was, too. But I saw him
only for a moment or two, and in the gloom of the
stable-yard I couldn't make out more." She giggled.
"But I did mark his eyes were close together as two
hazelnuts in an eggcup."

"Was he alone?"

"There was the coachmen, sir—and I think another
gentleman riding inside, but—"

"Did Mrs. Rogers see them?"

"Only for a few moments, sir. They were in a
shocking hurry..."

Hilda finished with the bath, dried me, helped me into clean pajamas, helped me stagger back to bed and tucked me in. I wanted to ask questions, but sleep came down over me like a flood from a broken dam.

The next time I woke up, I felt a little more normal. I got out of bed, tottered to the closet, found a suit of strange-looking clothes with narrow trousers and wide lapels, a shirt with ruffles at collar and wrist, shoes with tiny buckles.

But of course they weren't really strange, I corrected myself. Very stylish, in fact—and new, with the tailor's tag still in the breast pocket.

I closed the closet, went to the window for a look. It was still open, and late-afternoon sun glowed in the potted geraniums on the sill. Below was a tidy garden, a brick wall, a white picket fence, and in the distance, a tall openwork church spire. There was an odor of fresh-cut hay in the air. As I watched, Hilda came around the corner with a basket in her hand and a shawl over her head. She had on a heavy, ankle-length skirt and wooden shoes painted in red and blue curlicues. She saw me and smiled up at me.

"Hello there, sir! Have you have yer sleep out, now?" She came over, lifted the basket to show me a heap of deep red tomatoes.

"Aren't they lovely, sir? I'll slice ye some for dinner."

"They look good, Hilda," I said. "How long have I been asleep?"

"This last time, sir?"

"Altogether."

"Well, ye came about midnight. After we tucked ye in, ye slept all through the next day and night, and woke this morning about ten. After yer bath ye went back, and slept till now—"

"What time is it?"

"About five—so that's another six hours and more." She laughed. "Ye've slept like one drugged, sir..."

I felt a weight slide off me like thawed snow off a steep roof. Drugged! I wasn't sick—I was doped to the eyebrows.

"I've got to talk to Gunvor," I said. "Where is she?"

"In the kitchen, plucking a fine goose for yer dinner, sir. Shall I tell her—"

"No, I'm getting dressed. I'll find her."

"Sir, are ye sure ye're feeling well enough—"

"I'm fine." I turned back to the closet, fighting the drowsiness that washed around me like thick fog. I got out the clothes, donned underwear, a loose-sleeved silk shirt and tight black pants of heavy cavalry twill, eased my feet into the slippers. Out in the narrow not-quite-straight passage papered in woodland scenes and decorated with framed tintypes, I followed the sounds of clattering crockery, pushed through a swinging door into a low-ceilinged, tile-floored room with a big black coal range, stainless steel sinks where a teen-age girl soaped dishes before a window with a flower box just outside, a glass-paneled door, a display of copper pots on the wall, and a big scrubbed-looking wooden table where Gunvor stood, working over the goose.

"Why, it's Mr. Bayard!" She blew a feather off her nose, looking flustered.

I leaned on the table for support, trying not to think about the buzzing in my head.

"Gunvor, did the doctor give you any medicine for me?"

"He did indeed, sir. The little drops for yer soup, and the white powders for yer other dishes—though since ye've taken no solid food as yet—"

"No more medicine, Gunvor." Everything was blacking out around me. I planted my feet, tried to will away the dizziness.

"Mr. Bayard, yer not strong enough yet—ye shouldn't be on yer feet!"

"Not . . . going back to bed. Need to . . . walk," I got out. "Get me outside . . ."

I felt Gunvor's arm under mine, heard her excited voice. I was vaguely aware of stumbling up steps, then the coolness of out-of-doors. I tried again, drew a couple of deep breaths, blinked away the fog.

"Better," I said. "Just walk me . . ."

Gunvor kept a running string of clucks and suggestions that I lie down right away. I ignored her, kept walking. It was a nice garden, with brick walls curving and meandering among the vegetable plots, past a rose bed along the side, under fruit trees at the far end, by a tempting bench under a thick-boled oak, and back to the kitchen door.

"Let's go around again." I tried not to lean on Gunvor this time. I was stronger; I could feel faint stirrings of appetite. The sun was sinking fast, throwing long, cool evening shadows across the grass. After the third lap, I waited by the kitchen door while Gunvor fetched a pitcher from the brown wooden icebox and poured me a glass of cool cider.

"Now ye'll sit and wait for yer dinner, Mr. Bayard," Gunvor suggested anxiously.

"I'm all right now." I patted the hand she had laid on my arm.

She watched me anxiously as I started off. I breathed deep and tried to sort out my thoughts. Someone had brought me here, drugged, arranged to keep me that way—for how long I didn't know, but I could check that by examining Gunvor's medicine supply. Someone had also been tinkering with my memory. The question of who—and why—needed answering.

I made an effort to cut through the fog, place an authentic recollection. It was June here, I judged, from the tender leaves and the budding roses. Where had I been in May, or last winter? . . .

Icy streets, tall buildings grim in the winter night, but inside, warmth, cheer, color, the laughing faces of friendly people and the smile of a beautiful redhead, named . . . named . . .

I couldn't remember. The almost-recollection slipped away like a wisp of smoke in a sudden breeze. Someone had done a good job—using deep hypnotics, no doubt—of burying my recollections under a layer of false memories. Still, they hadn't done as well as they thought. It had taken me only a few hours to throw off the nebulous impressions of a dubious past. Perhaps—

I turned, hurried back to the house. Gunvor was hesitating over a plate of fresh-baked pastries. She ducked something under her apron as I stepped into the room.

"Oh! Ye startled me, sir . . ."

I went across and removed a saltshaker half-filled with a coarse white powder from her hand, tossed it into the wastebasket.

"No more medicine, I said, Gunvor," I patted her reassuringly. "I know the doctor gave you instructions, but I don't need it any more. But tell me, is there a..." I groped for a word. I didn't want to alarm her by asking for a brain doctor, and she wouldn't understand "psychiatrist." "A hypnotist?" I waited for signs of comprehension. "Someone who talks to troubled people, soothes them—"

"Ah, ye mean a mesmerist! But there's none here in the village, alas... Only Mother Goodwill," she added doubtfully.

"Mother Goodwill?" I prompted.

"I've nothing against her, mind ye, sir—but there's those that talk of witchcraft. And I was reading just the other day in the Paris *Match* that ye can develop serious neuroses by letting unqualified practitioners meddle with yer psyche."

"You're so right, Gunvor," I agreed. "But it's only a little matter of a faulty memory—"

"Are ye troubled with that too, sir?" Her face lit up. "I'm that forgetful meself, sometimes I think I should have something done—but then a regular mesmerist's so dear, and as for these quacks—"

"What about Mother Goodwill? Does she live near here?"

"At the other end of the village, sir. But I wouldn't recommend her—not for a cultured gentleman like yerself. Her cottage is very plain, and the old woman herself is something less than a credit to our village. Dowdy, she is, sir—no sense of style at all. And as for clothes—"

"I won't be overly critical, Gunvor. Will you take me to her?"

"I'll summon her here, sir, if ye're determined—but there's a licensed master mesmerist in Ealing, just an hour by coach—"

"Mother Goodwill will do, I think. How soon can you get her here?"

"I'll send Ingalill—but if it's all the same to ye, sir, let me have her up after dinner. I've just popped me goose in, and the pies are browning even now—"

"After dinner will be fine. I'll take a few more turns around the garden and develop an appetite worthy of your cooking."

After a second slab of blackberry pie buried in cream too thick to pour, a final mug of ground-at-the-table coffee, and a healthy snort of brandy with the flavor of a century in a dark cellar safely under my belt, I lit up a New Orleans cigar and watched as Hilda and Gunvor lit the oil lamps in the sitting room. There was a timid tap at the door, and Ingalill, the kitchen slavey, poked her face in.

"The old witch is here," she piped. "Gunvor, she's smoking a pipe. I think it's got ground-up salamander innards in it—"

"She'll hear ye, ye wretch," Hilda said. "Tell her to wait until her betters summon her—"

Ingalill yelped and jumped aside, and a bent-backed ancient in a poke bonnet pushed in past her, one gnarled hand gripping a crooked stick on which she leaned. Bright black eyes darted about the room, lit on me. I stared back, taking in the warty nose, toothless gums, out-thrust chin, and wisp of white hair hanging beside one hollow cheek. I didn't see a pipe, but as I watched she snorted a last wisp of smoke from her nostrils.

"Who has need of Mother Goodwill's healing touch?" she quavered. "But, of course, it'd be ye, sir, who's come such a strange, long way—and with a stranger, longer path still ahead..."

"Phooie, I told you it was the new gentleman," Ingalill said. "What's in the basket?" She reached to lift a corner of the red and white checked cloth covering the container, yelped as the stick cracked across her knuckles.

"Mind yer manners, dearie," Mother Goodwill said sweetly. She shuffled to a chair, sank down, put the basket on the floor at her feet.

"Now, Mother Goodwill," Gunvor said, sounding agitated. "The gentleman only wants a little help with—"

"He'd draw aside the veil of the past, the future to read more clearly," the crone piped. "Ah, he did well to call on old Mother Gee. Now..." her tone became more brisk. "If ye'll pour me a dram, Gunvor, to restore me strength a mite—and then ye'll all have to clear out—except m'lord, the new gentleman, o' course." She grinned at me like a meat-eating bird.

"I'm not interested in the future," I started—

"Are ye not, sir?" the old woman nodded as though agreeing. "Then it's a strange mortal ye are—"

"...But there are some things I need to remember," I bored on, ignoring the sales pitch. "Maybe under light hypnosis I can—"

"So...then it's the past ye'd glimpse, as I thought," she commented imperturbably. Gunvor was clicking glasses at the sideboard. She came over and handed the old woman a glass, then got busy clearing dishes from the table, with Ingalill and Hilda working silently beside her.

Mother Goodwill smacked her lips over the brandy, then waved an oversized brown-spotted hand.

"Away with ye, now, me chicks!" she quavered. "I feel the spirit coming over me! The power's flowing in the celestial field-coil! Strange visions are stirring, like phantom vipers in a pot! What's this! What's this! Ai, curious indeed, the things the spirits whisper to me now..."

"Hmmmp! Ye can skip the spirits routine," Hilda said. "All Mr. Bayard wants from ye—"

"Get along with ye, girl," the old woman snapped, "or I'll send a cramp that'll lock yer knees together that tight the fairest swain this side o' Baghdad'll not unlock 'em! All o' ye! Off, now!"

They went. Then the hag turned to me.

"Now, down to business, sir." She used a wheedling tone. "What were ye thinking o' giving the old woman for a handful of lost recollections? Is it a lover ye've forgot, the raptures of youth, the key to happiness once glimpsed and now forever gone a-glimmering?"

I was grinning at her. "You'll be well paid, but let's skip the rest of the routine. I'll get straight to the point. I have reason to believe I'm suffering from induced amnesia, probably the result of post-hypnotic suggestion. I'd like you to put me under and see if you can counter the block."

Mother Goodwill leaned forward, looked at me keenly.

"There's a strangeness about ye—something I can't put me finger on. It's as though yer eyes was focused on a horizon that other men can't see..."

"Granted I'm a strange character, but not so strange you can't hypnotize—or mesmerize me, I hope."

"Ye say ye've been tampered with, yer memories taken from ye. Who'd've done a thing like that to ye, lad—and why?"

"Maybe if you're successful, I'll find out."

She nodded briskly. "I've heard of such things. Spells of darkness, cast by the light of a bloodred moon—"

"Mother Goodwill," I cut in. "Let's get one thing straight: every time you mention spells, magic, dark powers, or geese, the fee goes down. I'm interested in straight scientific mesmerism. Okay?"

"What, good sir? Would ye tell the Mistress of Darkness how to ply her trade?"

The routine was beginning to get tiresome. "Maybe we'd better forget the whole thing." I reached in my pocket for a coin. "My mistake..."

"Are ye saying Mother Goodwill's a fraud, then?" Her voice had taken on a suspiciously mild note. I looked at her, caught a glint of light from an eye as black and bright as a polished opal. "D'ye think the old woman's out to trick ye, to play ye false, to gull ye fer a new fledged chick, to..." her voice droned on, coming from far away now, booming like surf in a sea cave echoing, echoing...

"...ten!"

My eyes snapped open. A woman with a pale, almost beautiful face sat, leaning pensively on one elbow, a cigarette in her hand, watching me. Her dark hair was done up in a tight bun. Her plain white blouse was open at the collar, showing a strong, graceful neck. There was one dark curl against her forehead.

I looked around the room; it was dark outside now; a clock was ticking loudly somewhere.

"What happened to the old beldame?" I blurted.

The woman smiled faintly, waved a well-manicured hand toward a black cape on the chair beside her, a gnarled stick leaning against it.

"Rather warm for working in," she said in a low voice. "How are you feeling?"

I considered. "Fine. But—" I caught a glimpse of a wisp of stringy grey hair under the edge of the cloak. I got out of my chair, went over and lifted it. There was a warty rubber mask, a pair of gnarly gloves.

"What's the idea of the getup?"

"I find it helpful in my...business. Now—"

"You fooled me in a bad light," I said. "I take it Gunvor and the others are in on the gag?"

She shook her head. "No one ever sees me in a good light, Mr. Bayard—and no one wishes to approach too close, even then. They're simple people hereabouts. In their thoughts, warts and wisdom go together—so I fit their image of a village mesmerist, else none would seek my skill. You're the only one who shares my little secret."

"Why me?"

She looked at me searchingly. "You are a most unusual man, Mr. Bayard. A true man of mystery. You talked to me—of many things. Strange things. You spoke of other worlds, like this our own familiar plane, but different, alien. You talked of men like animals, clothed in shaggy hair—"

"Dzok!" I burst out. My hands went to my head as though to squeeze the recollections from my brain like toothpaste from a tube. "The Hagroon, and—"

"Calmly, calmly, Mr. Bayard," the woman soothed. "Your memories—if true memories they are, and not fever fancies—are there, intact, ready to be recalled. Rest, now. It was not easy for either of us, this stripping away of veils from your mind. A master mesmerist indeed was he who sought to bury your visions of strange paradises and unthinkable hells—but all lies exposed now." I looked down at her and she smiled.

"I am no journeyman practitioner myself," she murmured. "But all my skill was challenged this night." She rose, went to a framed mirror on the wall, gracefully tucked back a strand of hair. I watched her without seeing her. Thoughts of Barbro, the flaming figure in the dark storeroom, the escape with Dzok from the Hagroon cell were jostling each other, clamoring to be remembered, thought about, evaluated.

Mother Goodwill plucked her cape from the chair, swirled it about her shoulders, hunching into the posture of the hag she had been. Her white hands slipped the mask in place, fitting it to her nose and mouth. The gloves and wig followed, and now the bright eyes gazed at me from the wrinkled face of age.

"Rest, sir," the ancient face cackled. "Rest, sleep, dream, and let those restless thoughts seek out and know their familiar places once again. I'll attend ye on the morrow—there's more that Mother Goodwill would learn of the universes ye've told me lurk beyond the threshold of this drab world."

"Wait," I said. "I haven't paid you . . ."

She waved a veined hand. "Ye've paid me well in the stuff visions are wrought on, sir. Sleep, I say—and awake refreshed, strong, with your wits keened to razor's edge. For ye'll be needing all yer strength to face what waits ye in the days yet undawned."

She went out then. I went along the hall to my dark room, threw my clothes on a chair, fell into the feather-mattressed bed, and sank down into troubled dreams.

CHAPTER SEVEN

IT WAS THREE DAYS before I felt strong enough to pay my call on Mother Goodwill. Her cottage was a thatch-roofed rectangle of weathered stone almost lost under a tangle of wrist-sized rose vines heavy with deep red blossoms. I squeezed through a rusted gate, picked my way along a path overhung with untrimmed rhododendron, lifted the huge brass knocker, clanked it against the low black oak door. Through the one small, many-paned window, I caught a glimpse of the corner of a table, a pot of forget-me-nots, a thick leather-bound book. There was a humming of bees in the air, a scent of flowers, and a whiff of fresh-brewed coffee. Not the traditional setting for calling on a witch, I thought...

The door opened. Mother Goodwill, looking neat in a white shirt and peasant skirt, favored me with a sad smile, motioning me in.

"No Halloween costume today," I commented.

"You're feeling better, Mr. Bayard," she said dryly.

"Will you have a mug of coffee? Or is't not customary in your native land?"

I shot her a sharp look. "Skeptical already?"

Her shoulders lifted and dropped. "I believe what my senses tell me. Sometimes they seem to contradict each the other." I took a chair at the table, glanced around the small room. It was scrupulously clean and tidy, furnished with the kind of rustic authenticity that would have had the ladies of the DAR back home oohing and aahing and overworking the word "quaint." Mother Goodwill brought the pot over, poured two cups, put cream and sugar on the table, then sat.

"Well, Mr. Bayard, is your mind clear this morning, your remembrance well restored?"

I nodded, tried the coffee. It was good.

"Don't you have some other name I could call you?" I asked. "Mother Goodwill goes with the fright wig and the warts."

"You may call me Olivia." She had slim, white hands, and on one finger a fine green stone twinkled. She sipped her coffee and looked at me, as though making up her mind to tell me something.

"You were going to ask me questions," I prompted her. "After I've answered them, maybe you'll clear up a few matters for me."

"Many were the wonders you babbled of in your delirium," she said. I heard a tiny clatter, glanced at her cup; a fine tremor was rattling it against the saucer. She put it down quickly, ducked her hands out of sight.

"Oft have I sensed that there was more to existence than this..." she waved a hand to take in everything. "In dreams I've glimpsed enchanted hills and my heart yearned out to them, and I'd wake with the pain of something beautiful and lost that haunted me long after. I think in your wild talk, there was that which made a certain hope spring up again—a hope long forgotten, with the other hopes of youth. Now tell me, stranger, that talk of other worlds, like each to other as new-struck silver pieces, yet each with a tiny difference—and of a strange coach, with the power to fly from one to the next—all this was fancy, eh? The raving of a mind sore vexed with meddling—"

"It's true—Olivia," I cut in. "I know it's hard to grasp at first. I seem to recall I was a bit difficult to convince once. We're accustomed to thinking we know everything. There's a powerful tendency to disbelieve anything that doesn't fit the preconception."

"You spoke of trouble, Brion . . ." she spoke my name easily, familiarly. I suppose sharing someone's innermost thoughts tends to relax formalities. I didn't mind. Olivia without her disguise was a charming woman, in spite of her severe hairdo and prison pallor. With a little sunshine and just a touch of makeup—

I pulled myself back to the subject at hand.

She listened attentively as I told her the whole story, from Richthofen's strange interrogation to my sentencing by the Xonijeelians.

"So I'm stuck," I finished. "Without a shuttle, I'm trapped here for the rest of my days."

She shook her head. "These are strange things, Brion, things I should not believe, so wild and fantastic are they. And yet—I do believe . . ."

"From what little I've learned of this world line, it's backward technologically—"

"Why, we're a very modern people," Olivia said. "We have steam power—the ships on the Atlantic run make the crossing in nine days—and there are the balloons, the telegraph, and telephone, our modern coal-burning road cars which are beginning to replace the horse in many parts of the colonies, even—"

"Sure, I know, Olivia—no offense intended. Let's just say that in some areas we're ahead of you. The Imperium has the M-C drive. My own native world has nuclear power, jet aircraft, radar, and a primitive space program. Here you've gone in other directions. The point is, I'm stranded here. They've exiled me to a continuum I can never escape from."

"Is it so ill then, Brion? You have a whole world here before you—and now that the artificial barriers have been cleansed from your mind, you'll freely recall these wonders you left behind!" She was speaking eagerly now, excited at the prospect. "You spoke of aircraft. Build one! How marvelous to fly in the sky like a bird! Your coming here could mean the dawn of a new Age of Glory for the Empire!"

"Uh-huh," I said ungraciously. "That's great. But what about *my* world? By now the Hagroon have probably launched their attack—and maybe succeeded with it! My wife may be wearing chains now instead of pearls!" I got up, stamped over to the window and stared out. "While I rot here, in this backwater world," I snarled.

"Brion," she said softly behind me. "You find yourself troubled—not so much by the threat of your beloved friends as by the quality of remoteness these matters have taken on..."

I turned. "What do you mean, remote? Barbro, my friends, in the hands of these ape-men—"

"Those who tampered with your mind, Brion, sought to erase these things from your memory. True, my skill availed to lift the curse—but 'tis no wonder that they seem to you now as old memories, a tale told long ago. And I myself gave a command to you while yet you slept, that the pain of loss be eased—"

"The pain of loss be damned! If I hadn't been fool enough to trust Dzok—"

"Poor Brion. Know you not yet it was he who gulled you while you slept, planted the desire to go with him to Xonijeel? Yet he did his best for you—or so your memory tells."

"I could have taken the shuttle back," I said flatly. "At least I'd have been there, to help fight the bastards off."

"And yet, the wise ones, the monkey-men of Xonijeel, told you that this Zero-zero world did not exist—"

"They're crazy!" I took a turn up and down the room. "There's too much here I don't understand, Olivia! I'm like a man wandering in the dark, banging into things that he can't quite get his hands on. And now—" I raised my hands and let them fall, suddenly inexpressibly weary.

"You have your life still ahead, Brion. You will make a new place for yourself here. Accept that which cannot be changed."

I came back and sat down.

"Olivia, I haven't asked Gunvor and the others many questions. I didn't want to arouse curiosity by my ignorance. The indoctrination Dzok and his boys gave me didn't cover much—just enough to get me started. I suppose they figured I'd get to a library and brief myself. Tell me something about this world. Fill me in on your history, to start with."

She laughed—an unexpectedly merry sound.

"How charming, Brion—to be called upon to describe

this humdrum old world as though it were a dreamer's fancy—a might-have-been, instead of dull reality."

I managed a sour smile. "Reality's always a little dull to whoever's involved in it."

"Where shall I begin? With Ancient Rome? The Middle Ages?"

"The first thing to do is establish a Common History date—the point at which your world diverged from mine. You mentioned 'The Empire.' What empire? When was it founded?"

"Why, the Empire of France, of course..." Olivia blinked, then shook her head. "But then, nothing is 'of course'," she said. "I speak of the Empire established by Bonaparte, in 1799."

"So far so good," I said. "We had a Bonaparte, too. But his empire didn't last long. He abdicated and was sent off to Elba in 1814—"

"Yes—but he escaped, returned to France, and led his armies to glorious victory!"

I was shaking my head. "He was free for a hundred days, until the British defeated him at Waterloo. He was sent to St. Helena and died a few years later."

Olivia stared at me. "How strange...how eerie, and how strange. The Emperor Napoleon ruled in splendor at Paris for twenty-three years after his great victory at Brussels, and died in 1837 at Nice. He was succeeded by his son, Louis—"

"The Duke of Reichstadt?"

"No; the Duke died in his youth, of consumption. Louis was a boy of sixteen, the son of the Emperor and the Princess of Denmark."

"And his Empire still exists," I mused.

"After the abdication of the English tyrant George,

the British Isles were permitted to enter the Empire as a special ward of the Emperor. After the unification of Europe, enlightenment was brought to the Asians and Africans. Today, they are semiautonomous provinces, administered from Paris, but with their own local Houses of Deputies empowered to deal with internal matters. As for New France—or Louisiana—this talk of rebellion will soon die down. A royal commission has been sent to look into the complaints against the Viceroy."

"I think we've got the C. H. date pretty well pinned down," I said. "Eighteen-fourteen. And it looks as though there's been no significant scientific or technological progress since."

This prompted questions which I answered at length. Olivia was an intelligent and well-educated woman. She was enthralled by my picture of a world without the giant shadow of Bonaparte falling across it.

The morning had developed into the drowsy warmth of noon by the time I finished. Olivia offered me lunch and I accepted. While she busied herself at the wood-burning stove, I sat by the window, sipping a stone mug of brown beer, looking out at this curious, anachronistic landscape of tilled fields, a black-topped road along which a horse pulled a rubber-tired carriage, the white and red dots of farmhouses across the valley. There was an air of peace and plenty that made my oddly distant recollection of the threat to the Imperium seem, as Olivia said, like a half-forgotten story, read long ago—like something in the book lying on the table. I picked up the fat, red leather-bound volume, glanced at the title:

THE SORCERESS OF OZ,
by Lyman F. Baum

"That's funny," I said.

Olivia glanced over at the book in my hands, smiled almost shyly.

"Strange reading matter for a witch, you think? But on these fancies my own dreams sometimes love to dwell, Brion. As I told you, this one narrow world seems not enough—"

"It's not that, Olivia. We've pretty well established that our C. H. date is early in the nineteenth century. Baum wasn't born until about 1855 or so—nearly half a century later. But here he is..."

I flipped the book open, noted the publisher—Wiley & Cotton, New York, New Orleans, and Paris—and the date: 1896.

"You know this book, in your own strange world?" Olivia asked.

I shook my head. "In my world he never wrote this one..." I was admiring the frontispiece by W. W. Denslow, showing a Glinda-like figure facing a group of gnomes. The next page had an elaborate initial "I" at the top, followed by the words: "'... summoned you here,' said Sorana the Sorceress, 'to tell you...'"

"It was my favorite book as a child," Olivia said. "But if you know it not, how then do you recognize the author's name?"

"He wrote others. THE WIZARD OF OZ was the first book I ever read all the way through."

"The Wizard of Oz? Not Sorceress? How enchanting it would be to read it!"

"Is this the only one he wrote?"

"Sadly, yes. He died the following year—1897."

"Eighteen ninety-seven; that could mean..." I trailed off. The fog that had been hanging over my mind for days since I had awakened here was rapidly dissipating in the brisk wind of a sudden realization: Dzok and his friends had relocated me, complete with phony memories to replace the ones they'd tried to erase, in a world-line as close as possible to my own. They'd been clever, thorough, and humane. But not quite as clever as they thought, a bit less thorough in their research than they should have been—and altogether too humane.

I remembered the photogram the councilors had shown me—and the glowing point, unknown to Imperial Net cartographers, which represented a fourth, undiscovered world lying within the Blight. I had thought at the time that it was an error, along with the other, greater error that had omitted—the Zero-zero line of the Imperium.

But it had been no mistake. B-I Four existed—a world with a Common History date far more recent than the 15th century—the C. H. date of the closest lines beyond the Blight.

And I was there—or here—in a world where, in 1897 at least one man known in my own world had existed. And if one, why not another—or two others: Maxoni and Cocini, inventors of the M-C drive.

"Could mean what, Brion?" Olivia's voice jarred me back to the present.

"Nothing. Just a thought." I put the book down. "I suppose it's only natural that even fifty years after a major divergence, not everything would have been affected. Some of the same people would be born..."

"Brion," Olivia looked at me across the room. "I won't ask you to trust me, but let me help you."

"Help me with what?" I tried to recapture the

casual expression I'd been wearing up until a moment before, but I could feel it freezing on my face like a mud pack.

"You have made a plan; I sense it. Alone, you cannot succeed. There is too much that is strange to you here, too many pitfalls to betray you. Let me lend you what help I can."

"Why should you want to help me—if I were planning something?"

She looked at me for a minute without answering, her dark eyes wide in her pale, classic face.

"I've spent my life in search for a key to some other world . . . some dreamworld of my mind. Somehow, you seem to be a link, Brion. Even if I can never go there, it would please me to know I'd helped someone to reach the unattainable shore."

"They're all worlds, just like this one, Olivia. Some better, some worse—some much, much worse. They're all made up of people and earth and buildings, the same old natural laws, the same old human nature. You can't find your dreamworld by packing up and moving on; you've got to build it where you are."

"And yet—I see the ignorance, the corruption, the social and moral decay, the lies, the cheats, the treachery of those who hold the trust of the innocent—"

"Sure—and until we've evolved a human society to match our human intelligence, those things will exist. But give us time, Olivia—we've only been experimenting with culture for a few thousand years. A few thousand more will make a lot of difference."

She laughed. "You speak as though an age were but a moment."

"Compared with the time it took us to evolve from

an amoeba to an ape—or even from the first Homo sapiens to the first tilled field—it *is* a moment. But don't give up your dreams. They're the force that carries us on toward whatever our ultimate goal is."

"Then let me lend that dream concrete reality. Let me help you, Brion. The story they told me—that you had fallen ill from overwork as an official of the Colonial Office, that you were here for a rest cure—'tis as thin as a Parisian nightdress! And, Brion..." She lowered her voice. "You are watched."

"Watched? By whom—a little man with a beard and dark glasses?"

"'Tis no jest, Brion! I saw a man last night lurking by the gate at Gunvor's house—and half an hour since, a man well muffled up in scarves passed in the road yonder, as you supped coffee."

"That doesn't prove anything—"

She shook her head impatiently. "You plan to fly, I know that. I know also that your visit to me will arouse the curiosity of those who prison you here—"

"Prison me? Why, I'm as free as a bird—"

"You waste time, Brion," she cut me off. "What deed you committed, or why, I know not; but in a contest between you and drab officialdom, I'll support your cause. Now, quickly, Brion! Where will you go? How will you travel? What plan will—"

"Hold on, Olivia! You're jumping to conclusions!"

"And jump you must, if you'd evade the hounds of the hunter! I sense danger, closing about you as a snare about the roebuck's neck!"

"I've told you, Olivia—I was exiled here by the Xonijeelian Council. They didn't believe my story—or pretended not to. They dumped me here to be rid of me—they fancy themselves as humane, you know. If they'd meant to kill me, they had every opportunity to do so—"

"They sought to mesmerize your knowledge of the past away; now they watch, their results to judge. And when they see you restive, familiar of a witch—"

"You're no witch—"

"As such all know me here. 'Twas an ill gambit that brought you here by daylight, Brion—"

"If I'd crept out at midnight, they'd have seen me anyway—if they're watching me as you seem to think—and they'd have known damned well I wasn't satisfied with their hand-painted picture of my past."

"In any case, they'll like it not. They'll come again, take you away, and once again essay to numb your knowledge of the worlds, and of your past."

I thought that over. "They might, at that," I said. "I don't suppose it was part of their relocation program to have me spreading technical knowledge among the primitives."

"Where will you go, Brion?"

I hesitated; but what the hell, Olivia was right. I had to have help. And if she intended to betray me, she had plenty on me already.

"Rome," I said.

She nodded. "Very well. What is the state of your purse?"

"I have a bank account—"

"Leave that. Luckily, I have my store of gold Napoleons buried in the garden."

"I don't want your money—"

"Nonsense. We'll both need it. I'm going with you."

"You can't—"

"Can, and will!" she said, her dark eyes alight. "Make ready, Brion! We leave this very night!"

"This is crazy," I whispered to the dark, hooded figure standing beside me on the shadowed path. "There's no reason for you to get involved in this..."

"Hush," Olivia said softly. "Now he grows restless. See him there? I think he'll cross the road now, more closely to spy us out."

I watched the dense shadows, made out the figure of a man. He moved off, crossed the road a hundred yards below the cottage, disappeared among the trees on our side. I shifted my weight carefully, itching under the wild getup Olivia had assembled for me— warty face, gnarly hands, stringy white hair, and all. I looked like Mother Goodwill's older brother—as ill-tempered an old duffer as ever gnashed his gums at the carryings-on of the younger generation. Olivia was done up like Belle Watling in three layers of paint, a fancy red wig, a purple dress that fit her trim figure like wet silk, and enough bangles, rings, beads and tinkly earrings to stock a gyfte shoppe.

"Hist—he steals closer now," my co-conspirator whispered. "Another half minute..."

I waited, listening to the monotonous chirrup of crickets in a nearby field, the faraway *oo-mau* of a cow, the yapping of a farm dog. After dark, the world belonged to the animals.

Olivia's hand touched mine. "Now..." I followed as she stepped silently off. I had to crouch slightly to keep below the level of the ragged hedge. There was no moon, only a little faint starlight to help us pick a way along the rutted dirt road. We reached the end of the hedge, and I motioned Olivia back, stole a look toward the house. A head was clearly silhouetted against the faint light from the small side window.

"It's okay," I said in a low voice. "He's at the window—"

There was a crunch of gravel, and a light snapped on, played across the ruts, flashed over me, settled on Olivia.

"Here, woman," a deep voice growled. "What're ye doing abroad after bell-toll?"

Olivia planted a hand on her hip, tossed her head, not neglecting to smile archly.

"Aoow, Capting," she purred. "Ye fair give me a turn! It's only me old gaffer, what oi'm seein orf to the rile-trine."

"Gaffer, is it?" The light dwelt on me again briefly, went back to caress Olivia's sequined bosom. "Haven't seen ye about the village before. Where ye from?"

"I float about, as ye might say, Major. A tourist, like, ye might call me—"

"On shank's mare, in the middle of the night? Queer idea o' fun, I call it—and with yer gaffer, too. Better let me see yer identity papers, ducks."

"Well, as it 'appens, I come away in such a rush, they seem to 'ave got left behind . . ."

"Like that, is't?" I heard a snort from the unseen man behind the light—one of the roving security police who were a fixture of this world, I guessed. "Run off with a fistful o' spoons, did ye? Or maybe lifted one purse too many—"

"Nofink o' that sort! What cheek! I'm an honest, licensed tart, plyin 'er profession and keeping her old gaffer, what oi'm the sole support of!"

"Never mind, love. I won't take ye in. A wee sample of yer wares, and I'll forget I ever saw ye." He came close, and a big hand reached out toward Olivia. She let out a sharp squeak and jumped back. The cop brushed past me. I caught a glimpse of a tricorn hat, a beak nose, loose jowls, a splash of color on the collar of the uniform. I picked my spot, chopped down hard across the base of his neck with the side of my hand. He yelped, dropped the light, stumbled to hands and knees. The stiff collar had protected him from the full force of the blow. He scrambled, trying to rise; I followed, kicked him square under the chin. He back-flipped and sprawled out, unconscious. I grabbed up the light and found the switch, flicked it off.

"Is he...badly hurt?" Olivia was staring at the smear of blood at the corner of the slack mouth.

"He'll have trouble asking for bribes for a few weeks." I pulled Olivia back toward the hedgerow. "Let's hope our snooper didn't hear anything."

We waited for a minute, then started off again, hurrying now. Far away, a spark of wavering, yellowish light moved across the slope of the hill beyond the village.

"That's the train," Olivia said. "We'll have to hurry!"

We walked briskly for fifteen minutes, passed the darkened shops at the edge of town, reached the station just as the puffing coal-burner pulled in. A severe-looking clerk in a dark uniform with crossed chest straps and coattails accepted Olivia's money, wrote out tickets by hand, pointed out our car. Inside we found wide seats upholstered in green plush. We were the only passengers. I leaned back in my seat with a sigh. The train whistle shrilled, a lurch ran through the car.

"We're on our way," Olivia breathed. She looked ecstatic, like a kid at the fair.

"We're just going to Rome," I said. "Not the land of Oz."

"Who can say whither the road of the future leads?"

Chapter Eight

AT THE ALBERGO ROMULUS, Olivia and I had adjoining rooms well up under the eaves, with ceilings that slanted down to a pair of dormer windows opening onto a marketplace with a handsome Renaissance fountain, the incessant flutter of pigeons' wings, and a day and night shrilling of excited Italian voices. We were sitting at the small table in my room, eating a late breakfast of pizzas, washed down with a musty red wine that cost so little that even the local begging corps could afford to keep a mild buzz on most of the time.

"The two men I'm interested in were born somewhere in northern Italy about 1850," I told Olivia. "They came to Rome as young men, studied engineering and electronics, and in 1893 made the basic discovery that gave the Imperium the Net drive. I'm gambling that if Baum managed to get himself born, and in the nineties was writing something pretty close to what he did in my world—and in the Zero-zero A-line too—then maybe Maxoni and Cocini existed here too. They didn't perfect the M-C drive, obviously—or if they did, the secret died with them—but maybe they came close. Maybe they left something I can use."

"Brion, did you not tell me that all the worlds that lie about your Zero-zero line are desolate, blasted into ruin by these very forces? Is it safe to tamper with such fell instruments as these?"

"I'm a fair shuttle technician, Olivia. I know most of the danger points. Maxoni and Cocini didn't realize what they were playing with. They stumbled on the field by blind luck—"

"And in a thousand million other worlds of might-have-been they failed, and brought ruin in their wake..."

"You knew all this when we left Harrow," I said shortly. "It's my only chance—and a damned poor chance it is, I'll admit. But I can't build a shuttle from scratch—there's a specially wound coil that's the heart of the field-generator. I've installed 'em, but I never tried to wind one. Maybe—if there was a Maxoni here, and a Cocini—and they made the same chance discovery—and they wrote up their notes like good little researchers—and the notes still exist—and I can find them—"

Olivia laughed—a charming, girlish laugh. "If the gods decree that all those *ifs* are in your favor—why then 'tis plain, they mean you to press on. I'll risk it, Brion. The vision of the Sapphire City still beckons me."

"It's the Emerald City, where I come from," I said. "But we won't quibble over details. Let's see if we can find those notes first. We'll have plenty of time then to decide what to do with them."

An hour later, at the local equivalent of a municipal

record center, a tired-looking youth in a narrow-cut black suit showed me a three-foot ledger in which names were written in spidery longhand—thousands of names, followed by dates, places of birth, addresses, and other pertinent details.

"*Sicuro, Signore,*" he said in a tone of weary superiority, "the municipality, having nothing to hide, throws open to you its records—among the most complete archives in existence in the Empire—but as for reading them..." he smirked, tweaked his hairline mustache. "That the Signore must do for himself."

"Just explain to me what I'm looking at," I suggested gently. "I'm looking for a record of Giulio Maxoni, or Carlo Cocini—"

"Yes, yes, so you said. And here before you is the registration book in which the names of all new arrivals in the city were recorded at the time identity papers were issued. They came to Rome in 1870, you said—or was it 1880? You seemed uncertain. As for me..." he spread his hands. "I am even more uncertain. I have never heard of these relatives—or friends—or ancestors—or whatever they might be. In them, you, it appears, have an interest. As for me—I have none. There is the book, covering the decade in question. Look all you wish. But do not demand miracles of me! I have duties to perform!" His voice developed an irritated snap on the last words. He strutted off to sulk somewhere back in the stacks. I grunted and started looking.

Twenty minutes passed quietly. We worked our way through 1870, started on 1871. The busy archivist peered out once to see what we were doing, withdrew after a sour look. Olivia and I stood at the wooden counter, poring over the crabbed longhand, each taking one page of about two hundred names. She was a faster reader; before I had finished my page, she had turned to the next. Half a minute later she gave a sharp gasp.

"Brion! Look! Giulio Maxoni, born 1847 at Paglio; trade, artificer—"

I looked. It was the right name. I tried not to let myself get too excited—but my pulse picked up in spite of the voice of prudence whispering in my ear that there might be hundreds of Giulio Maxonis.

"Nice work, girl," I said in a cool, controlled voice that only broke twice on the three words. "What address?"

She read it off. I jotted it down in a notebook I had thoughtfully provided for the purpose, added the other data from the ledger. We searched for another hour, but found no record of Cocini. The clerk came back and hovered, as though we'd overstayed our welcome. I closed the book and shoved it across the counter to him.

"Don't sweat it, Jack," I said genially. "We're just making up a sucker list for mailings on budget funerals."

"Mailings?" He stared at me suspiciously. "Municipal records are not intended for such uses—and in any event—these people are all long since dead!"

"Exactly," I agreed. "A vast untapped market for our line of goods. Thanks heaps. I'll make a note to give you special treatment when your time comes."

We walked away in a silence you could have cut into slabs with a butter knife.

Maxoni had lived at number twelve, Via Carlotti, fourth floor, number nine. With the aid of a street map purchased from an elderly entrepreneur in a beret and a soiled goatee who offered us a discount on racy postcards, which I declined with regret, we found it—a narrow alley, choked with discarded paper cartons, vegetable rinds, overflowing garbage barrels, and shoeless urchins who dodged madly among the obstacles, cheerfully exchanging badinage which would have made Mussolini blush. Number twelve was a faded late Renaissance front of rusticated granite wedged between sagging, boarded-up warehouses no more than a hundred or so years old. Maxoni, it appeared, had started his career in the most modest quarters available. Even a century ago, this had been a slum. I pushed open the caked door, stepped into a narrow hall reeking of garlic, cheese, decay, and less pleasant things.

"It looks terrible, Brion," Olivia said. "Perhaps we'd best make enquiries first—"

A door opened and a round, olive face set in cushions of fat looked out, and launched into a stream of rapid Italian.

"Your pardon, Madam," I replied in the courtly accents I had learned from the Roman Ambassador to the Imperial court. "We are but foreigners, visiting the Eternal City for the first time. We seek the apartment where once our departed relative dwelt, long ago, when the gods favored him with the privilege of breathing the sweet air of sunny Italy."

Her jaw dropped; she stared; then a grin the size of a ten lira pizza spread across her face.

"*Buon giorno, Signore e Signorina!*" She squeezed out into the hall, pumped our hands, yelled instructions back into her flat—from which a mouth-watering

aroma of ravioli emanated—and demanded to know
how she could serve the illustrious guests of fair
Italy. I gave her the number of the apartment where
Maxoni had lived, ninety-odd years before, and she
nodded, started up the narrow stair, puffing like the
steam-engine that we had ridden across Europe for
two days and nights. Olivia followed and I brought
up the rear; admiring the deposits of broken glass,
paper, rags and assorted rubbish that packed every
step and landing, with a trail winding up through
the center worn by the feet of centuries of tenants.
I would have given odds that the bits Maxoni might
have contributed were still there, somewhere.

At the top, we went along a narrow hall, past
battered-looking doors with white china knobs, stopped
at the one at the end.

"There is a tenant, Signore," the landlady said. "But
he is away now, at his job in the fish market that
I, Sophia Gina Anna Maria Scumatti, procured for
him! Believe me, if I hadn't given him an ultimatum
that the rent must be paid or out he'd go, he'd be
sleeping now, snoring like a serviced sow, while I,
Sophia Gina—"

"Undoubtedly the Signora has to endure much from
ungrateful tenants," I soothed. I had a hundred lira note
ready in my jacket pocket—the same oddly cut jacket
that had been in the closet at Gunvor's house. I fished
the bill out, tendered it with an inclination of the head.

"If the Signora will accept this modest contribution—"

Mama Scumatti puffed out her cheeks, threw out
her imposing bosom.

"It is my pleasure to serve the guest of Italy," she
started; I pulled the bill back.

"...but let it not be said that I, Gina Anna Maria Scumatti, was ungracious—" Fat fingers plucked the note from my hand, dropped it into a cleavage like the Grand Canyon. "Would the Signore and Signorina care to enter?" She fumbled a three-inch key from a pocket, jammed it into a keyhole you could have put a finger through, twisted it, threw the door wide. "Vidi!"

I looked in at a collapsed cot snarled with dirty blankets, a broken-down table strewn with garishly colored comics, empty coffee cups, stained, finger-greased glasses, and a half-loaf of dry-looking bread. There was a bureau, a broken mirror with racing tickets tucked under the frame, a wooden Jesus dangling on the wall, and an assortment of empty wine and liquor bottles bearing the labels of inferior brands, scattered about the room. The odor of the place was a sour blend of unlaundered bedding, old socks, and a distillery infested with mice.

I looked at Olivia. She gave me a cool smile, turned to our hostess.

"May we go in?"

Sophia Gina wrinkled her brow at me. "My sister would like to go inside and...ah...commune with the spirit of our departed progenitor," I translated freely.

The black, unplucked eyebrows went up. "But, as the Signore sees, the room is occupied!"

"We won't touch a thing; just look at it. A very emotional moment for us, you understand."

A knowing look crept over the round face. She gave Olivia, still wearing her makeup and rings, an appraising once-over, then looked me in the eye; one eyelid dipped in an unmistakable wink.

"Ah, but naturally, Signore! You and your...sister...

would of course wish to commune—in private. Another hundred lira, please." She was suddenly brisk. I forked over silently, trying to look just a little hangdog.

"I dislike to hurry the signore," the concierge said as she shook the second note down into the damp repository. "But try to finish in say two hours, *si*? There is the chance that Gino will be back for lunch." An elbow the size and texture of a football dug into my side. Two fat, broken-nailed hands outlined an hourglass in the air; two small black eyes rolled; then Mama Scumatti was waddling off, a hippo in a black skirt.

"What said the fat scoundrel?" Olivia demanded.

"Just admiring your figure," I said hastily. "Let's take a look around and see what clues we can turn up."

Half an hour later Olivia stood in the center of the room, still wrinkling her nose, hands on hips, a lock of hair curling down over her damp forehead.

"'Twas a hopeless quest from the first," she said. "Let's be off, before my stomach rebels."

I dusted off my hands, grimy from groping on the backs of shelves and under furniture. "We've looked in all the obvious places," I said. "But what about the unlikely spots? We haven't checked for loose floorboards, secret panels, fake pictures on the wall—"

"'Tis a waste of time, Brion! This man was not a conspirator, to squirrel away his secrets in the mattress! He was a poor young student, no more, living in a rented room—"

"I'm thinking of little things he might have dropped; a bit of paper that could have gotten stuck in the back of a drawer, maybe. Nobody ever cleans this place. There's no reason something like that couldn't still be here, even after all these years."

"Where? You've had the drawers out, rooted in the base of the chest, lifted that ragged scrap of rug, probed behind the baseboard—"

She trailed off; her eyes were on the boxed-in radiator set under the one small window. The wooden panels were curled, split, loose-fitting. We both moved at once. Olivia deftly set aside the empty Chianti bottles and the tin can half full of cigarette butts. I got a grip on the top board, lifted gingerly. The whole assembly creaked, moved out.

"Just a couple of rusty nails holding it," I said. "I'll lever it free..."

A minute later, with the help of a wooden coat hanger lettered "Albergo Torino, Roma," I had eased the housing away from the wall, revealing a rusted iron radiator, a few inches of piping, enough dust devils to fill a shoe box—and a drift of cigarette butts, ticket stubs, bits of string, hairpins, a playing card, paper clips, and papers.

"It was a good idea," I said. "Too bad it didn't pan out." Silently, I replaced the cover, put the bottles and ashtray back. "You were right, Olivia. Let's get back out in the street where we can get a nice wholesome odor of fresh garbage—"

"Brion, look!" Olivia was by the window, turning the blank scrap of paper at an angle to catch the sun. "The ink has faded, but there was something written here..."

I came over, squinted at the paper. The faintest of faint marks was visible. Olivia put the paper on the table, rubbed it gently over the dusty surface, then held it up to the mirror. The ghostly outline of awkward penmanship showed as a grey line.

"Rub it a little more," I said tensely. "Careful—that paper's brittle as ash." She complied, held it to the mirror again. This time I could make out letters:

Instituzione Galileo Mercoledi Guigno 7.
3 P.M.

"Wednesday, June 7th," I translated. "This just might be something useful. I wonder what year that was?"

"I know a simple formula for calculating the day on which a given date must fall," Olivia said breathlessly. "'Twill take but a moment..."

She nibbled at her lip, frowning in concentration. Suddenly her expression lightened. "Yes! It fits! June 7, 1871 fell on a Wednesday!" She frowned. "As did that date in 1899, 1911—"

"It's something—that's better than nothing at all. Let's check it out. The Galileo Institute. Let's hope it's still in business."

A dried-up little man in armbands and an eyeshade nibbled a drooping yellowed mustache and listened in silence, his veined hands resting on the counter top as though holding it in place as a barrier against smooth-talking foreign snoopers.

"Eighteen seventy-one. That was a considerable time in the past," he announced snappishly. "There have been many students at the Institute since then. Many illustrious scientists have passed through these portals, bringing glory to the name of Galileo." An odor of cheap wine drifted across from his direction. Apparently we had interrupted his midmorning snort.

"I'm not applying for admission," I reminded him. "You don't have to sell me. All I want is a look at the record of Giulio Maxoni. Of course, if your filing system is so fouled up you can't find it, you can just say so, and I'll report the fact in the article I'm writing—"

"You are a journalist?" He straightened his tie, gave the mustache a twirl, and eased something into a drawer out of sight behind the counter, with a clink of glass.

"Just give me the same treatment you'd accord any humble seeker after facts," I said loftily. "After all, the public is the owner of the Institute; surely it should receive the fullest attention of the staff whose bread and vino are provided by the public's largesse . . ."

That got to him. He made gobbling sounds, hurried away, came back wheezing under a volume that was the twin to the municipal register, slammed it down on the counter, blew a cloud of dust in my face, and lifted the cover.

"Maxoni, you said, sir. 1871 . . . 1871 . . ." he paused, popped his eyes at me. "That wouldn't be *the* Maxoni?" His natural suspicious look was coming back.

"Ahhh . . ." a variety of sudden emotions were jostling each other for space on my face. "*The* Maxoni?" I prompted.

"Giulio Maxoni, the celebrated inventor," he snapped. He turned and waved a hand at a framed daguerreotype, one of a long, somber row lining the room. "Inventor of the Maxoni churn, the Maxoni telegraph key, the Maxoni Improved Galvanic Buggy Whip—it was that which made his fortune, of course—"

I smiled complacently, like an inspector who has failed to find an error in the voucher files. "Very good. I see you're on your toes here at the Institute. I'll just have a look at the record, and then..." I let it trail off as Smiley·spun the book around, pointed out a line with a chewed fingernail.

"Here it is, right here. His original registration in the College of Electrics. He was just a lad from a poor farming community then. It was here at the Institute that he got his start. We were one of the first, of course, to offer lectures in electrics. The Institute was one of the sponsors of the Telegraphic Conference, later in that same year..." He rattled on with the sales pitch that had undoubtedly influenced many an old alumnus or would-be patron of the sciences to fork over that extra bundle, while I read the brief entry. The address in the Via Carlotti was given, the fact that Maxoni was twenty-four, a Catholic, and single. Not much help there...

"Is there any record," I inquired, "as to where he lived—after he made his pile?"

The little man stiffened. "Made his pile, sir? I fear I do not understand..."

"Made his great contribution to human culture, I mean," I amended. "Surely he didn't stay on at the Via Carlotti very long."

A sad smile twitched at one corner of the registrar's tight mouth.

"Surely the gentleman jests? The location of the Museum is, I think, well known—even to tourists."

"What museum?"

The gnome spread his hands in a gesture as Roman as grated cheese.

"What other than the museum housed in the former home and laboratory of Giulio Maxoni? The shrine wherein are housed the relics of his illustrious career."

Beside me, Olivia was watching the man's face, wondering what we were talking about. "Pay dirt," I said to her. Then:

"You don't have the address of this museum handy, by any chance?"

This netted me a superior smile. A skinny finger pointed at the wall beside him.

"Number Twenty-eight, Strada d'Allenzo. One square east. Any child could direct you."

"We're in business, girl," I said to Olivia.

"Ah . . . what was the name of the paper you . . . ah . . . claim to represent?" the little man's voice was a nice mixture of servility and veiled insolence. He was dying to be insulting, but wasn't quite sure it was safe.

"We're with the Temperance League," I said, and sniffed loudly. "The Maxoni questions were just a dodge, of course. We're doing a piece entitled: 'Drinking on Duty, and What it Costs the Taxpayer.'"

He was still standing in the same position, goggling after us, when we stepped out into the bright sunshine.

The Maxoni house was a conservative, stone-fronted building that would have done credit to any street in the East Seventies back home. There was a neglected-looking brass plate set above the inner rail beside the glass-paneled door, announcing that the Home and Laboratories of the Renowned Inventor Giulio Maxoni were maintained by voluntary contributions to the Society for the Preservation of Monuments to the Glory of Italy, and were open 9–4, Monday through Saturday, and on Sundays, 1–6 p.m. A card taped to the glass invited me to ring the bell. I did. Time passed. A dim shape moved beyond the glass, bolts rattled, the door creaked open, and a frowzy, sleep-blurred female blinked out.

"It's closed. Go away," said the voice like the last whinny of a dying plow horse. I got a foot into the narrowing space between the door and the jamb.

"The sign says—" I started brightly.

"Bugger the sign," the blurry face wheezed. "Come back tomorrow—"

I put a shoulder against the door, bucked it open, sending the charming receptionist reeling back. She caught her balance, hitched up a sagging bra strap, and raised a hand, fingers spread, palm facing her, opened her mouth to demonstrate what was probably an adequate command of Roman idiom—

"Ah—ah, don't say it," I cautioned her. "The Contessa here is unaccustomed to the vigor of modern speech. She's led a sheltered life, tucked away there in her immense palazzo at Lake Constance..."

"Contessa?" A hideous leer that was probably intended as a simper contorted the sagging face. "Oh, my, if I only would've known her Grace was honoring our little shrine with a visit—" She fled.

"A portal guarded by a dragon," Olivia said. "And the fair knight puts her to rout with but a word."

"I used a magic spell on her. You're promoted to Contessa now. Just smile distantly and act aloof." I looked around the room. It was a standard entry hall, high-ceilinged, cream-colored, with a stained-glass window shedding colored light across a threadbare, once-fine rug, picking up highlights on a marble-topped table in need of dusting, twinkling in the cut-glass pendants of a rather nice Victorian chandelier. A wide, carpeted stairway led up to a sunlit landing with another stained-glass panel. A wide, arched opening to the left gave a view of a heavy table with pots of wax flowers and an open book with a pen and inkpot beside it. There were rows of shelves sagging under rows of dusty books, uncomfortable looking horse-hair chairs and sofas, a fireplace with tools under a mantel on which china gimcracks were arranged in an uneven row.

"Looks like Maxoni went in for bourgeois luxury in a large way, once he got onto the buggy-whip boom," I commented. "I wonder where the lab is?"

Olivia and I wandered around the room, smelling the odor and age and dust and furniture polish. I glanced over a few of the titles on the shelves.

Experiments with Alternating Currents of High Potential and High Frequency by Nikola Tesla caught my eye, and a slim pamphlet by Marconi. Otherwise the collection seemed to consist of good, solid Victorian novels and bound volumes of sermons. No help there.

The dragon came back, looking grotesque in a housecoat of electric green—a tribute to Maxoni's field of research, no doubt. A layer of caked-looking makeup had been hastily slapped across her face, and a rose-bud mouth drawn on by a shaky hand. She laced her fingers together, did a curtsey like a trained elephant, gushed at Olivia, who inclined her head an eighth of an inch and showed a frosty smile. This example of aristocratic snobbishness delighted the old girl; she beamed so hard I thought the makeup was going to crack like plaster in an earthquake. A wave of an economical perfume rolled over me like a dust storm.

"Her Grace wishes to see the laboratories where Maxoni did his great work," I announced, fanning. "You may show us there at once."

She shouldered in ahead of me to get a spot nearer the duchess and with much waving of ringed hands and trailing of fringes, conducted us along a narrow hall beside the staircase, through a door into a weedy garden, along a walk to a padlocked shed, chattering away the whole time.

"Of course, the workrooms are not yet fully restored," she uttered, hauling a key from a baggy pocket. She got the lock open, stopped as she groped inside, grunted as she found the light switch. A yellowish glow sprang up. Olivia and I stared in at dust, lumpy shapes covered with tarpaulins, dust, heaped cartons, dust, grimed windows, and more dust.

"He worked *here*?"

"Of course it was not so cluttered then. We're short of funds, you see, your Grace," she got the sell in. "We haven't yet been able to go through the items here and catalogue them, dispose of the worthless things, and restore the laboratory to its original condition..." She chattered on, unabashed by Olivia's silence. I poked around, trying to look casual, but feeling far from calm. It was in this shed—or a near facsimile—that Maxoni had first made the breakthrough that had opened the worlds of alternate reality. Somewhere here, there might be...something. I didn't know what I was looking for: a journal, a working model not quite perfected...

I lifted the corner of the dust cover over a heaped table, glanced at the assortment of ancient odds and ends: awkward, heavy-looking transformers, primitive vacuum tubes, bits of wire—

A massive object at the center of the table caught my eye. I lifted the cover, reached for it, dragged it to me.

"Really, sir, I must insist that you disturb nothing!" my guardian hippo brayed in my ear. I jumped, let the tarp fall; dust whoofed into the air. "This is just as the professor left it, that last, fatal day."

"Sorry," I said, holding my face in what I hoped was a bland expression. "Looks like a collection of old iron to me."

"Yes, Professor Maxoni was a bit eccentric. He saved all sorts of odd bits and pieces—and he was forever trying to fit them together. He'd had a dream, he used to tell my departed Papa—when he was alive, of course—the professor, I mean—and Papa too, of course—"

"Your father worked for Maxoni?"

"Didn't you know? Oh, yes, he was his assistant, for ever so many years. Many's the anecdote he could tell of the great man—"

"I don't suppose he's still living?"

"Papa? Dear Papa passed to his reward forty-three—or is it forty-four...?"

"He didn't leave a journal, I suppose—filled with jolly reminiscences of the professor?"

"No—Papa wasn't what you'd call a lit'ry man." She paused. "Of course, the professor himself was most diligent about his journal. Five big volumes. It's one of the great tragedies of the Society that we've not yet had sufficient funds to publish."

"Funds may yet be forthcoming, Madam," I said solemnly. "The Contessa is particularly interested in publishing just such journals as you describe."

"Oh!" The painted-on mouth made a lopsided O to match the exclamation. "Your Grace—"

"So if you'd just fetch it along, so that her Grace can glance over it..." I left the suggestion hanging.

"It's in the safe, sir—but I have the key—I know I have the key, somewhere. I had it only last year—or was it the year before...?"

"Find it, my good woman," I urged her. "Her Grace and I will wait patiently here, thrilling to the thought that it was in this very room that the professor developed his galvanic buggy-whip."

"Oh, no, that was before he took this house—"

"No matter; the journals, please."

"Wouldn't you rather come back inside? The dust here—"

"As I said, we're thrilling to it. Hurry back..." I waved her through the door. Olivia looked at me questioningly.

"I've sent her off to find Maxoni's journals," I said. She must have noticed something in my voice.

"Brion, what is it?"

I stepped to the table, threw back the cover. The heavy assembly I had moved earlier dominated the scattering of articles around it.

"That," I said, letting the note of triumph come through, "is a Moebius-wound coil, the central component of the M-C drive. If I can't build a shuttle with that and the old boy's journals, I'll turn in my badge."

CHAPTER NINE

THE WORKSHOP I RENTED was a twelve-by-twenty space under a loft opening off a narrow alleyway that wound from the Strada d'Allenzo to a side-branch of the Tiber, a trail that had probably been laid out by goats, back before Rome was big enough to call itself a town. The former occupant had been a mechanic of sorts. There were rusty pieces of steam-engine still lying in the corners, a few corroded hand tools resting among the dust-drifts on the sagging wall shelves at one side of the room, odds and ends of bolts and washers and metal shavings trodden into the oil-black, hard-as-concrete dirt floor. The old fellow who leased the premises to me had grumblingly cleared away the worst of the rubbish, and installed a large, battered metal-topped table. This, plus the Moebius coil, which I had bribed the Keeper of the Flame into letting me borrow, and the journals, constituted my lab equipment. Not much to start moving worlds with—but still, a start.

Olivia had gotten us rooms nearby, cheaper and better quarters than the Albergo Romulus. There was a small hot plate in her room, charcoal-fired; we agreed to husband our meager funds by having two meals a day in, and the other at one of the small neighborhood pasta palaces where the carafes of wine were put on the table as automatically as salt and pepper back home.

I started my research program by reading straight through all five journals, most of which were devoted to bitter comments on the current political situation—the capital had just been moved to Rome from Florence, and it was driving prices up—notes on some seemingly pointless researches into magnetism, the details of a rather complicated but strictly Platonic affair with a Signora C., and worried budgetary computations that enlisted my fullest sympathy.

Only in the last volume did I start to strike interesting passages—the first, tentative hints of the Big Secret. Maxoni had been experimenting with coils; winding them, passing various types and amounts of electric current through them, and attempting to detect results. If he'd known more modern physics, he'd never have bothered, but in his ignorance, he persevered. Like Edison trying everything from horsehair to bamboo splints as filaments for his incandescent bulb, Maxoni doggedly tried, tested, noted results, and tried again. It was the purest of pure research. He didn't know what he was looking for—and when he found it, he didn't know what it was—at least not in this world. Of course, there had been no Cocini here. I didn't know what the latter's role had been back in the Zero-zero world line. It would be an interesting piece of reading for me when I got back— if I got back—if there were any place to get back to—

I let that line of thought die. It wasn't getting me anywhere. The last volume of the journal yielded up its secrets, such as they were—a few scattered and fragmentary mentions of the coil-winding, and a line or two regarding strange manifestations obtained with the gold-leaf electroscope when certain trickle currents were used.

A week had gone by, and I was ready to start the experimental phase. There were a few electrical supply houses in the city, mostly purveyors to the Universities and research institutes; electricity was far from the Reddy Kilowatt state in this world. I laid in a variety of storage batteries, oscillators, coils, condensers, vacuum tubes as big and clumsy as milk bottles, plus whatever else looked potentially useful. Then, at Olivia's suggestion, I let her mesmerize me, take notes as I repeated everything my subconscious had retained of the training I'd had in Net Shuttle technology—which turned out to be twice as valuable as Maxoni's notes.

They were pleasant days. I rose early, joined Olivia for breakfast, walked the two blocks to the shop, and toiled until lunch, recording my results in a book not much different from the ones Maxoni had used a century earlier. This was not a world of rapid change.

Olivia would come by at noon or a little after, looking fresh and cool, and healthier now, with the Roman sun giving her face the color it had lacked back in Harrow. The basket on her arm would produce sandwiches, pizzas, fruit, a bottle of wine. I had a couple of chairs by this time, and we'd spread our lunch on the corner of my formidable workbench, with the enigmatic bulk of the coil lying before us like some jealous idol in need of placating.

Then an afternoon of cut and fit and note, with

curious passerby pausing at the open door to look in
and offer polite greetings and shy questionings. By the
time a month had passed, I was deferred to by all the
local denizens as a mad foreigner with more than a suggestion of sorcerer about him. But they were friendly,
often dropping off a casual gift of a bottle or a salami
or a wedge of pungent cheese, with a flourish of Roman
compliments. Each evening, by the time the sun had
dropped behind the crooked skyline across the way, and
the shop had faded into deep shadow hardly relieved by
the single feeble lamp I had strung up, my eyes would
be blurring, my head ringing, my legs aching from the
hours of standing hunched over the table. I would solemnly close the door, attach the heavy padlock, ignoring
the fact that the door was nothing but a few thin boards
hung from a pair of rusted hinges held in place by bent
nails. Then walk home past the shops and stalls, their
owners busy closing up now, up the stairs to the flat for
a quick bath in the rust-stained tub down the hall, then
out with Olivia to the evening's treat. Sitting at the wob-
bly tables on the tile floors, often on a narrow terrace
crowded beside a busy street, we talked, watched the
people and the night sky, then went back to part at the
flat door—she to her room, I to mine. It was a curious
relationship, perhaps—though at the time, it seemed
perfectly natural. We were co-conspirators, engaged in a
strange quest, half-detectives, half researchers, set apart
from the noisy, workaday crowd all around us by the
fantastic nature of the wildly impractical quest we were
embarked on. She, for reasons of romantic fulfillment,
and I, driven by a compulsion to tear through the intangible prison walls that had been dropped around me.

My estimate of Olivia's age had been steadily revised

downward. At first, in the initial shock of seeing Mother Goodwill unmasked, I had mentally assigned her a virginal fortyishness. Later, bedizened in her harlot's finery—and enjoying every minute of the masquerade—she had seemed younger; perhaps thirty-five, I had decided. Now, with the paint scrubbed away, her hair cut and worn in a casual Roman style, her complexion warm and glowing from the sun and the walks, her figure as fine as ever in the neat, inexpensive clothes she had bought in the modest shops near our flat, I realized with a start one day, watching her scatter bread crumbs for the pigeons behind the shop and laughing at their clumsy waddle, that she was no more than in her middle twenties.

She looked up and caught me staring at her.

"You're a beautiful girl, Olivia," I said—in a wondering tone, I'm afraid. "What ever got you off on that Mombi kick?"

She looked startled, then smiled—a merrier expression than the Lady Sad-eyes look she used to favor.

"You've guessed it," she said, sounding mischievous. "The old witch in the *Sorceress of Oz*—"

"Yes, but *why*?"

"I told you: my business. Who'd patronize a Wise Woman without warts on her chin?"

"Sure—but why haven't you married?" I started to deliver the old saw about there being plenty of nice young men, but the look on her face saved me from that banality.

"Okay, none of my business," I said quickly. "I didn't mean to get personal, Olivia..." I trailed off, and we finished our walk in a silence which, if not grim, was certainly far from companionable.

Three weeks more, and I had assembled a formidable compilation of data—enough, I told Olivia when she came to the shop at ten PM to see what had kept me, to warrant starting construction of the secondary circuits—the portion of the shuttle mechanism with which I was most familiar.

"The big job," I said, "was to calibrate the coil— find out what kind of power supply it called for, what sort of field strength it developed. That part's done. Now all I have to do is set up the amplifying and focusing apparatus—"

"You make it sound so simple, Brion—and so safe."

"I'm trying to convince myself," I admitted. "It's a long way from simple. It's a matter of trying to equate a complicated assemblage of intangible forces; a little bit like balancing a teacup on a stream of water, except that I have a couple of dozen teacups, and a whole fire department's worth of waterworks—and if I threw full power to the thing without the proper controls..."

"Then what?"

"Then I'd set up an irreversible cataclysm—of any one of a hundred possible varieties. A titanic explosion, that keeps on exploding: an uncontrolled eruption of matter from another continuum, like a volcano pouring out of the heart of a sun—or maybe an energy drain like Niagara, that would suck the heat away from this spot, freeze the city solid in a matter of minutes, put the whole planet under an ice cap in a month. Or—"

"'Tis sufficient. I understand. These are fearsome forces you toy with, Brion."

"Don't worry—I won't pour the power into it until I know what I'm doing. There are ways of setting up auto-timed cutoffs for any test I run—and I'll be using trickle power for a long time yet. The disasters that made the Blight, happened because the Maxonis and Cocinis of those other A-lines weren't forewarned. They set her up and let her rip. The door to Hell has well-oiled hinges."

"How long—before you'll finish?"

"A few days. There isn't a hell of a lot to the shuttle. I'll build a simple box—out of pine slabs, if I have to—just something to keep me and the mechanism together. It'll be a big, clumsy setup, of course—not compact like the Imperial models—but it'll get me there, as long as the power flows. The drain isn't very great. A stack of these six volt cells will give me all the juice I need to get me home."

"And if the Xonijeel were right," she said softly, "if the world you seek lies not where you expect—what then?"

"Then I'll run out of steam and drop into the Blight, and that'll be the end of another nut," I said harshly. "And a good thing too—if I imagined the whole Imperium—"

"I know you didn't, Brion. But if, somehow, something has . . . gone wrong . . ."

"I'll worry about that when I get to it," I cut her off. I'd been plowing along, wrapping myself up in my occupational therapy. I wasn't ready yet to think about the thousand gloomy possibilities I'd have to face when I stepped into my crude makeshift and threw the switch.

It was three evenings later, and Olivia and I were sitting at a window table in one of our regular haunts, having a small glass of wine and listening to the gentle night sounds of a city without neon or internal combustion. She'd been coming by the shop for me every evening lately; a habit that I found myself looking forward to.

"It won't be long now," I told her. "You saw the box. Just bolted together out of wood, but good enough. The coil's installed. Tomorrow I'll lay out my control circuitry—"

"Brion..." her fingers were on my arm. "Look there!"

I twisted, caught a fleeting glimpse of a tall, dark figure in a long, full-skirted coat with the collar turned up, pushing past through the sparse pedestrian traffic.

"It was—him!" Olivia's voice was tight with strain.

"All right, maybe it was," I said soothingly. "Take it easy, girl. How sure are you—"

"I'm sure, Brion! The same terrible, dark face, the beard—"

"There are plenty of bearded men in Rome, Olivia—"

"We have to go—quickly!" She started to get up. I caught her hand, pulled her gently back.

"No use panicking. Did he see us?"

"I—think—I'm not sure," she finished. "I saw him, and turned my face away, but—"

"If he's seen us—if he *is* our boy—running won't help. If he didn't see us, he won't be back."

"But if we hurried, Brion—we need not even stop at the flat to get our things! We can catch the train, be miles from Rome by daylight—"

"If we've been trailed here, we can be trailed to the next town. Besides which, there's the little matter of my shuttle. It's nearly done. Another day's work and a few tests—"

"Of what avail's the shuttle if they take you, Brion?"

I patted her hand. "Why should anyone want to take me? I was dumped here to get rid of me—"

"Brion, think you I'm some village goose to be coddled with this talk? We must act—now!"

I chewed my lip and thought about it. Olivia wasn't being soothed by my bland talk—any more than I was. I didn't know what kind of follow-up the Xonijeelian Web Police did on their deportees, but it was a cinch they wouldn't look kindly on my little home workshop project. The idea of planting me here had been to take me out of circulation. They'd back their play; Olivia was right about that...

"All right." I got to my feet, dropped a coin on the table. Out in the street, I patted her hand.

"Now, you run along home, Olivia. I'll do a little snooping, just to satisfy myself that everything's okay. Then—"

"No. I'll stay with you."

"That's silly," I said. "If there *is* any rough stuff, you think I want you mixed up in it? Not that there will be..."

"You have some madcap scheme in mind, Brion. What is it? Will you go back to the workshop?"

"I just want to check to make sure nobody's tampered with the shuttle."

Her face looked pale in the light of the carbide lamp at the corner.

"You think by hasty work to finish it—to risk your life—"

"I won't take any risks, Olivia—but I'm damned if I'm going to be stopped when I'm this close."

"You'll need help. I'm not unclever in such matters."

I shook my head. "Stay clear of this, Olivia. I'm the one they're interested in, but you could get hurt—"

"How close are you to finishing your work?"

"A few hours. Then some tests—"

"Then we'd best be starting. I sense danger close

by this night. 'Twill not be long ere they close their noose."

I hesitated for just a moment, then took her hand. "I don't know what I've done to earn such loyalty," I said. "Come on, we've got work to do."

We went to the flat first, turned on lights, made coffee. Then, with the rooms darkened, took the back stairs, eased out into the cobbled alley. Half an hour later, after a circuitous trip which avoided main streets and well-lit corners, we reached the shop, slipped inside. Everything looked just as I'd left it an hour earlier: the six-foot-square box, its sides half-slabbed up with boards, the coil mounted at the center of the plank floor, the bright wire of my half-completed control circuits gleaming in the gloom. I lit a lamp, and we started to work.

Olivia was more than clever with her hands. I showed her just once how to attach wire to an insulator; from then on she was better at it than I was. The batteries required a mounting box; I nailed a crude frame together, fitted the cells in place, wired up a switch, made connections. Every half hour or so, Olivia would slip outside, make a quick reconnaissance—not that it would have helped much to discover any spy sneaking up on us. I couldn't quite deduce the pattern of their tactics—if any. If we had been spotted, surely the shop was under surveillance. Maybe they were just letting me finish before they closed in. Perhaps they were curious as to whether it was possible to do what I was trying to do with the materials and technology at hand...

It was well after midnight when we finished. I made a final connection, ran a couple of circuit checks. If my research had been accurate, and my recollection of M-C theory correct, the thing *should* work...

"It looks so...fragile, Brion." Olivia's eyes were dark in the dim light. My own eyeballs felt as though they'd been rolled in emery dust.

"It's fragile—but a moving shuttle is immune to any external influence. It's enclosed in a field that holds the air in, and everything else out. And it doesn't linger long enough in any one A-line for the external temperature or vacuum or what have you to affect it."

"Brion!" She took my arm fiercely. "Stay here! Risk not this frail device! 'Tis not too late to flee! Let the evil men search in vain! Somewhere we'll find a cottage, in some hamlet far from this scheming..."

My expression told her she wasn't reaching me. She stared into my eyes for a moment, then let her hand fall and stepped back.

"I was a fool to mingle dreams with drab reality," she said harshly. I saw her shoulders slump, the life go from her face. Almost, it was Mother Goodwill who stood before me.

"Olivia," I said harshly. "For God's sake—"

There was a sound from the door. I saw it tremble, and jumped for the light, flipped it off. In the silence, a foot grated on bricks. There was a sound of rusty hinges, and a lesser darkness widened as the door slid back. A tall, dark silhouette appeared in the opening.

"Bayard!" a voice said sharply in the darkness—an unmistakably Xonijeelian voice. I moved along the wall. The figure advanced. There was a crowbar somewhere near the door. I crouched, trying to will myself invisible, reached—and my fingers closed around the cold, rust-scaled metal. The intruder was two yards away now. I straightened, raised the heavy bar. He took another step, and I jumped, slammed the bar down solidly across the back of his head, saw a hat fly as he stumbled and fell on his face with a heavy crash.

"Brion!" Olivia shrieked.

"It's all right!" I tossed the bar aside, reached for her, put my arms around her.

"You have to understand, Olivia," I rasped. "There's more at stake here than anyone's dream. This is something I have to do. You have your life ahead. Live it—and forget me!"

"Let me go with you, Brion," she moaned.

"You know I can't. Too dangerous—and you'd halve my chances of finding the Zero-zero line before the air gives out." I thrust my wallet into her cloak pocket. "I have to go now." I pushed her gently from me.

"Almost . . . I hope it fails," Olivia's voice came through the dark. I went to the shuttle, lit the carbide running light, reached in and flipped the warm-up switch. From the shadows, I heard a groan from the creature I had stunned.

"You'd better go now, Olivia," I called. "Get as far away as you can. Go to Louisiana, start over—forget the Mother Goodwill routine . . ."

The hum was building now—the song of the tortured molecules as the field built, twisting space, warping time, creating its tiny bubble of impossible tension in the massive fabric of reality.

"Goodbye, Olivia . . ." I climbed inside the fragile box, peered at the makeshift panel. The field strength meter told me that the time had come. I grasped the drive lever and threw it in.

Chapter Ten

THERE WAS A WRENCHING sensation, a sputter of arcing current through untried circuits. Then the walls flicked from view around me, and I was looking out on the naked devastation of the Blight. No need for view-screens here. The foot-wide gaps between the rough slats gave me a panoramic view of a plain of rubble glowing softly under the light of the moon; a view that shifted and flowed as I watched, blackening into burned ruins, slumping gradually into a lava-like expanse of melted and hardened masonry and steel.

I unclenched my fists, tried a breath. Everything seemed all right. I was riding an egg crate across Hell, but the field was holding, leashed by the mathematical matrices embodied in a few hundred strands of wire strung just so from nail to nail around my wooden cage. The massive Moebius coil bolted to the floor vibrated nervously. I made an effort to relax; I had a long ride ahead.

My half-dozen jury-rigged instruments were obediently giving readings. I looked at the trembling needles and tried to think about what they represented. The only map I had was a fuzzy recollection of the photogram the Xonijeelians had showed me. If this *was* a fourth island in the Blight—and I had already decided not to question that assumption—then I was driving in what ought to be close to the correct "direction." Navigation in the Net depended on orientation with an arbitrary set of values—measurements of the strength of three of the seemingly infinite number of "fields" which were a normal part of the multiordinal continua. A reading of any three of these values should give a location. Noting the progressive changes in the interrelation of the values provided a pilot across the Net—maybe. There was the little matter of calibrating my instruments, estimating my A-entropic velocity, testing my crude controls to see how much steering I could do, and determining how to bring the shuttle into identity square on target when and if I had a target—and all of this before the air became too foul to breathe. There was no problem of food, water, or a place to sleep: I'd be dead long before any such luxuries became necessary.

My first rough approximation from the data on the dials told me that I was moving along a vector at least 150 degrees off the calculated one. I made a cautious adjustment to one of my crude rheostats, winced as the sparks flew, watched the dials to see the results.

They weren't good. Either I was misinterpreting my readings, or my controls were even worse than I'd thought. I scribbled down figures, made some hasty interpolations, and came up with the discovery that I was blasting along at three times my calculated Net velocity, on a course that seemed to be varying progressively. My hastily rigged untested circuitry was badly out of balance—not far enough out to spill the leashed entropic force in a torrent of destruction, but too far out to be soothing.

I made another haphazard adjustment, checked readings. The needles wavered, one back-tracking down the scale, two others moving steadily upward. I made a Herculean effort to recall all I'd ever known about emergency navigation, and concluded that I had described most of a full circle and was now headed back in the opposite direction. There wasn't much play left in my controls. I pushed the lever which served as rudder all the way to the left, watched as instruments responded—not enough.

Another ten minutes passed. My watch was ticking away, measuring off some unimaginable quality in my timeless, headlong plunge across the alternate realities. It was like the tooth-gritting wait while the lab technician probes around with his needle, looking for a vein. One second seemed to last forever.

Another reading. No doubt about it now, I was following a roughly spiral course—whether descending or ascending, I couldn't tell. The control circuits were sparking continuously; the stresses induced by the unnatural entropic loads were rapidly overheating the inadequate wiring. A junction box tacked to a two-by-four was glowing a dull red, and the wood under it was smoking, turning black. As I watched, pale flames licked, caught, ran up the wood. I pulled off my jacket, slapped at the fire uselessly. A wire melted through, dropped, spattered fire as it crossed other naked wires, then hung, welded into a new position.

For a heart-stopping instant, I braced myself for

the lurching drop into identity with the towering pillars of fire thundering silently outside—then realized that, miraculously, the shuttle was still moving. I rubbed smoke-stung eyes, checked dials; the course had changed sharply. I tried to reconstruct the erratic path I had taken, work out a dead reckoning of my position. It was hopeless. I could be anywhere.

The scene beyond the shuttle walls was strange, not like anything I remembered from Blight exploration films I'd seen. A row of steep-sided black cones stretched away to the horizon, each glowing dull red about its crater rim, over which continuous wellings of lava spilled, while vast bubbles burst, sending up dense belches of brown smoke that formed a cloud obscuring the moon. Here, it appeared, a new fault-line had been created in the planet's crust, along which volcanoes sprouted like weeds in a new-ploughed field.

I had been on my way for about forty minutes now. With a pang of homesickness I pictured Olivia, back at the flat, alone. Suddenly I was remembering the days, the evenings we'd spent together, her unfailing spirit, her gentle touch, the line of her throat and cheek as we sat at a table, raising glasses in the long Roman twilight...

I had had everything there a man needed for a good life. Maybe I'd been a fool to exchange it for this—a doomed ride on a hell-bound train to nowhere. Maybe. But there hadn't really been any choice. There were things in life a man had to do, or the savor was gone forever.

I was lost now, that was clear enough. For the last hour the shuttle had been charging across the continua blindly, describing an erratic course which varied every time a connection fused and created a new pattern in the control circuits. The post was still smoldering and smoking.

I had stretched out on the floor some time earlier, trying to find cleaner air. It was about gone now. I coughed with every breath, and my head kept up a steady humming, like a worn out transformer. I was picking up some interesting observations on the effects of modifying shuttle circuitry at full gallop—and observing some new country, never before explored by our Net Scouts—but the chances of my surviving to use it were dwindling with each passing minute. I had scratched a few line of calculations on the floor with a fragment of charred wood. At the rate I was moving, I was deep in the Blight by now. Outside the ruined worlds flowed past, a panorama of doomsdays. The volcanoes were gone, shrunken to fiery pits that sparked and hurled fountains of fire into the black sky. I blinked, peering through shrouding mists of steam and smoke. Far away, a line of dark hills showed—new hills, created by the upheavals of this world's crust. The smoke thinned for a moment, gave me a clearer glimpse of the distant landscape—

Was that a hint of green? I rubbed at my eyes, stared some more. The hills, dim in the moonlight, seemed to show a covering of plant life. The nearby fire pits seemed quieter now, stilling to glowing pools of molten lava, glazing over into dullness. And there—!! A scraggly bush, poking up at the rim of a crater— and another...

I drew a breath, coughed, got to hands and knees. The glow was fading from the scene. Unmistakable pinpoints of bright green were showing up everywhere.

A shoot poked through the black soil, rose, twisted, unfurled a frond, shot up higher, extending leaf after leaf, in a speeded-up motion-picture sequence of growth, each frame a glimpse of a different A-line, varying by a trifle from the next, creating a continuous drama of change—a change toward life.

In its erratic wandering, it appeared, the shuttle had turned back toward the edge of the Blight. I watched, saw new shoots appear, spring up, evolve into great tree-ferns, giant cattails, towering palm-like trunks, along whose concrete-grey surfaces vines crept like small snakes, to burgeon suddenly, embrace the vast tree in a smothering outburst of green, clamber over the crown, then sink down as the tree died and fell, only to turn on themselves, mound high, reach, capture a new host...

A jungle grew around me, nourished in the volcanic soil. Orchids as big as dinner plates burst like popcorn, dropped, were replaced by others as big as washtubs. In the bright moonlight, I saw a flicker of motion—a new kind of motion. A moth appeared, a bright speck, grew until he was two feet across. Then the vast flower on which he perched closed over him in a frantic flurry of gorgeous wings and flamboyant petals.

Nearby, a wall of foliage bulged, burst outward. A head thrust through—gaping jaws like those of an immense rat closed on vines that coiled, choking... The head changed, developed armor which grew out, blade-like, slicing through the ropes of living plant-fiber. Juice oozed, spilled; thorns budded, grew hungrily toward the animal, reached the furred throat—and recoiled, blunted, from armored hide. Then new leaves unfolded, reached to enfold the head, wrapping it in smothering folds of leathery green. It twisted, fought, tearing free only to be entoiled again, sinking down now, gone in a surging sea of green.

I coughed, choked, got to my feet, reached for the control panel—missed, and fell. The crack on the head helped for a moment. I tried to breathe, got only smoke. It was now or never. The worlds outside were far from inviting, but there was nothing for me in the shuttle but death by asphyxiation. I could drop into identity, make hasty repairs, study the data I had collected, decide where I was, and try again...

Back to hands and knees; a grip on a board; on my feet now, reaching for the switch, find it in the choking smoke, pull—

There was a shock, a whirling, then a blow that sent me flying against shattering boards, into rubbery foliage and a gush of fresh air...

I finished coughing, extricated myself from the bed of vines I found myself in, half expecting to see them reach for me; fortunately, however, the strange cause-and-effect sequences of E-entropy didn't apply here, in normal time.

In the gloom, I made out the shape of the flimsy box that had brought me here. It was canted against a giant tree trunk, smashed into a heap of scrap lumber. Smoke was boiling from under the heaped boards, and bright flames showed, starting along a wrist-thick vine, casting flickering lights and shadows on surrounding trees and underbrush. There was a board under my foot, still trailing a festoon of wires. I grabbed it up, struggled through to the fire, beat at the flames. It was a mistake—the bruised stems oozed a flammable sap which caught with bright poppings and cracklings. The main chassis of the broken shuttle was too heavy for me to try to drag back from the blaze. I tried to reach the coil, with some vague idea of salvage, but the fire was burning briskly now. The dry wood flamed up, sending fire high along the tree trunk, igniting more vines. Five minutes later, from a distance of a hundred yards, I watched a first-class forest fire getting underway.

The rain started then, too late to salvage anything from the shuttle, but soon enough to save the forest. I found shelter of sorts under a wide-leafed bush, listened for awhile to the drumming of the rain, then sank into exhausted sleep.

Morning dawned grey, wet, chilly, with water dripping from a billion leaves all around me. I crawled out, checked over assorted bruises, found everything more or less intact. I still had a slight rawness in the throat from the smoke, and somewhere I'd gotten a nice blister on the heel of my left hand, but that seemed a modest toll for the trip I had had.

The fire had burned out a ragged oval about a hundred feet across. I walked across the black stubble to the remains of the shuttle, surveyed the curled and charred boards, the blackened lump that had been the coil. The last, faint hope flickered and died. I was stranded for good, this time, with no handy museum to help me out.

There was a vague sensation in my belly that I recognized as hunger. I had a lot of thinking to do, some vain regrets to entertain, and a full quota of gloomy reflections on what was happening now back in the Imperial capital. But first, I had to have food—and, if my sketchy knowledge of jungles was any guide, a shelter of some sort against other inhabitants of the region that might consider me to be in that category.

And even before food, I needed a weapon. A bow and arrow would be nice, but it would take time to find a suitable wood, and I'd have to kill something for gut for the string. A spear or club was about all I'd be able to manage in my present state of technological poverty. And even for those, I'd need some sort of cutting edge—which brought me back to the stone age in two easy steps.

The ground had a slight slope to what I suspected was the east. I pushed my way through the thick growth—not as jungle-like as what I'd seen from the shuttle minutes before my crash landing, but not a nice picnicky sort of New English wood either. I kept to the down-slope, stopping now and then to listen for gurgling streams or growling bears. The Boy Scout lore paid off. I broke through into a swampy crescent hugging a mud flat, with a meandering current at its center, fifty feet distant. Tight-packed greenery hung over the far side of the watercourse, which curved away around a spit of more grey mud. There were no stones in sight. Still, there was plenty of clay—good for pottery making, perhaps. I squatted, dipped up a sample. It was thin and sandy muck—useless.

There was ample room to walk beside the stream. I followed the course for several hundred yards, found a stretch of higher ground where the water came close to a bank of grassy soil. This would make as good a campsite as any. I pulled off my shoes, eased over the edge into the water, sluiced the worst of the soot and mud from myself and clothes. Turning back, I noticed a stratum of clean yellowish clay in the bank. It was the real stuff: smooth, pliable, almost greasy in texture. All I needed was a nice fire to harden it, and over which to cook my roasts, chops, fish fillets, et cetera—as soon as I had acquired the latter, using the weapons I would make as soon as I had an axe and a knife . . .

It was almost sunset. The day's efforts had netted me one lump of flint, which I had succeeded in shattering into a hand axe and a couple of slicing edges that any decent flint worker would have tossed into the discard pile for archaeologists to quarrel over a few thousand years later. Still, they had sufficed to hack off two twelve-foot lengths of tough, springy sapling, remove the twigs and leaves, and sharpen the small ends to approximate points. I had also gathered a few handfuls of small blackberry-like fruits which were now giving me severe stomach pains, and several pounds of the pottery clay which I had shaped into crude bowls and set aside for air drying.

The skies had cleared off in the afternoon, and I had built a simple shelter of branches and large leaves, and dragged in enough nearly-dry grass for a bed of sorts. And using a strip of cloth torn from my shirt, I had made a small fire-bow. With a supply of dry punk from the interior of a rotted tree, and a more or less smooth stone with a suitable hollow, I was now preparing to make a fire. My hardwood stick was less hard than I would have liked, and the bow was a clumsy makeshift, but it was better than just sitting and thinking. I crumbled the wood powder in the hollow, placed the pointed end of the stick against it with the bow string wrapped around it, and started in.

Ten minutes later, with the bow twice broken and replaced, the stick dulled, and the punk and my temper both exhausted, I gave it up for the night, crawled into my cozy shelter. Two minutes later, a bellow like a charging elephant brought me bolt upright, groping for a gun that wasn't there. I waited, heard a heavy body crashing through underbrush nearby, then the annoyed growl that went with the kind of appetite that preferred meat. There were a number of large trees in the vicinity. I found one in the dark with amazing speed and climbed it, losing a trifling few square feet of skin in the process. I wedged myself in a high crotch and listened to stealthy footsteps padding under my perch until dawn.

I found the tracks the next morning when I half-climbed, half-fell from the tree. They were deeply imprinted, too big to cover with my spread fingers, not counting the claws—on the prints, that is. Some kind of cat, I guessed. Down at the water's edge were more tracks: big hoof-marks the size of saucers. They grew 'em big in these parts. All I had to do was bag one, and I'd have meat for as long as I could stand the smell.

I was getting really hungry now. Following the stream, I covered several miles to the south, gradually working my way into more open country. There were plenty of signs of game, including the bare bones of something not quite as big as a London bus, with condor-like birds picking over them half-heartedly. I had my two spears and my stone fragments, and I was hoping to spot something of a size and ferocity appropriate to my resources—say a half-grown rabbit.

There was a sudden rattle of wings just in front of

me, and a grousey-looking bird as big as a turkey took
to the air. I advanced cautiously, found a nest with
four eggs in it, speckled brown, three inches long. I
squatted right there and ate one, and enjoyed every
scrap. It would have been nice to have scrambled it
but that was a minor consideration. The other three
I distributed in various pockets, then went on, feeling
a little better.

The country here was higher, with less underbrush
and more normal-looking trees in place of the swampy
jungle growth I'd started from. During high water, I
imagined, the whole area where the shuttle lay would
be submerged. Now I had a better view, off through
the open forest, to what seemed like a prairie to the
south. That's where the game would be.

Another half hour's walk brought me to the edge
of a vast savannah that reminded me of pictures I'd
seen of Africa, with immense herds grazing under
scattered thorn trees. Here the trees were tall hard-
woods, growing in clumps along the banks of the
stream—and the animals were enough to make any
zoo-keeper turn in his badge and start keeping white
mice. I saw bison, eight feet at the shoulder; massive,
tusked almost-elephants with bright pink trunks and
pendulous lower lips; deer in infinite variety; and horses
built like short-necked giraffes, ten feet high in the
shoulder with sloping withers. There they were—and
all I had to do was to stick them with my spear.

There was a low snort from somewhere behind me.
I whirled, saw a head the size of a rhino's, set with
two rows of huge, needlesharp teeth in a mouth that
gaped to give me a view of a throat like the intake
duct on a jet fighter. There was a body behind the

head—ten feet or more of massively muscled tawny cat, with a hint of mane, faint stripes across the flanks, snow white throat, belly and feet. I took all these details in as the mighty carnivore looked me over, yawned, and paced majestically toward me, frowning across at the distant herds like a troubled politician wondering who to pay the bribe to.

He passed me up at a distance of thirty feet, moved out into the area, head high now, looking over the menu. None of the animals stirred. King Cat kept on, bypassed a small group of mastodons who rolled their eyes, switching their trunks nervously. He had his eye on the bison, among whom were a number of cuddly calves weighing no more than a ton. They moved restlessly now, forming up a defensive circle, like the musk-ox of the Arctic. The hunter changed his course, angling to the left. Maybe he was thinking better of it—

With the suddenness of thought, he was running, streaking across the grass in thirty-foot bounds, leaping now clear over the front rank of tossing horns to disappear as the herd exploded outward in all directions. Then he reappeared, standing over the body of a calf, one paw resting affectionately on the huddled tan corpse. The herd stampeded a short distance, resumed feeding. I let out a long breath. *That* was a hunter.

I jumped at a sound, spun, my hand with my trusty spear coming up automatically—

A brown rabbit the size of a goat stood poised on wiry legs, snuffling the air, showing long yellow rat-teeth. I brought the spear back, threw, saw it catch the creature in mid-leap as he whirled to flee, knocking him head over long white heels. I came pounding up, swung the second spear like a farmer's wife killing a snake, and laid him low.

Breathing hard, I gingerly picked up the bloody carcass, noting the gouge my spear had made. I looked around for a place to hole up and feast. Something black moved on my arm. A flea! I dropped the rabbit, captured the parasite, cracked him with a satisfying report. There were plenty more where that one came from, I saw, stirring around in the sparse hair on the foot-long ears. Suddenly I didn't want raw rabbit—or overgrown rat—for lunch.

As suddenly as that, the adrenalin I'd been getting by on for the past thirty-six hours drained away, left me a hungry, sick, battered castaway, stranded in a hell-world of raw savagery, an unimaginable distance from a home which I knew I'd never see again. I had been bumbling along from one fiasco to the next, occupying my mind with the trivial, unwilling to face reality; the chilling fact that my life would end, here, in solitude and misery, in pain and fear—and that before many more hours had passed.

I lay under a tree, staring up at the sky, resting—I told myself—or waiting for another cat, less choosy, to happen along. I had had my chances—more than one—and I'd muffed them all. I'd gotten away clean in the Hagroon shuttle—then let it carry me helplessly along to their den-city, permitted myself to be captured without a struggle, thinking I'd learn something from the gorilla men. And after a combination of the enemy's stupidity and my luck had given me a new chance, a new shuttle—I'd guessed wrong again, let Dzok beguile me along to be sentenced to life in exile. And a third time—after my wild guesses had paid off—I had panicked, run from the enemy without waiting to test my homebuilt shuttle—and ended here. Each time I had made what seemed like the only possible choice—and each time I'd gotten farther from my starting point. Not farther in terms of Net distance, perhaps, but infinitely farther from any hope of rescue—to say nothing of my hope of warning the Imperial authorities of what was afoot.

I got to my feet, started back toward where I'd left the wreckage of the shuttle, with some half-formed idea of searching through the wreckage again—for what, I didn't know. It was the blind instinct of one who had absorbed all the disaster he can for a while, and who substitutes aimless action for the agony of thought.

It was harder now, plodding back over the ground I'd already covered. Following the course of the river, I passed the huge skeleton—abandoned now by the birds—reached the mud flat where the trampled remains of my crude hut gave a clear indication of the inadequacies of my choice of campsites.

I had an idea of sorts then. Back at the shuttle there was a lump of metal—the remains of the original Maxoni coil. I might be able to use the material in some way—pound it out into spear-heads, or make a flint-and-steel for fire starting purposes...

The impulse died. My stomach ached, and I was tired. I wanted to go home now, have a nice hot bath, crawl into bed, and be joined there by someone soft and perfumed and cuddly who'd smooth my fevered brow and tell me what a hell of a guy I was...

It was easy to see the mechanics of schizophrenia at work here. From wishing, it was an easy jump to believing. I took a couple of deep breaths, straightened my back, and headed for the burn site. I'd try to retain my grip on reality a little longer. When it got unbearable, I knew the sanctuary of insanity would be waiting.

There were animal tracks across the blackened ground, hoof marks, paw prints, and—

I bent over, squinting to be sure. Footprints, human, or near enough. I knew how Robinson Crusoe had felt; the evidence of a fellow man gave me a sudden feeling of exposure along my backbone. I made it to the surrounding unburned wall of jungle in three jumps, slid down flat on the ground, and scanned the landscape. I tried to tell myself that this was a lucky break, the first real hope I'd had—but an instinct older than theories of the Brotherhood of Man told me that I had encountered the world's most deadly predator. The fact that we might be of the same species just meant competition for the same hunting ground.

My spear wasn't a handy weapon, and my skill with it wasn't anything to strike a medal in praise of. I checked my pocket for one of my stones, found a smashed egg. For a moment, the ludicrousness of the situation threatened to start me snickering. Then I heard a sound from nearby—in what direction, I wasn't sure. I eased back, rose up far enough to scan the woods behind me. I saw nothing. I tried to think the situation through. If I was right—if it was a man who'd visited here—it was important to establish contact. Even a primitive would have some sort of culture—food, fire, garments of sorts, shelter. I had skills: pottery making, basket weaving, the principle of the bow. We could work out something, perhaps—but only if I survived the first meeting.

I heard the sound again, saw a deer-like creature making its way across the burn. I let out a breath I didn't know I'd been holding. There was no way of knowing how long ago the man prints had been made. Still, I couldn't lie here forever. I emerged, made a quick check of the burned-out shuttle. Everything was as I'd left it.

I took another look at the footprints. They seemed to be made not by a bare foot, but by a flat sandal of some sort. They came across the burn, circled the shuttle, went away again. On the latter portion of the trail, they clearly overlay my own booted prints. Whoever my visitor had been, he was following me—or had started out on my trail. It was a thought that did nothing for my peace of mind.

I tried to calm the instinct that told me to get as far from the spot as possible. I needed to meet this fellow—and on terms that I could control. I didn't want to kill him, of course—but neither did I want to try the palm outward "I friend" routine. That left—capture.

It was risky business, working out in the open. But then being alive was a risky business. If the man tracking me had followed my trail, then lost it somewhere on the high ground, it might be a matter of many hours before he came back here to cast about again—and I was sure, for some reason, that he'd do that. And when he did—

I had been working hard for two hours now, setting up my snare. It wasn't fancy, and if my proposed captive were any kind of woodsman—which he had to be, to survive here—it wouldn't fool him for a moment. Still, it was action of a sort—occupational therapy, maybe, but better than hiding under a bush and waiting—and it was helpful to my morale to imagine that I was taking the initiative.

The arrangement consisted of a shallow pit excavated in the soft soil, covered over with a light framework of twigs and leaves, and camouflaged with a scattering of blackened soil. I had done the digging with my bare hands, helped out by a board from the wreck, and the dirt had been heaped under the brush, out of sight behind the wall of foliage. The hole was no more than four feet deep, but that was sufficient for my purpose—to throw the intruder off-balance, and give me the drop on him sufficiently to open negotiations.

I was hungry enough now to scrape one of the smashed eggs from the lining of my pocket and eat it. But first I had to select my hiding place and get ready to act when the victim stepped into the trap. I picked a spot off to the left, arranged myself so as to be able to jump out at the psychological moment, and settled down to wait.

The pit was dug just in front of the wreckage, at the point where the opening to the interior would lead an inquisitive victim. I had dropped a lacy-edged hanky just inside the opening as an added attraction. It was one Olivia had lent me to mop my forehead during that last all-night session, and it still held a whiff of a perfume that would attract a primitive more surely than a scattering of gold coins. I had done all I could. The next step was up to the opposition.

I awoke from a light doze to see that it was late evening. The trees were black lacework against a red-gold sky, and the chirruping of crickets and the shrill *tseet! tseet!* of a bird were the only sounds against an absolute stillness—

And then the crackle of underbrush, the snap of broken twigs, the sound of heavy breathing... I froze, trying to see through the gloom. He was coming. Hell, he was here! And making no effort at stealth. He was sure of himself, this native—which probably meant that here in his own stamping ground he was top carnivore. I tried to picture the kind of man who could stand up to the King Cat I'd seen, and gave it up as too discouraging. And this was the fellow I was going to trip up and then threaten with a broom handle...

I swallowed the old corn husks that had gotten wedged in my throat, squinted some more. I made out a tall figure coming across the burned ground, stooping, apparently peering around—looking for me, no doubt. The thought gave me no comfort. I couldn't see what kind of weapon he had. I gripped my spear, tried to hold my breathing to a deep, slow rhythm. He was close now, pausing to glance over the shuttle, then turning toward the entrance hold. The handkerchief would be visible in the dim light, and the scent...He took a step, another. He was close now, a vague, dark shape in deep shadow—

There was a choked yell, a crashing, a thud, and I was out of my hidey-hole, stumbling across a tangle of roots, bringing my spear up, skidding to a halt before the pale torso and dark head of the man who struggled, scrabbling for a handhold, hip deep in my trap.

"Hold it right there!" I barked through clenched teeth, holding the spear ready with both hands, poised over the man who stood frozen now, a narrow-shouldered, long-armed figure, his face a dark blob under a white headpiece—

"I say, Bayard," Dzok's voice came. "You've led me a merry chase, I must say!"

CHAPTER ELEVEN

"IT WASN'T EASY, OLD boy," Dzok said, offering me a second cup of a coffee-like drink he had brewed over the small fire he had built. "I can assure you I was in bad odor with the Council for my part in bringing you to Xonijeel. However, the best offense is a good defense, as the saying goes. I countered by preferring charges against Minister Sphogeel for compromise of an official TDP position, illegal challenge of an Agent's competence, failure to refer a matter of Authoritarian security to a full Board meeting—"

"I don't quite get the picture, Dzok," I interrupted. "*You* conned me into going to Xonijeel by promising me help against the Hagroon—"

"Really, Bayard, I promised no more than that I'd do my best. It was a piece of ill luck that old Sphogeel was on the Council that week. He's a notorious xenophobe. I never dreamed he'd go so far as to consign you to exile on the basis of a kangaroo hearing—"

"You were the one who grabbed my gun," I pointed out.

"Lucky thing, too. If you'd managed to kill someone, there'd have been nothing I could do to save you from being burned down on the spot. And I'm not sure I'd have wanted to. You *are* a bloodthirsty blighter, you know."

"So you followed me to B-I Four..."

"As quickly as I could. Managed to get myself assigned as escort to a recruitment group—all native chaps, of course—"

"Native chaps?"

"Ahhh...Anglics, like yourself, captured as cubs... er...babies, that is. Cute little fellows, Anglic cubs. Can't help warming to them. Easy to train, too, and damnably human—"

"Okay, you can skip the propaganda. Somehow it doesn't help my morale to picture human slaves as lovable whities."

Dzok cleared his throat. "Of course, old chap. Sorry. I merely meant—well, hang it, man, what can I say? We treated you badly! I admit it! But—" he flashed me a sly smile. "I neglected to mention your rather sturdy hypnotic defenses against conditioning. I daresay you'd have had a bit more trouble throwing off your false memories if they'd known, and modified their indoctrination accordingly. And to make amends I came after you, only to find you'd flown the coop—"

"Why so mysterious? Why not come right up and knock on the door and say all was forgiven?"

Dzok chuckled. "Now, now, dear boy, can you imagine the reaction of a typical Anglic villager to *my* face appearing at the door, inquiring after a misplaced chum?

I scratched at my jaw, itchy with two day's stubble. "All right, you had to be circumspect. But you could have phoned—"

"I could have remained hidden in the garret until after·dark, then ventured out to reconnoiter, which is precisely what I did," Dzok said firmly. "I was ready to approach you at Mrs. Rogers' house, when you slipped away from me. I located you again at the cottage at the edge of the woods, but again you moved too quickly—"

"We spotted you creeping around," I told him. "I thought it was the Xonijeelian Gestapo getting ready to revise the sentence to something more permanent than exile."

"Again, I was about to speak to you on the road, when that fellow in the cocked hat interfered. Then you fooled me by taking a train. Had a devil of a time learning where you'd gone. I had to return to Xonijeel, travel to Rome, reshuttle to your so-called B-I Four line, then set about locating you. Fortunately, we maintain a permanent station in Italy, with a number of trusties—"

"More natives, I presume?"

"Quite. I say, old man, you're developing something of a persecution complex, I'm afraid—"

"That's easy, when you're persecuted."

"Nonsense. Why, you know I've always dealt with you as an equal . . ."

"Sure, some of your best friends are people. But to hell with that. Go on."

"Umm. Yes. Of course, I had to operate under

cover of darkness. Even then, it was far from easy. The Roman police are a suspicious lot. I turned you up at last, waited about outside your flat, then realized what you were about, and hurried to your shop. You know what happened there..." He rubbed his round skull gingerly. "Still tender, you know. Fortunately for me I was well wrapped up—"

"If you'd just said something..." I countered.

"Just as I opened my mouth, you hit me."

"All right, I'm sorry—sorrier than you know, considering what I went through after that. How the hell did you trail me here?"

He grinned, showing too many even white teeth. "Your apparatus, old boy. Fantastically inefficient. Left a trail across the Web I could have followed on a bicycle."

"You came to B-I four ostensibly on a recruitment mission, you said?"

"Yes. I could hardly reveal what I had in mind—and it seemed a likely spot to find some eager volunteers for Anglic Sector duty—"

"I thought you had plenty of trusties you'd raised from cubs."

"We need a large quota of native recruited personnel for our Special Forces, chaps who know the languages and more of the Anglic lines. We're able to offer these lads an exciting career, good pay, retirement. It's not a bad life, as members of an elite corps—"

"Won't it look a little strange when you come back without your recruits?"

"Ah, but I have my recruits, dear boy! Twenty picked men, waiting at the depot at Rome B-I Four."

I took a breath and asked The Question: "So you

came to make amends? What kind of amends? Are you offering me a ride home?"

"Look here, Bayard," Dzok said earnestly. "I've looked into the business of Sphogeel's photogram—the one which clearly indicated that there is no normal A-line at the Web coordinates you mentioned—"

"So you think I'm nuts too?"

He shook his head. "It's not so simple as that..."

"What's that supposed to mean?" My pulse was picking up, getting ready for bad news.

"I checked the records, Bayard. Three weeks ago—at the time you departed your home line in the Hagroon shuttle—your Zero-zero line was there, just as you said. Less than twelve hours later—nothing."

I gaped at him.

"It can mean only one thing...I'm sorry to be the one to tell you this, but it appears there's been an unauthorized use of a device known as a discontinuity engine."

"Go on," I growled.

"Our own technicians devised the apparatus over a hundred years ago. It was used in a war with a rebellious province..."

I just looked at him, waiting.

"I can hardly play the role of apologist for the actions of the previous generation, Bayard," Dzok said stiffly. "Suffice it to say that the machine was outlawed by unanimous vote of the High Board of the Authority, and never used again. By us, that is. But now it seems that the Hagroon have stolen the secret—"

"What does a discontinuity engine do?" I demanded. "How could it conceal the existence of an A-line from your instruments?"

"The device," Dzok said unhappily, "once set up in any A-line, releases the entropic energy of that line in random fashion. A ring of energy travels outward, creating what we've termed a probability storm in each A-line as the wave front passes. As for your Zero-zero line—it's gone, old man, snuffed out of existence. It no longer exists..."

I got to my feet, feeling light-headed, dizzy. Dzok's voice went on, but I wasn't listening. I was picturing the Hagroon stringing wire in the deserted garages of the Net Terminal; quietly, methodically preparing to destroy a world...

"Why?" I yelled. "Why? We had no quarrel with them..."

"They discovered your Net capabilities. You were a threat to be eliminated—"

"Wait a minute! You said *your* bunch invented this discontinuity whatzit. How did the Hagroon get hold of it?"

"That, I don't know—but I intend to find out."

"Are you telling me they just put on false whiskers and walked in and lifted it when nobody was looking? That's a little hard to swallow whole, Dzok. I think it's a lot easier to believe you boys worked along with the Hagroon, hired them to do your dirty work—"

"If that were the case, why would I be here now?" Dzok demanded.

"I don't know. Why *are* you here?"

"I've come to help you, Bayard. To do what I can—"

"What would that be—another one-way ticket to some nice dead end where I can set up housekeeping and plant a garden and forget all about what might have been, once, in a world that doesn't exist anymore because some people with too much hair decided we might be a nuisance and didn't want to take the chance—" I was advancing on Dzok, with ideas of seeing if his throat was as easy to squeeze as it looked...

Dzok sat where he was, staring at me. "You don't have to behave like a complete idiot, Bayard, in spite of your race's unhappy reputation for blind ferocity— besides which, I happen to be stronger than you..." He took something from the pocket of his trim white jacket, tossed it at my feet. It was my slug gun. I scooped it up.

"Still, if you actually are a homicidal maniac, go ahead. Don't bother to listen to what I have to say, or to wonder why I came here."

I looked at him across the fire, then thrust the gun into my pocket and sat down. "Go ahead," I said. "I'm listening."

"I gave the matter considerable thought, Bayard," Dzok said calmly. He poured himself another cup of coffee, sniffed at it, balanced it on his knee. "And an idea occurred to me..."

I didn't say anything. It was very silent; even the night birds had stopped calling. Somewhere, far away, something bellowed. A breeze stirred the trees overhead. They sighed like an old man remembering the vanished loves of his youth.

"We've developed some interesting items in our Web Research Labs," Dzok said. "One of our most recent creations has been a special, lightweight suit, with its Web circuitry woven into the fabric itself. The generator is housed in a shoulder pack weighing only a few ounces. Its design is based on a new application of plasma mechanics, utilizing nuclear forces rather than the conventional magneto-electronic fields—"

"Sure," I snapped. "What does it have to do with me?"

"It gives the wearer Web mobility without a shuttle," Dzok continued. "The suit is the shuttle. Of course, it's necessary to attune the suit to the individual wearer's entropic quotient—but that in itself is an advantage: it creates an auto-homing feature. When the field is activated, the wearer is automatically transferred to the continuum of minimum stress—namely, his A-line of origin—or whatever other line his metabolism is attuned to."

"Swell. You've developed an improved shuttle. So what?"

"I have one here. For you." Dzok waved toward the bubble-shape of his standard Xonijeel model Web traveler—a far more sophisticated device than the clumsy machines of the Imperium. "I smuggled it into my cargo locker—after stealing it from the lab. I'm a criminal on several counts on your behalf, old fellow."

"What do I do with this suit? Go snark hunting? You've already told me my world is gone—"

"There is another development which I'm sure you'll find of interest," Dzok went on imperturbably. "In our more abstruse researches into the nature of the Web, we've turned up some new findings that place rather a new complexion on our old theories of reality. Naturally, on first discovering the nature of the Web, one was forced to accept the fact of the totality of all existence; that in a Universe of infinities, all possible things exist. But still, with the intellectual chauvinism inherent in our monolinear orientation, we assumed that the wavefront of simultaneous reality advanced everywhere at the same rate. That 'now' in one A-line was of necessity 'now' in every other—and that this was an immutable quality, as irreversible as entropy..."

"Well, isn't it?"

"Yes—precisely as irreversible as entropy. But now it appears that entropy can be reversed—and very easily, at that." He smiled triumphantly.

"Are you saying," I asked carefully, "that you people have developed time travel?"

Dzok laughed. "Not at all—not in the direct sense you mean. There is an inherent impossibility in reversing one's motion along one's own personal time track..." He looked thoughtful. "At least, I think there is—"

"Then what are you saying?"

"When one moves outward from one's own A-line, crossing other lines in their myriads, it is possible, by proper application of these newly harnessed subatomic hypermagnetic forces I mentioned to you, to set up a sort of—tacking, one might call it. Rather than traveling across the lines in a planiform temporal stasis, as is normal with more primitive drives, we found that it was possible to skew the vector—to retrogress temporally, to levels contemporaneous with the past of the line of origin—to distances proportional to the distance of normal Web displacement."

"I guess that means something," I said. "But what?"

"It means that with the suit I've brought you, you can return to your Zero-zero line—at a time prior to its disappearance!"

It was nearly daylight now. Dzok and I had spent the last few hours over a chart laid out on the tiny navigation table in his shuttle, making calculations based on the complex formulation which he said represented the relationships existing between normal entropy, E-entropy, Net displacement, the entropic quotient of the body in question—me—and other factors too numerous to mention, even if I'd understood them.

"You're a difficult case, Bayard," the agent said, shaking his head. He opened a flat case containing an instrument like a stethoscope with a fitting resembling a phonographic pickup. He took readings against my skull, compared them with the figures he had already written out.

"I think I've corrected properly for your various wanderings in the last few weeks," he said. "Since it's been a number of years since your last visit to your original A-line—B-I three—I think we can safely assume that you've settled into a normal entropic relationship with your adopted Zero-zero line—"

"Better run over those manual controls with me again—just in case."

"Certainly—but let's hope you have no occasion to use them. It was mad of you, old chap, to set out in that makeshift shuttle of yours, planning to navigate by the seat of your pants. It just won't work, you know. You'd never have found your target—"

"Okay, but I won't worry about that until after I find out if I'm going to survive this new trip. What kind of margin of error will I have?"

Dzok looked concerned. "Not as much as I'd like. My observations indicated that your Zero-zero line was destroyed twenty-one days ago. The maximum displacement I can give you with the suit at this range is twenty-three days. You'll have approximately forty-eight hours after your arrival to circumvent the Hagroon. How you'll do that—"

"Is my problem."

"I've given it some thought," Dzok said. "You observed them at work in null time. From your description of what they were about, it seems apparent that they were erecting a transfer portal linking the null level with its corresponding aspect of normal entropy—in other words, with the normal continuum. They'd need this, of course, in order to set up the discontinuity engine in the line itself. Your task will be to give warning, and drive them back when they make their assault."

"We can handle that," I assured him grimly. "The trick will be convincing people I'm not nuts..." I didn't add the disquieting thought that in view of the attitude of the Imperial authorities—at our last meeting—my own oldest friends included—it was doubtful whether I'd get the kind of hearing that could result in prompt action. But I could worry about that later too, after I'd made the trip—if I succeeded in finding my target at all.

"Now to fit the suit." Dzok lifted the lid of a wall locker, took out a limp outfit like a nylon driver's suit, held it up to me.

"A bit long in the leg, but I'll soon make that right..." He went to work like a skilled seamstress, using shears and a hot iron, snipping and re-sealing the soft woven plastic material. I tried it on, watched while he shortened the sleeves, and added a section down the middle of the back to accommodate my wider shoulders.

"Doesn't that hand-tailoring interfere with the

circuits?" I asked, as he fussed over the helmet-to-shoulder fit.

"Not at all. The pattern of the weave's the thing—so long as I make sure the major connecting links are made up fast..."

He settled the fishbowl in place, then touched a stud on a plate set in the chest area of the suit, looked at the meters mounted on a small test panel on the table. He nodded, switched off.

"Now, Bayard," he said seriously. "Your controls are here..."

It was full daylight now. Dzok and I stood on the grassy bank above the river. He looked worried.

"You're sure you understand the spatial maneuvering controls?"

"Sure—that part's easy. I just kick off and jet—"

"You'll have to use extreme care. Of course, you won't feel the normal gravitational effects, so you'll be able to flit about as lightly as a puff of smoke—but you'll still retain normal inertia. If you collide with a tree, or rock, it will be precisely as disastrous as in a normal entropic field."

"I'll be careful, Dzok. And you do the same." I held out my hand and he took it, grinning.

"Goodbye, Bayard. Best of luck and all that. Pity we couldn't have worked out something in the way of an alliance between our respective governments, but perhaps it was a bit premature. At least now there'll be the chance of a future rapprochement."

"Sure—and thanks for everything."

He stepped back and waved. I looked around for a last glimpse of the morning sun, the greenery, Dzok's transparent shuttle, and Dzok himself, long-legged, his shiny boots mud-spattered, his whites mud-stained. He raised a hand and I pressed the lever that activated the suit. There was a moment of vertigo, a sense of pressure on all sides. Then Dzok flickered, disappeared. His shuttle winked out of sight. The strange, abnormal movement of normally immobile objects that was characteristic of Net travel started up. I watched as the trees waved, edged about in the soil, putting out groping feelers toward me as though sensing my presence.

A hop, and I was in the air, drifting ten feet above the surface. I touched the jet-control and at once a blast of cold ions hurled me forward. I took a bearing, corrected course, and settled down for a long run.

I was on my way.

CHAPTER TWELVE

IT WAS A WEIRD trip across the probability worlds, exposed as I was to the full panoramic effects of holocausts of planetary proportions. For a while, I skimmed above a sea of boiling lava that stretched to the far horizon. Then I was drifting among fragments of the crust of a shattered world, and later I watched as pale flames licked the cinders of a burnt-out continent. All the while I sped northward, following the faint *be-beep!* of my autocompass, set on a course that would bring me to the site of Stockholm after four hours' flight. I saw great seas of oily, dead fluid surge across what had once been land, their foaming crests oddly flowing backwards, as I retrogressed through time while I hurled across A-space. I watched the obscene heaving and groping of monstrous life-forms created in the chaotic aftermath of the unleashed powers of the M-C field, great jungles of blood red plants, deserts of blasted, shattered stone over which the sun flared like an arc-light in a black, airless sky. Now and again there would be a brief uprising of almost normal landscape, as I swept across a cluster of A-lines which had suffered less than the others. But always the outré element intruded: a vast, wallowing animal form, like a hundred-ton dog, or a mountainous, mutated cow, with extra limbs and lolling heads placed at random across the vast bulk through which bloodred vines grew, penetrating the flesh.

Hours passed. I checked my chronometer and the navigational instruments set in the wrist of the suit. I was close to my target and, according to the positional indicator, over southern Sweden—not that the plain of riven rock below me resembled the warm and verdant plains of Scandia I had last seen on a hiking trip with Barbro, three months earlier.

I maneuvered close to the ground, crossed a finger of the sea that marked the location of Hykoping in normal space. I was getting close now. It was time to pick a landing spot. It wouldn't do to land too close to the city. Popping into identity on a crowded street would be unwise. I recognized the low, rolling country south of the capital now; I slowed my progress, hovered, waiting for the moment...

Abruptly, light and color blazed around me. I threw the main control switch, dropped the last few feet to a grassy hillside. It took me a moment to get the helmet clear; then I took a deep breath of cool, fresh air—the air of a world regained from twenty-two days in the past.

Down on the road, with the suit bundled under my arm, I flagged a horse-drawn wagon, let the driver ramble on with the assumption that I was one of those crazy sky-diver fellows. He spent the whole trip into town telling me how you'd never get him up in one of those things, then asked me for a free ride. I promised to remember him next time I was up, and hopped off at the small-town post office.

Inside, I gave a rambling excuse for my lack of funds to an ill-tempered looking man in a tight blue uniform, and asked him to put through a call to Intelligence HQ in Stockholm. While I waited, I noticed the wall calendar—and felt the sweat pop out on my forehead. I was a full day later than Dzok had calculated. The doom that hung over the Imperium was only hours away.

The plump man came back, with a thin man in tow. He told me to repeat my request to his superior. I began to get irritated.

"Gentlemen, I have important information for Baron Richthofen. Just put my call through—"

"That will not be possible," the slim fellow said. He had a nose sharp enough to poke a hole through quarter-inch plywood. It was red on the end, as though he'd been trying.

"You can charge the call to my home telephone," I said. "My name is Bayard, number 12, Nybrovagen—"

"You have identity papers?"

"I'm sorry; I've lost my wallet. But—"

"You place me in a difficult position," the thin fellow said, with a smile that suggested that he was enjoying it. "If the Herr is unable to identify himself—"

"This is important!" I rapped. "You have nothing to lose but a phone call. If I *am* on the level, you'll look like a damned fool for obstructing me!"

That got to him. He conferred with his chubby chum, then announced that he would check with the number I had given him in Stockholm, supposedly that of Herr Bayard...

I waited while he dialed, talked, nodded, waited, talked some more in an undertone, placed the receiver back on the phone with a triumphant look. He spoke briefly to the other man, who hurried away.

"Well?" I demanded.

"You say that *you* are Herr Bayard?" he cooed, fingertips together.

"Colonel Bayard to you, Buster," I snapped. "This is a matter of life and death—"

"Whose life and death, ah...*Colonel* Bayard?"

"To hell with that..." I started around the counter. He leaned on one foot and I heard a distant bell sound. The fat man reappeared, looking flushed. There was another man behind him, a heavy fellow in a flat cap and gunbelt, with cop written all over him. He put a gun on me and ordered me to stand clear of the wall. Then he frisked me quickly—missing the slug gun which Dzok had restored—and motioned me to the door.

"Hold on," I said. "What's this farce all about? I've got to get that call through to Stockholm—"

"You claim that you are Colonel Bayard, of Imperial Intelligence?" the cop rapped out.

"Right the first time," I started.

"It may interest you to know," the thin postal official said, savoring the drama of the moment, "that Herr Colonel Bayard is at this moment dining at his home in the capital."

Chapter Thirteen

THE CELL THEY GAVE me wasn't bad by Hagroon standards, but that didn't keep me from pounding on the bars and yelling. I had my slug gun, of course—but since they wouldn't recognize it as a weapon even if I showed it, there was no chance of bluff. And I wasn't quite ready yet to kill. There were still several hours to go before the crisis and my call wouldn't take long—once they saw reason.

The fat man had gone away, promising that an official from the military sub-station at Sodra would be along soon. Meantime I pounded and demanded that another call be put through—but nobody listened. Now my chance to use the gun was gone. The man with the keys kept to the outer office.

A slack-looking youth in baggy pants and wide blue and yellow suspenders brought me in a small smorgasbord about noon. I tried to bribe him to make the call for me. He gave me a crooked smile and turned away.

It was well after dark when there was a sudden stir in the outer room of the jail. Then the metal door clanged open and a familiar face appeared—a field agent I had met once or twice in the course of my duties with Intelligence. He was a tall, worried-looking man, wearing drab civvies and carrying a briefcase. He stopped dead when he saw me, then came on hesitantly.

"Hello, Captain," I greeted him. "We'll all have a good chuckle over this later, as the saying goes, but right now I need out of here fast..."

The cop who had arrested me was behind him, and the fat man from the post office.

"You know my name?" the agent asked awkwardly.

"I'm afraid not—but I think you know me. We've met once or twice—"

"Listen to the fellow," the fat man said. "A violent case—"

"Silence!" the agent snapped. He came up close, looked me over carefully.

"You wished to place a call to Intelligence HQ," he said. "What did you wish to speak about?"

"I'll tell them myself," I snapped. "Get me out of here, Captain—in a hell of a hurry! This is top priority business!"

"You may tell me what it is you wished to report," he said.

"I'll report directly to Baron Richthofen!"

He lifted his shoulders. "You place me in an awkward position—"

"To hell with your position! Can't you understand plain Swedish? I'm telling you—"

"You will address an officer of Imperial Intelligence with more respect!" the cop broke in.

The agent turned to the two men behind him. "Clear out, both of you!" he snapped. They left, looking crestfallen. He turned back to me, wiped a hand across his forehead.

"This is very difficult for me," he said. "You bear a close resemblance to Colonel Bayard—"

"Resemblance! Hell, I *am* Bayard!"

He shook his head. "I was assured on that point, most specifically," he said. "I don't know what this is all about, my friend, but it will be better for you to tell me the whole story—"

"The story is that I have information of vital importance to the Imperium! Every minute counts, man! Forget the red tape! Get me a line to Headquarters!"

"You are an imposter. We know that much. You asked to have a call placed. A routine check at Colonel Bayard's home indicated that he was there—"

"I can't try to explain all the paradoxes involved. Just put my call through!"

"It is not possible to route every crank call to the Chief of Intelligence!" the man snapped. "What is this message of yours? If it seems to warrant attention, I will personally—"

"Let me talk to Bayard, then," I cut in.

"Ah, then you abandon your imposture?"

"Call it what you like. Let me talk to him!"

"That is not possible—"

"I didn't know we had anyone in the service as stupid as you are," I said clearly. "All right, I'll give

you the message—and by all you hold sacred, you'd
better believe me."

He didn't. He was polite, and heard me all the
way through. Then he signaled for the jailer and got
ready to leave.

"You can't walk out of here without at least checking
my story!" I roared at him. "What kind of intelligence
man are you? Take a look at the suit I had with me,
damn you! That will show you I'm not imagining the
whole thing!"

He looked at me, a troubled look. "How can I
believe you? Your claim to be Bayard is a lie, and the
story you tell is fantastic! Would *you* have believed it?"

I stared back at him.

"I don't know," I said, honestly. "But I'd at least
have checked what I could."

He turned to the cop, who was back, hovering at
the door.

"You have this...shuttle suit?"

The cop nodded. "Yes, sir. I have it here on my
desk. I've checked it for..." his voice faded as he and
the agent went out and the door shut behind them.
For another half hour I paced the cell, wondering
whether I should have shot a couple of them and
tried to scare the cop into unlocking me; but from
what I knew of the men of the Imperium, it wouldn't
have worked. They were too damned brave for their
own good.

Then the door clanged open again. A stranger was
there this time—a small man with a runny nose and
eyes, and glasses as thick as checkers.

"...very odd, very odd," he was saying. "But meaningless, of course. The circuitry is quite inert..."

"This is Herr Professor Doctor Runngvist," the agent said. "He's checked your ... ah ... suit, and assures me that it's crank work. A homemade hoax of some sort, incapable of any—"

"Damn you!" I yelled. "Sure the suit's inert—without me in it! I'm part of the circuitry! It's attuned to me!"

"Eh? Tuned to you? A part of the circuitry?" The old man adjusted his glasses at an angle to get a better view of me.

"Look, pops, this is a highly sophisticated device. It utilizes the wearer's somatic and neural fields as a part of the total circuitry. Without me inside, it won't work. Let me have it. I'll demonstrate it for you—"

"Sorry, I can't allow that," the agent said quickly. "Look here, fellow, hadn't you better drop this show now, and tell me what it's all about? You're in pretty deep water already, I'd say, impersonating an officer—"

"You know Bayard on sight, don't you?" I cut in.

"Yes ..."

"Do I look like him?"

He looked worried. "Yes, to an extent. I presume it was that which inspired this imposture, but—"

"Listen to me, Captain," I said as levelly as I could through the bars. "This is the biggest crisis the Imperium has faced since Chief Inspector Bale ran amok ..."

The captain frowned. "How did you know of that?"

"I was there. My name's Bayard, remember? Now get me out of here—"

There was a shrilling of a telephone bell in the outer room. Feet clumped. Voices rumbled. Then the door flew open.

"Inspector! It's a call—from Stockholm ..."

My inquisitors turned. "Yes?"

"That fellow—Colonel Bayard!" an excited voice said. Someone shushed him. They stood in the hall, conversing in whispers. Then the intelligence captain came back with the cop behind him.

"You'd better start telling all you know," he snapped, looking grimmer than ever.

"What happened?"

"Stockholm is under attack by an armed force of undetermined size!"

It was close to midnight now. I had been looking for a chance for a break for the past hour, but Captain Burman, the agent, was taking no chances. He had locked the outer door to the cell block and nobody was allowed even to come close to my cell. I think he was beginning to suspect that everything wasn't as simple as it appeared.

I watched the door across the aisle as a key clattered in it and it swung wide. It was Burman, white-faced, and two strangers, both in civilian clothes. My wrist tensed, ready to flip the gun into my palm, but they kept their distance.

"This is the man." Burman waved at me like a tenant complaining about a prowler. "I've gotten nothing from him but nonsense—or what I thought was nonsense, until now!"

The newcomers looked me over. One was a short, thick-set, hairless man in wide lapels and baggy-kneed pants. The other was trim, neat, well set up. I decided to make my pitch to the former. No underling could afford to look that messy.

"Listen, you," I started. "I'm Colonel Bayard, of Imperial Intelligence—"

"I will listen, of that you may be assured," the little man said. "Start at the beginning and repeat what you have told the Captain."

"It's too late for talk." I flipped the gun into my hand. All three of them jumped, and a heavy automatic appeared in the snappy dresser's hand.

"Ever seen one of these before?" I showed the slug gun, keeping the armed man covered.

The thick man jerked his head in a quick nod.

"Then you know they're only issued to a few people in Net Surveillance work—including me. I could have shot my way out of here when I first arrived, but I thought I'd get a fair hearing without killing anybody. Now it's too late for humanitarianism. One of you open up, or I start shooting—and I'm faster than you are, Buster," I added for the benefit of the tall man with the gun.

"Here, you're only making it worse—"

"It couldn't be worse. Get the key. Call that dumb flatfoot out front."

The thick man shook his head. "Shoot then, sir. Major Gunnarson will then be forced to return your fire, and so two men will die. But I will not release you."

"Why not? You can watch me. All I want to do is call Intelligence—"

"I do not know what set of signals you may have worked out, or with whom, and I do not intend to find out at the expense of Imperial security."

"There's not any Imperial security, as long as you keep me here. I've told my story to Burman! Take action! Do something!"

"I have already attempted to relay your statement to Baron Richthofen at Stockholm," the rumpled man said.

"What do you mean, attempted?"

"Just that. I was unable to get through. All telephonic connection is broken, I found. I sent a messenger. He failed to return. Another messenger has reached me but now. He was dispatched an hour ago, and heard the news over his auto radio set just before..."

"Just before what?"

"Before the gas attack," he said in a harsh voice. Abruptly there was a gun in his hand—a heavy revolver. He had drawn it so quickly that I couldn't even say where he'd gotten it.

"Now, tell me all you know of these matters, Mr. Bayard, or whatever your name might be! You have ten seconds to begin!"

I kept my gun on his partner. I knew that if I moved it as much as a millimeter, the baggy man would gun me down. I tried to match the steely look in his eye.

"I told Burman the whole story. If you choose not to believe it, that's not my fault. But there may still be time. What's the situation in the city?"

"There is *no* time, Mr. Bayard. No time at all..." To my horror I saw a tear glisten at the corner of the thick man's eye.

"What..." I couldn't finish the question.

"The invaders have released a poisonous gas which has blanketed the city. They have erected barricades against any attempt at relief. Strange men in helmeted suits are shooting down every man who approaches..."

"But what about...the people...What about my wife? What—"

He was shaking his head. "The Emperor and his family, the government, everyone, all must be presumed dead, Mr. Bayard, inside the barricaded city!"

There was a shattering crash from the outer room.

The thick man whirled from me, jumped to the door, shot a look out, then went through at a dead run, Burman at his heels. I yelled at Major Gunnarson to stop or I'd shoot, but he didn't and neither did I. There was a clatter of feet, a crash like breaking glass, a couple of shots. Someone yelled "The ape-men!" There were more shots, then a heavy slam like a body hitting the floor. I backed into the corner of my cell, cursing the fatal mistake I'd made in letting myself get cornered here. I aimed at the door, waited for the first Hagroon to come through—

The door flew open—and a familiar narrow-shouldered figure in stained whites sauntered into view.

"Dzok!" I yelled. "Get me out of here—or—" A horrible suspicion dawned. Dzok must have seen it in my face.

"Easy, old fellow!" he shouted as my gun covered him. "I'm here to give you a spot of assistance, old chap—and from the looks of things, you can jolly well use it!"

"What's going on out there?" I yelled. There was someone behind Dzok. A tall young fellow in a green coat and scarlet knee pants came through the door, holding a long-barreled rifle with a short bayonet fixed to the end of it. There were white facings on the coat, wide loops of braid, and rows of bright gold buttons. There was a wide cocked hat on his head, with a gold fringe and a crimson rosette, and he wore white stockings and polished black shoes with large gilt buckles. The owner of the finery flashed me a big smile, then turned to Dzok and gave a sloppy salute with the palm of his hand out.

"I reckon we peppered 'em good, sor. Now what say ye we have a look about out back here for any more o' the gossoons as might be skulkin' ready to do in a honest man?"

"Never mind that, sergeant," Dzok said. "This is a jail delivery, nothing more. Those chaps out there are our allies, actually. Pity about the shooting, but it couldn't be helped." He was talking to me now. "I attempted to make a few inquiries, but found everyone in a state of the most extreme agitation. They opened fire with hardly a second glance, amid shouts of 'hairy ape-men'! Disgraceful—"

"The Hagroon have hit the capital," I cut him off. "Laid down a gas attack, barricaded the streets, everybody presumed dead..." I wasn't thinking now—just reacting. The Hagroon had to be stopped. That was all that mattered. Not that anything really mattered any more, with Barbro gone with the rest—but she was a fighter. She'd have expected me to go on fighting, too, as long as I could still move and breathe.

Dzok looked stricken. "Beastly, old fellow! I can't tell you how sorry I am..." He commiserated with me for awhile. Then the sergeant came back from the outer room with a key, opened my cell door.

"And so I came too late," Dzok said bitterly. "I had hoped..." He let the sentence trail off, as we went into the outer room.

"Who are these fellows?" I gaped at the half-dozen bright-plumaged soldiers posted about the jail covering the windows and the door.

"These are my volunteers, Bayard—my Napoleonic levies. I was on a recruiting mission, you'll recall. After I left you, I went back and loaded these chaps into my cargo shuttle, and returned to Zaj—and found—you'll never guess, old fellow!"

"I'll take three guesses," I said, "and they'll all be 'the Hagroon.'"

Dzok nodded glumly. "The bounders had overrun Authority headquarters, including the Web terminal, of course. I beat a hasty strategic retreat, and followed your trail here..." he paused, looking embarrassed. "Actually, old chap, I'd hoped to enlist the aid of your Imperium. We Xonijeelians are ill-equipped to fight a Web war, I'm sorry to say. Always before—"

"I know. They caught us off-guard too. I wondered all along why you figured you were immune—"

"The audacity of the blighters! Who'd have expected—"

"You should have," I said shortly.

"Ah, well, what's done is done." Dzok rubbed his hands together with every appearance of relish. "Inasmuch as you're not in a position to assist me, perhaps my chaps and I can still be of some help here. Better start by giving me a complete resumé of the situation..."

After ten minutes' talk, while the troops kept up a sporadic fire from the jail windows, Dzok and I had decided on a plan of action. It wasn't a good one, but under the circumstances it was better than nothing. The first step was to find the S-suit. We wasted another ten minutes searching the place before I decided to try the vault. It was open, and the suit was laid out on a table.

"Right," Dzok said with satisfaction. "I'll need tools, Bayard, and a heat source and a magnifying glass..."

We rummaged, found a complete tool kit in a wall

locker and a glass in the chief's desk drawer. I made a hasty adaptation of a hot plate used for heating coffee, while Dzok opened up the control console set in the chest of the suit.

"We're treading on dangerous ground, of course," he said blandly, while he snipped hair-fire wires, teased them into new arrangements. "What I'm attempting is theoretically possible, but it's never been tried—not with an S-suit."

I watched admiring the dexterity of his long grayish fingers as he rearranged the internal components of the incredibly compact installation. For half an hour, while guns cracked intermittently, he made tests, muttered, tried again, studying the readings on the miniature scales set on the cuff of the suit. Then he straightened, gave me a wry look.

"It's done, old chap. I can't guarantee the results of my makeshift mods, but there's at least an even chance that it will do what we want."

I asked for an explanation of what he had done, followed closely as he pointed out the interplay of circuits that placed stresses on the M-C field in such a way as to distort its normal function along a line of geometric progression leading to infinity...

"It's over my head, Dzok," I told him. "I was never a really first-class M-C man, and when it comes to your Xonijeelian complexities—"

"Don't trouble your head, Bayard. All you need to know is that adjusting this setting..." he pointed with a pin drill at a tiny knurled knob—"controls the angle of incidence of the pinch-field—"

"In plain English, if something goes wrong and I'm not dead, I can twiddle that and try again."

"Very succinctly put. Now let's be going. How far did you say it is to the city?"

"About twelve kilometers."

"Right. We'll have to commandeer a pair of light lorries. There are several parked in the court just outside. Some sort of crude steam-cars, I think—"

"Internal combustion. And not so crude; they'll do a hundred kilometers an hour."

"They'll serve." He went into the guard room, checked the scene from the windows.

"Quiet out there at the moment. No point in waiting about. Let's sally at once." I nodded and Dzok gave his orders to the gaily costumed riflemen, five of whom quietly took up positions at the windows and door facing the courtyard, while the others formed up a cordon around Dzok and me.

"Hell, we may as well do our bit," I suggested. There were carbines in the gun locker. I took one, tossed one to Dzok, buckled on a belt and stuffed it with ammo.

"Tell your lads to shoot low," I said. "Don't let anybody get in our way, but try not to kill anybody. They don't know what's going on out there—"

"And there's no time to explain," Dzok finished for me, looking at his men. "Shoot to wound, right, lads? Now, Sergeant, take three men and move out. Cover the first lorry and hold your fire until they start something. Mr. Bayard and I will come next, with ten men, while the rest of you lay down a covering fire. Those in the rear guard stand fast until number two lorry pulls up to the door, then pile in quickly and we're off."

"Very well, sor," the sergeant said. He was working

hard on a plug of tobacco he'd found in the police chief's desk drawer. He turned and bawled instructions to his men, who nodded, grinning.

"These boys don't behave like recruits," I said. "They look like veterans to me."

Dzok nodded, smiling his incredible smile. "Former members of the Welsh regiment of the Imperial Guard. They were eager for a change."

"I wonder what you offered them?"

"The suggestion of action after a few months changing of the guard at Westminster was sufficient."

The sergeant was at the door now, with two of his men. He said a quick word, and the three darted out, sprinted for the lorry, a high-sided dark blue panel truck lettered flottsbro polis. A scattering of shots rang out. Grass tips flew as bullets clipped the turf by the sergeant's ankle. The man on his left stumbled, went down, rolled, came up limping, his thigh wet with a dark glisten against the scarlet cloth. He made it in two jumps to the shelter of the truck, hit the grass, leveled his musket and fired. A moment later, all three were in position, their guns crackling in a one-round-per-second rhythm. The opposing fire slackened.

"Now," Dzok said. I brought the carbine up across my chest and dashed for the second truck. There was a white puff of smoke from a window overlooking the courtyard, a whine past my head. I ducked, pounded across the grass, leaped the chain at the edge of the pavement, skidded to a halt beside the lorry. Dzok was there ahead of me, wrenching at the door.

"Locked!" he called, and stepped back, fired a round into the keyhole, wrenched the door open. I caught a glimpse of his shuttle, a heavy passenger-carrying job, parked across a flowerbed. He followed my gaze.

"Just have to leave it. Too bad..." He was inside then, staring at the unfamiliar controls.

"Slide over!" I pushed in beside him, feeling the vehicle lurch as the men crowded in behind me, hearing the *sprang!* as a shot hit the metal body. There were no keys in the ignition. I tried the starter; nothing.

"I'll have to short the wiring," I said, and slid to the ground, jumped to the hood, unlatched the wide side panel, lifted it. With one hard jerk, I twisted the ignition wires free, made hasty connections to the battery, then grabbed the starter lever and depressed it. The engine groaned, turned over twice, and caught with a roar. I slammed the hood down as a bullet cut a bright streak in it, jumped for the seat.

"Who's driving the second truck?"

"I have a chap who's a steam-car operator—"

"No good. I'll have to start it for him..." I was out again, running for the other lorry, parked twenty feet away. A worried-looking man with damp red hair plastered to a freckled forehead was fumbling with the dash lighter and headlight switch. There was a key in the switch of this one; I twisted it, jammed a foot against the starter. The engine caught, ran smoothly.

"You know how to shift gears?"

He nodded, smiling.

"This is the gas pedal. Push on it and you go faster. This is the brake..." He nodded eagerly. "If you stall out, push this floor button. The rest is just steering."

He nodded again as glass smashed in front of him, throwing splinters in our faces. Blood ran from a cut across his cheek, but he brushed the chips away, gave me a wave. I ran for it, reached my truck, slammed it in gear, watched a moment to see that the redhead picked up the rear guard. Then I gunned for the closed iron gates, hit them with a crash at twenty miles an hour, slammed through, twisted the wheel hard left, and thundered away down the narrow street.

It took us twenty minutes to cover the twelve kilometers to the edge of the city. For the last hundred yards, we slowed, steered a course among bodies lying in the street, pulled up at a rough barricade of automobiles turned on their sides and blackened by fire, bright tongues of flame still licking over the smouldering tires. A church tower clock was tolling midnight—a merry sound to accompany the cheery picture.

I looked at the dark towers of the city behind the barrier, the dark streets. There were at least a dozen men in sight, sprawled in the unlovely attitudes of violent death. None was in uniform or armed; they were bystanders, caught in the clouds of poison that had rolled out from the city's streets. There were no Hagroon in sight. The streets were as still as a graveyard.

There was a sound to the left. I brought my carbine up, saw a hatless man in a white shirt.

"Thank God you've got here at last," he choked. "I got a whiff—sick as a dog. Pulled a couple back, but..." he coughed, retched, bending double. "Too late. All dead. Gas is gone now, blown away..."

"Get farther back," I said. "Spread the word not to try to attack the barricades." There was another man behind him, and a woman, her face soot-streaked.

"What do you want us to do?" someone called. They clustered around the car, a dozen battered survivors, thinking we were the police, and ready to do whatever had to be done to help us.

"Just stay back, keep out of harm's way. We're going to try something—"

Someone yelled then, pointing at Dzok. A cry went through the crowd.

"Everybody out—fast!" I barked to the men in the rear of the truck. Then: "This is a friend!" I yelled to the crowd. I jumped down, ran around to the side where the man had raised his first outcry, caught him by the arm as he jerked at the shattered door handle.

"Listen to me! This isn't the enemy! He's an ally of the Imperium! He's here to help! These are his troops!" I waved at the ten costumed soldiers who had formed a rough circle around the truck. The headlights of the second truck swung into view then. It growled up beside the first, chugged to a stop and stalled out. The doors flew open and men swarmed out.

"He's got hair on his face—just like the others—"

"You saw them?"

"No—but I heard—from the man I pulled back from the barricade—before he died—"

"Well, I don't have hair on my face—unless you want to count three days' beard. This is Commander Dzok! He's on our side. Now, spread the word! I don't want any accidents!"

"Who're you?"

"I'm Colonel Bayard, Imperial Intelligence. I'm here to do what I can—"

"What can we do?" several voices called. I repeated my instructions to stay back.

"What about you?" the man who had spotted Dzok asked me. "What's your plan, Colonel?"

Dzok was out of the car now. He handed the modified S-suit to me, turned and bowed in courtly fashion to the crowd.

"Enchanted, sirs and madams, to make your acquaintance," he called. Someone tittered, but Dzok ignored it. "I have the honor, as Colonel Bayard has said, to offer my services in the fight against the rude invader. But it is the Colonel himself who must carry out our mission here tonight. The rest of us can merely assist..."

"What's he going to do?"

I had the suit halfway on now. Dzok was helping me, pulling it up, getting my arms into the sleeves, settling the heavy chest pack in place, zipping long zippers closed.

"Using this special equipment," Dzok said in his best theatrical manner, "Colonel Bayard will carry out a mission of the utmost peril..."

"Skip the pitch and hand me the helmet," I interrupted him.

"We want to help," someone called.

"I'd like to go along," another voice said.

"Our chief need at the moment," Dzok's voice rang above the rest, "is a supply of coffee. My brave lads are a trifle fatigued, not having rested since leaving their home barracks. For the rest, we can only wait—"

"Why can't some of us go along, Colonel," a man said, stepping close. "You could use an escort—and not those overdressed fancy dans, either!"

"The Colonel must go alone," Dzok said. "Alone he will carry out a spy mission among the enemy—on the other side of time!" He turned to me, and in a lower voice said: "Don't waste any time, old fellow. It's after midnight now—in about two hours the world ends..."

The transparent helmet was in place, all the contacts tight. Dzok made a couple of quick checks, made me the O sign with his fingers that meant all systems were go. I put my hand on the "activate" button and took my usual deep breath. If Dzok's practice was as good as his theory, the rewired S-suit would twist the fabric of reality in a different manner than its designers had intended, stress the E-field of the normal continuum in a way that would expel me, like a watermelon seed squeezed in the fingers, into that curious non-temporal state of null entropy—the other side of time, as he poetically called it.

If it worked, that was. And there was only one way to find out. I pressed the button—

Chapter Fourteen

THERE WAS A MOMENT of total vertigo; the world inverted itself around me, dwindled to a pinhole through which all reality flowed, to expand vastly, whirling...

I was standing in the street, looking across at the black hulks of burned-out cars glowing with a bluish light like corpses nine days under water. I turned, saw the empty police lorries, the dead bodies in the street, the stark, leafless trees lining the avenue, the blank eyes of the houses behind them. Dzok, the soldiers, the crowd—all of them had vanished in the instant that the suit's field had sprung into being—or, more correctly, I had vanished from among them. Now I was alone, in the same deserted city I had seen when I awakened after my inexplicable encounter with the flaming man in the basement of Imperial Intelligence Headquarters.

I looked again at the clock on the church tower: the hands stood frozen at twelve twenty-five. And the clock I had seen in the office just after the encounter had read twelve-o-five. I was already too late to intercept the flaming man before he did whatever he had been there to accomplish.

But I wasn't too late to spy out the Hagroon position, discover where the discontinuity engine was planted, then return, lead an assault force...

There were too many variables in the situation. Action was the only cure for the hollow sensation of foredoomed failure growing in the pit of my stomach.

A pebble hopped suddenly, struck the toe of my shoe as I took a step. Small dust clouds rose, swirled toward my feet as I crossed the dry, crumbling soil where grass had grown only moments before. The eerie light that seemed to emanate from the ground showed me a pattern of depressions in the soil that seemed to form before my foot reached them...

I looked behind me. There were no prints to show where I had come, but a faint trail seemed to lead ahead. A curious condition, this null time...

I crossed the sidewalk, skirted a dead man lying almost on the barricade. I clambered over the burned wreck of a car, a boxy sedan with an immense spare tire strapped to the rear. There were more bodies on the other side—men who had died trying to climb the wall, or who had chosen that spot to make a stand. Among them a lone Hagroon lay, the bulky body contorted in the heavy atmosphere suit, a bloody hole in the center of his chest. Someone on the Imperial side had drawn enemy blood. The thought was cheering in this scene of desolation. I went on, glanced up at the tower clock as I passed—

The hands stood at one minute after twelve. As I watched, the minute hand jerked back, pointed straight up.

And suddenly I understood. Dzok's changes to the S-suit had had the desired effect of shifting me to null time. But both of us had forgotten the earlier adjustment he had made to the suit's controls—the adjustment that had caused the suit to carry me in a retrograde direction, back along the temporal profile, during my trip from the jungle world. Now, with the suit activated, holding me in my unnatural state of anti-entropy, the retrograde motion had resumed. I was traveling backward through time!

I walked on, watching the curious behavior of objects as they impinged on the E-field of the suit, or crossed from the field to the external environment. A pebble kicked by me took up a motion, flew from the field— where it resumed its natural temporal direction, sprang back, seemed to strike my foot, then dropped from play. The air around me whispered in constant turmoil as vagrant currents were caught, displaced backward in time, only to be released, with the resultant local inequalities in air pressure. I wondered how I would appear to an outside observer—or if I could be seen at all. And my weapon; what effect would—or *could* it have, fired in the future, dealing death in the past—

Soundlessly, a figure backed into view around a corner two blocks away, walked briskly toward me, the feet moving back, the arms swinging—like a movie in reverse. I flattened myself against a wall, watched as the walker came closer. A Hagroon! I felt my hackles rise. I flipped the slug gun into my hand, waited...

He stepped past me, kept going, his head turning as though scanning the sidewalk for signs of life—but he paid no attention to me. I looked around. There were none of his fellows in sight. It was as good a time as any to make a test. I stepped boldly out, aimed the gun at his retreating chest at a distance of twenty feet, twenty-five...

There was no reaction. I was invisible to him, while he, somehow, remained visible to me. I could only assume that light rays striking me were affected by the field, their temporal progression reversed, with the effect of simply blanking them off, while normal light emanating from the scene to me...

But how could I see, with light traveling *away* from my eyes...

I remembered a statement made by an Imperium Net physicist, explaining why it was possible to scan the continua through which a moving shuttle passed in an immeasurably short instant of time: "Light is a condition, not an event..."

Whatever the reason, the Hagroon couldn't see me. A break for our side at last. Now to see what I could accomplish on the strength of one small advantage and whatever luck I could find along the way.

It was half an hour's walk to the Net Garages. There were few corpses in the street along the way. Apparently the people had been caught in their beds by the attack. Those few who had been abroad had fallen back toward the barricades—and died there. I passed a pair of Hagroon, walking briskly backward, then a group of a half dozen, then a column of twenty or thirty, all moving in the opposite direction from my own course, which meant that, in normal progression, they were headed for the area of the Net Garages, coming from the direction of the Imperial HQ.

Two blocks from there, the crowd of Hagroon almost filled the street.

Moving with the stream—which seemed to part before me, to the accompaniment of perplexed looks on the Hagroon faces I glimpsed through the dark faceplates—I made my way across the North Bridge, through the dim-glowing wrought-iron gates before the looming bulk of the headquarters building. The mob of Hagroon here was tight-packed, a shoving, sullen mass of near-humanity—jostling their way backward through the wide doors, overflowing the gravel walks and the barren rectangles of dry dirt that were immaculately manicured flower beds in normal times. I caught a glimpse of a clock in the front of a building across the plaza—eleven fifteen.

I had moved back through time three-quarters of an hour, while thirty subjective minutes passed.

I made my way through the streaming crowd of suited Hagroon, reached the door, slipped through into the same high-ceilinged foyer that I had left, alone, six weeks earlier. Now it was crowded with silent Hagroon masses, overseen by two heavily brassed individuals who stood on the lower steps of the flight leading to the upper floors, waving their arms and grimacing. Sound, it appeared, failed to span the interface between "normal" null time and my reversed field effect.

The stream pressed toward a side corridor. I made my way there, reached a small door set in the hall with the sign service stair beside it—

I remembered that door. It was the one through which I had pursued the flaming man, so many weeks before. I pushed through it, felt the ghostly jostle of Hagroon bodies that seemed to slip aside an instant before I touched them, descended one flight, followed the direction of the stream of aliens along to a door—the one beyond which the fiery man had turned at bay...

The stream of Hagroon was smaller now, less tightly packed. I stood aside, watched as the creatures shuffled backward through the narrow entry into the small room—and more and more, packing into the confined space...

It wasn't possible. I had seen hundreds of the brutes in the streets, packing the entryway, crowding the corridors, all streaming here—or *from* here in the normal time sequence—from this one small room...

There were only a few Hagroon in the hall now, standing listening to a silent harangue from a brass-spangled officer. They shuffled back, almost eagerly passed into the room. The officers appeared from above, joined in a brief huddle, backed through the door into the gloom. I followed—and stopped dead.

A glistening, ten-foot disk of insubstantiality shimmered in the air, floating an inch or two above the dull stone floor, not quite grazing the dusty beamed ceiling of the abandoned storeroom. As I watched, one of the remaining Hagroon officers backed quickly to it, crouched slightly, leaped backward through the disk—and disappeared as magically as a rabbit into a magician's hat. There were only two Hagroon left now. One of them backed to the disk, hopped through. The last spoke into a small hand-held instrument, stood for a moment gazing about the room, ignoring me utterly. Then he too sprang through the disk and was gone.

I was seeing wonders, which, by comparison, the shuttles of the Imperium were as prosaic as wicker baby buggies, but there was no time to stand in awe, gaping. This was an entry portal from some other space to null-time Stockholm. The Hagroon had entered through it; from where, I didn't know. There was a simple empirical method of answering that question...

I went to the disk—like the surface of a rippled pond, upended in gloom. There was another visible beyond that mysterious plane. I gritted my teeth, took an instant to hope I was guessing right, and stepped through.

I knew at once that I was back in normal time—still running backwards, doubtless, still in the same room—but I was standing in honest darkness, away from the pervasive death light of null time. There were Hagroon all about me, bulky, suited figures, almost filling the confined space of the room, overflowing into the corridor, seemingly unbothered by the lack of illumination. I recognized the officers I had seen moments before, the last to pass through the portals—or the first, in normal time: the pioneers sent through ahead of the main body to reconnoiter—before the horde poured through, to stream back to the Net Garages. Six weeks earlier—or tonight; either way of looking at it was equally valid—I would meet them there, embarking in their shuttles to return to the Hagroon world line, their job here finished. But now, because of the miracle of my retrograde motion in the time stream, I was seeing the play acted out in reverse; watching the victorious troops, flushed from their victory over the sleeping city, about to back out into the streets, and re-enact their gas attack.

Many of the Hagroon, I noted, carried heavy canisters. Others, as I watched, took empty containers from a heap in the corridor, hitched them into place on their backs. They were filing away now, by two's and three's, backing out into the corridors, up the stairs, back into the dead streets. I started to follow—then checked myself. There was something tugging at the edge of my awareness. Something I must do, now—quickly—before my chance slipped away. Events were flowing inexorably toward their inevitable conclusion, while I hesitated, racking my brain. It was hard to think, hard to orient my thoughts in the distorted perspective of reversed time; but I had to stop now, force myself to analyze what I was seeing, reconstruct the attack.

The Hagroon had arrived at the Net Garages. I had seen their shuttles there. It was the perfect spot for an assault in force via shuttle, and due to the characteristic emanations of the Net communicator carriers, easy to pinpoint for navigation purposes.

Once there, they had marched across the empty null-time city to Intelligence Headquarters, a convenient central location from which to attack, and with plenty of dark cellar rooms—and perhaps there was also an element of sardonic humor in their choice of staging areas...

Then the troops had poured through the portal, emerged into the midnight streets of the real-time city, spewing gas—the attack the end of which I was now witnessing.

Then they had returned through the portal, crossed to their shuttles again in null time—the exodus I had just witnessed...

But why the gas attack on a city about to suffer annihilation along with the rest of the planet?

Simple: The Hagroon needed peace and quiet in which to erect the discontinuity engine—and they needed the assurance that the infernal machine would remain undisturbed for the necessary time to allow them to pass back through their portal into null time, regain their shuttles, and leave the doomed A-line. By gassing the city, they had ensured their tranquility while they perpetrated the murder of a universe.

Because it was more than a world they killed. It was a planet, a solar system, a sky filled with stars, to the ends of conceivable space and beyond—a unique, irreplaceable aspect of reality, to be wiped forever from the face of the continuum, because one world, one tiny dust-mote in that universe posed a possible threat to Hagroon safety. It was an abominable plot—and the moments during which I could take action to thwart it were fast slipping away. Somewhere, at this moment, a crew was at work, preparing the doomsday device. And if I delayed, even for minutes, in finding it—it would be too late or (too early!). The machine would be separated into its component parts, carried away to the shuttles by backward-walking men, transported out of range—

I had to find the engine—now!

I looked around. Hagroon laden with empty canisters were still backing away along the corridor. Their officers waved their arms, mouths moving behind faceplates. One individual, helmetless, caught my attention. He came from the opposite direction along the narrow hall, stepping briskly up to the Hagroon directing the canister operation. Two rank-and-file Hagroon preceded him. They turned away, joined a group plucking empty canisters from a heap and fitting them on their backs. The helmetless one talked to the officer; both nodded, talked some more; then the former backed away down the dark hall—away from the stair. I hesitated a moment, then followed.

He backed off fifty feet, turned into a storeroom much like the one in which the portal had been erected. There were four other Hagroon there, crouching around a heavy tripod on which a massive construction rested, its casing lying on the floor to one side.

Luck was with me. I had found the discontinuity engine.

The next step was clear to me in the same instant that I saw the engine. As two of the Hagroon paused, staring with comically puzzled expressions, I went to the stand, planted my feet, gripped the massive casing, and lifted. It came away easily. My slightly accelerated time rate, although reversed, gave me an added quota of brute strength. I stepped back, hugged the horror device to my chest, feeling the buzz of its timer—and to my blank amazement, saw it still resting where it had been—while I held its counterpart in my hands. The Hagroon technicians were working away, apparently undisturbed. But then, I hadn't yet appeared, to create paradox before their startled eyes...

I turned to the door, made my way along the corridor, climbed the steps, set off at the fastest dog trot I could manage for the Net Garages.

I made it in twenty minutes, in spite of the awkward burden, forcing myself to ignore the gas attack going on all around me. Suited Hagroon clumped backward through the well-lit streets under a vague cloud of brownish gas that seemed to slowly coalesce, drawing together as I watched. I half-ran, half-walked, shifting my grip on the heavy casing, sweating heavily now inside the suit. The gas was all around me, and I hoped the seals of my garment were as secure as Dzok had assured me they were.

At the garages, a few morose-looking Hagroon loitered about the parked shuttles, peering out through the wide doors toward the sounds of action in the city streets. I passed them unnoticed, went to the last shuttle in line—the same machine I had ridden once before. I knew it had preset controls, which would automatically home it on its A-line of origin—the Hagroon world. I pulled open the door, lowered my burden to the grey metal floor, pushed it well inside, then checked the wall clock. Dzok and I had calculated that the engine had gone into action at two AM precisely. It was now ten forty-five; three hours and fifteen minutes until M minute.

And the transit of the shuttle from the Zero-zero line to the Hagroon line had taken three hours and twenty-five minutes.

I had ten minutes to kill...

The discontinuity engine was already counting down toward its moment of cataclysmic activity—the titanic outpouring of energy which would release the stasis which constituted the fabric of reality for this line of alternate existence. I had plucked it from the hands of its makers just as they were completing their installation. When the time came, it would perform. The shuttle was the problem now. I climbed inside, looked over the controls. They, at least, were simple enough. A trip wire, attached to the main field switch...

I went back out, found a length of piano wire on a workbench at one side of the garage, secured it to the white painted lever that controlled the shuttle's generators, led the wire out through the door. Five minutes to go, now. It was important to get the timing as exact as possible. I watched the hands of the clock move back: ten thirty-four; ten thirty-three; ten thirty-two; ten thirty-one. There was a faint vibration from the shuttle...

I closed the door carefully, checked to be sure the wire was clear, then gripped it, gave it a firm pull. The shuttle seemed to waver. It shimmered, winked for an instant—then sat, solid and secure, unmoving. I let out a breath; the example of the engine had forewarned me. The results of my actions on external objects weren't visible to me, but I had sent the shuttle on its way. This was its past reality I saw before me now.

CHAPTER FIFTEEN

BACK IN THE STREET, the attack was in full swing. I saw a man lying in the gutter rise, like a dummy on a rope, clutch at his throat, run backwards into a building—a corpse risen from the dead. The brown cloud hung low over the pavement now, a flat stratum of deadly gas. A long plume formed, flowed toward a Hagroon, whipped into the end of the hand-held horn of his dispenser. Other plumes shaped up, flowed toward other attackers. I was watching the gas attack in reverse—the killers, scavenging the streets of the poison that would decimate the population. I followed them as the poisonous cloud above gathered, broke apart, flowed back into the canisters from which it had come. I saw the invaders, laden now, slogging in their strange reverse gait back toward the dark bulk of Intelligence HQ. And I followed, crowding with them along the walk, through the doors, along the corridor, down the narrow steps, back to the deserted storeroom where they poured in a nightmare stream through the shining disk, back to null time and their waiting shuttles.

There was a paralyzing choice of courses of action open to me now—and my choice had to be the right one—with the life of a universe the cost of an error.

The last of the Hagroon passed through the portal, returning to null time, to march back to the Net Garages, board their shuttles and disappear back toward their horrendous home world. The portal stood deserted in the empty room, in a silence as absolute as deafness. I stood by it, waiting, as minutes ticked past—minutes of subjective time, during which I moved inexorably back, back—to the moment when the Hagroon had first activated the portal—and I saw it dwindle abruptly, shrink to a point of incredible brilliance, wink out.

I blinked my eyes against the darkness, then switched on a small lamp set in the suit's chest panel, intended as an aid in map and instrument reading during transit through lightless continua. It served to show me the dim outlines of the room, the dusty packing cases, the littered floor—nothing else. The portal, I was now certain, required no focusing device to establish its circle of congruency between null and real time.

I waited a quarter of an hour to allow time for the Hagroon to leave the vicinity of the portal, studying my wrist controls and reviewing Dzok's instructions. Then I twisted the knob that would thrust me back through the barrier to null time. I felt the universe turn inside out while the walls whirled around me; then I was standing in null time, alone, breathing hard, but all right so far.

I looked around, and saw what I was looking for—a

small, dull metal case, perched on a stand, half-obscured behind a stack of cases—the portal machine. I went to it, put a hand on it. It was humming gently, idling, ready to serve its monstrous owners when they arrived, minutes from now in normal time.

There were tools in a leather case clipped to the arm of my suit. I took out a screwdriver, removed the screws. The top of the case came off, showed me a maze of half-familiar components. I studied the circuits, recognized an analog of the miniature moebius-wound coil that formed the heart of my S-suit. The germ of an idea was taking shape—a trick probably impossible, certainly difficult, and very likely impractical, even if I had the necessary technical knowledge to carry it out—but an idea of such satisfying scope that I found myself smiling down in Satanic anticipation at the machine in my hands. Dzok had told me a little about the working of the S-suit—and I had watched as he had modified the circuits on two occasions. Now it was my turn to try. If I could bring it off...

Twenty minutes later I had done what I could. It was simple enough in theory. The focusing of the portal was controlled by a simple nuclear-force capacitor, tuned by a cyclic gravitational field. By reversing contacts, as Dzok had done when adjusting the suit to carry me backward in time as I crossed the continua, I had modified the orientation of the lens effect. Now, instead of establishing congruency at a level of temporal parity, the portal would set up a contact with a level of time in the future—perhaps as much as a week or two. I could go back now, reverse the action of the suit, and give my warning. With two weeks or more to convince Imperial Intelligence that I was something other than a madman with a disturbing likeness to one B. Bayard, I could surely make them see reason. True, there would be a number of small problems, such as the simultaneous existence of two battered ex-diplomats of that name—but that was a minor point, if I could avert the total destruction that waited in the wings.

I replaced the cover, for the first time feeling a throb of hope that my mad gamble could pay off— that in moving back through time to a point before the Hagroon attack, I might actually have changed the course of coming events. If I was right, it meant that the invaders I had seen pouring through the portal would never come—had never come; that the gas attack was relegated to the realm of unrealized possibilities; and that the city's inhabitants sleeping peacefully now would wake in the morning, unaware of the death they had died and risen from...

It was a spooky thought. I had done what I could here. Now it was time to go. I braced my stomach against the wrench of the S-suit's null-time field, reversed the control...

I blinked, letting my senses swim back into focus. I was back in real time, in the dark, deserted store-room. There was no sign of the portal—and now, if my guesses were right, there wouldn't be for many days—and then the startled Hagroon would emerge into a withering fire from waiting Imperial troops.

Back in the hall, I licked my lips, suddenly as dry as a mummy's. The next step was one I didn't like. Tampering with my suit was dangerous business, and I'd had my share of daring experimentation for the night. But it had to be done.

The light here was dim—too dim for fine work. I went up the stairs to the ground floor corridor, saw a group of men back across the entry hall, walk backwards up the stairs that led to the second floor. I stifled the impulse to rush out with glad cries; they wouldn't hear me. They were as impervious to sounds coming from the past as the Hagroon. I was a phantom, moving in an unreal world of living memories, unreeled in reverse like a glimpse of an old album, riffled through from back to front. And when I had reversed the action of the S-suit, I'd still have the problem of making someone believe me.

It was hard, admittedly, for anyone to take my story seriously when my double—another me—was available to deny my authenticity. And nothing would have changed. I—the "I" of six weeks ago, minus the scars I had collected since then, was at home—now—dining in my sumptuous villa, with the incomparable Barbro, about to receive a mysterious phone call—and I would appear—a dirt-streaked man in torn clothing of outlandish cut, needing a shave and a bath, and talking nonsense. But this time at least I'd have a few days to convince them.

I stepped back into the cross corridor, found an empty office, closed and locked the door and turned on the light. Then, without waiting to consider the consequences of a miscalculation, I switched off the suit's power-pack. I unzipped, lifted the light helmet off, pulled the suit off, looked around the room. Everything seemed normal. I reached to the desk, gingerly lifted the black-handled paper knife that lay there—and with a sinking sensation saw it, still lying on the desk—the duplicate of the one in my hand. I tossed the knife back to the desk—and it winked out of existence—gone along the stream of normal time.

It was what I had been afraid of: even with the suit off, I was still living backwards.

Again, I got the miniature tool kit, used it to open the chest control pack. I knew which wires to reverse. With infinite care, I shifted the hair-fine filaments into new positions, guessing, when my recollection of Dzok's work failed. If I had known I'd be doing this job alone, I could have had Dzok run through it with me, even made notes. But both of us, in the excitement of the moment, had forgotten that I would slide away into past time as soon as the suit was activated. Now he was out of reach, hours in the future.

I finished at last, with a splitting headache, and a taste in my mouth like an abandoned rat's nest. My empty stomach simultaneously screeched for food and threatened violence if I so much as thought about the subject. I had been operating for the best part of forty-eight hours now without food, drink, or rest.

I pulled the suit back on, zipped up, too tired now even to worry, flipped the control—and knew at once that something was wrong—badly wrong.

It wasn't the usual nauseous wrench that I had come to expect; just a claustrophobic sense of pressure and heat. There was a loud humming in my ears, and a cloying in my throat as I drew a breath of scalding air.

I stepped to the desk, my legs as sluggish as lead castings. I picked up the paperweight—strangely heavy—

It was hot! I dropped it, watched it slam to the desk top. I dragged in another breath—with a sensation of

drowning. The air was as thick as water, hot as live
steam...

I exhaled a frosty plume of ice crystals. The sleeve
of the suit caught my eye. It was glazed over with a
dull white coating. I touched it with a finger, felt the
heat of it, the slickness. It was ice—hot ice, forming
on my suit! Even as I watched, it thickened, coating
my sleeve, building up on my faceplate. I bent my
arm to wipe it clear, saw crusts break, leap toward
the floor with frantic speed. I managed to get one
finger-swipe across the plastic visor. Through the clear
strip, I saw a mirror across the room. I started for
it—my legs strained uselessly. I was rooted to the
spot, encased in ice as rigid as armor!

My faceplate was frosted over solidly now. I tried to
move an arm; it was rigid too. And suddenly, I understood. My tinkering with the suit's circuits had been less
than perfect. I had re-established my normal direction
of temporal progression—but my entropic rate was only
a fraction of normal. I was an ice statue—an interesting
find for the owner of the office when he broke the door
down in the morning, unless I could break free fast!

I tensed my legs, threw my weight sideways—and
felt myself toppling, whipping over to slam stunningly
against the floor. My ice-armor smashed as I hit, and
I moved quickly, brought one numbed arm up, groped
for the control knob, fumbled at it with half-frozen
fingers, twisted—

There was a sudden release of pressure. The faceplate cleared, dotted over with water droplets that
bubbled, danced, disappeared. A blinding cloud was
boiling up from me as the ice melted, flashed away
as steam. I thrust against the floor, felt myself bound

clear, rise halfway to the ceiling, then fall back as leisurely as an inflated balloon. I landed on one leg, felt the pressure build as the ankle twisted. I got my other foot under me, staggered, regained my balance, cursing between clenched teeth at the agony in the strained joint. I grabbed for the control, fumbled over the cold surface—

The control knob was gone. The twist I had given with numbed fingers had broken it off short!

I limped to the door, caught the knob, twisted—

The metal tore; pain shot through my hand. I looked at my palm, saw ripped skin. I had the strength of a Gargantua without the toughness of hide to handle it. I had overcontrolled. Now my entropic rate was double or triple the normal one. My body heat was enough to boil water. The friction of my touch bubbled paint! Carefully I twisted the door's lock, pulled at the crushed knob. The door moved sluggishly, heavy as a vault. I pushed it into the hall—and lurched to a stop.

A seven-foot specimen of the Hagroon species stood glowering from a dark doorway ten feet across the corridor.

I backed away, flattened myself against the wall. This boy was a factor I hadn't counted on. He was a scout, probably, sent through hours ahead of the main column. I had seen the last of his fellows leave, and watched the portal blink out. On the strength of that, I had assumed they were all gone. But if the portal had been activated briefly, an hour earlier, as a test . . .

Another academic question. He was here, as big as a grizzly and twice as ugly, a broad, thick troll in a baggy atmosphere suit, raising an arm slowly, putting a foot forward, heading my way—

I jumped aside, almost fell, as the Hagroon slammed heavily against the wall where I'd been standing—a wall charred black by the heat of my body. I moved back again, carefully this time. I had the speed on him, but if he caught me in that bonecrusher grip...

He was mad—and scared. It showed in the snarling expression I could dimly see through the dark faceplate. Maybe he'd already been down to the portal room, and found his escape hatch missing. Or maybe the follow-up invasion force was behind schedule now...

I felt my heart take a sudden leap as I realized that I'd succeeded. I had worked over the suit for an hour, and perhaps another half-hour had gone by while I floundered in my slow-time state, building up a personal icecap—and they hadn't appeared on the scene. I could answer the theorists on one point now: a visitor to the past *could* modify the already-seen future, eliminate it from existence!

But the Hagroon before me was unaware of the highly abnormal aspects of his presence here. He was a fighter, trained to catch small hairless anthropos and squeeze their necks, and I fitted the description. He jumped again—a curiously graceless, slow-motion leap—hit and skidded, whirling ponderously to grab again—

I misjudged my distance, felt his hand catch at my sleeve. He was fast, this hulking monster. I pulled away, tore free—and stumbled as I skidded back, felt my feet go out from under me—

He was after me, while I flailed the air helplessly. One huge hand caught my arm, hauled me in, gathered me to his vast bosom. I felt the crushing pressure, almost heard the creak of my ribs as blood rushed blindingly to my face—

The fabric of his suit was bubbling, curling, blackening. His grip relaxed. I saw his face, his mouth open, and distantly, through his helmet and mine, I heard his scream of agony. His hands came up, fingers outspread, blistered raw by the terrible heat of my body. Even so, he ripped with them at his suit, tearing the molten plastic from his shaggy chest, exposing a bleeding second degree burn from chin to navel.

I continued my fall, took the shock on my outstretched hands, felt the floor come up and grind against my chin, felt the skin break, the spatter of hot blood. Then there was only the blaze of stars and a soft bottomless blackness...

I lay on my back, feeling an Arctic chill that gripped my chest like a cold iron vise. I drew a wheezing breath, pressed my hands against the floor. They were numb, as dead as a pair of iceman's tongs, but I managed to get my feet under me, stagger upright. There were blackened footprints burned against the polished wood of the floor, and a larger black area where I had lain—and even as I burned the surfaces I touched, they bled away my heat, freezing me.

The Hagroon was gone. I saw a bloody hand-print on the wall, another farther along. He had headed for the service stair, bound no doubt for the storage room where the portal had been. He'd have a long wait...

I leaned against the wall, racked with shivering, my teeth clamped together like a corpse in rigor. I had had enough of lone world-saving missions. It was time for someone else to join the party, share the honor—and incidentally, perform a delicate operation on my malfunctioning S-suit before I froze solid, fell on my face, and burned my way through to the basement.

I turned toward the front hall with a vague idea of finding someone—Richthofen, maybe. He was here tonight. Sure, good old Manfred, sitting at his desk upstairs, giving the third degree to a poor slob named Bayard, hauled on the carpet because some other poor slob of the same name was in jail a few miles away, claiming he was Bayard, and that the end of the world was nigh!

I reached the corner, staggered, feeling the hot flush of fever burning my face, while the strength drained from my legs, sucked away by the terrible entropic gradient between my runaway E-field and the normal space around me.

Bad stuff, Mr. B, tinkering with machines you don't understand. Machines made by a tribe of smart monkey-men who regard us sapiens as little better than homicidal maniacs—and with good reason, good reason . . .

I had fallen, and was on hands and knees watching the smoke curl up from between my numbed fingers. It was funny, that. Worth a laugh in anybody's joke book. I clawed at the wall, bubbling paint, got to my feet, made another yard toward the stair . . .

Poor old Bayard; me. What a surprise he'd get, if he walked into that little room down below, and encountered one frightened, burned, murder-filled Hagroon—a pathetic leftover from a so-carefully-planned operation that had gotten itself lost along the way because it had overlooked a couple of small factors. The Hagroon, self-styled tough guys. Ha! They didn't know what real bloodthirstiness was until they ran up against good old Homo sap. Poor little monsters, they didn't have a chance . . .

Down again, and a mouthful of blood. Must have hit harder that time, square on the face. A good thing, maybe. Helps to clear the head. Where was I going? Oh, yes. Had to go along and warn poor old B. Can't let the poor fellow walk in all unsuspecting. Have to get there first...still have the slug gun... finish off bogie man...

I was dimly aware of a door resisting as I leaned against it, then swinging wide, and I was falling, tumbling down stairs, bouncing, head over heels, slow and easy like a pillow falling—a final slam against the gritty, icy floor, the weight, and the pain...

A long trip, this. Getting up again, feeling the cold coming up the legs now like slow poison...cloud of brown gas, spreading up the legs, across the city. Have to warn them, tell them...

But they don't believe. Fools. Don't believe. God, how it hurts, and the long dark corridor stretching away, and the light swelling and fading, swelling again—

There he is! God, what a monster. Poor monster, hurt, crouched in the corner, rocking and moaning. Brought it on himself, the gas-spreading son of a bearskin rug! Sees me now, scrambling up. And look at those teeth! Makes old Dzok look like a grass-eater. Coming at me now. Get the gun out, feel it slap the palm, hold it, squeeze—

The gun was falling from my numbed hand, skidding on the floor, and I was groping for it, feeling with hands like stumps, seeing the big shape looming over me—

To hell with the gun. Can't press the firing stud anyway. Speed, that's all you've got now, m'lad. Hit him low, let his weight do the job, use your opponent's strength against him, judo in only five easy lessons, class starts Monday—

A blow like a runaway beer truck and I was skidding across the floor, and even through the suit I heard the sickening *crunch!* as the massive skull of the Hagroon struck the corner of a steel case, the ponderous *slam!* as he piled against the floor. I was on hands and knees again, not feeling the floor anymore, not feeling anything—just get on your feet once more and make sure...

I pulled myself up with the help of a big box placed conveniently beside me, took three wavering steps, bent over him. I saw the smear of blood, the thin ooze of fluid from the gaping wound above the ear, the black-red staining the inside of the helmet. Okay, Mr. Hagroon. You put up a good scrap, but that low block and lady luck were too much for you, and now—

I heard a noise from the door. There was a man there, dim in the wavering light of fading consciousness. I leaned, peering, with a strange sense of *déjà vu*, the seen-before...

He came toward me in slow-motion, and I blinked, wiped my hand across the steamed-over faceplate. He was in midair, in a dream leap, hands reaching for me. I checked myself, tried to back away, my hand outflung as though to hold back some unspeakable fate—

Long, pink sparks crackled from his hand to mine as he hung like a diver suspended in midair. I heard a noise like fat frying, and for one unbelievable instant glimpsed the face before me—

Then a silent explosion turned the world to blinding white, hurling me into nothingness.

Chapter Sixteen

IT WAS A WONDERFUL bed, wide and cool and clean, and the dream was wonderful too. Barbro's face, perfect as an artist's conception of the goddess of the hunt, framed by her dark red hair in a swirl of silken light. Just behind the rosy vision there were a lot of dark thoughts clamoring to be dragged out and reviewed, but I wasn't going to get hooked on that one. No sir, the good old dream was good enough for me, if only it wouldn't go away and leave me remembering dark shapes that moved in foul tunnels—and pain, and loss, the sickness of failure and dying hope—

The dream leaned closer and there were bright tears in the smoke-grey eyes, but the mouth was smiling, and then it was against mine, and I was kissing warm, soft lips—real lips, not the dream kind that always elude you. I raised a hand, felt a weight like an anvil stir, saw a vast bundle of white bandage swim into view.

"Barbro!" I said, and heard my voice emerge as a croak.

"Manfred! He's awake! He knows me!"

"Ah, a man would have to be far gone indeed to fail to know you, my dear," a cool voice said. Another face appeared, less pretty than the other, but a good face all the same. Baron von Richthofen smiled down at me, looking concerned and excited at the same time.

"Brion, Brion! What happened?" Barbro's cool fingertips touched my face. "When you didn't come home, I called, and Manfred told me, you'd gone—and then they searched the building and found footprints, burned—"

"Perhaps you'd better not press him now," Manfred murmured.

"No, of course not." A hot tear fell on my face, and Barbro smiled and wiped it away. "But you're safe now, that's all that matters. Rest, Brion. You can think about it later..."

I tried to speak, to tell her it was all right, not to go...

But the dream faded, and sleep washed over me like warm, scented soapsuds, and I let go and sank down in its green depths.

The next time, I woke up hungry. Barbro was sitting by the bed, looking out the window at a tree in full spring leaf, golden green in the afternoon sun. I lay for a while, watching her, admiring the curve of her cheek, the line of her throat, the long, dark lashes—

She turned, and a smile like the sun coming out after a spring rain warmed me all the way to my bandaged heels.

"I'm okay now," I said. This time the voice came out hoarse but recognizable.

There was a long, satisfying time then, of whispered

words and agreeable nonsense, and as many feather-soft kisses as we could fit in. Then Manfred came in, and Hermann, and Luc, and things got a bit more brisk and businesslike.

"Tell me, Brion," Manfred said mock-sternly. "How did you manage to leave my office, disappear for half an hour, only to be discovered unconscious beside some sort of half-ape, and dressed like a wanderer from a fancy dress ball in a variety of interesting costumes, wearing a three-day beard, with twenty-seven separate and distinct cuts, abrasions, and bruises, to say nothing of second-degree burns, frostbite, and a broken tooth?"

"What day is it?" I demanded.

He told me. I had been unconscious for forty-eight hours. Two days since the scheduled hour for the invasion—and the Hagroon hadn't appeared.

"Listen," I said. "What I'm going to tell you is going to be a little hard to take, but in view of the corpse you found beside me, I expect you to do your best..."

"A truly strange creature, Brion," Hermann said. "It attacked you, I presume, which would account for some of the wounds, but as for the burns..."

I told them. They listened. I had to stop twice to rest, and once to eat a bowl of chicken broth, but I covered everything.

"That's it," I finished. "Now go ahead and tell me I dreamed it all. But don't forget to explain how I dreamed that dead Hagroon."

"Your story is impossible, ridiculous, fantastic, mad, and obviously the ravings of a disordered mind," Hermann said. "And I believe every word of it. My technicians have reported to me strange readings on the Net Surveillance instruments. What you have said fits the observations. And the detail of your gambit of readjusting the portal, so as to shunt the invading creatures into a temporal level weeks in the future; I find that of particular interest—"

"I can't know how far I deflected them," I said. "Just be sure to station a welcoming party down there to greet them as they arrive."

Hermann cleared his throat. "I was about to come to that, Brion. You yourself have commented on the deficiencies in your qualifications for the modification of sophisticated M-C effect apparatus—and by the way, I am lost in admiration of the suit you have brought home from your travels. A marvel—but I digress.

"You adjusted the portal, you said, to divert the Hagroon into the future. Instead, I fear, you have shunted them into a past time-level of our Zero-zero line..."

There was a moment of silence. "I don't get that," I said. "Are you saying they've already invaded us—last month, say?"

"The exact temporal displacement, I cannot yet state. But it seems clear, Brion, that they went back, not forward..."

"Never mind that," Barbro said. "Wherever they are, they are not troubling us now—thanks to your bravery, my hero!"

Everybody laughed and my ears got hot. Manfred stepped in with a comment on the fiery figure.

"A strange sensation, my friend, to meet yourself face to face..."

"Which reminds me," I said in the sudden silence. "Where's the ... ah ... other me?"

Nobody said anything. Then Hermann snapped his fingers.

"I think I can tell you the answer to that! It is an interesting problem in the physics of the continuum—but I think it can be accepted as axiomatic that the paradox of a face-to-face confrontation of identities is intolerable to the fabric of simultaneous reality. Hence, when the confrontation occurs—something must give! In this case, the intolerable entropic stress was relieved by the shunting of one aspect of this single ego into the plane you have called null time—where you encountered the Hagroon, and embarked on your strange adventure."

"Your friend, Dzok," Barbro said. "We must do something, Manfred, to help his people in their fight against these shaggy monsters. We can send troops—"

"I fear the implications of what Brion said regarding the disposition of the discontinuity engine have escaped you, my dear," Hermann said. There was a glint of ferocious amusement in his eyes. "From the care with which he timed his operation, I should imagine that the Hagroon shuttle bearing the apparatus of destruction arrived on schedule in the Hagroon world-line—just as the timer actuated it. The Xonijeelians have nothing to fear from invading Hagroons. Our Brion has neatly erased them from the roster of the continuum's active menaces."

"Dzok was right," Manfred said sadly. "We *are* a race of genocides. But perhaps that is a law of the nature that produced us..."

"And we must help the poor peoples of these sub-technical A-lines," Barbro said. "Poor Olivia, dreaming of a brighter world, and never to know it, because we selfishly reserve its treasures for ourselves—"

"I agree, Barbro," Manfred said. "There must be a change in policy. But it is not an easy thing to bring what we think of as enlightenment to a benighted world. Whatever we do, there will be those who oppose us. This Napoleon the Fifth, for example. How will he regard a proposed status as vassal of our Emperor?"

Barbro looked at me. "You were half in love with this Olivia, Brion," she said. "But I forgive you. I am not such a fool as to invite her to be our houseguest, but you must arrange to bring her here. If she is as lovely as you say, there will be many suitors—"

"She wasn't half as gorgeous as you are," I said. "But I think it would be a nice gesture."

There was a clatter of feet at the door. A young fellow in a white jacket came in, breathing hard.

"A call for you, Herr Goering," he said. "The telephone is just here along the hall."

Hermann went out, and we talked—asking lots of questions and getting some strange answers.

"In a way," Manfred said, "it is a pity that these Hagroon were so thoroughly annihilated by your zeal, Brion. A new tribe of man only remotely related to our own stock, but having high intelligence, a technical culture—"

Hermann came back, pulling at his earlobe and blinking in a perplexed way.

"I have spoken to the Net Laboratory just now," he said. "They have calculated the destination of your unhappy party of invading Hagroon, Brion. They worked from the brief traces recorded by our instruments over the period of the last five years—"

"Five years?" several voices echoed.

"From the date on which our present improved

Net instrumentation was installed," he said, "there have been a number of anomalous readings, which in the past we were forced to accept as a normal, though inexplicable deviation from calculated values. Now, in the light of Brion's statements, we are able to give them a new interpretation."

"Yes, yes, Hermann," Manfred urged. "Spare us the dramatic pause-for-effect..."

"The Hagroon, to state it bluntly, Barbro and gentlemen, have been plunged over fifty thousand years into past time by our clever Brion's adjustment to their portal!"

There was a moment of stunned silence. I heard myself laugh, a wild-sounding cackle.

"So they made it—just a little early. And if they tried to go back—they jumped off the deep end into an A-line that had been pulled out from under them..."

"I think they did not do that latter," Hermann said. "I believe that they safely reached the Neolithic era—and remained there. I think they adapted but poorly to their sudden descent to a sub-technical status, these few hundreds of cast-aways in time. And, I think, never did they lose their hatred of the hairless hominids they found there in that cold northland of fifty millennia past.

"No, they were safely marooned there in the age of mammoths and ice. And there they left their bones, which our modern archaeologists have found and called Neanderthal..."

ASSIGNMENT IN NOWHERE

PROLOGUE

HE SAT ASTRIDE THE great war-horse, in the early morning, looking across the field toward the mist-obscured heights where the enemy waited. The chain-mail coif and hauberk weighed heavy on him; and there was another weight within him: a sense of a thing undone, a duty forgotten, of something valuable betrayed.

"The mist clears, my lord," Trumpington spoke at his side. "Will you attack?"

He looked up at the sun, burning through the mist. He thought of the green vales of home, and the sense grew in him that death waited here on this obscure field.

"No. I'll not unsheathe Balingore this day," he said at last.

"My lord—is all well with you?" There was concern in the young squire's voice.

He nodded curtly. Then he turned and rode back through the silent, staring ranks of his panoplied host.

CHAPTER ONE

AT MOLLY'S PLACE, THE jukebox was breaking its heart over a faithless woman, but there was nobody listening but a few conchs sitting out on the rickety porch under the yellow bug lights, nursing beers and catching the breeze moving in off the gulf. It was after nine p.m. and the heat of the day was gone from the beach, and the surf coming up on the sand sounded lonesome and far away, like an old man's memories.

I took a stool at the bar and Molly put a bottle of wine in front of me, with the seal still intact.

"Johnny, it happened again today," she said. "I found a platter I swear I broke last month, right there in the sink, not a chip out of it. And the whiskey stock is different—stuff I never ordered there, and not a sign of the Red Label—and you know I know my stock. And three heads of cabbage, fresh yesterday—rotten in the cooler!"

"So—your last order was mixed up—and the vegetables weren't as fresh as they looked," I said.

"And toadstools growing in the corners?" she said. "I guess that's natural too? You know better'n that, John Curlon! And how about this?" She brought a heavy cut-glass cup up from behind the bar. It was about one-quart capacity, rounded on the bottom, with a short stem.

"This was here when I came in this evening. It's worth money. How'd it get here?"

"Impulse shopping," I suggested.

"Don't kid me, Johnny. There's something happening—something that scares me! It's like the world was shifting right under my feet! And it's not just here! I see things all around—little things—like trees are in different places than they used to be—and a magazine I started reading; when I came back to it—there wasn't any such story in the book!"

I patted her hand and she caught my fingers. "Johnny—tell me what's happening—what to do! I'm not losing my mind, am I?"

"You're fine, Molly. The glass was probably the gift of some secret admirer. And everybody loses things sometimes, or remembers things a little differently than they really were. You'll probably find your story in another magazine. You just got mixed up." I tried to make it sound convincing, but it's hard to do when you're not sure yourself.

"And Johnny—what about you?" Molly was still holding my hand. "Have you talked to *them* yet?"

"Who?" I asked.

She gave me a hot look from a pair of eyes that had probably been heartbreakers back before the Key West sun had bleached the fire out of them. "Don't act like you don't know what I mean! There was another one in today asking for you—a new guy, one I never saw before."

"Oh—them. No, I haven't had time—"

"Johnny! Smarten up! You can't buck that crowd. They'll smash you so flat you could slide under the linoleum without making a bump."

"Don't worry about me, Molly—"

"Sure, grin! Johnny Curlon, six foot three of bone and muscle, the fellow with the bullet-proof hide! Listen, Johnny! That Jakesy's a mean one—especially since they put the wire in his jaw. He'll chop you into cutbait—" she broke off. "But I guess you know all that. I guess nothing I can say is going to change you." She turned and picked a Remy Martin bottle from the back bar.

"Like you said, it's just a glass. Might as well use it." She poured brandy into the chalice and I picked it up and looked into the glint of amber light inside it. The glass was cool and smooth and heavy against my palms...

Seated in my great chair, I looked down at the narrow, treacherous face of him I had loved so well, saw hope leap up in those crafty eyes.

"My lord king," he started, and shuffled toward me on his knees, dragging the chains that he bore. "I know not why I was cajoled to embark on such rude folly. 'Twas but a fit of madness, meaning naught—"

"Three times ere now have you sought my throne and crown," I cried, not for his ears alone, but for all those who might murmur against that which I knew must be. "Three times have I pardoned thee, lavished anew my favor on thee, raised thee up before loyal men."

"Heaven's grace descend on thy Majesty for thy great mercy," the glib voice babbled, and even in that moment I saw the hunger in his eyes. "This time, I swear—"

"Swear not, thou who are forsworn!" I commanded him. "Rather think on thy soul, to tarnish it no more in these thy final hours!"

And I saw fear dawn at last, driving out the hunger and all else save lust for life itself. And I knew that lust to be foredoomed.

"Mercy, brother," he gasped, and raised his manacled hands to me as to a god. "Mercy, out of memory of past joys shared! Mercy, for love of our mother, the sainted Lady Eleanor—"

"Foul not the name of her who loved thee!" I shouted, hardening my heart against the vision of her face, pale under the hand of approaching death, swearing me to the eternal protection of him who knelt before me.

He wept as they bore him away, wept and swore his true allegiance and love for me. And later in my chambers, drugged with wine, I wept, hearing again and ever again the fall of the headsman's ax.

They told me that at the end, he found his manhood, and walked to the block with his head held high, as befits the son of kings. And with his last words, he forgave me.

Oh, he forgave me...

A voice was calling my name. I blinked and saw Molly's face as through a haze of distance.

"Johnny—what is it?"

I shook my head and the hallucination faded. "I don't know," I said. "Not getting enough sleep, maybe."

"Your face," she said. "When you took the glass in your hands and held it up like that, you looked—like a stranger..."

"Maybe it reminded me of something."

"It's getting to you too, isn't it, Johnny?"

"Maybe." I drank the brandy off in a gulp.

"The best thing for you would be to go away," she said softly. "You know that."

"And if they don't?"

"You can't have everything," I said.

She looked at me and sighed.

"I guess I knew all along you'd go your own way, Johnny," she said.

I felt her eyes following me as I pushed through the screen door and out into the cool evening air.

A heavy fog had rolled in from the gulf, and down at the pier the big merc lamps were shining through the mist like a bridge out into nowhere. At the end of it, my boat floated in fog. She was a sweet forty-footer, almost paid for, riding low in the water with full loads in her four hundred-gallon tanks. The pair of 480 Supermarine Chryslers under her hatches were old, but in top condition; I'd rebuilt them myself. They'd always gotten me where I was going, and back again.

I went up past the gear locker by the pole and two men separated themselves from the shadows and stepped out to block my way. One of them was the big ex-pug, the one they call Jakesy. The other was a foxy little bird in racetrack clothes. He flipped a cigarette away and pinched the knot in his tie and shook out his cuffs like a card shark getting set for a fast shuffle.

"This here is Mr. Renata, Curlon," Jakesy said.

Somebody had hit him in the throat once and his voice was a foghorn whisper. "He came down from Palm special to talk to ya."

"A pleasure, Mr. Curlon," the foxy man put out a long narrow hand like a monkey's. I didn't look at it.

"I told you not to hang around my boat," I said.

"Don't get tough, Curlon," Jakesy said. "Mr. Renata's a big man, he come a long way——"

"The Fishermen's Protective Association's an important organization, fella," Renata spoke up. "A man can save hisself a lot of trouble by signing up."

"Why would I want to save myself trouble?"

He nodded, as if I'd said something reasonable. "Tell you what, Curlon," he said. "To show our good will, we'll waive the three hundred initiation fee."

"Just stay out of my way," I said, and started past him.

"Wait a minute, conch," Jakesy growled. "Mugs like you don't talk to Mr. Renata that way."

"Take it easy, Jakesy," Renata said softly. "Mr. Curlon's too smart a man to start any trouble."

I looked the way his eyes had flicked and saw the car that had eased up across the street. Two men had gotten out and were leaning against the front fender with their arms folded.

"You got to move with the times, Curlon," Renata said, and showed me some teeth that needed work. "A guy on his own ain't got a chance nowadays. The competition is too tough." He took some papers out of an inside pocket and held them out. "Sign 'em, fella. It's the smart thing to do."

I took the papers and tore them across the middle and tossed them away. "Anything else before you go?"

I asked him. His face got nasty, but he put out a hand to hold Jakesy back.

"That's too bad, Curlon. Too bad." He took out his show hanky and flapped it and I stepped in fast past him and left-hooked Jakesy before his hand had time to finish its sweep up from his hip. The blackjack went flying and Jakesy took two off-balance steps back and went over the side and hit with plenty of splash. I grabbed for Renata, and a small automatic fell out of his clothes; he dived for it and ran into the toe of my shoe. He flopped out on his back, spitting blood and mewling like a wet kitten. The two back-up men were coming at a run. I grabbed up the gun and started to say something to Renata about calling them off, but a gun flashed and coughed through a silencer and a slug cut air past my right ear. I fired twice from the hip and a man skidded and went down and the other hit the planks. I caught Renata's collar and hauled him to his feet.

"Any closer and you're dead," I said; he kicked and tried to bite my hand, then squalled an order.

"The lousy punk got Jimmy," the yell came back.

Renata yelled again and one of the gunnies got to his feet, slowly.

"Jimmy, too," I said. Renata passed the word. The man on his feet tried to lift his partner, couldn't make it, settled for getting a couple of handfuls of coat and dragging him. After a minute or two I heard the car start up, gun away into the fog.

"OK—now gimme a break," Renata said. I pushed him away. "Sure," I said, and hit him hard in the stomach, and when he bent over, I slammed a solid one to the chin. I left him on the dock and went on out and started up. I used my old knife to cut her stern line; in two minutes I was nosed out into the channel, headed for deep water. I watched the beach lights sliding away into the mist that covered the decay and the poverty and just left the magic of a harbor at night. And the smell of corruption; it couldn't cover that.

I ran due west for five hours, then switched off and sat on deck and watched the stars for an hour, listening for the sound of engines, but nobody was chasing me.

I put out a sea anchor and went below and turned in.

There was a low mist across the water when I rolled out just before dawn. My shoulder was aching, and for a minute that and the feel of the clammy fog against my face almost reminded me of something: the glint of light on steel and a pennon that fluttered in the breeze, and the feel of a big horse under me; and that was pretty strange, because I've never been on a horse in my life.

The boat was dead still on the flat sea, and even through the mist the sun already had some heat in it. It looked like another of those wide, blue days on the gulf, with the sea and sky empty to the far horizon. Out here, Jakesy and his boss Renata seemed like something out of another life. I started for the galley to rustle some ham and eggs, noticed a curious thing: little clumps of fungus-like stuff, growing on the mahogany planking and on the chrome rail. I kicked it over the side and spent half an hour swabbing her down and polishing her brass, listening to a silence as big as the world. Afterward, I lifted the hatch and checked the engines over, screwed the grease cups on the stuffing boxes down a turn or two. When I came back up on deck, there was a man standing by the port rail, looking at me over the sights of a gun.

He was dressed in a tight white uniform with little twists of gold braid at the cuffs. His face was lean, hard, not sunburned; a city man. The thing in his hand wasn't like any gun I had ever seen, but it had that functional look; and the hand that pointed it at my face was as steady as it needed to be. I looked past him, all around the boat. There was no other boat in sight—not even a rubber raft.

"Smooth," I said. "How did you manage it?"

"This is a neurac—a nerve-gun," he said in a matter-of-fact tone. "It is indescribably painful. Do exactly as I tell you and I won't be forced to use it." He motioned me back toward the hatch. He had a strange accent— British, and yet not quite British. I moved back a step or two and he followed, keeping the distance between us constant.

"There is a fuel-pump valve located at the left of the water manifold," he said, in the same tone you might ask to have the sugar passed. "Open it."

I thought of things to say then, but the gun was the answer to all of them. I climbed down and found the valve and opened it; diesel fuel gushed out, making a soft splashing sound hitting the water on the port side. Three hundred gallons of number two, spreading out oily on the flat water.

"Open the forward scuttle valve," the man with the gun said.

He moved with me as I lifted the hatch, watched me open the valve to let the green water boil in. Then we went aft and opened the other one. The water made a cool, gurgling sound coming in. I could see it in the open engine hatch, rising beside the big cylinder blocks, with bits of flotsam swirling on the dark surface. In two minutes she was down by the stern, listing a little to port.

"It's a cumbersome way to commit suicide," I said. "Why not just go over the side?"

"Close the aft valve," he said. He was braced against the side of the cockpit, cool and calm, a technician doing his job. I wondered what the job might be, but I went aft fast and closed the valve. Then the forward one. By then, she was riding low, her gunwales about six inches out of the water. The smell of the oil was thick in the air.

"If the wind comes up, under we go," I said. "And with no fuel, that means no pumps—"

"Lie down on the deck," he cut me off.

I shook my head. "I'll take it standing up."

"As you wish." He dropped the gun muzzle and I tensed and shifted my weight to make my try and the gun made a sharp humming noise and liquid fire smashed into me and tore my flesh apart.

... I was lying with my face against the deck, quivering like a freshly amputated leg. I got my knees under me and got to my feet.

The man in the white uniform was gone. I was alone on the boat.

I went over her from bow to transom—not that I thought I'd find him hiding in the bait locker. It was just something to do while I got used to the idea of what had happened. I finished that and leaned against the deckhouse while a spell of pain-nausea passed. The spot I'd picked to ride out the night hours was sixty miles south of Key West, about forty north of the Castillo del Morro. I was afloat, as long as the wind didn't rise enough to put a riffle on the water. I had plenty of food, and water for two days—maybe three if I stretched it. The man with the gun had fixed my radio before he left; I checked and found a tube missing. There was no spare. That meant my one chance was to stay afloat until somebody happened past who could put a line on me. It would mean losing the boat—but she was as good as lost now, unless I could save her fast.

There wasn't much I could do in that direction: the hand pump in the bilge was under two feet of water. I spent an hour rerigging it on deck, and put in another hour working the handle before it broke. I may have lowered the level an eighth of an inch—or maybe it was just the light. I bailed for a while with a bait bucket, doing math in my head: at six buckets a minute, figuring three gallons to a bucket, how long to pour ten thousand gallons over the side? Too long, was the answer I came up with. By noon, the wind was starting to stir, and the level was down about an inch. I fished a canned ham and a bottle of beer out of the water sloshing around in the galley, then sat on the shady side of the cockpit and watched the pale clouds piling up far away across the brassy water, and thought about sitting in the cool dimness of Molly's bar, telling her about how a mysterious man in a dapper white suit had aimed something he called a nerve-gun at me and told me to dump her fuel and scuttle her, and then disappeared while I was lying down...

I got up and checked the spot where he'd been

standing. There was nothing there to prove he hadn't been an illusion. He'd walked me forward, and then aft again, but that hadn't left a trail, either. I had opened the dump valve myself, flooded her myself. There was still the missing radio tube, but maybe I'd sneaked in and done that, too, while I wasn't looking. Maybe the hot tropical sun had finally crisped my brains, and the shot from the nerve-gun, which I could still feel every time I moved, had been the kind of fit people have after they've lost their grip on reality.

But I was just talking to myself. I knew what I'd seen. I remembered that hard, competent face, the way the light had glinted along the barrel of the gun, the incongruously spotless whites with the shiny lapel insignia with the letters TNL in blue enamel on them. I got my bucket and went back to work.

A breeze sprang up at sunset, and in ten minutes she had shipped more water than I had bailed in ten hours. She wallowed in the swells, logy as a gravid sea cow. She'd swamp sometime in the night, and I'd swim for a while, and after that...

There wasn't any future in that line of thought. I stretched out on my back on top of the deckhouse and closed my eyes and listened to her creak, as she moved in the water with all that weight in her...

...And came awake, still listening, but to a new sound now. It was full dark, with no moon. I slid down to the deck and solid water came over the gunwale and soaked me to the knees.

I heard the sound again; it came from forward—a dull *thunk*! like something heavy bringing up solid against the decking. I reached down inside the cockpit and brought out the big six-cell flash I keep clamped to the wall beside the chart board and flicked it on and shone it up that way, and a voice out of the dark said, "Curlon—kill that light!"

I went flat against the house and flashed the beam along the rail and found his feet, raised it and put it square in his eyes. It wasn't the man who'd used the pain-gun on me. He was tall, gray-haired, wearing a trim gray coverall. His hands were empty.

"Put the light out," he said. "Quick! It's important!"

I switched off the flash. I could still see him faintly.

"There's no time to explain," he said. "You'll have to abandon her!"

"I don't suppose you brought a boat with you?" More water came over the side. She shuddered under me.

"Something better," he said. "But we'll have to make it fast. Come on forward!"

I didn't answer because I was halfway to him. I tried to find his silhouette against the sky, but it was all the same color.

"She's sinking fast," he said. "Jumping me won't change that."

"Her fuel and water tanks are dry," I said. "Maybe she'll float." I gained another yard.

"We don't have time to wait and see. There are only a few seconds left."

He was standing on the forehatch, half turned to the left, looking out into the dark as though there were something interesting out there he didn't want to miss. I followed the way he was looking and saw it.

It was a platform, about ten feet on a side, with a railing around it that reflected faint highlights from what looked like a glowing dish perched on a stand in the center. It was about a hundred yards away, drifting a few feet above the water. There were two men on it, both in the white suits. One of them was the man who'd scuttled my boat. The other was a little man with big ears: I couldn't see his face.

"What's the hurry?" I said. "I see a man I need to have a talk with."

"I can't force you," the man in gray said. "I can only tell you that this time they're holding all the cards. I'm offering you a chance at a new deal. Look!" He hooked a thumb over his shoulder. At first I didn't see anything; then I did: a rectangle, six feet high, two feet wide, like an open doorway into a room where a dim candle burned.

"I can't afford to be caught," the man in gray said. "Follow me—if you decide to trust me." He turned and stepped up into the ghost-door hanging in the air and was gone.

The platform was coming up fast now; the lean man was standing at the forward edge with the nerve-gun in his hand. "Give me ten seconds," I said to the hole in the air.

I went back along the pilot-house, dropped down into hip-deep water in the cockpit. I felt around up above the dead binnacle light, found the leather belt and sheath, strapped it on. As I swung back up, I felt her start to go. White water churned up around my waist, almost broke my grip on the rail. The glowing doorway was still there, hanging in the air six feet away. I jumped for it as she slid under. There was a sensation like needles against my skin as I crossed the line of light; then my feet struck floor, and I was standing in the strangest room I ever saw.

Chapter Two

IT WAS ABOUT EIGHT feet by ten, carpeted with curved white-painted walls lined with the glitter of screens, dials, instrument faces, more levers and gadgets than the cockpit of a Navy P2V. The man in gray was sitting in one of two contoured bucket seats in front of an array of colored lights. He flashed me a quick glance, hit a button at the same time. A soft humming sound started up; there was an indefinable sense of motion, in some medium other than space.

"Close, but I don't think they saw us," he said tensely. "At least there's no tac-ray on us. But we have to move out fast, before he sets up a full-scale scan pattern." He was looking into a small, green-glowing screen, the size of a flight-deck radarscope, flipping levers at the same time. The scanning line swept down from top to bottom, about two cycles per second. I'd never seen one like it. But then I'd never seen anything like any of what had happened in the last few minutes.

"Who are they?" I said. "What are they?"

He gave me a fast up-and-down look. "For the moment, suffice it to say they're representatives of someone who seems to have taken a dislike to you." He flipped a switch and the lights dimmed down almost to nothing. On a big screen, six feet square, a picture snapped into sharp focus. It was the platform, hovering above the choppy water about fifty feet away, receding. The view was as clear as though I were looking out through a picture window. One of the men in white was playing a powerful beam of bluish light across the waves. My boat was gone. There was nothing in sight but a few odds and ends of gear, bobbing on the black water.

"You dropped off his tracer cold," the man in gray said. "He won't like that very well—but it couldn't be helped. By picking you up, I've put myself in what one might call an impossible position." He eyed me as if he were thinking over how much more to tell me.

"After what's already happened, that's not a word I'd use lightly," I said. "What are you—FBI? CIA? Not that they'd have anything like this." I nodded at that fantastic control panel.

"My name is Bayard," he said. "I'm afraid you're going to have to take me on trust for a while, Mr. Curlon."

"How do you know my name?"

"I've been following them," he nodded at the screen. "I've learned a number of things about you."

"Why did you pick me up?"

"Curiosity is as good a word as any."

"If you were tailing them, how did you manage to get here first?"

"I extrapolated their route and got ahead of them. I was lucky; I spotted you in time."

"How? It's a dark night, and I was showing no lights."

"I used an instrument which responds to . . . certain characteristics of matter."

"Make that a little plainer, will you, Bayard?"

"I'm not being intentionally mysterious," he said, "but there are regulations."

"Whose regulations?"

"I can't tell you that."

"So I just ask you to drop me at the next corner, and go on home and have a couple of drinks as if nothing had happened. By tomorrow the whole thing will seem silly—except for my boat."

He stared at the screen. "No, you can't do that, of course." He gave me a sharp stare. "Are you sure you're not holding something back? Something that would shed some light on all this?"

"You're the man of mystery, not me. I'm just a fisherman—or was until today."

"Not just any fisherman. A fisherman named Richard Henry Geoffrey Edward Curlon."

"I didn't think there was anyone alive who knew I had three middle initials."

"He knows. He also knows something that makes you important enough to be the object of a full-scale Net operation. I'd like to know what it is."

"It must be a case of mistaken identity. There's nothing about me to interest anyone except a specialist in hard-luck cases."

Bayard frowned at me. "Do you mind if I run a few tests on you? It will only take a minute or two. Nothing unpleasant."

"That will be a nice change," I said. "What kind of tests, for what purpose?"

"To find out what it is about you that interests

them," he nodded at the screen. "I'll tell you the results—if any." He took out a gadget and ran it over me like a photographer checking light levels.

"If the word hadn't already been overworked," he said, "I'd call these readings impossible." He pointed to a green needle that wavered, hunting around a luminous dial, like a compass at the North Pole. "According to this, you're in an infinite number of places at the same time. And this one—" he indicated a smaller dial with a glowing yellow arrow, "says that the energy levels concentrated in your area are of the order of ten thousand percent of normal."

"Your wires are crossed," I suggested.

"Apparently," he went on thinking out loud, "you represent a nexus point in what is known as a probability stress pattern. Unless I miss my guess, a major nexus."

"Meaning what?"

"That great affairs hinge on you, Mr. Curlon. What, or how, I don't know. But strange things are happening—and you're at the center of them. What you do next could have a profound effect on the future of the world—of many worlds."

"Slow down," I said. "Let's stick to reality."

"There is more than one reality, Mr. Curlon," Bayard said flatly.

"Who did you say you were again?" I asked him.

"Bayard. Colonel Brion Bayard of Imperial Intelligence."

"Intelligence, eh? And Imperial at that. Sounds a little old-fashioned—unless you're working for Haile Selassie."

"The Imperium is a great power, Mr. Curlon. But please accept my word that my government is not inimical to yours."

"Nowadays, that's something. How is it you speak American without an accent?"

"I was born in Ohio. But let's leave that aside for the moment. I've bought some time by whisking you out from under his nose, but he won't give up. And he has vast resources at his disposal." I still had the feeling he was talking to himself.

"All right, you've bought time," I prompted him. "What are you going to do with it?"

Bayard pointed to a dial with a slim red needle that trembled over a compass face. "This instrument is capable of tracing relationships of a high order of abstraction. Given a point of fixture, it indicates the position of artifacts closely associated with the subject. At the moment, it indicates a distant source, to the east of our present position."

"Science, Mr. Bayard? Or witchcraft?"

"The wider science ranges, the more it impinges on the area of what was once known as the occult. But after all, occult merely means hidden."

"What does all this have to do with me?"

"The instrument is attuned to you, Mr. Curlon. If we follow it, it may lead us to the answers to your questions. And mine."

"And when we get there—then what?"

"That depends on what we find."

"You don't give away much, do you, Colonel?" I said. "I've had a long day. I appreciate your picking me off my boat before she went under—and I suppose I owe you some thanks for saving me from another taste of that nerve-gun. But the question-and-no-answer game is wearing me down."

"Let's reach an understanding, Mr. Curlon," Bayard

said. "If I could explain, you'd understand—but the explanation would involve telling you the things I can't tell you."

"We're talking in circles, Colonel. I suppose you know that."

"The circle is tightening, Mr. Curlon. I'm hoping it isn't a noose that will choke us all."

"That's pretty dramatic language, isn't it, Colonel? You make it sound like the end of the world."

Bayard nodded, holding his eyes. In the varicolored light from the instrument panel, his face was hard, set in lines of tension.

"Precisely, Mr. Curlon," he said.

The moon rose, painting a silver highway across the water. We bypassed Bermuda, saw the light of the Azores in the distance. Two more hours passed, while the ocean unrolled under us, until the shore of France came into view dead ahead.

"The proximity sensors are registering in the beta range now," Bayard said. "We're within a few miles of what we're looking for."

He moved a lever and the moonlit curve of the shore dropped away under us. It was swift, noiseless, smooth. We leveled off at a height of a couple of hundred feet over tilled fields, swung over the tiled rooftops of a small village, followed a narrow, winding road that cut through a range of wooded hills. Far ahead, a wide river glittered against the black land.

"The Seine," Bayard said. He studied the illuminated chart that unrolled on a small screen before him, with a red dot in the center that represented our position.

"The indicator is reading in the red now. Not much farther."

Ahead, the river curved between high banks. At the widest point, there was a steep, tree-covered island.

"Does any of this look familiar to you?" Bayard asked. "Have you ever been here before?"

"No. It doesn't look like much. A river, and an island."

"Not just an island, Mr. Curlon," Bayard said. "Take a closer look." There was a note of suppressed excitement in his voice.

"There's a building," I said. I could make it out now: a massive pile of stone, topped by castellated towers.

"A rather famous building—known as Chateau Gaillard," Bayard said. He glanced at me. "Does the name mean anything to you?"

"I've heard of it. Pretty old, isn't it?"

"About eight hundred years." All the while we talked, the shuttle was gliding in across the river, toward the stone walls and towers of the fortress. Bayard adjusted levers and we stopped, hanging in empty air about fifty feet from the face of the high wall. There was ivy growing there, and in the spaces between the dark leaves the stone looked as old as the rocks below.

"We're within five hundred feet of the center of resonance," Bayard said. "It's somewhere below us." The wall in front of us slid upward as the shuttle dropped vertically. There were narrow loopholes in the stonework, between weathered buttresses that gripped the rockface like talons. We leveled off at the base of the wall.

"Our target is some twelve feet below this point, and approximately sixteen feet to the north-northeast," Bayard said.

"That puts it somewhere in the foundations," I said. "It seems we're out of luck."

"You're about to have another unusual experience," Mr. Curlon," Bayard said. "Hold on to your equanimity." He flipped a switch. The view on the screen faded into a sort of luminous blue, the color of a gas flame, and about as solid-looking. He moved the controls, and the ghost-wall slid upward. The line of rubble that was the surface slid past, like water rising over a periscope, and the screen went solid blue, with clearly defined stratum lines running across it at an angle. There were a few embedded stones, a darker shade of blue, like lumps of gelatin floating in an aquarium, some gnarled roots, pale and transparent, pieces of broken pottery. The screen went darker, almost opaque.

"We're into the solid rock now," Bayard said in a tone as calm as if he were pointing out movie stars' homes. We stopped, and I felt a few million tons of the planet pushing in at me. It gave me a strange, insubstantial feeling, as if I were nothing but a pattern drawn in smoke, like the gaseous granite just beyond the thin hull.

"As I said, quite a machine," I grunted. "What else will she do?"

Bayard showed me a faint smile and touched the controls. The texture of the rock swirled around us like muddy water with a dim light shining through it. We eased forward about ten feet, and slid out through a wall and were in a small room, stone walled and floored, windowless, thick with dust. It was almost bright here, after the trip through the rock. There were things in the room: the tattered shreds of a rotted tapestry on the wall, a wooden bench, crudely made from rough planks, heaped with dust; some metal plates and mugs ornately decorated with colored stones, pieces of gaudy jewelry, lumps of rusted iron.

"I think maybe we've found something, Mr. Curlon," Bayard said, and now he didn't sound quite so calm. "Shall we step out and have a closer look?"

Bayard did things with his levers and a soft hum I'd forgotten I was hearing ran down the scale, and the scene on the viewplate faded, as if a projector had been switched off. He snapped another switch and a harsh white light glared against the bleak walls, casting black shadows in the corners. The panel slid back and I stepped out after him. The dust was a soft carpet underfoot; the odor of age in the air was like all the musty books in all the forgotten libraries.

"An old storeroom," Bayard said in the kind of hushed voice that went with a disturbed grave. "Sealed up, probably centuries ago."

"It could do with a sweeping," I said.

"The cloth and wood and leather have rotted away, except for the heavier pieces. And most of the metal has oxidized."

I stirred a heap of rust with my foot. A flake the size of a saucer crumbled off. Bayard went to one knee, poked at the corrosion, lifted the curved piece clear.

"This is a *genouillère*," he said. "A knee guard; part of a suit of chain armor."

He had an instrument like a Geiger counter in his hand, with a pointer on a cable that he aimed around the room.

"There are extraordinary forces at work here," he said. "The Net tension reading is off the end of the scale."

"Meaning?"

"The fabric of reality is stretched to the breaking

point. It's almost as if there were a discontinuity in the continuum—a break in the entropic sequence. Forces like these can't exist, Mr. Curlon—not for long—not without neutralization!"

He changed the settings on the gadget he was holding, swung around to point it at me.

"You seem to represent the focus of a strongly polarized energy flow," he said. He came closer, pointed the instrument at my face, waved it down across my chest, stopped with the thing aimed at my left hip.

"The knife," he said. "May I see it?"

I took it out and handed it over. It was nothing much to look at: a wide, thick blade, about a foot long, ground to a rather crude point, with a stubby cross-guard and an oversized, leather-wrapped handle. It wasn't the handiest scaling knife in the world, but I'd had it a long time. Bayard held the metal pointer against it and looked incredulous.

"Where did you get this, Mr. Curlon?"

"I found it."

"Where?"

"In a trunk, in an attic, a long time ago."

"Whose trunk? Whose attic? Think carefully, Mr. Curlon. This may be of vital importance."

"It was my grandfather's attic, the day after he died. The trunk had been in the family a long time; the story was it belonged to a sea-faring ancestor, back in the eighteen hundreds. I was rummaging in it and turned the knife up. I kept it. I don't know why. It's not much, as knives go, but it seemed to fit my hand pretty well."

Bayard looked closely at the blade. "There's lettering here," he said. "It looks like Old French: *Dieu et mon droit*."

"We didn't come all this way just to study my knife," I said.

"Why keep calling it a knife, Mr. Curlon?" Bayard said. "We both know better." He gripped the hilt of the weapon and hefted it. "It's much too massive for a knife, too clumsy."

"What would you call it?"

"It's a broken sword, Mr. Curlon. Didn't you know?" He offered it to me, hilt first. As I took it, Bayard looked at his dials. "The reading went up into the blue when you took it in your hand," he said in a voice that was as taut as a tow-cable.

In my hand, the hilt of the knife seemed to tingle. It tugged, gently, as if invisible fingers were pulling at it. Bayard was watching my face. I felt sweat trickle down across my left eyebrow. Hackles I didn't know I had were trying to rise. I took a step and the pull became stronger. A vivid blue spark, like static electricity, played across a lump of rusted iron on the bench. Another step, and a faint blue halo sprang up around the end of the knife. From the corner of my eye, I saw that objects all around the room were glowing softly in the gloom. Dust trickled from the bench; something stirred there, rotated a few inches, stopped. I took a step sideways; it pivoted, following me.

Bayard stirred the dust with his finger, lifted a piece of pitted steel about three inches by six, beveled along both edges, with a groove along the central ridge.

"Just a piece of scrap iron," I said. "What made it move?"

"Unless I'm mistaken, Mr. Curlon," Bayard said, "it's a piece of your broken sword."

CHAPTER THREE

"I DON'T BELIEVE IN magic, Colonel," I said.

"Not magic," Bayard said. "There are subtle relationships between objects, Mr. Curlon; affinities between people and the inanimates that play a role in their lives."

"It's just old iron, Bayard. Nothing else."

"Objects are a part of their environment," Bayard said flatly. "Every quantum of matter-energy in this Universe has been here since its inception. The atoms that make up this blade were formed before the sun was formed; they were there, in the rock, when the first life stirred in the seas. Then the metal was mined, smelted, forged. But always, the matter itself has been a part of the immutable sum total of this material plane of reality. Complex inter-relationships exist among the particles of a given world-line—relationships which are affected by the uses to which the matter they comprise are put. Such a relationship exists between you and this ancient weapon."

Bayard was grinning now—the grin of an old gray

wolf who smells blood. "I'm beginning to put two and two together: you—with that red mane, that physique—and now this. Yes, I think I'm beginning to understand who you are, Mr. Curlon—*what* you are."

"And what am I?"

Bayard made a motion that took in the room, and the massive pile above it. "This chateau was built in the year 1196 by an English king," he said. "His name was Richard—known as the Lion-Hearted."

"That's what *he* was. What am I?"

"You're his descendant, Mr. Curlon. The last of the Plantagenets."

I laughed aloud at the letdown. "I suppose the next move is to offer me a genuine hand-painted reconstruction of the family coat of arms, suitable for framing. This must be your idea of humor, Colonel. And even if it were true, after thirty generations, any connection between him and a modern descendant would be statistically negligible."

"Careful, Mr. Curlon; your education is showing," Bayard's smile was grim. "Your information is correct—as far as it goes. But a human being is more than a statistical complex. There are linkages, Mr. Curlon—relationships that go beyond Mendel and Darwin. The hand of the past still reaches out to mold the present—and the future—"

"I see. The lad with the nerve-gun is running me down to collect a bill that Richard the First owed his tailor—"

"Bear with me a moment, Mr. Curlon. Accept the fact that reality is more complex than the approximations that science calls the axioms of physics. Every human action has repercussions that spread out across a vast continuum. Those repercussions can have profound effects—effects beyond your present conception of the exocosm. You're not finished with all this yet. You're involved—inevitably, like it or not. You have enemies, Mr. Curlon; enemies capable of aborting every undertaking you attempt. And I'm beginning to get a glimmering of an idea why that might be."

"I'll admit somebody sank my boat," I said. "But that's all. I don't believe in vast plots, aimed at me."

"Don't be too sure, Mr. Curlon. When I discovered that missions were being carried out in B-I Three—the official designation of this area—I looked into the matter. Some of those missions were recent—within the last few weeks. But others dated back over a period of almost thirty years."

"Which means someone has been after me since I was a year old? I ask you, Colonel: Is that reasonable?"

"Nothing about this affair is reasonable, Mr. Curlon. Among other curiosa is the fact that the existence of B-I Three wasn't officially known to Intelligence HQ until ten years ago—" He broke off, shook his head as though irritated. "I realize that everything I say only compounds your confusion—"

"Am I the one who's confused, Colonel?"

"Everything that's happened has a meaning—is a part of a pattern. We must discover what that pattern is, Mr. Curlon."

"All this, on the basis of a fishknife and a piece of rusty metal?"

I put out my hand and he put the piece of iron in it. The upper end was broken in a shallow V. There was a gentle tugging, as if the two pieces of metal were trying to orient themselves in relation to each other.

"If it's all my imagination, Mr. Curlon," Bayard said softly, "why are you fighting to hold the two pieces apart?"

I let the smaller shard turn, brought it slowly across toward the point of the knife. When it was six inches away, a long pink spark jumped across the gap. The pull increased. I tried to hold them apart, but it was no use. They moved together and touched ... and a million volts of lightning smashed down and lit the room with a blinding glare.

The rays of the late sun shone fitfully from a cloud-serried sky, and shadows fled across the sward, across the faces of those who stood before me, swelled up in arrogance, petty men who would summon a king to an accounting. One stood forth among them, a-glitter in rich stuff, and made much of flourishing the scrolls from which he spelled out those demands by which they thought to bind my royal power.

To the end I let him speak his treason, for all to hear. Then I gave my answer.

From the dark forest roundabout my picked archers stepped forth, and in a dread silence bent their bows. And my heart sang as their shafts sang, finding their marks in traitors' breasts. And under my eyes were the false barons slain, every one, and when the deed was done I walked forth from my pavilion and looked on their dead faces and spurned with my foot that scrap of parchment they called their Charter.

The voices and the faces faded. The shadowed walls of the old storeroom closed in around me. But it was as though years had passed, and the room was a forgotten memory from some distant life, lived long ago.

"What happened?" Bayard's voice rasped in the silence.

"I . . . know not," I heard myself say, and my own voice sounded strange in my ears. "'Twas some fit took hold on me." I made an effort and shook the last of the fog out of my brain. Bayard was pointing at me—at what I held in my hand.

"My God, the sword!"

I looked—and felt time stop while my pulse boomed in my ears. The broken blade, which had been a foot long, was half again that length now. The two pieces of metal had welded themselves together into a single unit.

"The seam of the joining is invisible," Bayard said. "It's as though the two parts had never been separated."

I ran my fingers over the dark metal. The color, the pattern of oxidation was unbroken.

"What did you experience while it was happening?" Bayard asked.

"Dreams. Visions."

"What kind of visions?"

"Not pleasant ones."

Bayard's eyes went past me to the wall beyond.

"The sword wasn't the only thing that was affected," he said in a tight voice. "Look!"

I looked. Against the stones, where only tatters had been, a faded tapestry hung. It showed a dim, crudely worked design of huntsmen and hounds. There was nothing remarkable about it—except that it hadn't been there five minutes ago.

"Notice the pattern," Bayard said. "The big figure in the center is wearing a cloak trimmed in ermine tails—a symbol of royalty. My guess is that's Richard himself." He looked around the room, bent and picked up the *genouillère*. The metal was dark with age, but there was no rust on it now.

"What happened here had an effect on the fabric of the continuum itself," Bayard said. "Reality is being reshaped as the Net tensions resolve themselves. There are fantastic powers in balance, Mr. Curlon, ready for a touch to send them tumbling one way—or another." His eyes held on mine. "Someone is working to upset that balance. I think we can take it as axiomatic that we must oppose him."

As he finished speaking, a bell clanged from the shuttle. Bayard leaped to the panel, hit the switches.

"There's a tracer locked on us at close range!" he snapped. "They followed us here! The energy discharge must have given them a fix to home on." The familiar humming sound started up, but this time it had a groaning note, as if it was working under an overload. I smelled hot insulation, and smoke curled from behind the panel.

"Too late," Bayard said. "He's holding a suppressor beam on us. We can't shift out of identity with this line. It looks like we're trapped!"

A deep thrumming sound started up somewhere. I could feel it vibrating through the floor of the room. Dust floated from the cracks in the walls, rose from the floor. A metal ornament made a soft thump falling off the bench.

"He's right above us," Bayard said. "He doesn't have half-phase capability; he'll use a force probe to dig his way down to us."

"All right," I said. "Let him. Two against two is fair odds."

"I can't take the chance," Bayard said. "It's not just you and me—it's the machine. It's unique, a special model. And if what I'm beginning to suspect is true, letting it fall into Renata's hands would be a major disaster."

"Renata?" I started to ask all the questions, but Bayard pulled a ring from his finger, handed it to me. "This is a control device governing the half-phase unit. With it, you can hold the machine clear until he's gone. You'll know, when the red light goes off—"

"Where will you be?"

"I'll meet him, try to steer him away from you. If he has any suspicion of what's happened, he'll be able to detect the shuttle, and grapple it."

"I'll stay, Bayard," I said. "I have a bone to pick with Mr. Renata."

"No—there's no time to argue! Do as I ask, Curlon, or he'll take both of us!" He didn't wait for an answer; he stepped out of the shuttle and the entry snapped shut behind him. His image appeared on the screen.

"Now, Mr. Curlon!" his voice came through the speaker. "Or it will be too late for both of us!"

A crack had already appeared in the wall he was facing. The time for talk had all run out. I pressed the stone set in the ring and heard a soft *click!* and felt space twist between my bones.

A soft, high-pitched whine started up, went up and off into the supersonic. Bayard's outline turned transparent blue, like the wall behind him. To him, the shuttle was invisible now.

"Good man," he said. His voice had a whispery quality but it was clear enough. He turned and faced the wall. A section of it bulged and fell in. A beam of dazzling light played through the opening. A man stepped through. It was Renata, the foxy man I'd left unconscious on the dock at Key West a couple of short lifetimes ago; there was no doubt about it: the sharp eyes, the narrow jaw, the slick black hair. But now he was in a swank white uniform that he wore as if he'd been born to it. But it was his face that bothered me most. I'd hit him hard, but there was no mark on him to prove it. He looked around the room, then at Bayard.

"You seem to be a long way from home, Colonel," he said, in a casual drawling voice—nothing like Renata's throaty whine.

"About the same as you, Major," Bayard said.

"Why did you come here—to this particular spot? And how did you get in? I see no entrance from the outside—other than the one I used."

Bayard glanced at the broken wall. "Your tactics seem a little rough for use in an interdicted area, Major. Are you acting on orders—or have you gone in business for yourself?"

"I'm afraid for the present you'll answer the questions, Colonel. You're under arrest, of course. Where have you left your shuttle?"

"I lent it to a friend."

"Don't fence with me, Bayard. It dropped completely off my screens less than half a minute ago—just as it did earlier, in the Gulf of Mexico. It seems you have equipment in your possession unknown to Imperial Intelligence. I shall have to ask you to lead me to it."

"I can't help you."

"You realize I must use force, if necessary. I can't permit the subject Curlon to slip out of my hands."

"I'm afraid you already have."

The little man half turned his head. "Lujac," he called. Another man came in through the hole in the wall. It was the fellow who'd used the nerve-gun on me. He had it in his hand now.

"Level three," the major said. Lujac raised the gun and pressed the firing stud on the side. Bayard staggered and doubled over.

"Enough," the little man said.

"Colonel, you're in considerable difficulty: absence from your post of duty without leave, interference with an official Net operation, and so on. All this will be dealt with in due course—but if you'll cooperate with me now, I think I can promise to make it easier for you."

"You don't know...what you're doing," Bayard got the words out. It wasn't easy; I knew what he was going through then. "There are forces...involved..."

"Never mind what's involved," the major snapped. "I don't mean to let the man slip through my fingers. Speak up, now! How did you do it? Where is he hidden?"

"You're wasting...your breath," Bayard said. "You know damned well you can't break my conditioning. Face it, Major; he got away from you. What are you going to do about it?"

"Don't be a fool, Bayard! You know the Imperium faces a crisis—and you're well aware that I'm acting on orders from a very high ranking official! You're throwing away not only your career, but your life, if you oppose me! Now—I want an explanation of why you came to this spot, what you expected to accomplish here—and where you've sent the man I want!"

"I'll bet you do," Bayard said. "Try and get it."

"Let me deal with the swine," Lujac said, and took a quick step forward, but Renata waved him back.

"I'm taking you in to Stockholm Zero-zero," he told Bayard. "You'll face a firing squad for this night's work—I promise you that!" He put cuffs on him and they went out through the hole in the wall. Half a minute later the red telltale light went off, meaning Renata's shuttle was gone. I flipped the switch that shifted me back to full-phase identity, waited for the color to come back into things, then stepped out and switched the machine back to half-phase. It shimmered like a mirage and winked out. The air was still swirling from that when the tunnel mouth exploded. When the dust cleared, it was packed solid with broken rock. The major had taken the precaution of closing the route behind him.

CHAPTER FOUR

IT TOOK ME FOUR hours of shifting sharp-edged rock fragments before I pushed aside the last slab and poked my head out into the open air beside the old stone wall rising up from a tangle of untrimmed shrubbery. I climbed out and breathed some fresh night air and tried to shake off the feeling that I was dreaming the whole thing. The Occam principle told me that the simplest explanation was that I was strapped into a jacket in some quiet rest home, living out a full-fledged delusional system. But if I was dreaming it, the dream was still on. Ten feet from the hole I'd crawled out of, I found a set of booted footprints which led a few yards to the imprint of a set of skids. That would be where the major's shuttle had been parked—if there had been a major, and he had a shuttle, and it had been parked.

And while I was still following that one through, I got the proof I'd been wanting: The man called Lujac stepped out from black shadows and for the second time I felt the bone-crushing agony of the nerve-gun sweep over me.

I came to lying on the floor in front of the control panel of a shuttle with my arms clamped behind me. It wasn't Bayard's machine, but there was no mistaking the sweep of unfamiliar dials and the big pink-glowing screen, or the hum that went between my bones until it rose out of the audible range. On the screen, things were happening. The old walls rising on the left of the screen flickered and sank down into heaps of rubble, with weeds poking out from between the stone slabs. The weeds withered and the rubble blackened into cokelike ash, then glowed blue and slumped into puddled lava. The river was rising, it welled out over its banks and became an oily black sea that stretched away to a row of volcanic cones that shed red light on the far horizon. Green slime crawled up on the rocks that showed above the surface. It changed into moss that grew into toadstools fifty feet high that jostled and thrust for footing. The water receded, and new plants swarmed up out of the sea; a vine-thing like writhing snakes threw itself over the jungle and tiny black plants sprang up along its tendrils, eating at it like acid. Broad leaves poked out from under the rotted vegetation and wrapped themselves around the black vine-eaters. I saw all this through a sort of purple haze of pain that did nothing to brighten the nightmare.

Animal life appeared: Strange creatures with deformed limbs and misshapen bodies like melting wax statues posed among the cancerous plants. The leaves grew huge and curled and fell away, and scaly, deformed trees rose up, and all the while the creatures didn't move. They swelled, twisted, flowed into new shapes. A forty-foot lizard was locked in the clutch of a plant with rubbery, spike-studded branches that wound around the bossed hide until the hide grew its own spikes that impaled the thorn tree, and it shriveled and fell away and the lizard dwindled into a crouching frog-thing that bloated into a stranded tadpole the size of a cow and sank into the ooze.

For a while, night glowed like day under a radio-active moon; and then the ground dissolved and the shuttle was hanging in black space, with the glare of the sun coming from behind to illuminate the undersides of the dust and rock fragments that arched up and over in a pale halo that must have dwarfed Saturn's rings. Then land appeared again: a dusty plain where small plants sprouted and grew thicker and turned into tangled underbrush dotted with small, cancerous trees. They grew taller and developed normal bark and green leaves, and slowly the atmosphere cleared and the moon was riding high and white in a dark sky full of luminous clouds.

Lujac switched off and the sound of the drive dwindled down to a low growl and died. He pointed the nerve-gun at me, gestured toward the exit. I made it to my feet, stepped out onto a trimmed green lawn beside a high stone wall that was the same one we'd started from. But now there was ivy growing there, and lighted windows, up high. There were flowerbeds along the base, and a tended path led off down the slope toward the moonlit water of the river below. The trees were gone, but other trees grew in places where there had been no trees. Across the river, the lights of a town glowed, not quite where the town had been before.

We went along the path to a broad, paved walk, rounded the front of the building. Light blazed from a wide entry with glass doors set in the old stone. Two sharp-looking troopers in white jodhpurs snapped to and passed us into a high marble hall. Nobody seemed to think there was anything exceptional about a prisoner in cuffs being gun-walked here. We went along a corridor to an office where neat secretaries sat at typewriters with only three rows of keys. A lean, worried-looking man exchanged a few words with Lujac, and passed us into an inner office where Major Renata sat at a desk, talking into a recorder microphone. He twitched his sharp mouth into a foxy smile when he saw me and motioned Lujac out of the room.

This wasn't the same man I'd known back at Key West, I saw that now. It was his twin brother, better fed, better bred, but with the same kind of mind behind the same sly face. Not a man I'd ever really take a liking to.

"You led me quite a chase, Mr. Curlon," he said. "It's unfortunate that events fell out as they did; I had hoped to handle matters more subtly. You understand that I require certain information from you as the first order of business. Let's begin with the matter of Colonel Bayard's involvement. When did he first contact you, and what was his proposition?"

"Where is he now?"

"Never mind that!" Renata rapped. "Don't be confused by any false sense of misguided loyalty, Mr. Curlon. You owe him nothing! Now—answer my questions fully and promptly, and I give you my assurance that you will be in no way held accountable for his crimes."

"Why did you sink my boat?"

"It was necessary. You will be reimbursed, Mr. Curlon. As a matter of fact, you are an extremely lucky man. When this matter is finished up to the satisfaction of, ah, Imperial authorities, you'll find yourself in a most comfortable situation for the rest of your life."

"Why me?"

"I'm acting on instructions, Mr. Curlon. As to precisely why you were selected for this opportunity, I can't say. Merely accept your good fortune and give me your cooperation. Now, kindly begin by telling me precisely how Bayard contacted you and what he told you of his plans."

"Why not ask him?"

"Mr. Curlon, please limit your comments to answering questions for the present. Later, all your questions will be answered—within the limits of Imperial security requirements, of course."

I nodded. I was in no hurry. What came next probably wouldn't be as much fun.

"I know about your good intentions," I said. "I've met your lieutenant, the fellow with the nerve-gun."

"It was necessary to insure there'd be no unfortunate accident, Mr. Curlon. You're a powerful man, possibly excessively combative. There was no time for explanations. And you've suffered no permanent injury. Oh, by the way: where did Bayard secrete the shuttle?"

"You mean the amphibious car he picked me up in?"

"Yes. It's Imperial property, of course. By helping

me to recover it, you'll be reducing the charges against Bayard."

"He must have parked it out of sight."

"Mr. Curlon..." Renata's face tightened. "Perhaps you don't understand the seriousness of your situation. Cooperate, and your rewards will be great. Fail to cooperate, and you'll live to regret it."

"It seems you're always offering me a proposition, and I'm always turning it down," I said. "Maybe you and I just weren't meant to get together, Renata."

He took a breath as though he were about to yell, but instead he thumbed a button on his desk, savagely. The door opened and a couple of the armed troops were there.

"Place this subject in Class Three quarters, MS block," he snapped. He favored me with a look like a poison dart. "Perhaps a few days of solitary contemplation will assist you in seeing the proper course," he snapped, and went back to his paper work.

They marched me along halls, down steps into less ornately decorated halls, down more steps, along a passage with no pretensions of elegance at all, stopped before a heavy iron-bound door. A boy with blond fuzz on his chin opened up. I stepped through into the dim light of a shielded bulb and the door closed behind me with a solid sound. I looked around and put my head back and laughed.

I was back in the underground room I'd started from all those hours before.

It was the same, and yet not quite the same. The floor was swept, and the litter of dust and rusty junk was gone. But the tapestry was still on the wall, more complete now than it had been.

I prowled around the room, but aside from a chair and a cot, I didn't find anything that hadn't been there before. I rapped on the walls, but no sliding panels opened up on hidden stairways with daylight showing at the top of them. I looked at the tapestry, but it didn't tell me anything. The central figure was a tall, red-bearded man with a bow slung at his back, a sword at his side. His horse was pawing the air with one hoof and the hounds were leaping up, as if they were eager to be off. I knew how they felt. I was ready to travel myself. But this time there was no convenient tunnel waiting to be dug out. It was too bad Renata hadn't tossed Bayard in the same VIP cell. Maybe he'd have had another trick ring up his sleeve. I looked at the one wedged on my little finger and felt a prickling along my scalp line at the thoughts I was thinking. I wondered if I was missing some angle that was too obvious to see, but if I was, it was still invisible.

I pushed the stone and got ready for nothing to happen. For five seconds, nothing did. Then air *whooshed* around me and the shuttle winked into existence, with the door open and the soft light gleaming from inside.

I stepped into the shuttle and sat in the chair facing all those dials, packed in the panel like chrome and glass anchovies. I tried to remember which ones Bayard had used, and a trickle of sweat went down the side of my face when I thought about all the things that could go wrong if I made a mistake. But thinking at a time like this was a mistake. It would be too bad if I cross-controlled and stalled out in the middle of the solid rock, but chances like this didn't come along every day. I pushed the half-phase switch and the walls faded to electric blue. The first lever I pushed did nothing that was visible. I worked another one and had a short heart attack when the shuttle started to sink through the floor. I moved it the other way and moved up like a balloon rising through dense blue fog. Seconds later, I popped through the surface. I was behind a dense clump of trees, just a few feet from the spot where I'd seen the runner-marks. Just a few feet, and at the same time, in some way I wasn't ready to try to put into words yet, as far away as you could get. And that brought me to the question of my next move.

For the moment, I was in the clear. If my operating the shuttle had registered on any meters in the vicinity, it wasn't apparent. The obvious thing for me to do was to return the machine to half-phase, get off the premises as fast as I could, and forget about a stranger named Bayard and his story of a probability crisis coming that would turn the world into bubbling chaos.

On the other hand, I was sitting on a device which, according to its previous owner, was something out of the ordinary, even among the men in the white Imperial uniforms. And those same high-powered operators owed me a few things, including one boat of which I'd been rather fond. I had an advantage now; they didn't know where the shuttle was, where I was. And I could watch them, without being seen.

There was just one catch: It meant operating a machine that was more sophisticated than a jet fighter, and potentially more dangerous. I'd watched Bayard at the controls; I had a rough idea of how he had maneuvered it. The big white lever marked DR-MAIN was the one that started everything working. It had a nice feel to it under my hand: smooth and cool, a lever that wanted to be pulled.

I was still sitting there, looking into the screen and thinking these thoughts when lights came on over a side entry fifty feet along the wall. The door opened and Major Renata stepped out, carrying a briefcase and talking over his shoulder to a harassed-looking adjutant with a notebook. My reaction was automatic: I punched the half-phase switch and the scene faded out to the transparent blue that meant I was invisible.

A big, boxy staff-car pulled up along the drive and Renata and four others got in and the car pulled away. I remembered the controls Bayard had used to maneuver on half-phase. I tried them; the shuttle glided away as smoothly as oil spreading out on water. I followed the car down the winding drive through parklike grounds, past a gate where a sentry yawned as I slid by two feet from him, across a bridge and through the village. On the open highway, he opened up, but I had no trouble staying with him.

I trailed the car for half an hour, until it pulled through a gate in a wire fence around a small grassed airstrip. Renata got out and his aides scuttled around, readying a big, fabric-covered prop-driven airplane with wings the size of barn roofs. There were handshakes and some heel-clicking from a couple of Germanic-looking fellows; then Renata and one other climbed in and the plane taxied out and headed into the wind.

I'd spent the time looking over the controls, and was ready when the plane revved up and started its run. It took me three tries to match my rate of ascent to the airplane's, but I managed it, then maneuvered into a spot a quarter of a mile astern. So far, it had been easy; all I'd had to do was steer. For all I knew, the instruments were indicating ten different critical overloads, but I'd worry about that when I had to. The theory of a shuttle was a complex thing, but straight-line operation was simple enough.

It was a three-hour flight over rolling farmland straight into the rising sun, then out across water that had to be the English Channel. The plane began letting down toward a city that had to be London, circled a field a few miles out from the center of the city, landed and taxied up to a small operations building with rbaf-northolt lettered across it. I had a bad few seconds when the pavement washed up around me like muddy water, but I managed to level the shuttle out a foot above the pavement.

Renata climbed down, and a car pulled out and collected him. By now I was getting used to the capabilities of my little machine; I didn't bother with the gate, just slid across through the fence and fell in behind the car as it picked up speed along a broad parkway that led straight toward the towers of the city.

It was a fast twenty-minute trip. Renata's car, with a few touches of a siren that sounded like a ghost wailing through the audio pickup, cleared traffic, making speed through narrow, twisting streets, crossed the Thames on a bridge with a fine view of the House of Commons, swung into a stone-walled courtyard behind a big, grim fortress. Renata stepped out and headed for a small door under a big wrought-iron lantern, and I followed him through the wall. The sun winked out and I was in a wide, well-lit corridor lined with open doors where people in uniform did what people do in government offices. Renata took a sudden corner, and I over-corrected, found myself in solid rock that must have been five feet thick. By the time I'd maneuvered back into the open, he was out of sight.

For the next hour, I cruised through the building like a mechanized ghost, looking into big offices with ranks of filing cabinets and desks under banks of fluorescents, into smaller offices with deep carpets and solemn-looking bureaucrats admiring their reflections in the picture windows, into storerooms, a message center. I tried the lower levels, found dead-record storage, a still, some grim-looking cells. There was nothing for me there. I took a shortcut through a wall and was in an eight-foot-square room with rusty manacles and a hole in the floor for plumbing. It had everything a medieval dungeon needed except a couple of human skeletons chained to the wall.

I slid through the wall and was in a hollow in the masonry with rough steps leading up. It didn't look like a much-traveled way. I followed the route, found an intersecting passage above. It led to another. The walls of the old building were riddled with hideaways, it seemed. I found exits into a dozen rooms, a hidden door into the gardens at the bottom. But none of this was getting me any closer to Renata.

Back on the upper level, I checked out more VIP offices, and in the tenth or twelfth one found my quarry, sitting on the edge of a chair across from a big-shouldered, gray-haired man with career military written all over him. He didn't look pleased.

". . . difficult to explain to the Baron just how it was this subject was able to appear and disappear at will," he was growling. "No one outside Operation

Rosebush was aware of the existence of the sub-HQ at the chateau. Yet Bayard was found there; and later, the subject pops up—from nowhere! This is an unacceptable report, Major." He slammed a piece of paper to the desk in front of him and stared at Renata with less than a friendly look.

"My report is factual, Colonel," the little man said. He didn't seem to be much intimidated by the eyebrow treatment. "The fact that I have no hypothesis to offer in explanation doesn't alter my observations."

"Tell me more about the security arrangements you made for holding the subject," the colonel rapped.

"The man is under close guard in a maximum security cell under the chateau," Renata said crisply. "I'll stake my career on that."

"Better not," the colonel said.

Renata shifted in the chair. "Would the colonel care to explain?"

"He's gone. Half an hour after your departure, a routine check showed the cell empty."

"Impossible! I—"

"You're a fool, Renata," the colonel snapped. "The man had already demonstrated that he had unusual resources at his command. Yet you persisted in dealing with him in a routine way."

"I followed service procedures to the letter," Renata came back. Then a thought hit him. "What about Colonel Bayard? He's not . . . ?"

"He's here. I've taken the precaution of cuffing him to his bedstead, and posting two armed guards in the room with him."

"He must be questioned! His conditioning will have to be broken—"

"I'll make that decision, Major! Bayard enjoys a rather special status with top headquarters—"

"Break him, Colonel! He'll confirm what I've told you—and I think he can also offer an explanation of this subject's apparently miraculous powers!"

The colonel picked up a cigar, rolled it between his fingers, then snapped it in two.

"Renata, what the devil is behind this? What's Baron van Roosevelt planning? How does Bayard tie in—and just how much bearing does Richthofen's sudden illness have to do with it?"

"I'm not at liberty to discuss Baron van Roosevelt's plans," Renata said, and returned the colonel's look with interest.

"I'm still your superior officer," the colonel barked. "I demand to know what's going on under my nose!"

"I showed you my report out of courtesy," Renata stood. "I'll make further report to Baron General van Roosevelt, and no one else."

"We'll see about that, Major!" As the colonel jumped to his feet, a red telephone on his desk clanged. He grabbed it up, listened. His expression changed. He looked around the room.

"Right," he said. "I understand."

I moved the shuttle closer, until half of the desk was inside with me, turned up the audio to maximum. Among the crackling and hissing static, I caught the words from the telephone:

"... as though you suspected nothing! It will take us another thirty seconds to bring the suppressor into focus..."

That was enough for me. I backed off, sent the shuttle out through the side wall, shot through another office where a fat man was kissing a girl, on out through the exterior wall and was hovering over a city park, with hedges, a fountain, winding paths. There was a sharp crackling from the panel, and all my meters jumped at once. The hum of the drive faltered, took on a harsh note. I dropped the shuttle to ground level in a hurry; a power failure in mid-air would be messy. When I tried to head across the park, the shuttle moved six feet and halted with a jolt. The smell of hot wiring was strong now. Flames spouted from behind the panel. I slammed the drive switch off; I was caught but there still might be time to accomplish some denial to the enemy. I switched to full phase, and the color flooded back into the scene on the screen. It took me another five seconds to cycle the door open, jump clear, and thumb the ring switch. The shuttle wavered and faded from view, and dry leaves swirled where it had been a moment before. Then there were white uniforms all around me, closing in with drawn nerve-guns.

The building looked different in normal light. My escort walked me along a white-floored hall, up a wide staircase to a big white door flanked by sentries.

Everything in sight was smooth and efficient, but I could feel the tension in the air: a sort of wartime grimness, with lots of hurrying feet in the middle distance. And in the midst of all that spit-and-polish, a curious anomaly caught my eye: a patch of what looked like yellow toadstools, growing in a corner where the marble floor met the wall.

A fellow with a bundle of silver braid looped under his epaulet popped out of the door and we went in. It was a big office with dark-paneled walls and gold-framed paintings of tough-looking old birds in stiff uniform collars, and a desk the size of a bank vault. I looked at the man sitting behind it and met a pair of eyes that literally blazed with power.

"Well, Mr. Curlon," he said in a voice like the dirge notes on an organ. "We meet at last."

He was a big man, black-haired, with a straight nose and a firm mouth and eyes with a strange, dark shine. He motioned with one finger and the men who had brought me in disappeared. He stood and came around the desk and looked me up and down. He was as tall as I was, which made him over six three, and about the same weight. Under the smooth gray uniform he wore, there was plenty of muscle. Not the draft-horse kind; more like an elegant tyrannosaurus in tailored silk.

"Major Renata made a number of mistakes," he said. "But in the end—you're here, safe and sound. That's all that counts now."

"Who are you?" I asked him.

"I am Baron General van Roosevelt, Chief of Imperial Intelligence—Acting Chief, I should say, during the temporary indisposition of Baron Richthofen." He gave me one of those from-the-neck-up bows and a smile that was like the sun coming through a black cloud. He clapped me on the shoulder and laughed.

"But between you and myself, Mr. Curlon, formalities are unnecessary." He looked me in the eye, and the smile was gone, but a merry glint still burned there. "I need you, Curlon. And you need me. Between us, we hold the destiny of a world—of many worlds—between our fingers. But I'm being obscure—and I don't mean to be." He waved me to a chair, went to a liquor cabinet and poured two drinks, handed me one, and sat behind the desk.

"Where to begin?" he said. "Suppose I start by assuming that Colonel Bayard has told you nothing— that you have guessed nothing. Listen, then, and I'll tell you of the crisis we face now, you and I..."

Chapter Five

"THE CONTINUUM OF MULTI-ORDINAL reality is a complex structure, but for purposes of simplicity we can consider it as a bundle of lines stretching from the remote past toward the unimaginable future. Each line is a world, a universe, with its own infinitude of space and stars, separated from its sister worlds by the uncrossable barriers of energy that we know as entropy.

"Uncrossable, that is, until the year 1897, when two Italian scientists, Maxoni and Cocini, stumbled on a principle which changed the course of history—of a billion histories. They created a field in which the energy of normal temporal flow was deflected at what we may consider right angles to the normal direction. Objects and individuals enclosed in the field then moved, not forward in time as in nature, but across the lines of alternate reality. From that beginning grew the Imperium—the government claiming sovereignty over the entire Net of alternate worlds. Your world—which is known to us as Blight Insular Three—is but one of the uncountable parallel universes, each differing only infinitesimally from its neighbors. Like this world, it lies within the vast disaster area we call the Blight, a desert formed when an unfortunate miscarriage in early experimentation with the M-C principle led to the utter destruction of a vast complex of worlds, to the abortion of their destinies into the chaos which you no doubt saw as you crossed that area coming here.

"Among the relationships existing between parallel lines are those linking individuals, Mr. Curlon. Think for a moment: If two worlds differ by only the disposition of two grains of sand on a beach—or of two molecules within a grain of sand—then it follows that analogues of individuals will exist in all those world-lines whose date of common history—the date at which their histories diverged—is later than the birth date of the individual in question. Your case, Mr. Curlon, is an exception—and that fact is at the root of the problem. Your world is an island in the Blight, surrounded not by viable parallel worlds, but by a desert empty of normal life. You are unique, Mr. Curlon—which renders the present situation all the more poignant."

"That's a mild adjective, General," I said. "I'm still listening for what's going to make sinking my boat sound like a friendly move."

"As I said, Major Renata made a number of errors—but his intentions were good. He'd been working here with me, under great strain, for many weeks. As for his mission, consider, Mr. Curlon: You are a man destined for a role in great affairs—yet what did I know of you? Nothing. And time was short. It was necessary—unfortunate, but absolutely necessary—to put you to the test. I apologize for the Major's excessive zeal. Of course, he wasn't aware of the full ramifications of the situation—of your importance to the present contretemps."

"That makes a pair of us."

Roosevelt's expression flickered; there were emotions boiling under that bland façade, but he wasn't the man to show them.

"In the lost worlds of the Blight, your family loomed like a colossus, Mr. Curlon. Now, of all that mighty stock, only you remain." His eyes held me. "The destinies of many men died in the holocaust of the Blight—and human destiny is a force equal to the evolutionary pressure of the Universe itself. Remember: the vast energies choked off by the disaster were not destroyed, but instead shunted into the orgy of patternless vitality that characterizes the Blight. Now those energies seek to reorient themselves, to force a pattern on reality. Unless this power is channeled, guided, given form—our worlds will be engulfed in the cancer of the Blight. Already, signs of the coming plague are here!"

He waved a hand at the gold and royal blue seal on the wall behind him. There were flecks of green on the gilding, and at one corner a tiny crust of mold had formed.

"That crest was polished this morning, Mr. Curlon. And observe this." He pointed to the gold wire insignia on his collar: it was pitted by tarnish. "And this!" he pushed a leather-bound folder across the table. The regal coat of arms embossed on it in silver was bubbly with corrosion.

"Symbols—but symbols that represent the fixed

parameters of our cosmos—and those parameters are being eroded, Mr. Curlon!" He leaned back, forced the fire out of his eyes, his voice.

"Unless something is done now, at once, to reinforce the present reality, existence as we know it is doomed, Mr. Curlon."

"All right, General," I said. "I've listened. I don't understand all this, but I've seen enough in the last few hours to keep me from calling you crazy to your face. What is it you want from me? What do you expect me to do about the toadstools growing in your corridors?"

He stood and walked the length of the room, turned and paced back, stopped beside me.

"My plan is a dangerous one; you may think it fantastic, Captain Curlon . . ." I looked the question at him; he nodded and smiled. "I've ordered that you be commissioned in the Imperial Service, and gazetted to my staff," he said casually.

"Thanks, General," I said. "But you can skip the fancies. I'll settle for facts."

He looked disturbed for an instant. "This isn't intended as a bribe," he said, and picked up a thick parchment from the desk. "It's already accomplished—"

"Not without some kind of commitment on my part, it isn't," I said. "Not in any army I ever heard of."

"The oath is required, of course," he said. "A mere formality—"

"A symbol, I believe you said, General. For what it's worth, I'm still a civilian."

"Very well," he tossed the fancy commission aside in a way that I sensed wasn't quite as casual as it looked. "As you wish. Perhaps something Colonel Bayard said has prejudiced you—"

"By the way, where is Bayard now? The last I saw of him he was having a set of stomach cramps brought on by Major Renata's itchy trigger finger."

"Colonel Bayard was misguided. His intentions were good, no doubt, but he was uninformed. I don't wonder that he formed a false impression of the operation on the basis of the few facts he stumbled on."

"I'd like to see him."

"That won't be possible at present; he's in the hospital. However, I contemplate no action against him for breach of discipline, if that's what concerns you. He has an excellent record—until now. He was merely overzealous in this instance."

"You said something about working together. What is it you want from me?"

He stood, came around the desk and clapped me on the shoulder.

Come along, Captain," he said. "I'll show you."

The room he took me to was an underground vault, guarded by three relays of white-jacketed troopers with guns in their hands. One high wall was filled by a ground-glass screen, on which lines and points of light twinkled.

"This is a chart of the Net, covering the area lying within the hundred-thousand-year CH range," Roosevelt said. He picked up a pointer, indicated a red light at the exact center. "This is the Zero-zero world-line of the Imperium. Here"—he showed me another glowing point, not far away—"is your home-line, B-I Three. Note that all around these isolated lines, for a vast area, there is nothing—a desert. This, Mr. Curlon, is the Blight. Calculations by our physicists tell us that the probability imbalance, dating from the original cataclysm that formed the Blight some seventy years ago, is now seeking equilibrium. Fantastic energies are trapped there in a precarious stasis; energies of the kind that generate reality instant by instant as normal entropy progresses. I needn't tell you of the inconceivable potency of such powers. Consider only that in each instant of time the Universe is destroyed and recreated—and that here, in this blighted region, that process has been aborted, blocked like a choked volcano. For seven decades the pressure has mounted. Now it will no longer be denied. A great probability storm rages at the centroidal point of the Blight. When it blasts through, unless we take some action first, it will carry our world—and all other worlds within a vast range—with it into a limbo of probability disaster which beggars the imagination. Even now, probability waves are moving outward from the holocaust, with results that anyone can see—a mere hint of the holocaust to come."

He grounded the pointer, looked at me long and hard.

"Your destiny is interwoven with that of your world, Mr. Curlon—your fate, your history, are a part of the basic warp of the fabric of the reality we know. We have to seize on that thread—and every other thread we know of, few though they are—and from them, attempt to reweave a viable matrix into which the trapped energies can drain."

I had the feeling he was oversimplifying the problem; but even so, it was too dense for me.

"Keep talking, General," I said. "I'm trying to grope along with you."

"Our lives don't exist in a vacuum, Curlon. We have

pasts, roots, antecedents. Actions of men of a thousand years ago affect our lives today, just as our actions of today will repercuss down the ages that come after. Napoleon, Hitler, Caesar, affected their times and all the times to follow. But we stand at a moment where the very texture of existence is strained to the breaking point. What we do, far beyond the ordinary measure of the potency of key individuals, will determine the shape of the world to come. We must act promptly, decisively, correctly. We can afford no weakness, no mistake."

"You're building up to something, General. Why not come to the point."

He pushed a button on a console and the map winked out and another diagram took its place. This one showed an amoeba of pink and red lines twitching and writhing over a grid dotted with glowing points.

"This is a close-range energy chart of the Blight," he said. "Here you see the shifting of the lines of quantum demarcation, as they seek to adjust to the abnormal pressures exerted by the probability storm. In every world-line adjoining the Blight, objective reality is in flux. Objects, people, landscapes, are shifting, changing from moment to moment, day to day. I need not detail for you the pandemonium thus produced. So far we've felt the effects less, here; the Zero-zero line is a stable one firmly rooted in past history by a series of powerful key events. The same is true of your line, B-I Three. For the Blight to engulf these lines would entail the obliteration of basics of human cultural development as powerful as the discovery of fire."

He switched again, this time to a view of a blazing roil like a close-up of the sun.

"This is the center of the probability storm, Mr. Curlon. We've pinpointed its location, in a world-line that was once the seat of a great culture. This is where the key to the crisis will be found. I propose to go there, Mr. Curlon, to find that key."

"It looks as though that would be a lot like jumping down the throat of a live volcano."

"This diagram represents the turmoil of probability energies," Roosevelt said. "On the surface, to an observer within the A-line itself, the storm is not directly apparent. Abnormalities, freaks, impossibilities, the suspension of natural law, the distortion of reality under your very eyes, yes; but the tempest itself rages at a level of energy detectible only to specialized instruments. A man can go there, Mr. Curlon; the dangers he faces will be beyond description—but not perhaps beyond overcoming."

"Once there, then what?"

"Somewhere in that line is a key object, an artifact so inextricably interwoven with the past and future of the line, and of the quantum it controls, that all major probability lines must pass through it, in the way that lines of magnetic force flow through the poles of a magnet. I propose to find and identify that object, and remove it to a safe place."

"Go ahead," I said. "Spell the rest of it out."

"What more is there to say, Mr. Curlon?" Roosevelt gave me the sunny smile again, and his eyes had that dangerous twinkle of a man in love with danger. "I want you with me. I need you—the powers you represent—at my side."

"What makes you think I'll go?"

"I ask you to go—I can't, wouldn't attempt to force

you. That would be worse than useless. But remembering the greatness of your line, I believe you'll know where your duty lies."

"Now it's my duty, eh?"

"I think it is, Captain Curlon." He rose and gave me the smile again. This was a man I would have to love or hate; there'd be no middle ground.

"You needn't make your decision now," he said easily. "I've arranged for quarters for you here in my apartments. Get a night's rest; then we'll talk again." His eyes strayed down over my sweater and dungarees, fixed on the knife stuck through my belt.

"I shall have to ask that you leave the, er, weapon with me," he said. "Technically, you're under what is known as RIA—routine interrogational arrest. No point in causing talk."

"I'll keep it," I said. I don't know why. He had an army at his disposal to take it away from me if he felt like it. He leaned forward and frowned at me. His eyes were showing a little controlled anger now.

"Be kind enough to save unpleasantness by placing the knife on my desk," he said.

I shook my head. "It's a sentimental hang-up I have, General. I've carried it so long I'd feel naked without it."

His eyes locked on mine like electronic gun-pointers; then he relaxed and smiled.

"Keep it, then. Now go along and think over what I've said to you. And by tomorrow I hope you've decided to do as I ask."

The room they took me to was a little small for a diplomatic reception, but otherwise would have filled the bill OK. After my escort left I poked into a dressing room fit for a Broadway star, a closet that could have slept six with room left over for an all-night poker game, stuck a finger in a bed that looked like an Olympic wrestling mat with tassels. It was fancier than my usual style, but I had an idea I'd be able to sleep on it all right.

I took a shower in a bathroom full of gold faucets and pink marble, and put on the fresh clothes that were laid out for me, after which a waiter in black knee pants and a gold vest arrived with a cart loaded with pheasant on translucent china and wine and paper-thin glasses. While I tucked away I thought about what I'd learned from Roosevelt. The surface part—the story about parallel worlds and the disaster hanging over them unless he and I did something about it—was all right; as all right as insanity ever is. I didn't understand it, would never understand it—but the evidence was here, all around me. It was the other parts of the general's presentation that bothered me.

Once, when time hung heavy on my hands in a flat-top ready room, I spent some time reading up on games theory. The present situation seemed susceptible to analysis in the light of what I learned then. Roosevelt had tried three gambits: First, when he'd eased the commission at me. Second, when he'd tried to get my agreement to go along with him, in the blind, on a mission into the Blight. And third, when he'd tried to separate me from the knife. I'd resisted all three moves, more by instinct than any logic or plan.

I walked over to the window and looked down at a wall and a cobbled street. The big trees threw shadow patterns over the grass strips and flowerbeds, and the wide sidewalks were full of pretty women and men in bright uniforms with horsetail plumes and buttons that sparked under the lights. Across the park there were shops with bright-lit windows full of plush merchandise, and cafés with open-air terraces and awnings and tables and an odor of fresh-ground coffee and fresh-baked bread. From a bandstand somewhere you could hear an orchestra playing a Straussy sort of waltz—one that had never been heard, back where I came from.

I wondered what Bayard was doing now and what he'd have to say about the latest developments. I'd accepted him at face value, mostly on the basis of the fact that he'd snatched me off my boat just before I started the long swim. But if Roosevelt was telling the truth—if the whole thing had been designed just to test my reactions before pulling me into a key role in world-shaking events...

In that case I should tell Roosevelt all I'd seen at Chateau Gaillard. Maybe there was a clue there for someone who knew how to use it. Or misuse it.

Bayard had known a lot more about the situation than I did, and he hadn't trusted Renata, or Renata's boss. I wished he could have heard Roosevelt's pitch and given me the other side of the story.

What I needed now was information about Roosevelt, about Bayard, about what was going on and most of all, information about my place in all this—and the meaning of the old piece of steel with the magical property of pointing to other old pieces of steel.

I went to the door and eased it open; there was a guard in a white and gold uniform standing at a rigid parade rest at the far end of the passage. He

looked my way and I gave him an offhand wave and
he went back to eyes-front. I wasn't exactly under
arrest, but they were keeping an eye on me. I started
to close the door—and heard a scream like a gutted
horse from the room next to mine. The sentry yanked
a shiny chrome-plated gun from a polished holster
and came on at a run. I took two jumps to the door
the yell had come from and jerked at the knob, then
stepped back and kicked it open and was looking at
a white worm the size of a fire hose looped like a
boa constrictor around the crushed body of a man.

He was an old man with a purple face and white
hair and popped-out eyes and tongue. I was holding
the broken sword in my hand; I didn't remember
drawing it. It made a sound like an ax hitting a saddle
when I brought it down on the worm. It cut through
it like cheese, and the severed end whipped around,
splattering foul-smelling juices. Something boomed
like a cannon behind my ear, and a chunk of worm
flew. A ten-foot piece was flapping across the floor
and the gun boomed again and it flew up in the air,
whipping, while I hacked at another loop that was
weaving around on end like a charmed snake. There
were four pieces of the thing now and more boiling
out through the bathroom door. I heard a gun click
on an empty chamber and the guard swore and ended
on a gurgling note. I chopped my way through to him,
but I was too late. He was wrapped like a mummy
and his head was at an angle that meant he'd made
his last formation. There were yells from the passage,
and the sound of running feet and shots. I cut my
way across and into the bathroom. The jade green
marble tub was full of worm, writhing up through the

drain. I hacked it off, grabbed up a long-handled bath brush and rammed it down the drain, then chopped my way back through the flopping sections and into the hall. What was there was worse than the worm. It looked like a mass of raw meat, bulging up from the stairwell halfway down the corridor. Two men were firing into it, but it didn't seem to mind that much. I came up on it from the side and carved a slice off, and the mass of rubbery stuff recoiled, oozing pink blood. It didn't like cold steel.

"Get knives and swords!" I yelled. "You're wasting time firing slugs in it!"

The mass had bulged along the hall far enough to half cover a door. It burst inward, and I got a glimpse of a woman standing there before it welled through and blocked the opening. I caught just a faint echo of her scream. It took a half a dozen good chops to amputate the mass in the door, but I was too late again. All I could see of the girl was a pair of slippered feet sticking out from under the thing like a careless mechanic under a slipped jack.

Back in the hall I saw Roosevelt, in his shirt-sleeves, his teeth bared in what might have been a grin, hewing away at the thing with a two-handed sword. He saw me and yelled, "Curlon, to me!"

Uniformed men were doing what damage they could with ceremonial short-swords, but it was Roosevelt who was driving the thing back. It had bulged in to form a pocket, and he was wading into the pocket, while the rest of the thing bulged alongside, flanking him. I hit it on his left, hacked away a chunk the size of a Shetland pony just as the other side folded in, almost caught him. He stabbed at it, and I cut a swath through and got a stance back to back with him. He seemed to be trying to cut his way to a door that was two-thirds covered and starting to sag. We cleared it, and by then there were a dozen men working on the outer perimeter with swords they'd pulled off walls somewhere. We were ankle-deep in the thin pink blood that drained from every cut we made. I smelled smoke, and saw a pair of firemen in protective suits coming up the stair with oversized blowtorches. The thing flowed away ahead of them, turning black and shriveling. In another minute or two it was all over. I looked at Roosevelt through the smoke and the stink, past him along the corridor that was splashed to the ceiling and reeking like a slaughterhouse.

"Nice," I said, and discovered I was as winded as if I'd just run the four-minute mile. "What was it?"

Roosevelt grinned at me. He was breathing hard, and there was blood on his face, but incredibly, he looked like a man having fun.

"A brisk hour and a quarter," he said. "I congratulate you, Captain. You matched me blow for blow. Not many could have done it." It was a brag, but somehow it didn't sound arrogant. Just truthful.

"You didn't answer the question, General," I said.

His eyes went past me to the foul bulk spread across the blue Oriental carpeting.

"I don't really know," he said. "This was the worst attack so far. The periodicity has decayed to ninety-one hours and the intensity is increasing logarithmically. It doesn't seem to be an animal, in the normal sense of the word—merely a mass of flesh, growing wild."

"What kind of flesh?" I growled. It made my skin crawl to look at it.

His eyes met mine. "Human flesh, Mr. Curlon," he said.

I nodded. "I'm still not sure about all this, General; but if this is what you're fighting, I'm with you."

He gave me the smile, reached out and caught my hand with a grip like a rock-crusher.

"With you behind me—"

"Beside you," I cut in.

He nodded, still smiling. "Beside me, then. Perhaps we can yet prevail."

I didn't get much sleep for the next couple of nights. When I wasn't busy bone-bending with an unarmed combat master named Lind, I was listening to lectures on field operation, and doing my napping with a hypnotaper strapped to my skull, pumping me full of background data on the history of the Blight.

There were a few other trainees around. One was a beautiful Oriental-looking girl from an A-line where the Chinese had settled America back in the ninth century, and had met the Romans head-on along the Mississippi in 1776. She was headed for a place where a horde of backward, matriarchal Mongols were getting ready to sweep across a feudal Europe. It seemed that she fitted the bill of particulars for the incarnation of the goddess Chiu-Ki, a sort of celestial Dragon Lady. And a big coal-black man with a fierce look— maybe because of the stainless steel peg through his nose—had been recruited from a Zulu-ruled African empire to help organize a grass-roots resistance to a murder-suicide cult that was decimating the enslaved blacks in a line where the Greeks had developed science in the pre-Christian era and used it to conquer the known world before stagnation set in. I met one fellow who was a classic example of the Australian Bushman—but in his line his tribe had made it big on the mainland. He had a hard time not wrinkling his flat nose at the strange odors, but he was a gentleman. He treated us like equals.

During the week, I tried several times to see Bayard, but Roosevelt always put me off. The colonel was a sick man, he said. Pneumonia had set in, as it often did after a taste of the neurac. He was in an oxygen tent, and no visitors allowed.

Then the day came when the general came down and watched for half an hour while Lind tried to throw me on my ear; but I got lucky and threw him instead.

"You're ready," Roosevelt said. "We'll leave at midnight."

The shuttle terminus was a huge bright-lit room with a polished white floor marked off in orange lines, with shuttles ranked between the lines. There were little one-man scouts and big twenty-man passenger transports, some bare, functional boxes, some fancy VIP jobs, some armored, some fitted up to look like moving vans or delivery trucks. There was a steady, high-pitched whine, and a constant booming and buffeting from air displacement as shuttles came and went. I'd never seen any of it before, but it was all familiar from the sessions under the hypnotaper.

Technicians in white coveralls worked over machines, standing at little desks that were spaced along the aisles. Across the room I saw a party of men in costumes like Spanish conquistadors, and another group in Puritan black.

"Protective coloration," Roosevelt said. "Our agents always try to blend with the background. In our case, no disguises are necessary. As far as I know, there's no human life left where we're going."

The technicians fitted us into our suits—old-fashioned flyers' outfits with lightweight diving helmets. They checked us over with a minimum of formality, and we strapped in and closed the hatch. Roosevelt looked sideways at me and gave me the thumbs-up sign. "Ready?"

"It's your show, General," I said. He nodded and threw in the drive control. The whining hum started up; the light outside faded. The walls and roof quivered and disappeared, and we were perched two feet above a vacant lot full of weeds and blown dust under the open sky.

CHAPTER SIX

WE DIDN'T TALK MUCH, crossing the Blight, following the *beep-beep!* of the tracer tuned to our target. I watched the blasted landscape flow past while Roosevelt monitored fifty dial faces at once and corrected the control settings from time to time for no reason I could make out. For a while we skimmed above a plain of shattered rock, where smoke boiled up from fumaroles and volcanic cones that threw a red glow across the sky. Then there was an ocean of oil, scummed fluid that broke in sluggish foamy waves. And then land again: cinder-black, with pale flames licking over it until it coalesced into a sea of lava, dull-red and bubble-pocked. All the while, the clouds over the moon never moved.

The lava darkened, hardened, turned to a dusty plain. Green appeared, and strange, scabbed trees shot up in clumps of two or three. Vines spread, and ruins poked up among them. A slab of rock came into view, tilted up by the roots of a fifty-foot dandelion with hooks all along the stem. "We're close," Roosevelt said. "That's the highway leading into the city of Fontrevrault."

He corrected course to bring us in over the old road leading off through the nightmare jungle, between fallen walls and rusted steel frameworks that were trellises now for ropes of flesh entwined with warty vines with leaves like rotted canvas curving over clusters of over-sized, blind rodent-heads like bunches of fruit. They had no eyes, but there were plenty of teeth showing, set in the husks of the plants that nourished them.

The forest opened out, thinned. Tall ochre and rust buildings loomed up on both sides, like jungle temples in Yucatan. Fungus grew on the granite and marble, and the bronze statues of gods and goddesses were overgrown with cancerous-looking corrosion. The forest retreated to expose a paved plaza, and a mountain of marble chips and tiles and glass behind a set of hundred-foot columns tangled in vines.

Some of the discolored blotches faded from the marble; the wide sweep of the plaza smoothed minutely. A fountain at the center that had been scattered slid back into shape, all but the head of the mermaid at the center. Then there was a sharp *be-beep!* and the amber light went on on the panel. We had arrived in the eye of the probability storm.

Roosevelt slung an instrument pack over his shoulder and checked the dials on it.

"You and I will be the first men ever knowingly to set foot in the Blight," he said. "And if we do anything wrong—make the slightest error—we'll be the last. One mistake here could send our entire cosmos tumbling."

"Fair enough," I said. "Just one question: How do we know what might be a mistake?"

"Follow your instinct, Mr. Curlon," Roosevelt said and gave me a smile that seemed to be loaded with obscure significance. Then he opened up and we stepped out into a nightmare fantasy.

All around, tall buildings reared up against a sky of broken clouds over a yellow moon. The nearest was made of polished crimson stone, carved into patterns where huge vines clung, casting black shadows. From it, white marble steps led down to a walk lined with giant oaks on which green orchids grew. Vivid-colored birds sang in branches that arched across the tiled avenue. And behind this island of comparative order, the jungle loomed like a besieging army.

"Amazing," Roosevelt said in a low voice. "It's almost intact, Curlon—almost as it was in the days of its glory! There is the Summer Palace—and there the Cathedral—and the Académie des Artes—still standing, in the midst of carnage!"

"Hard to believe we're in the center of a storm," I said. "It's as peaceful as a graveyard."

"A mighty empire died here," Roosevelt said. "Where we stand, triumphal armies marched, with kings at their heads. The fairest women in any universe rode their carriages along these avenues. Here art and culture rose to their highest peak—to be dashed to the lowest depths. Grieve for it, Curlon; for magnificence, lost forever."

"For now I'll settle for finding what we came for."

"Quite right," Roosevelt said in a suddenly brisk tone. He checked the dials strapped to his wrist, then tilted back his helmet.

"The air is all right," he said. I tried it. It was hot, steamy, like a greenhouse at night. There was a steady surf-roar of sound: the rustle and scrape of leaves, the rasp and creak of stems bending in the breeze, the cluck and groan and hiss and whine and bleat of animal voices, as if we were in the middle of the world's biggest zoo, and all the inmates were having bad dreams. The tiled pavement under our feet was chipped and shattered, but navigable. Lichenous vines as big as your wrist snaked across it, and the moonlight glinted on spines like poniards that bristled along them.

"To protect the shuttle, I'm putting it on an oscillatory circuit that will prevent it from phasing into identity with any A-line," Roosevelt said. "When we're ready to leave, I can recall it with a remote signaler."

I watched as it winked out of sight with a boom of imploding air. As we started off, something moved among the greenery; a thing like a hairy snake dragged its length over a fallen tree-trunk, gaping a dog's head at us. At first I thought there were no legs, but then I saw them—dozens of them, all sizes, growing out of the ten-foot body at random angles. A vine hissed and struck at it, and the jaws snapped and another ten feet of body flopped into view, with more heads, all biting at once. The vine took a few more loops around the wormlike body and squeezed. Somewhere a cat yowled, and underbrush crashed and the yowl became a scream.

"Don't use your gun except in extremity," Roosevelt warned. "To take life here—any life—is to interfere with the probability equation. Even the slightest realignment could interfere with the shuttle recall signal."

There was an archway across the avenue ahead almost lost under its load of washtub-sized toadstools, but across the top carved figures and flowers were still visible. Roosevelt consulted his dials again.

"Our destination appears to be the Royal Archives," he said. "It's just ahead."

The side street faced a wall of foliage that had been a park. On our side, there was a monumental façade, festooned with ragged vines. Some of the windows still had glass in them, but most of them were blind, like eyes afflicted with green cataracts. Where the door had been, there was a gap in the screen of vines.

"Something's been using that entrance," I said. "Something the size of a rhinoceros."

"Still—that's where we must go," Roosevelt said, and pushed through a screen of limp, yellow-spotted leaves the size of garrison flags. There was a path through the mat of moss on the floor, where tiles showed. We followed it fifty feet to a dead end. Roosevelt unshipped a handlight and played it over a wall of impacted vines.

"We'll have to cut through." He changed the torch setting, and the beam dimmed to deep red, sliced through the tangled growth. In half a minute he had cut a hole big enough to climb through.

He clipped the torch to his belt and went ahead. I started after him, and heard a rumble like a Bengal tiger disturbed at his nap. I came through fast, grabbing for my gun, and saw moonlight on low walls, black lawn, a fountain with water. Roosevelt was backed against the carved Neptune, facing something right out of the fairy-tale books. It had a long, feline body, a maned neck, a beak like an eagle—if eagles had beaks two feet long. The legs were scaled from the midpoint down and ended in talons like the big claw in a wrecking yard. It was a griffin, half lion and half eagle, and both halves were closing in for the kill.

I yelled and fired high to distract the thing. It reared up and danced around on its hind legs to face me, showing an expanse of snow-white underbody and giving me a good look down the red throat behind the beak. The eyes were the size of Dixie cups, three concentric circles around yellow irises. The outer circle was scales—iridescent silver ones. Darker scales ran back across the face and ended where the white mane began. A pointed black tongue licked out like a snake between the halves of the knife-edged beak. I saw all this in a couple of fast seconds while I backed away and wondered just what Roosevelt would call an extremity.

"Hold your fire!" he called. "It's tame!" I started to ask him what his idea of wild was, when I saw what he meant. There was a harness strapped around the thing's chest, almost hidden under the mane. Silver ornaments dangled from the black leather, jingled as it moved. It dropped down to all fours less than ten feet from me, gave a scream that ended in a yowl, and sat down on its haunches. Its timing was good; in another half second I'd have blown its chest open. Which would have been a serious mistake, because just then the owner came walking out of the shadows.

CHAPTER SEVEN

I'D GAPED PRETTY HARD at the snake-dog, and the griffin had held my attention, too; but neither of them was anything at all to what I saw now.

It was a girl: tall, high-bosomed, long-legged, with skin as white as the fallen marble columns, and dark copper hair piled up high over a face that was like the one you dream about, that smiles and is lost forever, and you wake up sick with yearning. She was dressed in a flimsy swath of white gauzy stuff that clung to her hips and thighs like wet tissue paper and floated when she moved. She came straight up to the thing that had me cornered and said, "Aroint thee, Vrodelix! An ill greeting for visitors!" It dropped its head and whined like an overgrown puppy.

The girl pushed the monster aside and looked at me. Her eyes were dark blue, and they glistened in the moonlight. I knew those eyes; I'd seen them in the dream.

"Are you a man?" she said. "Or a god?" Her tone

indicated that both choices were equally likely. I told her and she nodded.

"I'm glad. I am a mortal woman." She looked across at Roosevelt, who had come up to us. He gave her a courtly bow and the smile.

"But *you* are a god," she said.

"Only a man, my dear," he said. "Pieter Roosevelt, at your service—and this is Richard Curlon."

She smiled at him, and I felt a strange feeling that somehow I'd missed out on something rare and valuable.

"And I am Ironel, Pieter," she said.

"You live here alone?" Roosevelt was asking.

"Oh, no. Vrodelix is with me." She ran a hand along the sleek, curved neck of the nightmare animal. "And I have other friends—and now, two new ones!" She caught Roosevelt's hand and then mine and smiled from one to the other of us, and we grinned back.

"Tell me about your other, ah, friends, Ironel," Roosevelt said in the gentle, fatherly tone he had adopted with her.

"Of course, Pieter! There is Ronizpel the Climber, and Chazz the Dweller Below, and Arnq of the Spines—and many more!"

"All animals?"

She had to think that one over. "Mostly," she said. "Except for Chazz—I think. But you'll meet them soon. Oh, how glad they'll be you've come!" She stopped, as if she had just remembered something. "But Old Garff—I'm not sure *he'll* be pleased."

"How long have you lived here?" Roosevelt wanted to know.

"Why—forever." She sounded surprised at the silly question.

"Where are your parents?"

"What are parents?"

"The people who raised you—taught you to speak, to dress yourself so prettily?"

"Why . . . 'tis a novel thought, Pieter! Must one *learn* to talk as I taught Arnq to weave his nets o'er the Dark Places?" She touched the soft fold of the cloth she wore. "As for my garment—'tis made for me by Arnq, of course." She looked at Roosevelt's nylon suit, touched my sleeve. "I must show him your weaver's work; 'twill set him a task, to make stuff like it." She laughed, pleased by the idea.

"Are there no other people here—like you, and us?" Roosevelt persisted.

"But—we are not like!" Ironel laughed. "You are taller than I, and your hair is short, and your shoulders wide and your chest flat—not like me." She touched her body, ran her hand down her slim waist as if to sense the differences with her fingertips.

"We're men," Roosevelt said, smiling faintly. "You're a woman. Are there other humans of either sex here?"

That seemed to puzzle her. "No, none," she said.

"What do you eat? How do you keep warm in winter?"

"Why—Chazz brings me roots from the deep earth, and Ronizpel knows where the grapes and melons ripen soonest. And when the whiteness falls, I dwell indoors, and Arnq swathes the windows with his finest weaving to hold back the cold."

Vrodelix whined, and while the girl was soothing him, Roosevelt stepped close to me.

"Are we to believe this poor natural maid lives all alone here as she says? Is it possible?"

"It looks that way. For some reason the Blight seems to stay clear of this little patch of ground. You said it was the eye of the storm. The eye of a hurricane is a dead calm."

Ironel was back beside us, smiling. "Come," she said. "Now I'll show thee my playthings!" She towed us across a flagstone walk between tended flowerbeds where black and gold fungus blossoms grew between roses and daisies. We went through an archway and across a tiled hall and up stairs into a wide, shadowy corridor that was blocked twenty feet away by fallen masonry; but the part that was clear was swept clean. She opened a door on a room with a deep black carpet and high, glassless windows with curtains of the same gauzy stuff as her clothing. There was a high bed with a white silk canopy over it, decorated with a floral design in gold thread. She knelt by a big chest with a carved lid and opened it and lifted out a bolt of scarlet cloth.

"Is it not pretty?" she said and stretched a length of it across her body. I had to agree it was pretty.

She took out a smaller box and poured gold coins out on the rug. I knelt to gather them up and discovered that the rug was a layer of moss, as smooth and even as black velvet.

"And these!" she dumped jewels among the coins; they sparkled like hot embers.

"And these are my dearest treasures!" she said, and spilled colored seashells out among them.

She laughed. "And now we must sort them, and put them away. Is it not a fine game?"

Roosevelt picked up a big square-cut ruby with an incised crest.

"Where did you get this?" his voice grated roughly. His eyes bored into hers. She didn't seem to notice the change of pace.

"In the Pretty Place," she said. "There are many more, but I liked these the best."

"Show me!" he snapped.

"Easy, General," I said. "We play the young lady's game first, then yours."

For a moment his eyes clashed with mine; then he relaxed, smiled, laughed aloud. He got down on his knees and started picking up seashells and placing them in a careful heap.

She led us down into a wide, moonlit avenue, almost roofed over by vines. Vrodelix paced beside her, making hissing sounds and acting increasingly nervous as we came closer to the fallen buildings at the far end.

"Poor beast, he remembers the Thing-with-eight-legs and the Fanged Ones," Ironel said. "They frightened him, ere he slew them."

She pointed to a tall, mold-blackened building nestled up against the barricade of rubble. "Vrodelix mislikes me to go there—but with you by me, naught can imperil us."

"The State Museum," Roosevelt said. He looked at the instrument strapped to the underside of his wrist, but if it told him anything he didn't say so.

We went through a weed-choked entrance, crossed a hall that was carpeted and walled with vines, went up a wide, curved staircase. The second floor was in better condition. There were glass-topped cases here, dusty but intact. Old paintings hung on the walls, mold-spotted faces in strange ruffs and plumed helmets peering down from leafy shadows, but their stiff expressions looked more frightened than arrogant. We went on into the next room, where formerly elaborate uniforms with knee-boots and capes with moth-eaten tiger-skin facings hung on decaying dummies with vacant, horrified faces. Fancy saddles and tattered regimental flags were displayed along with lances and dueling pistols and hand-tooled matchlocks, all draped with spiderwebs.

"Now—you must close your eyes," Ironel said, and took our hands. Her fingers were slim and cool and soft. She watched to make sure I followed instructions, then led the way up three steps, and across more floor, around obstructions, then down again. I was just beginning to wonder how long the blindman's bluff went on when she stopped and said, "Open your eyes!"

Colored moonlight streamed down through a stained-glass window on a gray stone floor leading away to an altar with slim columns and a gold canopy and silver candlesticks. A silver-mounted reliquary box lay there. There was a stone sarcophagus before the altar, with the carved figure of a Crusader on it, dressed in full armor, his hands crossed over the hilt of his sword that lay on his chest like a crucifix.

"Dost like my Pretty Place?" Ironel asked in a breathless voice.

"We like it very much indeed," Roosevelt said softly. "Will you show me where you found the signet stone?"

"Here." Ironel turned to a brass-bound coffer sitting on wooden trestles to the left. Roosevelt lifted the lid. The soft light winked on rings and armlets and brooches—a magpie's trove of trinkets. Ironel lifted a chain of soft gold links and held it against her, then dropped it and took a tiny silver chain with a dangling amethyst.

"This is prettier," she said. "Do thee not think so, Pieter?"

"Much prettier, my dear." His eyes moved past her, roving over the details of the little chapel, back to the dial on his wrist. He started toward the altar, and Ironel made a distressed sound and caught at his hand.

"Pieter—no! Thou must approach no closer!"

He gave her a smile that was more grim than comforting.

"It's all right," he said in a soothing tone. "I mean only to have a look at it." He brushed her hand away.

"Pieter—you mustn't! Bad things will happen if we intrude there! Canst thou not feel it in the very air?"

He wasn't listening. He took another step—and stopped. Far away, something rumbled. The floor trembled, and a piece of glass cracked in the window. I stepped to his side.

"You're a guest here," I said. "Maybe you'd better play house rules."

He shot me a look like a harpoon. "I'll decide that," he said, and started on.

I caught his arm. It was like grabbing an oak rail. He strained to pull free and I strained to hold him back. Neither of us seemed to be gaining.

"The girl says 'no,' General," I said. "Maybe she has a reason."

"Come to your senses, Curlon," he said, still sounding calm. "Remember what we came here to find!"

"You said yourself the equation is in delicate balance," I said. "Take it slowly, until you know what you're doing."

There was another rumble, closer this time. I felt the floor move under my feet. The griffin raked his talons on the floor and yowled. Ironel whimpered; I heard a sound from above, looked up in time to see a safe-sized stone dropping at me. I dived to the side; the smash was like switch-engines colliding. Rock chips flew like shrapnel. Roosevelt whirled and ran for the altar. The griffin hissed and reared to strike at him, but Ironel shrieked and the animal crouched back, his ears flat and Roosevelt ran past him. I started after him and a marble pilaster crashed down between us. The floor was heaving like jelly, with broken stone and fragments of ceiling mosaic and stained glass and ironwork and chunks of statuary dancing on it like water drops in a hot skillet. Roosevelt ran into the thick of it; stones fell around him like bomb fragments. A small one hit him on the shoulder, but he stayed on his feet, staggering now but still trying to reach the altar. He was six feet from it when the canopy over it sagged and went down. One of the columns fell. It barely brushed him, but it threw him ten feet. He skidded in the dust and lay still, a broken doll. The rumble died away. A few stray pebbles clattered down into silence.

Ironel went to her knees beside Roosevelt. She touched his face. "Is he dead?" she whispered.

I checked him over. There was a nasty dent in his skull. His breathing was shallow and rasping, but his pulse was solid.

"He's badly hurt," I said. "But not dead—yet."

With Ironel's help I got him on my back, carried him back to her sleeping room, and laid him out on the bed in the dark.

CHAPTER EIGHT

DAYLIGHT CAME AFTER A long time. Ironel was asleep, her head on Roosevelt's bed. When I woke her, she smiled at me.

"He still lives, Richard," she said. I checked his pulse again. It was still there, but his breathing was shallow and ragged. I touched the depressed fracture over his eye.

"I've got to do something about this," I said. "Do you have any way to make fire?"

"Ronizpel fears the fire," she said. "But he will bring it to me."

I examined the wound. There was one main bone splinter, with some smaller fragments. Ironel came back with a shallow brass tray with glowing embers in it. I didn't ask questions, just added some wood to the coals and got a brisk fire going, and sterilized my knife blade in it.

I made an incision across the wound, crossed it with another, and folded back the flaps of skin. Ironel stepped in like a trained nurse, following every step, acting without even words from me. While she held the incision open, I used a hook bent from wire and heat-sterilized to lift the big splinter back into position, then probed for the others. After a while I was finished. I closed the wound and he was still breathing. Ironel used red silk thread to stitch up the cuts. She finished and then sat beside him, watching his face. I found a corner and went to sleep.

I woke up with light in my face; Ironel was beside me; her face was cameo-pale against the shadows.

"Richard—I am afraid for Pieter."

I got up and went to him. He lay on his back on the bed. His eyes were closed and sunken, his face drawn into a tortured rictus. He snarled between his locked teeth, and his hands raked at the coverlet.

"No," he ground out the words. "Never . . . bend the knee . . . better . . . eternal destruction . . ." His voice ran off into a mutter.

I put my fingers against his neck. He was hot as new-cast iron. The wound in his forehead was swollen and inflamed.

"I'm sorry," I said. "We need medicines we don't have."

"Richard," the girl said. "Chazz says we must bring Pieter to him."

I looked at her. Her eyes were big and dark, her hair red-black, a damp curl against her white skin.

"We shouldn't move him."

"But—Chazz cannot come here, Richard!"

I looked at Roosevelt. I didn't know much about medicine, but I'd seen a dying man before. I lifted him and the girl led the way down through the dark halls among the black vines and the fallen statuary and out into the perfumed night.

Stone mermaids cavorted in a dry fountain at the center of a weed-choked garden. Ironel pulled aside the leafy branch of a twisted bush that grew up through a crack in the basin, exposing an opening. Stone steps led down at a steep angle into an odor of mushrooms and wet clay. Ironel led the way. In a room at the bottom, she flashed my handlight on sagging shelves loaded with dusty wine bottles. At the far side the wall was broken away by what looked like a giant rat-hole. The odor that came from it was like the ape-house at the zoo.

Ironel didn't seem to notice. She went to the opening, called:

"Chazz—it's I, Ironel—and Richard, my friend. We've brought Pieter!"

A sound came back, like boulders grinding together under the earth. Ironel turned to me.

"Chazz says we may bring him in."

I went down through the opening; it was a smooth-walled tunnel cut through damp earth. It curved, dipped, ended at a complicated wall of lumpy wet leather that blocked the tunnel. Ironel put the light on the wall and I saw it was a face, six feet high, six feet wide, with a vast hooked nose, sunken eyelids that lifted to show the glint of eyes the size of basketballs. There was matted hair as coarse as mammoth fur on the cheeks and on the sloping, wrinkled forehead. Where there wasn't hair, the skin was black, scaled, and creased like a rhino's hide. The edges of broken teeth the size of bargain tombstones showed under the purple edge of the lip. The mouth opened and the voice rumbled forth.

"He says to put him down here," Ironel relayed. I did as she asked. Roosevelt lay like a corpse, death-pale now. The big eyes roved over him. A tongue like a pink feather blanket peered out from the vast mouth, tested the air, went in again.

"This one made the rocks fall," the big voice boomed out, clearer now—or maybe I was just getting used to hearing an earthquake talk.

"He didn't know, Chazz dear," Ironel said in a pleading tone. "He meant no harm."

"A stone hurt me," Chazz said. He rotated his huge skull, and the edge of a black-crusted cut big enough to lay an arm in came into view.

"Poor Chazz—did it hurt very much?"

"Not much, Ironel." The face came back up and a tear that would have filled a teacup splashed down across the leather face. "Don't feel bad for Chazz. Chazz is all right, Ironel."

"And—can you help Pieter?"

Again the incredible eyeballs rotated, stared at the unconscious man. The lids came down, half-covering them like wrinkled leather blinds.

"I can try," the monster rumbled. "I feel the hurt place . . . there. Bad, bad hurt—but it's not that which is killing Pieter. No—it's the things that pull—there and there! But I push . . . push against them . . . ." his voice went into a mutter like a glacier breaking apart in a spring thaw. Roosevelt stirred, made vague sounds. Ironel put her hand on his forehead. I held the light and saw the color come slowly back into his face. He sighed and his hands moved restlessly, then lay still. His breathing eased.

"Ahhh," Chazz groaned. "Bad things still there,

Ironel! I fix him—but I feel bad things stir there still!
Better I kill him now—"

"Chazz—no!" Ironel threw herself half across Roosevelt. "You mustn't!"

"I feel things there, inside him," Chazz said. "Things
that make me afraid!"

"He's only a man, Chazz—he said so himself. Like
Richard! Tell him, Richard!" Ironel caught at my arm.
"Tell Chazz that Pieter is our friend!"

"What kind of bad things do you feel inside him,
Chazz?" I asked the big face. He rolled his whale's
eyes at me.

"When the stones fell, I felt them," he said. "And
when I reached into him—I felt them again. Black
things prowl there, in the red caverns of his sleeping
brain, Richard. He would mold all the world to an
image he keeps secret there."

"Back home, he's an important man," I said. "He
came here to try to save his world. He made a mistake, and it almost killed him. I don't think there's
any harm in him now."

Chazz groaned. "I have known him in my dreams, as
I slept here under the earth. Why does he come, Richard? And why you? For of you, too, I have dreamed,
moving across the bright restless pattern of the world.
A doom hangs about your head, and about his. But I
cannot tell which doom is the stronger." He groaned
again. "I fear him, Richard. But for Ironel's sake, I give
him his destiny. Now take him from me. His mind stirs
and the pain of that stirring cuts to my heart."

I lifted Roosevelt and carried him back through
the stinking tunnel and up to Ironel's room.

She woke me with half a golden melon on a gold

plate and a cluster of red grapes the size of plums. Roosevelt was better, now, she said. I went over and looked at him, lying there on his back, still unconscious. He didn't look any different to me, but his temperature seemed to be normal, and his pulse and breathing too. Maybe I was a better brain surgeon than I thought.

Ironel took me for a tour of her kingdom: the lower floors of the building where she slept, the garden, what was left of the street the earthquake had shaken up. With the early morning light slanting down through the leaves that overgrew it, it had a sort of eerier, silent beauty. Ironel led me by the hand, showed me little clumps of flowers growing in hidden places, a clear pool in a basin that must have been a beautiful fountain once, led me to where there were pretty stones lying scattered in the rank grass—the fragments of an alabaster statue.

We went down chipped marble steps under huge old trees and bathed in a black pool, climbed up in a ruined tower, and looked out through a stone-filigreed window at the view of other towers thrusting up through the jungle. In the evening, we sat on a bench in the garden and listened to the hooting and screeching and hissing of night things that prowled just beyond the borders of the garden. Sometimes she talked, chattered away about her friends and her games; other times she sang strange little tuneless songs. And sometimes, she just smiled into the vague distance, like a flower, glad to be alive. There were a lot of questions I wanted to ask, but I didn't ask them. She was like a sleeping child; I didn't want to wake her. That night she came to my bed and slept with me, like a child.

The second day passed, and Roosevelt woke up, gave us a faint smile, and went back to sleep. The next day he stayed awake. He seemed to be his old self, assurance and all—except for the hollow-cheeked look. He professed to have no recollection of anything from the time we'd met the girl.

He mended fast then. On the fourth day, he was up and walking. On the fifth day, on my way back from an expedition to the edge of the jungle to gather fruit, I heard an angry yowl from the direction of the park, followed by shots. I knew that yowl—it was Vrodelix, and he was mad. I dropped the red and yellow mangoes I had collected and ran for the gates. Ten feet inside the park, I found the griffin, stretched beside the dolphin fountain, with three holes in him. He moaned and tried to get up, and fell back, dead, his beak gaping. I ran on across the park, up the steps. I shouted for Ironel, but there was no answer. Something made a soft sound behind me, and I turned to see Roosevelt come out of shadows with his nerve-gun aimed at my head.

"I'm sorry, Curlon," he said. "But there's no other way." He pulled the trigger and the world blew up in my face.

I was lying on my back, dreaming that Roosevelt was bending over me. His face was thin, hollow-cheeked, and the wound over his eye stood out like a big X marked in lipstick. His voice came from someplace as far away as the stars, but the words were clear enough.

"Get on your feet, Curlon. I've paralyzed your volitional centers, but you can hear me. We have a duty to perform."

I felt myself climbing to my feet. They seemed to

be miles below my head, which floated all alone in a rarified level high above the clouds that drifted just at the edge of vision. My hands were wired together in front of me.

"That way," Roosevelt said. We went out across the garden, past the gentle, dead monster lying on the flagstones, into the ruined street. There was a high, humming noise inside my head, and the light was strange, as though there were an eclipse in progress. We entered the museum, went up the stairs littered with plaster and fragments of a skylight, into the big hall where the armored manikins lay strewn around like disaster victims. In the chapel, the sun came through the broken window like a spotlight. The altar was still standing, with the ruins of the golden canopy around it. There was a feeling in the air as if the whole world was a bowstring, stretched to the breaking point.

"Go ahead of me," Roosevelt ordered. I picked my way through the rubble, stepped over the broken sarcophagus, brushed away the rotted strands of a velvet cape, stopped in front of the altar.

"Take the box," Roosevelt ordered. I picked it up awkwardly in my wired hands. It was heavy, and the surface tingled as though an electric current was running through it. I felt the current in my feet, too. The floor vibrated under me. There was a rumbling around, like distant thunder. Roosevelt's face was strained in a tight, bared-teeth look that wasn't a smile.

"Give it to me," he said. I handed it over as the rumble grew louder.

"Lo, the very heavens attend our enterprise," he said, sounding as though he meant it. "But we have what we want. Now we'll go."

He turned away and I followed. A section of carved stone toppled from up high, smashed down a few feet away from us. Other things fell, but none of them touched us. As we reached the door, the roof came down behind us. On the stair, I felt the stones breaking up under my feet, but they held until we were down in the big hall; then they came tumbling down.

Outside, the street was a sea of heaving rubble. The building across the way sagged and leaned and fell into the plaza.

We jumped across broken pavement slabs that tilted and ground together like an ice floe breaking up. A tree fell, trailing a snarl of vines, and back in the jungle something as massive as an apartment house loomed up, bellowing.

"The centroid of the probability storm is moving, following us," Roosevelt called to me. "It's success, Curlon—if we can reach the shuttle before this enclave of antiprobability collapses! Stay close to me!" He ran, and I ran with him, while the world came apart around us.

In the clearing where we'd left the shuttle on half-phase, Roosevelt took the signaler from the pouch clipped to his belt. I saw something moving in the trees just above him, but I made no effort to say anything. It eased out from under a spray of tent-sized leaves, a spider with a body as big as a bathtub, thick, bristly legs, faceted eyes the size of dinner plates. It swung out on a clotted, grayish cord, a pair of pinchers at its fore end cocked and ready.

"No, Ronizpel!" Ironel's voice cried out behind us, and the spider-thing checked just long enough for Roosevelt to draw his gun and fire a burst of mini-slugs into the swollen abdomen ten feet above him. The thing fell, thrashing its eight legs and Ironel screamed and rushed to it while Roosevelt pumped more rounds into the dying thing. He jumped past her, knocking her aside, pressed the recall button of the signaler. I felt the buzzing in the air around me, saw the light darken, taking on a tarnished tinge like the light before a thunderstorm. A gust of air whirled leaves up, and the shuttle phased into identity, low, black, deadly-looking. Its door slid open to spill white light out into the gloom.

"Curlon—get in!" Roosevelt shouted. The ground shook under me as I walked past the weeping girl and the gutted spider. To my left, the jungle crashed and burst open and the ground rose up and split and the head of Chazz rose up into view, squinting against the light. His eyes went to the girl, and his mouth opened in a howl of rage. Roosevelt brought the gun up and fired into the big face, and chunks of flesh flew and black blood welled out of the craters, and Chazz bellowed in agony; then I was inside, and Roosevelt was behind me, slamming the hatch. He produced handcuffs, chained me to the contoured seat. The screen glowed pink, then cleared to a view of the outside. Chazz had forced his shoulders up through the earth, and his hands, huge and gnarled with chipped black nails as big as coal scuttles, groped out toward the girl. He touched her with one finger, and then the giant head slumped, and Roosevelt threw the drive switch in and the scene flowed like wax in the sun, as the jungle closed in over the spot where Ironel's garden had been.

CHAPTER NINE

I CAME UP OUT of a drugged sleep to see early morning sunshine glowing through curtains at an open window. I had a headache like a cracked anvil. Roosevelt was sitting in a brocaded chair beside the bed, dressed in a fantastic outfit that somehow, on him, looked natural enough: a short, loose coat with a fur collar, tight breeches, slippers with jeweled pompons, a big gold chain across his chest, and jewels everywhere, stitched to his sleeves, sparkling in finger rings.

He said "Good morning" in a cheery tone and passed me a cup of coffee. "We've been through a difficult time," he went on. "But it's over now, Curlon. I regret the necessity for the things I was forced to do—but I had no choice. And we succeeded, you and I. Now the victory and all its fruits are ours." He said this in a low voice, but his black eyes glowed like a man looking at visions.

I tried the coffee. It was hot and strong, but it didn't help my head any.

"You understand, don't you?" His eyes probed mine. "A great new destiny is taking shape—for you as well as me. Think of it, Curlon! Who hasn't wished to seize the sorry scheme of things entire, and mold it nearer to his heart's desire? We—we've done it—together! Out of the ashes of the old, a new world rises—a world in which our fates loom like colossi over the faceless mob! The world that should have been, Curlon, a world of might and glory, such as has never before been seen—spread at our feet like a carpet! We've turned back the clock of fate, set history back on a course that seemed doomed forever!"

"What about the girl?" I asked.

"I'm sorry; she was a shadow in a twilight world. And you, I'm afraid, were caught up in her spell. I did what I had to do. I would have brought her with us, but it was impossible. The fabric I'm weaving is too fragile at this stage to support the transfer of a key figure from a peripheral A-line."

"I don't know what you're doing, Roosevelt," I said. "But whatever it is, the price is too high."

"One day you'll understand, Curlon. Of all mankind you'll understand best. Because, out of all the millions of pawns on the board, you alone are my compeer; like mine, your destiny is entwined with that of the new world that's taking shape."

"Count me out, General," I said. "I want no part of your operations. If you'll tell me where my pants are, I'll be going now."

Roosevelt shook his head, smiling a little. "Curlon, don't talk like a fool. Do you have any idea where you are?"

I got out of bed, shakily, and went to the window

and looked down on lawns and flowerbeds that were almost familiar.

"This is a world-line far removed from the turmoil of the Blight," Roosevelt said as I dressed in the loose shirt and tight pants laid out for me. "Its common-history date with your world is 1199 A.D. We're in the city of Londres, capital of the province of New Normandy, an autonomous duchy under the French king, Louis Augustus. Great affairs are afoot here, Curlon. Rebels challenge the power of the Emperor, loyalists are charged with treason, and across the Channel, Louis waits, ready to land forces at Harwich and Dover and Newcastle if needed. A touch would send the situation crashing into war. It's what which we must prevent."

"And what's in it for you, General?"

"I'm known here; I enjoy the confidence of both Viceroy Garonne and important members of the rebellious faction. My hope is to prevent bloodshed, stabilize the situation. A strongly established A-line is necessary to contain the vast energies I've channeled here. You'll recall what I told you of key objects, key lines. New Normandy will become the key line of its probability quantum, with the aid of the artifact we brought here. And with the rise of the new master-line, our stars too will ascend!"

"And where do I come in?"

"Ten days ago, Duke Richard fell dead at a public ceremony in full view of the populace. Murdered, they say. The rebels charge the loyalists with eliminating the natural leader of the Britons; the loyalists in turn charge the rebels with killing a man they regarded as no more than a vassal of the French king. The tension has reached crisis level; it must be relieved."

"I still haven't heard anything illuminating."

"It's really quite obvious," Roosevelt said. "As a Plantagenet born and bred, you'll step forward to take up the role of the Duke of Londres."

"You're out of your mind, General," I told him.

"Nothing could be simpler," he said with a wave of the hand. "No one could deny that you look the part; you're enough like the departed Duke to be his brother. However, we shall present you in the role of a more distant relation, raised secretly north of the Scots border. Your appearance will satisfy the most fanatical rebel, and of course you'll make suitably defiant pronouncements to satisfy that clique. More discreetly, you'll engage in dialogues with Viceroy Garonne aimed at easing the crisis and restoring civil order."

"What's going to make me do all this?"

"This is the drama of life itself—and you were a part of it from the moment you were born—and before. Like me, you're the inheritor of a mighty dynasty. All that you might have been—that your analogs, those close to you might have done—all the vast repercussions across time and history of every act of that great clan, chopped down in the prime of their strength—all those aborted probability energies must find their expression in you—and in the world you help create!"

"What about my own world?"

"The new master-line will dominate the quantum," Roosevelt said flatly. "In the readjustment that accompanies its establishment, lesser lines must of necessity be sacrificed. The Imperium and the Blight-Insular lines will go under. But that's a matter of no moment to you, Mr. Curlon—or to me. Our destinies lie elsewhere."

"You have it all figured out," I said. "There's just one weak point."

"Which is?"

"I won't play."

Roosevelt looked grim. "Understand me, Curlon: I want you as my willing ally; but willing or not, you'll help me."

"You're bluffing, Roosevelt. You need a walking, talking puppet, not a man with wires on his wrists."

He made an impatient gesture. "I told you I regretted that, and the need for drugging you to bring you here. But I'd do it again, ten thousand times, if that were the only way! The Old Empire *will* rise again! We're not discussing *if*, Curlon; only *how*. Meet this challenge—lend me your full support, and your future will be of a splendor unimaginable to you now. Defy me, and you'll walk like a corpse through what would have been your triumph. Which do you want, Curlon? Honors, or rotted rags? Majesty, or misery?"

"You've worked your story out pretty carefully, General. But it still doesn't make sense."

"The rebels are strong," Roosevelt said grudgingly. "They have all the strength on their side, if the truth were known. They could seize power any time they chose. They lack only one thing: leadership. They'll rally to you, Curlon—but instead of leading them to victory, you'll cool their revolutionary fervor. Because if they should rise up and cast out the French, a major branching of the line will result! Seven hundred years of stable history would be shattered, creating a whole new probability spectrum. I need not detail the effect this would have on my plans for New Normandy!"

I smiled a smile I didn't feel. "You're in trouble,

aren't you, Roosevelt? You need me—and not just to carry a spear in the third act of some farce to fool the locals. What is it? What's the real reason for trying to drag me into this paranoid fantasy-system of yours?"

"I've told you! We're linked, you and I, all down through the corridors of past time, on every world within a thousand years of common history. As your fortunes wax, so do mine. I can force you, Curlon—but to the extent that I must break you to my will our joint stature is diminished. Join with me freely, lend your *mana* to mine—and anything we desire is within our grasp!"

"And if I don't?"

"I want your willing aid," he said in a steely voice. "But your broken mind and body, dangling from the strings, will serve if need be."

"Everything you say confirms the one clear idea I've gotten from all this, Roosevelt. Whatever this fight is, you're on one side, and I'm on the other."

"I can break you, Curlon. The stronger man can always break the weaker. A simple demonstration will suffice to prove my point." He took a stance with his feet apart and raised his arms until they were level with his shoulders, smiling.

"The first to drop his arms acknowledges the other man his superior—at least in one small way."

I put my arms out. The effort made my temples pound, but I didn't burst into tears. If Roosevelt wanted to play little games I was willing to go along. The hamburger machines could wait.

"In every world, in every time, the will of some man has shaped reality," Roosevelt said suddenly. "Here, now, that old rule is still in force—but made more potent by the existence of titanic new forces. Those forces are at the command of whoever can master them. Fate is a fragile thing, Curlon. A mindless thing, controlled by the whim of a strong man. Let an Alexander set out to conquer the world; the world becomes what he makes it. Without Alexander, there would have been no Caesar, no Attila, no Muhammad, no Hitler in your world, no Guglielmo Maxoni in the Zero-zero line. Men make fate, Curlon, not the other way around. You saw that demonstrated when we fought together, back to back. We two form islands of stability about ourselves, even in a sea of formlessness.

"But only one of us can shape the cosmos to his will. That one will be me. I'll dominate you—not because I hate you—I have no cause for enmity. But because I must—as an Alexander must destroy a Darius."

"Funny," I said. "I never had any interest in shaping the cosmos to my will. But I'm not willing to see it shaped to yours. Home was never much to me, but I'm not ready to see it flushed down the drain to give you a roost to rule."

Roosevelt nodded. "I suppose it's a thing outside both of us, Curlon, written in the stars, as they say. For seven hundred years, your ancestors and mine fought to rule the quantum. Think of it, Plantagenet! In a thousand billion alternate world-lines, each differing from the others in some greater or lesser degree, your clan and mine, striving, down through the centuries, each to dominate his world, none knowing of the others, all driven by the common instinct to fulfill the potentiality inherent in them. And then—the day of cataclysm, when the Blight swept in to wipe them out, root, stem and branch—all but one man of my line, and one of yours."

It had been about ten minutes since the game had begun. Fiery pains were shooting along the backs of my arms and shoulders. Roosevelt was still standing as rigid as a statue. His arms hadn't quivered.

"They tell me the blight dates back to the nineties," I said. "You're a little young to be remembering it—unless your Imperium has face-lift techniques that beat anything Hollywood's come up with."

"I'm telling you what I've learned—what my researchers have revealed, what I was told—" He cut himself off.

"I thought this was all your own idea, Roosevelt."

"Told—by my father," Roosevelt said. "He devoted his life to the conviction that somehow—somewhere—our time would come again. His world was gone—but how could such glory be forever vanished? He worked, studied, and in the end made his discovery. He was old then, but he passed the charge on to me. And I've made it good! I worked first to gain a powerful position within Imperial Intelligence—the one organization that knew the secrets of the Net. This gave me a platform from which to prepare this line—New Normandy—to be the vessel that would contain and shape the forces of the Blight."

I had to concentrate on keeping my arms at shoulder level. Somehow, it seemed important not to lose at Roosevelt's game. If he was suffering, he didn't show it.

"Are you tiring?" he asked in a conventional tone. "Poor Mother Nature, so blind in her efforts to protect the body. She sends pain as a warning, first. Then little by little, she'll numb the nerves. Your arms will begin to sag. You'll try, with all your will, to hold them high—to outdo me, your inevitable master. But you'll fail. Oh, the strength is there—but Nature forces you to husband your strength. So though you might be willing of yourself, to endure the torture of fatigue until death from exhaustion—she won't let you. You'll suffer—for nothing. A pity, Mr. Curlon."

I was glad he felt like talking. It kept my mind off the hot clamps set in the back of my neck. I tried to fan a little spark of anger alive—another of Mother Nature's tricks, this one on my side. I wanted to keep him chattering, but at the same time coax along the frustration I hoped he was beginning to feel.

"Seeing you drop will be worth waiting for," I said.

"But you won't. I'm stronger than you are, Mr. Curlon. Since childhood I've trained every day in these exercises—and the mental control that goes with them. At the age of seven I could hold a fencing foil across my palm at arm's length for a quarter of an hour. For me, this is literally child's play. But not for you."

"There's nothing to this," I said breezily. "I can stand here all day."

"So far, you've endured it for less than a quarter of an hour. How will you feel fifteen minutes from now, eh, Mr. Curlon? And half an hour after that?" He smiled—not quite the easy smile he'd have liked. "In spite of yourself, you'll have failed long before then. A simple demonstration, Curlon—but a necessary one. You must be brought to realize that in me you've met your superior."

"There must be a catch to it," I said. "Maybe this is supposed to keep my attention occupied while your pals aim a spy beam at my brains—or whatever it is mad scientists do."

"Don't talk like a fool, Curlon," Roosevelt almost

snapped the words. "Or—why, yes, I see." He smiled and the strain went out of his face. "Very good, Mr. Curlon. You were almost beginning to irritate me. A well-designed tactic. Such distractions can appreciably sap endurance. By the way, how are your arms feeling? A trifle heavy?"

"Fine," I said in what I hoped was a light tone. "How about yours?" The lines of fire were lancing out into my trapezius muscles, playing around my elbows, tingling in my fingertips. My head ached. Roosevelt looked as good as new. He stared across at me, silent now. That bothered me. I wanted him to talk.

"Keeping up the patter's hard work, eh? But I'll tip you, Roosevelt. You picked the wrong man. I'm a fisherman. I'm used to fighting the big ones eight hours at a stretch. For me, this is a nice rest."

"A flimsy lie, Curlon. I expect better of you."

"The circulation is the weak point," I said. "Soldiers who could march all day in the sun under a full pack used to drop out in a dead faint on parade. Standing at attention, not moving, restricted the flow of blood to the brain—and all of a sudden—blackout. Some fellows couldn't take it. Nothing against them, just a peculiarity of the metabolism. It never bothered me. Good circulation, you know. How's yours?"

"Excellent, I assure you."

"But you're not talking." I gave him a grin that cost me a year off the end of my life.

"I've said what I intended."

"I don't believe you. You had canned lecture number three all ready to go. I can see it in your eyes."

Roosevelt laughed—a genuine laugh. "Mr. Curlon, you're a man after my own heart. I wish we could have met in another time at another place. We might have been friends, you and I."

Neither of us said anything after that. I discovered I was counting off the seconds. It had been about twenty minutes now, maybe a little more. I realized one hand was sagging and brought it back up. Roosevelt smiled a faint smile. More time passed. I thought about things, then tried not to think about things. It occurred to me that the ancient Chinese had wasted a lot of time and effort designing iron maidens and chipping bamboo splinters. Torture was a sport you could play without equipment. And Roosevelt's version was a double challenge, because the only one forcing me was me. I could quit now and laugh it off and call for the next round.

That was the catch. There'd be a next round—and one after that. And if I quit on the first, I'd quit sooner on the second, until I refused to meet his challenge—and that was what he wanted.

That was his swindle. To make me think that if I lost—I'd lost. But it wasn't true. Losing was nothing. Only surrender counted.

And once I understood that, I felt better. The pain was like flaying knives, but it was just pain, something to be endured until it ended. I hitched my arms back up into line and stared across at him through the fading light...

...and came to, lying on the floor. Roosevelt was standing over me. His face looked yellowish and drawn.

"A commendable effort, Curlon," he said. "One hour and twelve minutes. But as you see—you lost. As you must always lose—because it's your destiny to lose to me. Now—will you join with me willingly?"

I climbed back to my feet, feeling dizzy, and with slow fires still burning in my shoulders, I raised my arms to the crucifix position.

"Ready to try it again?" I said. Roosevelt's face twitched before he laughed.

I grinned at him. "You're afraid, aren't you, Roosevelt? You see your grand scheme coming apart at the seams—and you're afraid."

He nodded. "Yes—I'm afraid. Afraid of my own weakness. You see—incredible though it may seem to you—I truly wanted you to be a part of it, Plantagenet. A foolish sentimentality—but you, like me, are a man of the ancient stock. Even a god can be lonely—or a devil. I offered you comradeship. But at the first trial, you turned against me. I should have known then. And now I've learned the lesson. I have no choice left to me. My course is plain now."

"You're a flawed devil, Roosevelt," I said. "A devil with a conscience. I pity you."

He shook his head. "I want none of your pity, Plantagenet. As I can have none of your friendship. What I want from you, I'll take, though the taking will destroy you."

"Or you."

"That's a risk I'll run." He motioned to the waiting guards; they closed in around me. "Spend these next hours in meditation," he said. "Tonight you'll be invested with the honors of a dukedom. And tomorrow you'll be hanged in chains."

The dungeons under the viceregal palace were everything that dungeons should be, with damp stone walls and iron doors and unshielded electric lights that were worse than smoky flambeaux. The armed men in Swiss Guard uniforms that had herded me down the upper levels waited while a burly man with a round, oily, unshaven face opened a barrel grill on a six-by-eight stone box with straw. I didn't move fast enough for him; he swung a kick to hurry me along, but it never landed. Roosevelt showed up in time to slam the back of his hand across the fat face.

"You'd treat a royal duke like a common felon?" he barked. "You're not fit to touch the floor he stands on."

Another man grabbed up the fat man's keys, led the way along the narrow passage, opened an oak door on a larger cell with a bed and a loophole window.

"You'll meditate here in peace," Roosevelt told me, "until I have need of you."

I lay on the bed and waited for the pounding in my head to retreat to a bearable level.

. . . and woke up with a voice that wasn't in my head, whispering, "Plantagenet! Be of good cheer! Wait for the signal!"

I lay where I was and waited for more, but there wasn't any more.

"Who's that?" I whispered, but nobody answered. I got up and examined the wall by my head, and the bed itself. It was just a wall, just a bed. I went to the door and listened, pulled myself up and looked out the six-inch slit at a light-well. There were no lines dangling there with files tied to them; no trap-doors opened up in the ceiling. I was locked in a cell, with no way out, and that was that. The voices were probably courtesy of the management, another of Roosevelt's subtle moves to either wear me down or convince me I was crazy. He was doing pretty well on both counts.

I was having a fine dream about a place where flowers as big as cabbages grew on trees beside a still lake. Ironel was there, walking toward me across the water, and the water broke into a sea of glass splinters, and when I tried to reach her, the flowers turned to heads that shouted threats and the branches were arms that grabbed at me, and shook me—

Hands shook me awake; lights shone in my face. Men with neat uniforms and unholstered nerve-guns took me along passages and up stairs to a room where Roosevelt waited, rigged out in purple velvet and ermine and loops of gold cord. A jewel-covered sword as big as a cased garrison flag hung at his side as if it belonged there. He didn't talk, and neither did I. Nobody was interested in the condemned man's last words.

Servants clustered around, fitting me with heavy garments of silk and satin and gold thread. A barber trimmed my hair, and poured perfume on me. Someone fitted red leather shoes to my feet. Roosevelt himself strapped a wide, brocaded baldric around my waist, and the tailor's helper attached a jeweled scabbard to it. The hilt that projected from it was unadorned and battered. It was my old knife, looking out of place in all this magnificence. The armorer complained, offered a shiny sword, but Roosevelt waved him away.

"Your sole possession, eh, Curlon?" he said. "It shares your aura strongly. You'll keep it by you—in your moment of glory."

A procession formed up in the wide corridor outside, with the gun-handlers sticking unobtrusively close to me. Roosevelt was beside me as we walked up a wide staircase into an echoing hall hung with spears and banners and grim-faced paintings. Wigged and spangled and beribboned people filled the room. Beyond an arched opening, I saw a high, stained-glass window above a canopied altar. I knew where I was then.

I was standing in the spot where I had stood with Ironel, with the griffin, Vrodelix, beside us, just before Roosevelt had tried the first time to reach the altar. Now the floor was carpeted in gold rose, and there was an odor of incense in the air, and the woodwork gleamed with the dull shine of wax—but it was the same room—and not the same. Not by a thousand years of history.

We halted, and priests in red robes and dry-faced old men in ribbons and fluffy little wigs went into action, handing ritual objects back and forth, ducking their heads at each other, mumbling incantations. I suppose it was an impressive ceremony, there in the ancient room under the damask-draped, age-blackened beams, but I hardly noticed it. I kept remembering Ironel, leading Roosevelt to her Pretty Place, so that he could destroy it.

The odor of incense was strong; strong enough to burn my eyes. I sniffed harder and realized I was smelling something more than scented smoke; it was the real kind, that comes from burning wood and cloth and paint. There was a faint, brassy haze in the air. Roosevelt was looking back; the head priest interrupted his spiel. The gun-handlers jostled in close to me, looking worried. Roosevelt snapped off some orders, and I heard yells from outside the big room. A wave of heat rolled at us then, and the party broke up. Four guns prodded me toward the archway. If this was a signal, it was a dandy, but there wasn't much I could do about it. The nerve-gun squad cut a path through the notables who were dithering, coughing, half headed one way and half the other. We reached the low steps, and two new guards came in from the flank and there was some fast footwork, and they were close to me, and the crowd was closing around us, fighting for position. An old boy in pink and gold, with his wig askew, thrust his face close to mine.

"Favor the left, y'r Grace," he hissed in my ear. I was still working on that one when I saw the nearest guard put his nerve-gun in his partner's kidney and press the button. Two more men in uniform came from somewhere; I heard a thud behind me, and then we were clear, peeling off from the edge of the main crowd, heading right into the smoke.

"Only a few yards, y'r Grace," the little old man squeaked. A door opened and we were in a cramped stairway, leading down. On the landing, all four guards stripped off their uniform jackets and tossed their caps aside and pulled on workmen's coveralls from a stack behind the door. The old fellow ditched his wig and cape and was in a footman's black livery. They handed me a long gray cloak. The whole operation was like a well-practiced ballet. It didn't take twenty seconds.

On the next floor down, we pushed out into a concourse full of spectators, firemen, a few belted earls and mitred priests, none of them looking at a repair crew in dirty overalls. The old man led the way to a passage where a lone sentry stood, looking anxious. He stepped in front of us, and the old boy raised a finger and drew him around to the right while one of the others expertly sapped him back of the ear. Then we were in the passage and running.

Two startled scrubwomen watched us cross the

kitchen and duck out a door between garbage cans into an unlit alley. The truck parked there started up with a lot of valve click and black kerosene exhaust. I went over the tailgate and the old man scrambled up behind me and pulled the canvas flap down as the truck pulled away. Three minutes later, it slowed, stopped. I heard voices up front, the clatter of a gun, leather boots on cobbles. After a minute, gears clashes and we went on. On the bench opposite, my new friend let out a held breath and grinned from ear to ear.

"Worked like a charm," he said. He cackled and rubbed his hands together. "Like a bloody charm, beggin' y'r Grace's pardon."

The old man's name was Wilibald. "Our friends are waiting for y'r Grace," he said. "True Britons, they are, every man Jock o' 'em. Simple men, y'r Grace, but honest! Not like those treasonous palace blackguards in their silks and jewels!" He gnashed his gums and wagged his head.

"That was a neat play, Wilibald," I said. "How did you manage it?"

"There's true men among the Bluecoats, y'r Grace. The jailor was one. He tried to lodge y'r Grace in a safe cell—one we'd a tunnel to—but his high and mightiness the Baron would ha' none o't. So it took a little longer. But here y'r Grace be now, all the same!" He cackled and rasped his hands together like a cricket's wings.

"You're with the rebel party?"

"Some call us rebels, y'r Grace—but to honest men, we're patriots, pledged to rid these islands o' the French pox!"

"Why did you spring me?"

"Why? Why?" the old man looked astonished. "When word went abroad the Plantagenet was housed in the viceregal tombs, what other course could a loyal Briton follow, y'r Grace? Did y'r Grace deem we'd leave ye there to rot?"

"But I'm not—" I started and left it hanging.

"Not what, y'r Grace?" Wilibald asked. "Not surprised? Of course not. There's ten million Britons in this island, sworn to free the land o' tyranny!"

"Not going to waste any time," I finished. "We'll strike immediately."

The traffic on the road was a mixed bag of horse carts, big solid-tired trucks with open cabs, little droop-snoot cars that looked as if they came in cereal boxes and more than a sprinkling of blue-painted military vehicles. According to Wili, the viceroy was concentrating his forces around the fortified ports, ready to cover the landing of reinforcements if the talk of rebellion crystallized into action. The place we were headed for was the country seat of Sir John Lackland.

"A dark-avised gentleman," Wili said. "But moneyed, and of the ancient stock." He rambled on for the next hour, filling me in on the local situation. The rebels, he swore, were ready to move. And according to Roosevelt, if they moved, they'd win.

"You'll see," Wili told me. "Loyal Britons will rise to a man and flock to y'r Grace's standard!"

After an hour's run, we turned down a side road and swung in between brick pillars, went along a drive that led through tended woods into a cobbled yard fronting a three-story house with flower boxes and leaded windows and half-timbered gables that looked like the real thing. Steps went up to a broad veranda. An old

man in a fancy vest and black pants and house slippers
let us in. His eyes bugged when he saw me.

"'Is Grace must see Sir John at once," Wili said.

"Sir John's been abed this twoday wi' a touch o'
the ague. He's had no callers—"

"He has now," Wili cut him off.

The old fellow dithered, then led the way into a
dark room full of books, and shuffled away.

I looked at the books on the shelves, mostly leather-
bound volumes with titles like *Historic Courts* and
Campaigns Among the Quanecticott. After five minutes
or so the door opened and the old fellow was back,
piping that Sir John would see us now.

The master of the house was in a bedroom on the
top floor, a lean-faced sharp-nosed old aristocrat with
a silky black eyebrow-moustache and a matching fringe
of hair around a high bald dome. He was propped up
in a bed no larger than a skating rink, half buried in
a violet satin pillow with an embroidered monogram
and more lace than a Hollywood bishop. He had a
tan woolen bathrobe with satin lapels wrapped around
him, and a knitted shawl over that, and even so, the
end of his nose looked cold. When he saw me, he
nearly jumped out of bed.

"What—now . . . ?" he stared from me to Wili and
back. "Why did you come here—of all places?"

"Where else would I be more likely to find friends?"
I came back.

"Friends? I'd heard that the viceregent had declared
a pretender heir to the dukedom, but I scarce expected
to see him present himself *here* in that guise."

"How do you know I'm the man—or that I'm an
imposter?"

"Why—why—who else would you be?"

"You mean you're accepting me as genuine? I'm glad, Sir John. Because the time has come for action."

"Action? What action?"

"The liberation of Briton."

"Are you mad? You'd bring destruction down on my house—on all of us! We Plantagenets have always lived on sufferance! The murder of Duke Richard shows us all how precarious our position is—"

"Who killed him?"

"Why—Garrone's men, of course."

"I wonder about that. From the viceroy's point of view, it was a foolish move. It aligned the Britons against him more solidly than Richard ever did alive."

"Conjecture. Idle conjecture," Sir John barked. "You come here, unbidden, preaching treason! What do I know about you? You imagine I'll place our trust in an upstart, a stranger?"

"Hardly that, Sir John," Wili said indignantly. "One glance at him—"

"What do you know of him, fellow? Is any oversized carrot-locked bumpkin who cares to lay claim to the dukedom to be accepted without question?"

"That's hardly fair, Sir John—"

"Enough! The matter will have to wait for resolution until I can summon certain influential men! In the meantime, I'll give you sanctuary. I can do no more." Lackland gave me a look like a dagger in the ribs and yanked at his bellcord. The old footman popped in with a speed that suggested he'd been standing by not far away.

"Show milord to his suite," Lackland got out between lips as stiff as a Hoover collar. "And quarter Master Wilibald below stairs."

I followed my guide along the corridor to a high-ceilinged, airy room with big windows and a sitting room and bath opening from it. The old fellow showed me the soap and towel and then paused at the door and gave me a sly look.

"It did me heart proud to hear y'r honor gi' a bit o' the rough to his Lordship," he cackled. "It's been a weary time since a real fighting duke put foot o' these old boards, beggin' y'r Honor's pardon."

"You listen at keyholes, eh?" But I grinned at him. "Wake me as soon as the clan's gathered. I wouldn't want to miss anything."

"Rely on me, y'r Grace," he said and went out and I pulled off my boots and lay in the dark and slid off into a dream about knights on horseback riding with leveled lances into the fire of massed machine guns.

I came back from somewhere a long way off with a hand shaking my shoulder and a thin old voice saying, "They're here, y'r Grace! Milord Lackland's wi' 'em i' the study this minute—and unless I mistake me, there's mischief afoot!"

"Does Lackland know you're here?"

"Not 'em, y'r Grace."

We went down the stairs and across the hall to a door that was standing ajar. When Wili got close he turned and gave me a quick jerk of the head, cupping his ear.

"...imposter, gentlemen," Lackland was saying. "No true Briton, but a hireling of Garrone, bought with French gold and sent here to betray us all—"

I pushed the door open and walked in. The talk cut off as if a switch had been thrown. There were about a dozen men grouped around a long table with

Lackland seated at the head. They were dressed in a variety of costumes, but all of them featured fur and brocades and a sword slung at the hip. The nearest was a big, wide-shouldered, neckless man with a curly black beard and ferocious eyes. He took a step back when he saw me, looked me up and down, surprised.

"Don't be beguiled by his face and stature!" Lackland spat the words. "He'd seize control of the rebellion, and turn coat, come to terms with Garrone! Can he deny it?" He was pointing at me with a finger that quivered with rage.

I didn't answer immediately. What he was saying was precisely what Roosevelt had proposed. There seemed to be a message for me in that somewhere, but it wouldn't come clear.

"You see?" Lackland crowed. "The treacher dares not deny it!"

The black-bearded man drew his sword with a skin-crawling rasp.

"A shrewd stroke!" he said in a high, rasping voice. "With a Plantagenet puppet to dance on his strings, he'd accomplish what the Louis have dreamed of for seven centuries! The total subjugation of Briton!" More swords were out now, ringing me in.

"Spit him, Tudor!" Lackland screamed.

"Stop!" Wilibald stood in the doorway with fire in his old eye. "Would you murder our Duke in cold blood? In the name of Free Briton, I say he deserves a better hearing at your Lordship's hands than this!"

For an instant, nobody moved—and in the silence I heard a droning sound, far away but coming closer. The others heard it, too. Eyes swiveled to stare at the ceiling as if they could see through it. A man rushed to the window, threw back the long drapes to stare out. Another jumped for a wall switch. Tudor didn't move as the chandelier went dark, leaving just what light filtered in from the hall.

"An aircraft!" a man at the window called. "Coming straight in over us!"

"It was a trick to get us here together!" a lean man in yellow snarled, and drew back his sword for a cut. I saw this from the corner of my eye; it was Tudor I was watching. His jaw had set harder, and the tendons beside his neck tensed and I knew the thrust was coming.

I twisted sideways and leaned back and the point ripped through the ruffles on the front of my shirt; my back-handed swing caught him across the cheek-bone, knocked him backward into the table as the room went pitch dark. The engines sounded as if they were right down the chimney. A piece of bric-a-brac fell from the mantle.

The *to-to! to-to!* marched across off to the right and the engine sound was deafening, and then receding. I heard glass tinkling, but the ceiling didn't fall in. I slid along the wall toward the door and heard feet break for it and a chair went over. Somebody slammed into me and I grabbed him and threw him ahead of me. I found the door and got through it, and could see the big hall faintly by the moonlight coming through the stained glass along the gallery. There was a lot of yelling that was drowned by the bomber's engines. Then a flash lit the room and the wall seemed to jump outward about a foot. When things stopped falling, I was bruised, but still alive. Wilibald was lying a few feet away, covered with dust and brick chips. There was a timber across his legs above the ankle; by the time I got it clear the plane was making its third run. With the old man over my shoulder, I reached the rear hall just as the front of the house blew in. I made it out through the kitchen door, went across grass that was littered with bricks. Blood from a cut on my scalp was running into my eyes. I made it to a line of trees before my legs folded.

The roof was gone from the house and flames were leaping up a hundred feet high and boiling into smoke clouds that glowed orange on their undersides. The shells of the walls that were still standing stood up in black silhouetted against the fire, and the windows were bright orange rectangles cut in the black.

Then there was a sound and I tried to get up and made it as far as my hands and knees, and three men with singed beards and torn finery and bare swords in their hands came out of the darkness to surround me.

One of the men was Tudor; he stepped in close and drew his arm back, and I was bracing myself for the thrust when all three of them turned and looked toward the house. Light flickered from among the trees lining the drive; pieces of bark jumped from the bole of the tree beside me and the man nearest it went over backward and the man beside him spun and fell, and Tudor turned to run, but it was the wrong reflex. I saw the bullets smack into him, throw him six feet onto his face.

There were men on the drive, coming up at a run—men in blue uniforms. I started to crawl and suddenly old Wilibald was there, his thin hair wild, soot on his face. He had been below the line of fire, like me; he was all right.

"Run, Wili!" I yelled. He hesitated for a moment, then turned and disappeared into the woods. Then the soldiers were all around me, grim and helmeted, smoking guns ready. And I waited for what came next.

Chapter Ten

THIS TIME, I GOT to ride up front. The countryside was pretty, but the towns were as deserted as Mexican villages at siesta time. You could feel in the air that a storm was about to break, and the populace had taken cover. If the rebels were as strong as Roosevelt said, it didn't show. The roads were full of military traffic in the blue paint of the French king. I wondered how much my short-lived escape had to do with that. I tried to pump the man beside me, but he didn't answer.

When we rolled into the outskirts of Londres, the town was carrying on some semblance of business as usual. The shops were open, and big canvas-topped buses rumbled along the streets, half full. We passed a big market square, lined with stalls with bright-colored awnings and displays of flowers and vegetables. At one side a raised platform was roped off. Half a dozen downcast-looking men and women in drab gray stood there, under a sign above the platform that said bullman & windrow—chattels. It was a slave market.

We swung into a cobbled courtyard ringed in by high walls. I was hustled inside, along a corridor full of the smell of government offices.

An officer in shirt-sleeves stepped out of a door ahead, swiveled hard when he saw me. He rattled off a question in strange-sounding French that sounded like "Where are you taking him?"

"*A la général, mon major.*"

"*No, c'est la province du demiregent. Laissez les cordes!*"

"*J'ai les ordeurs direct—*"

"*A diable avec vos ordeurs! Fair que je dit, vite!*"

The sergeant in charge of my detail put a hand on his holstered pistol. The major shouted to someone inside the room. Two sharp-looking lads in khaki with holstered side arms appeared behind him. That ended the argument. One of the new men cut the ropes off. Then they formed up a new procession and marched me off in a new direction.

We rode up in an elevator, went along a lushly carpeted hall, into a fancy outer office. A young fellow in a shiny blue uniform with aide's aglets ducked in through the inner door, came back and made an ushering motion to me. I walked through and was looking at Garonne, the French viceroy.

He was a pouch-eyed fellow in his late forties or early fifties, with thick gray hair, a large, rather soft-looking mouth with a quirk at one end registering benign intentions grown weary. He wore Ben Franklin glasses over a pair of sharp black eyes. His clothes were plain, his fingers lean and competent and without rings.

"I regret the discomfort you were forced to undergo,

milord," he said, in straight New Norman without a trace of French accent. His voice was deep as a bullfrog's. "In view of the great importance of time just now, I asked that you be brought directly to me. A discussion between us might yet retrieve the unfortunate situation that now obtains."

"How does Baron General van Roosevelt feel about that?" I asked. It didn't mean anything. I was just probing.

"Some of my lieutenants are overzealous," he said cryptically. "It is a matter I must deal with. However, the business of the moment takes precedence. I am empowered, your Grace, by His Most Christian Majesty, to offer certain emoluments to loyal liegemen who support his efforts to calm the present unrest. Among them, greater internal autonomy for the island, with offices to deserving servants; various tax and import benefits, revised trade regulations, including issuance of import licenses to men of proven character. For yourself, a royal patent as Prince Imperial of the New Normandy provinces, together with the grant of estates and pensions appropriate to your station. And of course, full recognition of your status as inheritor of the ancient honors of your House."

"What do I do to earn all this?" I stalled.

"You will accept appointment, under his Majesty, as emergency peace marshal of New Normandy. You will appear on telescreen and wireless and instruct all loyal New Normans to return to their homes, and exhort all subjects of his Majesty to observe his laws regarding assembly and bearing of arms. In short, only those acts which I feel certain your own good judgment would dictate, once freed from the pressures placed on you by incendiary elements: the exercise of your influence toward the achievement of civil stability and order."

"In other words, just sell out the Britons."

Garrone narrowed his eyes at me. He leaned across the desk. "Don't waste my time. I'm sure you'll find my offer preferable to a miserable death in the interrogation section."

"You wouldn't murder me, Monsieur Garonne," I said, trying to sound as if I believed it. "I'm the people's hero, remember?"

"We can drop all that nonsense between us," Garonne said in a flat tone. "I'm aware of your masquerade. There was no Lady Edwinna, no secret hideaway in Scotland, no long-lost heir of the bastard honors of Plantagenet! Who are you? Where do you come from? Who sent you here?"

"Whoever I am," I said, "you need me all in one piece."

"Nonsense. Modern methods of persuasion don't rely on thumbscrews. In the end you'll babble whatever I choose for you to babble. But if you'll act as I command—now—lives will be saved. His Majesty's offer still stands. Now, again: Who are you? Who sent you?"

"If I'm a fake, what makes you think what I say will help you?"

"Rumors of your presence are abroad here—a Plantagenet of the Old Mark, as Duke Richard was, but without his shabby record of failure and compromise. If word spreads that you've been killed, the countryside will rise—and I'll have no choice but to crush the revolt."

"That might not be easy. The guerrillas—"

"There are no guerrillas, no irregulars, no rebel organization. These are fictions, fabricated by myself." He nodded. "Yes, myself. Consider the facts: New Normandy has been the scene of increasing unrest for decades now, most particularly since the Continental Wars of 1917-1919, with its Prussian dirigible raids, and the less than glorious peace that ended it. The old cries of Saxon unity were revived—idiotic nonsense, of course, based on imaginary blood-ties. I needed a force which would bring the provinces back under tight control. Duke Richard was the perfect foil. By his loose living, he had discredited himself with the islanders, of course—but a rousing call to ancient loyalties served to unite popular sentiment behind him. Then—with all New Normandy pledged to follow him—the final stroke would have been the 'compromise,' granting the hollow honors he craved— and placating the revolutionary spirit with fancied autonomy. His murder destroyed a scheme ten years in the building."

"You murdered him yourself."

"No. It was not I who killed him! He was a valuable tool—and unless you—whoever you are, whatever your original intentions—can be brought to see the wisdom of cooperation—I foresee tragedy!"

"You have proof of this?"

"I have Duke Richard's seal on the secret agreement between us. I have the records of payments to him, of subsidies to him and to various *agents provocateurs* working ostensibly for his underground organization. Of course, they might be counterfeit— how can I demonstrate otherwise? My best evidence is the inherent logic of my version of affairs, as opposed to the romantic nonsense you've been deluded into accepting! Face facts, man! You have the opportunity laid at your feet to spring from obscurity to princely rank overnight. Your best—your *only* interest lies in cooperation!"

"I don't believe you. The rebels can win."

"Nonsense." He pointed to a wall map, showing blue arrows aimed across the channel from Dunkirk to Brest.

"His Majesty's forces are overwhelmingly powerful. The only result of war would be a murderous guerrilla delaying action, profitable to no one."

"Why not give the Britons their independence and save all that?"

Garonne was wagging his head in a weary negative. "Milord, what you propose is, has always been, an economic and political fantasy. These islands, by their very nature, are incapable of pursuing an independent existence. Their size alone would preclude any role other than that of starveling dependent, incapable of self-support, at the mercy of any power which might choose to attempt annexation. A Free Briton, as the fanatics call it, is a pipe dream. No, milord: France will never give up her legitimate interests here. In conscience, she cannot. To discuss such fantasies is a waste of valuable time. You've heard His Majesty's most gracious offer. As we sit here, time is passing— time that takes us closer to the brink of tragedy with each instant. Accept His Majesty's generosity, and in an hour you'll be installed in your own apartments in the town, secure in your position as chief local magistrate of new Normandy, with all the honors and privileges appertaining thereunto; refuse your duty to your sovereign, and your end will be a miserable one! The choice is yours, milord!"

He was staring across the desk at me, waiting. The ormolu clock on the marble mantel behind him ticked loudly in the silence. Things were coming at me too fast; there was something I was missing, or forgetting. I needed time to think.

The door opened; a small, dried-up footman with a little white peruke and ribbons on his knees came into the room. He doddered across to the table beside the big desk, put a tray down on it. There was a squat brown bottle, a pair of long-stemmed glasses, a big white napkin folded into a peak. The old fellow lifted the napkin, and scooped a small, flat automatic pistol from under it. He turned and fired three shots into Garonne's chest from a distance of six feet.

I saw the stiff black brocade of the viceroy's coat jump as the bullets hit, saw splinters of pinkish mahogany fly from the chair back, heard the dull smack of the slugs as they lodged in the plaster. The pistol had made a soft unimportant sound as it fired: a silencer, or maybe compressed gas. Garonne jerked and threw his arms up and flopped forward with his face on the fancy leather-bound blotter. The old man pulled off the peruke and I saw it was Wilibald. He shrugged out of the long-skirted coat, all gold and blue with little pink flowers. He was wearing plain gray under it, not too clean. He grinned a toothless grin and said, "We'd best be off direct, m'lord?" He tucked the gun away and went past me, around the end of the desk where a brilliant scarlet stain was growing, and pulled back the drapes gathered at the end of the

big window. There was a dark opening in the paneled
wall behind them. His flashlight beam showed me
rough brickwork and time-blackened timber, a narrow
passage leading off into darkness.

"This way, y'r Grace. No time to waste!" There was
a sharp note in his voice; an impatient note. I hadn't
moved since the shots were fired.

"What's your hurry, Wili?" I said. "No one's going to
burst in on the viceroy, in conference—except maybe
a trusted servant with his ten o'clock tea."

"How's that? Beggin' y'r Grace' pardon—but that's
a dead man lying there! The penalty for murder is
hanging! If y'r caught here—"

I went to him and instead of going past him into
the passage I caught his wrist.

"What if we're both caught here, Wili? Would that
spoil the scheme?"

"We'd hang!" He tried to jerk free, but I held him.

"They all know I was with him. When he's found
dead, it will be an open-and-shut case, eh, Wili?"

"What matter if it is? Ye'll be far away by then—"

"Who are you working for, Wili? Roosevelt? He
let me escape last time, didn't he? Why? So I could
stir up the populace? Why did he bomb Lackland's
house? But it was a fake raid, wasn't it? Just a flock
of near misses—with the machine guns to clean up
the witnesses, including Lackland."

"It was Lackland called the attack down on the
house!" Wili croaked. "He was a creeping spy and
telltale for the Louis, hoping to see y'r Grace killed—
but he paid for his crimes! Aye, he paid—"

"Don't kid me—he was working for Roosevelt. I
guess he'd outlived his usefulness."

"Shameful times we've fell on," Wili babbled on. "But what was he but a Black Plantagenet, eh? But now it's needful we make our escape. I've a car waiting—"

"Very convenient, you and your cars. It hardly fits in what I've seen of the Organization here. I suppose we'll breeze right through the police lines, just like we did last time, thanks to Roosevelt."

"The Organization—"

"Is a lot of hot air, Wili. Roosevelt sent you here to kill Garonne, and arranged for it to look as though I'd done the job—just as he killed Duke Richard and spread the word Garonne was guilty. Why? The situation was already balanced on a knife-edge. Why did he tell me the rebels had the winning hand? That was another lie. They're evenly matched at best. But he wants them to make their try, wants to see the country cut to pieces in a civil war that won't end until both factions are ruined. Why, again?"

"Y'r daft!" Wili yelped. "Let go, you fool! They'll be here at any instant—"

"Who tipped them this time, you? Better start talking, Wili—and it had better be good—"

I was watching his free hand; it dipped to his pocket and I grabbed it as it came out with the automatic. He was strong, but I was lots stronger.

"I'm going to spoil the play, Wili," I told him. "I'm a little slow, but after awhile even I catch on. Your boss has been dancing me on the strings from the beginning, hasn't he? Every move has been planned: getting me here on my own initiative, the dramatic escape complete with voices coming out of the walls, then letting Garonne's men have me. What's planned for me next? Maybe I'm supposed to get on a horse and lead the peasants into battle, is that it? But I'm breaking the chain, Wili. The moves are too subtle for me, but that doesn't matter. A fancy knot cuts as easy as a simple one—"

His knee came up, almost fast enough. As I took it on the thigh, he put everything he had into twisting the gun around. It wasn't enough. The muzzle was pointing to his own chest when it coughed. He went slack, fell backward into the room. He tried, tried hard to speak, but I couldn't make out the words. Then his eyes went dull and blank. I dragged the body into the passage, felt over the wall until I found the lever that closed the panel behind me.

"Good-bye, Wili," I said. "You were loyal to something, even if it was the wrong thing." I left him there and started off in what I hoped was the right direction.

It was different, picking my way in the dark through the network of hidden passages that I had traced out once before in the shuttle, on half-phase. I made a wrong turning, bumped my head and barked my shins, retraced my steps and tried again. It took me hours— I don't know how many—to find the passage I was looking for: the one that led to Roosevelt's quarters.

I found the lever and eased the panel back and was looking down from over the fireplace into the quiet luxury of the spacious study. It was empty. Roosevelt would be fully occupied elsewhere for a while, working out an explanation of the locked-door murder of the viceroy.

It was a difficult room to search. Every door and drawer was locked, and there were a lot of them. I levered them open one by one, looked at books and papers and boxed records, and drew a blank.

The next room was the Baron's sleeping chamber. I started in the closet, worked my way through two large bureaus and a wardrobe, and in the last drawer, found a flat, paper-wrapped bundle. It was my broken sword. I wondered what it meant to Roosevelt that had made him squirrel it away here, but that was a problem I could solve later—maybe. I buckled it on, and the weight of it felt good at my hip. It wasn't much of a weapon, but it was better than nothing, if they walked in and found me here.

Ten minutes later, in a cubicle almost hidden in a shadowy corner, I found what I was looking for: the silver-mounted reliquary box that Roosevelt had destroyed a world to get.

There was a silver lock on the silver hasp that closed the lid. I hated to destroy such a handsome piece of workmanship, but I put the edge of the sword under it and levered and it shattered. The lid came up; inside, in a bed of yellowed satin, lay a rusted slab of steel, a foot long, three inches wide, beveled on both edges. It was another piece of the broken sword.

I picked it up, felt the same premonitory tingle in my hand that I'd felt that other time, in the underground room beneath the old chateau. Like that time, I brought the scrap of metal to the broken blade, saw the long, blue spark jump between them as they came together—

The world exploded in my face.

I sat astride a great war-horse, in the early morning. I felt the weight of the chain armor on my back, the drag of the new-forged sword at my side. Beside me, Trumpington turned in his saddle to look across at me. He spoke, but I gave him no answer. A strange vision was upon me. Though I was here, a part of me was elsewhere, observing...

My vision widened, and I seemed to see myself riding away from the field of Chaluz, my mind unbloodied. More ghostly images flocked in my mind. I saw the lean face of John my brother, hungry-eyed, silky-bearded, as he knelt before me, pleading for his life. And the sudden look of fear, as I, who had always before been merciful of his treacheries, hardened my heart.

I heard the thunk of the headsman's ax...

Then it seemed I sat in my pavilion on the island of Runnymede, summoned there by my rebellious barons. They stood before me in their arrogance, and presented to me, their sovereign lord, the perfidious writing of their demands. And again, I saw their looks of triumph change to the knowledge of death as my hidden bowmen stepped forth and loosed their clothyard shafts into the false hearts of my forsworn vassals...

Scenes of warfare passed before my eyes. I saw the walls of Paris go down before me, saw the fires that blazed up from the cathedrals of Madris, saw the head of him who once had been a king, impaled on a pike and borne before me. Faces crowded around me, fair women and ambitious men, praising me. There was revelry, and riding behind the baying hounds, and roasted venison before the roaring blaze; and tuns of wine broached, and the passing of days, years of gluttony and lechery and sloth, until the time when my hand no longer sought the sword. Swollen with excess, rotten with disease, I cowered in my palace while my picked retainers parleyed with the invaders at my gates. Parleyed, and sold their kingdom and its king for their own vile lives. But no viler than mine,

when I knelt, weeping, at the feet of the stripling
whose father I had hanged on his own gates, and
swore to him on my sword the eternal servility of
all my house…

I swam back from across a gulf wider than the
Universe and was standing in the room I remembered
from an eon—or a second—before. The sword burned
hot in my hand—no longer an awkward stub, but a
blade four feet long, ending in a blunt, broken tip.
The cross-guard was different: longer, the quillons
curving out above carved knuckle-bows. There were
traces of gold on the grip, and a single jewel glinted
in the pommel. It was the same magic I'd seen before,
all the talk in the world about probability stresses and
the reshaping of reality couldn't make it anything else
for me. I groped after the dream that had filled my
head a moment before: a panorama of faces and sounds
and vain regrets; but it faded, as dreams do, and was
gone. Then my reverie was shattered into small pieces
as the door to the next room slammed open and feet
came across the rug toward the bedroom.

"Milord Baron," a familiar voice called. "An emergency in the Net! The stasis has been broken! The
probability storm will strike within hours!"

His rush had carried him past me where I had
flattened myself to the wall beside the door. He
halted when he saw the room was empty, spun, saw
me, yelled.

"Thanks for the information, Renata," I said, and
laid the flat of the sword against the side of his head
with all the power in my arm. I didn't wait to see if
I had broken his skull. I went across the study and
was back inside my private tunnel before the first of

his men had gotten up his nerve to enter without knocking.

An hour or two of exploring the tunnel system turned up plenty of side-branches, some secret rooms with tables and rotted bedding, a cramped stairway leading down to ground level; but there seemed to be no direct way into the other wing of the palace and the exit behind the rhododendrons. I thought about coming out and trying it in the open, but there were too many sounds of activity beyond the walls to make that seem really attractive. The whole building seemed to be in a state of uproar. That wasn't too hard to understand. With a dead viceroy to handle, and a probability storm coming on, it looked like a busy day.

My break came when I found a shaft with a rusty ladder bolted inside it.

The rungs were too close together, and scaled with rust, and the bore was barely big enough to give me operating space. It seemed to get smaller as I went down. It ended on a damp floor that I recognized as running behind the rank of cells where I'd once been a guest. I started along the two-foot-wide passage, in near pitch-dark. What light there was came from chinks in the mortar between the stones. If night fell while I was still here, the going would be rough.

I followed the passage fifty feet to a dead end. I turned back, and after thirty feet, encountered an intersection that I would have sworn hadn't been there two minutes before. The right-hand branch led to an uncovered pit that I discovered by almost falling in it. The other spiraled down, debouched into a circular room lined with dark openings. I turned my back, and when I looked again, everything had changed. This time I was sure; where the passage I had entered by had been there was a solid wall of stone. I knew now what Roosevelt meant by a probability storm. Subjective reality had turned as insubstantial as a dream.

The next passage I tried ended in a blank wall of wet clay. When I came back into the circular room it was square, and there were only two exits now. One led to a massive iron-bound door, locked and barred. I retraced my steps, but instead of a room I came into a cave with water trickling across its floor and a single dark opening on the far side. I went into it, and it widened and was a carpeted hall, faced with white doors, all locked. When I looked back, there was only a gray tunnel, cut through solid rock.

For a long time, I wandered through dark passages that closed behind me, looking for a way up. And then, in a tunnel so low that I had to duck my head, I heard the clank of chains, not far away.

I listened hard, heard heavy breathing, the rasp of feet on stone, another clank. It wasn't what would ordinarily be considered an inviting sound, but under the circumstances I was willing to take the risk. I pushed ahead ten feet and saw dim light coming through a crack in the wall. It was a loose stone slab, three feet on a side. I put my eye to the crack and looked into a cell with windowless walls, a candle on a table, a straw pallet. An old man stood in the center of the room. He was as tall as I was, wide through the shoulders, with big, gnarled hands, a weather-beaten complexion, pale blue eyes with a hunted look. He was dressed in tattered blue satin knee-pants, a wine and rose brocaded coat with wide fur lapels, a flowered vest, scuffed and worn shoes that had once been red. The chains were on his ankles. He looked around, scanning the walls as if he knew I was there.

"Geoffrey," he said, in a hoarse, old voice that I'd heard before, in a dream, "I feel you near me."

I got a grip on the stone and slid it aside and was looking through a barred opening. The old man turned slowly. His mouth opened and closed.

"Geoffrey," he said. "My boy..." He put out a hand, then drew it back. "But my boy is dead," he told himself. "Forever dead." A tear ran down the leathery cheek. "Who are you, then? His cousin, Henry? Or Edward? Name yourself, then!"

"Curlon is my name. I'm lost. Is there a way out of here?"

He ignored the question. "Who sent you here? The black-hearted rogues who slew Geoffrey?" He caught at the bars, and the sleeve of his coat fell back. There was a welted, two-inch-wide scar all the way around his wrist.

"No one sent me," I said. "I managed it on my own."

He stared at me and nodded. "Aye—you're of the blood—I see it in your face. Are you, too, caught in his traps?"

"It looks that way," I said. "Who are you? Why are you here?"

"Henry Planget is my name. I claim no other honor. But I'll not fall in with his schemes, though all the devils in hell come to haunt me!" He shook his fist at the wall. "Do your damnedest, rascals! But spare the boy!"

"Snap out of it, old man!" I said roughly. "I need your help! Is there a way out of here?"

He didn't answer. I drew the broken sword and

levered at the bars. They were solid, an inch thick, set in barred sockets.

"My help?" His rheumy eyes held on mine. "A Planget never calls for help—and yet . . . and yet, perhaps it would have been better if we had, so long ago . . ."

"Listen to me, Henry. There's a man called Roosevelt—Baron General Pieter van Roosevelt. He's crazy enough to think he can remake the Universe according to a private set of specifications and I'm crazy enough to believe him. I'd like to stop him, if I can. But first, I have to break out of this maze. If you know the way—tell me!"

"The maze?" The old man looked at me vaguely; then as if he were shaking off a weight, he straightened his back; his eyes cleared and vitality came into them.

"The maze of life," he said. "The maze of fate. Yes, we must break out!" He stopped, staring at the broken sword. His hand went out to it, but stopped, not touching it.

"You bear Balingore?" his voice quavered. His eyes met mine, and now fire flashed in them. "A miracle passes before my eyes! For these same eyes saw Balingore broken and cast into the sea! And now . . . he lives again!"

"I'm afraid it's just a broken sword," I said, but he wasn't listening.

"Balingore lives again!" he quavered. "His strength runs in you, lad! I sense it! And still the powers draw at you across the veils of the worlds! I've seen them—yes, he showed me, long ago, when he plied me with fine words and talk of glories vanished. There are more worlds than one, and they call to me—and to you, too! Can you feel them, the voices that cry out of darkness, summoning you? Go! Go to them! Break the ring of fate that forever doomed our house!"

"How do I do that, Henry?"

He clung to the bars and I could see the fight he was having to hold to the glimmer of sanity that had come to him—if that was what it was.

"I must speak quickly, before the veils descend again," he said. His voice was steadier now. "This is the tale that he told me:

"Long ago, a king of our line bore Balingore into battle, and with him built a mighty empire across the world. But in the end, he turned aside from honor. Balingore passed to the hands of another, and for seven centuries, served the cause of evil. But at last the usurper's greed undid him. His wise men built a strange machine in which a man might leave his proper frame of fate and walk in worlds of might-have-been. He sought to use this wonder as a weapon, to spread his black dream of empire—but he failed. And in his failure, he brought down the very skies about him!"

"The machine was called a shuttle," I said. "It used the MC-drive to move across the alternate world-lines. I've heard that the Blight was caused by the drive running out of control."

"Nay—it was no accidental havoc! Van Roosevelt knew what he did when he unleashed its power on the world! And now his spawn seeks again to mold the cosmos to his liking! But this is a task too great for him alone! He needs the might of Angevin beside him. This much he told me when he snatched me from my manor house in the far world of my birth. But I defied him! As you must!"

"Who is he, Henry? What is he?"

"A fallen angel; a man so evil that the world cannot contain his malice! Even now it melts and flows—as I have seen it melt and flow before! Run, lad! Flee this pit of horrors before you find yourself forever lost...as I was lost, so long ago..."

"You were telling me about the sword," I reminded him.

"Many things have I learned, strange beyond belief," Henry mumbled. "And yet you must believe them!" The fire came back into his tone. "There are many worlds, many lines of fate that grow across the walls of time like so many vines of ivy! Once there were many Balingores, each holding some fraction of the power that was once welded into one. But in the disaster that overtook the world, all were lost, save two: One, in the hands of the devil, Roosevelt. And another, which hung on the high wall of my house, in a far land I shall never see again!" Knuckles whitened as he gripped the bars. "Once, this was my house, these chambers my cellars. Then *he* came. His talk beguiled me, in my ignorance. At his behest, I took down the ancient blade of my ancestors, and would have put it in his hand. But at his touch, it shattered.

"He raged, blamed me for the miracle. But I took new pride from the sign given me. I defied him, then! Too late, I defied him! He brought me here, told me his tale—and his lies. He swore I was the key to his greatness, that together we would rebuild his world— that other world, so like mine, and yet so different. I would not listen. I saw the sword he bore—the other Balingore, so long ago dishonored—but I sensed that the true power flowed not in it. He needed me, in truth—but what he did not know was that I had saved one fragment of the true sword. I hid it away from him, and when he scattered the shards in the salt sea, there to corrode to nothing, one piece was left behind..."

"There were more than two Balingores," I said. "I have part of one. And I found another part, in a ruined city in the Blight—"

"Listen to me!" Henry's voice shook. "I feel the red darkness returning! Time is short! Go to my world, Curlon! Find my house of the high stone walls and the red towers; and there, in the chapel dedicated to St. Richard, search beneath the altar-stone. But beware the False Balingore! Now go—before the world melts away into a tortured dream!"

"I'll try, Henry," I said. "But I can't leave you here. I'll try to find something—some way to release you." I went back along the passage, feeling the walls, with the vague idea I might find a ring of keys hanging there; but there was nothing.

When I came back to the barred window, the candle still burned on the table; but the room was empty. Only the rusted shackles lay on the floor among scattered bones.

For a long time, I stood in the dark, watching the candle burn down and gutter out. Then I went on. I don't know how many hours later it was that I came into a room where light filtered down from a heavy oak door, half-smashed from its hinges. I went up stone steps into late afternoon light in a kitchen that looked as though it had been fought through. There was shooting going on outside, not far away.

The door opened into a bricked alley under high

walls. A dead man in a blue uniform lay on his back a few feet from it. I picked up his gun and moved up to cross the street without any unnecessary noise. In the distance, big guns rumbled and boomed, and flashes showed against the colors of early dusk. I knew where I was now. I had covered several city blocks, underground. The viceregal palace was in the next square, a hundred yards away.

A sudden burst of gunfire nearby made me flatten myself against the wall. I heard running feet, and three blue-uniformed Imperial guards dashed out of a doorway, heading across the street. There was more gunfire, from up high, and one of them fell. A shell shrieked, and a section of street blew up and blanketed the scene with dust. When it cleared, a dead civilian with a bandolier across his shoulders lay near the dead soldier. The revolution was in full swing, but somehow I had a feeling that in spite of that, things hadn't turned out the way Roosevelt had wanted them. The thought warmed me, and turned my mind to what I had to do next.

I left my cubbyhole, made it across the street, and into a narrow street that led to the delivery yard at the back of the palace. I went along it with the machine pistol ready; I didn't want to be gunned down, by either side. Near the gate, I heard feet coming up behind me. I threw the gun away and went over the wall and was in the viceregal gardens, fifty feet from the spot where I had left the shuttle on half-phase.

The shadowy trees and bushes looked different somehow; wild flowers of a kind I'd never seen before sprouted in the tended beds. Somewhere a nightingale was singing his heart out, ignoring the gunfire.

I was still wearing the ring Bayard had given me, the one with the miniaturized shuttle recall signaler set inside the synthetic ruby. I had left the shuttle in another world-line, with Imperial suppressor beams holding it pinned down like a butterfly on a board but this wasn't the time to pause and consider things like that. If the signaler worked, I was on the board for another round; if not, the game was finished now. I pressed the stone.

The bird sang. A breeze stirred the long grass. At the far side of the garden, a man stepped into view, capless, dressed in sweat-stained blues. He stopped when he saw me, shouted, and started for me at a run. He was halfway there when the shuttle shimmered and phased into solidity with a rush of displaced air. I stepped inside and flipped the half-phase switch. On the screens, the twilit garden faded to eerie blue. The man who had been running skidded to a stop, raised his gun and fired a full clip into the spot the shuttle occupied. The gun made a remote, flat sound. Then the man threw the gun down and laughed a wild laugh. He turned and wandered away. I could sympathize with him. I knew how he felt. The world had come apart around his ears, and there was no place to turn.

The telltale light on the panel was blinking on, off, on. It was the tracer that had been locked to Roosevelt's shuttle. It still was—and the target was moving.

Again, I didn't stop to calculate the odds. I threw in the drive lever and set off in pursuit.

I had seen it before, but it was a thing that could never lose its fascination. All around me, as the hours passed, the world changed and flowed. I knew now that what I was seeing was a simultaneous sequence of A-lines, each differing only slightly from the next, like the frames of a movie film. Nothing really moved; no normal time elapsed during a transdimensional crossing. But the eerie pseudo-activity of E-entropy went on; plants jostled each other for favorable positions; vines attacked trees; weeds swelled and crowded out other weeds. The ivy-covered walls of the palace shrank, broadened, became a fortress ringed with a moat. The walks shifted position, slid away, became footpaths. The trees moved back, gliding slowly through the turf that parted like water, until the shuttle was perched in an open field edged by an ancient forest. The fort had become a stone manor house, with mansard roofs and chimneys poking up into the unchanging sky; the chimneys drew together and merged, became towers of brick with castellated tops.

Suddenly, the hum of the drive whined down-scale and ceased. The scene stabilized. I was looking across a tilled field of grain toward the lone house occupying the top of a low rise among tall trees.

A high stone house with brick towers. Bricks would be red in normal light. Out of all the possible destinations in all the Universes, Roosevelt had led me to the house of Henry Planget.

I waited until full dark before I switched the shuttle back to full-phase and stepped out, then shifted it back. The soft *boom!* of imploding air had a lonely sound of finality.

For the past hour, a steady stream of men had come and gone around the big house. Couriers had galloped up on horseback, and others had ridden away down the unpaved road with full saddlebags slapping at their mounts' flanks. Lights burned in all the ground-floor windows. Sentries paced in front of the main door. Everything about the place spelled military headquarters. Somewhere inside, Roosevelt would be cooking up the last ingredients of his grand scheme for the world.

I skirted the house, came up in the shelter of a row of poplars until I could see through the nearest set of casement windows. A group of men in ornate green uniforms clustered around a table on which a map was spread, under a gas-burning chandelier. Roosevelt wasn't among them. It was the same in the next room, except that the men wore plain khaki and were working over what might have been manning documents or supply lists. I worked my way halfway around the house, using the hedges for concealment, before I found my man. He was sitting alone at a table, writing rapidly with a ball-point pen—a curious anomaly in the old-fashioned setting. He was smiling a little as he wrote. There was a small cut on his forehead. He was still wearing the fancy outfit he had donned for the ceremony back in New Normandy, now stained and powder-burned. It seemed the general had seen some close action before he had left the scene of battle.

He finished writing and left the room. I closed in and checked the windows. It was a mild evening, and they stood open half an inch. Ten seconds later, I was inside.

I listened at the door, heard nothing, opened it, and took a look along the papered hallway glowing softly in the light of a single gas jet. A sentry stood at the far end, all shiny leather and brass, with a musket over his shoulder. I tried to pretend I was a shadow moving along the hall, sliding into the recess of a stairwell. He never turned his head.

There was red carpeting on the stairs, a polished mahogany rail. On the landing, I gave a listen, then went on up into a dark corridor, door-lined. I was standing there, waiting for instinct to whisper instructions in my ear, when I felt a touch at the hip. I came around fast, and my hand went to the sword-hilt before I understood. The touch had been the sword, tugging gently at my side. I drew it, following the direction of the pull.

At the end of the corridor, three steps led up to double doors of carved oak. I pushed through them, stood in moonlight shining through a rose window. It wasn't a room that I had ever seen before—and yet it was. I knew, without knowing how I knew, that it was the analog of the chapel from which Roosevelt had stolen the reliquary box. This room was smaller, simpler, almost unadorned. But somehow, in the abstruse geography of the Net of alternate reality, it occupied the same position. The altar under the high window consisted of two heavy oak uprights with a flat slab of rough stone across them, but somehow, it was the same altar. In the dim light, it looked like a sacrificial block. I started forward and the door made a soft sound behind me. I turned, and Roosevelt stood there. His black eyes seemed to blaze across the darkness at me, as armed men spread out behind him.

"You see, Plantagenet?" he said softly. "Struggle as you will, your fate must deliver you into my hands."

"I misjudged you when we met," Roosevelt said. "And again, in New Normandy. You should have seized on the chance to escape, filled with the zeal to set a nation free. The countryside would have risen at your call; you'd have ridden into glory with your followers at your back and the bright sun overhead. Why didn't you?"

"You're a clever man, Roosevelt," I said. "But not clever enough to play God. Men aren't cardboard cutouts for you to arrange to suit yourself."

"Men are tools," Roosevelt said flatly. "As for you— you're a tool that turns in the hand, and your edges are surpassingly sharp." He shook his head. "You're supposed to be a man of emotion and action, Plantagenet, not thought!"

"Stop second-guessing me, Roosevelt. Your scheme's blown up in your face. You've failed—the way your father failed with Henry Planget." It was a shot in the dark, just something to say. For a moment, he looked startled. Then his teeth flashed in a smile.

"It was my grandfather," he said. "I wonder how you learned of that? But it doesn't matter now, does it? You've come here, to the one place you had to come to—and found me waiting and ready."

"Not so ready. I could have shot you while you were writing at your desk."

"I fail to see the weapon." He was still smiling an almost gentle smile. "No, Plantagenet, it's not your destiny to shoot me in the back. We'll have our meeting face to face—and the fateful time is now." He drew the heavy longsword slung at his side. The light winked on the jewels that crusted the pommel and grip and *pas-d'âne*. The men behind him stood silent, drawn guns in their hands.

"You like to talk about fate, Roosevelt," I said. "It's

a lot of hot air. A man determines his own fate." I was watching the long blade, ready to ward off a blow with the broken weapon in my hand. Roosevelt looked at it and laughed, a low chuckle.

"Like your blade, Plantagenet, you're incomplete! You know a little—though even that little surprises me—but not enough. Don't you recognize the weapon you face?"

"It's a fancy piece of iron," I said. "But a weapon is as good as the man behind it."

"Look on Balingore!" Roosevelt held the sword out so that the blade caught the light. It was a slab of edged and polished steel, six feet long, as wide as my hand, and Roosevelt's brawny arm held it as though it were a stick of wood. "It was forged for your once-great ancestor, Richard of the lion-heart. It served him well—but he was a greedy man. He went too far, grew fat on gold and wine. Richard Bombast, they called him in the end. He lay drunk in his chamber while the French attacked the walls of London and his people opened the gates to them. He bought his life with this. He handed it, hilt-first, to the Dutch mercenary who led the forces of Louis Augustus, and swore the submission of himself and his house, to the end of time!"

"Fairy tales," I said.

"But a fairy tale you believe in." Roosevelt tilted the sword, made light wink in my eyes. "I know why you're here, Plantagenet."

"Do you?"

He nodded somberly. "Somehow—and later you'll tell me how—you learned that Balingore was the key object through which the lines of power run. You imagined you could steal it, and win back all that you lost, so long ago." He shook his head. "But the weapon is mine, now! Its touch would shrivel your hand. All the probability energies built up in seven hundred years of history flow through this steel, and every erg of that titanic charge denies your claim. I offer you your last chance for life and its riches. Plantagenet! Submit to me now, and you'll stand first below the throne in the new order. Refuse, and you'll die in an agony beyond your comprehension!"

"Dead is dead," I said. "The method doesn't matter much. Why don't you go ahead, do it now? You've got the weapon in your hand."

"I should have killed you," he said between his teeth. "I should have killed you long ago!"

"You kept me alive for a reason," I said raggedly. "But it wasn't your reason, Roosevelt. All along, you've thought you were in charge, but you weren't. Maybe fate isn't as easy to twist as you thought it was—"

One of the men behind Roosevelt gave a muffled yell; a rat as big as a tomcat scuttled out between his feet. Roosevelt cut at it with the sword—and I whirled and sprinted for the altar.

I expected gunfire to racket, a bullet in the spine, a wash of agony from a nerve-gun; but Roosevelt shouted an order to his men to hold their fire. I jumped up on the low platform, gripped the altar-stone, and heaved at it. I might as well have tried to lift the columns of the Parthenon. Roosevelt was coming toward me at a run. I jammed the broken sword in under the rock, felt it clash on metal—

The Universe turned to white fire that fountained round me, then dwindled away to misty gray...

"My lord, will you attack?" Trumpington's voice came from beside. I looked up at the sun, burning through the mist. I thought of England's green fields, and the sunny vineyards of Aquitaine, of the empire I might yet win. I looked across toward the place where the enemy waited, where I knew death waited with a message for me.

"I will attack," I said.

"My lord," Trumpington's voice was troubled. "Is all well with you?"

"As well as can be with mortal man," I said, and spurred forward toward the high gray walls of Chaluz.

The chapel of St. Richard swam back into solidity. Roosevelt was running toward me; behind him, his men were spreading out; one brought his gun up and there was a vivid flash and I felt a smashing blow in my shoulder that spun me back and down...

Roosevelt was standing over me, the bared sword in his hand.

"You can't die yet, Plantagenet," he said in a voice that seemed to ring and echo like a trumpet. "Get on your feet!"

I found my hands and knees, dragged them under me. My body was one pulsating agony...like the other time, when Renata had shot me with the nerve-gun. Remembering Renata helped. I stood.

"You're a strong man and a proud one," Roosevelt said; his voice swelled and faded. My hand burned and tingled. I remembered the sword, blinked the haze away, saw it still projecting from under the altar-stone where I had jammed it just before somebody shot me. I wished I could get my hands on it.

"You've run a long way, Plantagenet," Roosevelt

was saying. "I think you knew how it would end, but still you fought. I admire you for that—and soon I'll let you rest. But first—make your submission to me!"

"You're still afraid..." I got the words out. "You can't swing it...on your own."

"Listen to me," Roosevelt said. "The storm is all around us; it will reach us here, soon. You've seen it, seen what the Blight is! Unless we resolve the probability flaw now, it will engulf this world-line along with all the rest! You're holding the fault-line open with your stubbornness! In the name of the future of humanity, give up your false pride!"

"There's another solution," I said. "You can submit to me."

"Not though the pit should open to swallow me alive," Roosevelt said, and brought the sword up, poised—

I used the last ounce of strength in my legs to lunge for his wrist, caught it, held him. I reached past him, toward the scarred hilt of my weapon. His hand closed on my wrist. We stood there, locked together, his black eyes inches from mine.

"Stand back!" Roosevelt shouted as his men came close. "I'll break him with my own hands!"

My fingers were six inches from the hilt of the sword. I could feel a current, not a physical pull, but a force as intangible as hate or love flowing from my hand to it.

"Strive, Plantagenet," Roosevelt hissed in my ear, and threw his weight against me. My hand was forced back, away from the sword...

"Balingore!" I shouted.

The sword moved, leaped across the intervening space to my hand.

There was a sensation as though fire poured through my arm, not burning, but scouring away the fatigue. I threw Roosevelt back, and swung six feet of scarred and rusted steel in my two hands. He backed away, his eyes fixed on the old sword, nicked and blunted, but complete now. An expression passed across his face like a man who's looked into the furnace doors of Hell. Then his eyes met mine.

"Again, I underestimated you," he said. "Now I begin to understand who you really are, Plantagenet, *what* you are. But it's far too late to turn back. We meet as we were doomed to meet, face to face, your destiny against mine!" He lunged, and the False Balingore leaped toward me, and the True Balingore flashed out to meet it. The two blades came together with a ring like a struck anvil and the sound filled the world...

...I saw the shaft leap toward me out of the dust, felt the hammer blow in my shoulder that almost struck me from the saddle.

"Sire—you're hit!" Trumpington shouted, and reined closer to me in the press of battle. For an instant weakness swept over me, but I kept my seat, spurred forward.

"My lord—you must retire and let me tend your wounds!" Trumpington's voice followed me; but I did not heed him. He galloped abreast, seeking to interpose himself between me and the enemy.

"Sire—turn back!" he shouted. "Even a king can die!"

For a moment we faced each other among the plunging mounts and struggling men.

"More than other men, a king knows how to die," I said. "And when, as well." Then the charge of the enemy host separated us, and I saw him no more...

I saw the change come into Roosevelt's eyes, locked on mine as we strained together, chest to chest. He staggered back, staring unbelievingly at his empty hands. Under my eyes, his face withered, his cheeks collapsed, his silks and brocades turned to gray rags that dropped away to expose gaunt ribs, the yellow skin of age. He fell, and his toothless mouth mumbled words, and his hands, like the claws of a bird, scrabbled for a moment at the stone floor. Then there were only bones that dwindled to dust.

The sword burned in my hands. I looked at it and saw how the light shone along the flawless length of the perfect blade, how the jeweled hilt glittered. I sheathed it and walked down the length of the empty chapel and out into the sunlight.

CHAPTER ELEVEN

COLONEL BAYARD WAS WAITING for me in the Imperial Shuttle Garages when I rode the homing beacon back. I spent a week in a nice bed under the care of as pretty a nurse as ever raised a temperature. Bayard spent a lot of time with me, filling in the details.

"We've pieced together most of the story," he told me. "Seventy years ago, when the Blight wiped out most of our quantum of alternate world-lines, one man escaped from the general destruction. He was a high official in the government of the key world-line of the Blighted area. He'd been instrumental in the misguided shuttle experimentation that led to the disaster. He managed to coax a crude experimental machine across the Net to the Zero-zero line—one of the very few with a stable enough probability framework to survive the disaster.

"It wasn't a world to his liking. At home, he'd been a power behind the throne of Orange that ruled half the planet. Here he was a nobody—though not without ability. In time, he rose to a top position in the Imperial Trans-Net Liaison Service. But his heart was never in his work. His real ambition was to reestablish the old empire. In his lifetime, he didn't succeed, but he passed the charge on to his son and to his grandson after that.

"Obviously, it was impossible for one man to overthrow the Imperial government single-handed. The van Roosevelts needed another line, outside the Blight, in which to carry out their plan. They picked New Normandy. It was at an adequate technical level, was politically unstable and ripe for a strong hand—and it had a suitable historical base on which to build. Roosevelt's intention was to foment rebellion, play the French against the Britons, and when both sides were exhausted and discredited, step in with a small but highly organized band of irregulars and take over.

"He soon learned the undertaking wasn't as easy as he had supposed. The Duke of Londres was a powerful key figure, not easy to manipulate. He killed him—and discovered that by his interference from outside the line, he'd created a massive probability imbalance with the results you saw here, and at home. He had to restore stability. That meant stamping out the power of the Plantagenets, once and for all, because as long as one of them was alive, anywhere, the probability forces would concentrate in him, force him into the theater of events, and create a probability subnucleus around him. Roosevelt couldn't have that: he needed all the probability energy he could command to make his chosen line stable enough to stand against the Blight.

"Just killing off the Plantagenets wouldn't do. He needed their strength, their *mana*, added to his. That was where you came in. He used some very special instruments that his grandfather had brought with him in his original shuttle from the Orange line to trace the affinities across the Net—and found you. I know you're just a fisherman, you know nothing about the Plantagenets. But the probability lines were concentrated around you. He intended to use you as a figurehead to restore the stability of the New Normandy line, let you destroy your power in a hopeless war, then offer you escape. The price would be your acknowledgement of his as master.

"He made his first mistake when he secretly arrested the Chief of Intelligence, Baron von Richthofen. Manfred has friends; we weren't content with Roosevelt's story of a sudden stroke. Either he was too soft-hearted, or he was afraid to break too many important life-lines in the Imperium. He should have killed him, and me, too. But he didn't.

"They broke me out of the cell I was in a few hours after he left with you on his mission into the Blight. We tried to follow, but the storm blew up, and we barely made it back. When Roosevelt didn't return, we started searching. Our instruments pinpointed him in New Normandy. When I arrived, it was all over—as you know. We haven't found a trace of Roosevelt. I suppose he was killed in the fighting. You're lucky to be alive yourself."

There were a few holes in Bayard's version of what had happened, but that was all right. It covered the main points; it seemed to satisfy everybody. With Roosevelt's death, the storm had blown itself out. There were no more toadstools sprouting in the archives. And Imperial umpires were rapidly pacifying New Normandy under a free parliament.

But there was still something bothering Bayard. When I left the hospital, he showed me the city, took me to restaurants and concerts, fixed me up with a nice little apartment for as long as I wanted it. He didn't mention taking me back home, and neither did I. It was as though we were both waiting for something impending hanging over everything.

We were sitting at a table at a terrace restaurant in Uppsala when I asked him about it. At first he tried to pass it off lightly, but I caught his eyes and held them.

"You'll have to tell me sooner or later," I said. "It concerns me, doesn't it?"

He nodded. "There's still an imbalance in the Net. It's unimportant now, but in time it will grow until it threatens the stability of the Imperium—and of B-I Three, and New Normandy; of every viable line in the quantum. The Blight is a cancer that can never be contained permanently. There's an incompleteness there, and like an electric circuit, it must complete itself."

"Go on."

"Our instruments indicate that the aborted lines center on you, and in the sword Balingore."

I nodded. "I'm not a part of the line, is that it? You'll have to take me back to Key West, then, and let me get on with my fishing."

"It's not as simple as that. Seven hundred years ago a key figure in the ancestral line entered into a course of action that ended by creating the holocaust. Stability will never be attained until the probability lines that were scattered then are led back to their source."

That was all he said, but I understood what he was trying to tell me.

"Then I have to go back," I said. "Into the Blight."

"It's your decision," he said. "The Imperium won't try to force you."

I stood up. The sunset colors had never looked lovelier, the distant music more appealing.

"Let's go," I said.

The technicians who checked us into the shuttle worked silently and efficiently. They shook hands all around and we strapped in, Bayard and I.

"Our target is the former master-line of the quantum," Bayard said. I didn't tell him I'd been there before. The shapes and colors of the Blight flowed around us, but for once I didn't notice.

"What will happen afterward?" I asked.

"Our hope is when the Blight energies are canceled, the Blight itself will dissipate instantly. The ruined worlds will no longer exist in the Net."

We didn't talk any more after that. It seemed like only minutes before we clocked down and the hum of the drive died.

"We've arrived," Bayard said. He cycled the lock open and I looked out into shifting fog. It shifted and blew away and the jungle and the ruins were gone, and gleaming towers rose up into sunlight, above green lawns and the play of light in fountains. Far away, a woman was singing.

"I wish there was something I could say," Bayard said. "But there isn't. Good-bye, Mr. Curlon."

I stepped down onto the ground, and the door closed behind me. I waited until the shuttle had vanished in a shimmer of light. Then I walked forward along a flower-bordered path toward the sound of Ironel's voice.

Epilogue

Baron von Richthofen, Chief of Imperial Intelligence, looked at Bayard across the polished expanse of desk.

"Your mission was successful, Brion," he said quietly. "At the instant the subject entered the Blighted line, the stress indicators dropped to zero readings across the board. The peril to the Net is ended."

"I wonder," Bayard said, "what he felt, in those last seconds?"

"Nothing. Nothing at all. In one silent instant of readjustment, the continuum closed in to seal the scar. The probability equation is satisfied." Richthofen paused a moment. "Why? Did you see something there?"

"Nothing," Bayard said. "Just fog, as dense as concrete, silent as death."

"He was a brave man, Brion. He fulfilled his destiny."

Bayard nodded, frowning.

"Brion, is there something else—something that troubles you?"

"We've always held the theory that history is immutable," Bayard said. "Perhaps I'm just deluding myself. But I seem to remember a story of King Richard's massacre of the barons at Runnymede. I checked the references to make sure, but I was wrong, of course."

Richthofen looked thoughtful. "The idea has a certain feel of familiarity . . . but that's illusory, of course," he added. "It was King John who met with the barons—and signed their Magna Charta."

"Where did I get the idea that John was executed by Richard in 1201?"

Richthofen started to nod, then checked himself. "For a moment—but no, I recall now. Richard was no longer living then. He was killed by a cross-bow bolt in a minor skirmish at a place called Chaluz, in 1199." He looked thoughtful. "Curious . . . there was no need for him to have taken part in the engagement at all—and after he was wounded, he refused all medical aid. It was almost as though he sought death in battle."

"It was all so clear," Bayard said. "How he lived to a ripe old age—an overripe old age—lost his crown, died in disgrace. I'd swear I read it as a kid. But none of that's in the books. It never happened."

"No," Richthofen said. "It never happened. If it had, the worlds we know would never have existed."

"Still—it's strange."

"Every phenomenon in the space-time probability continuum is strange, Brion—one no more than another."

"I suppose it was just a dream," Bayard said. "A vivid dream."

"Life itself is a dream, they say," Richthofen sat

up, suddenly brisk. "But this is the dream we're in, Brion. And we have work waiting for us."

Bayard returned his smile.

"You're right," he said. "One dream is enough for any man."

AFTERWORD

The next volume of Baen Books' reissue of the writings of Keith Laumer is entitled *Earthblood & Other Stories*. The centerpiece of the volume is one of Laumer's very few collaborations, the novel *Earthblood*, which he co-authored with Rosel George Brown.

Also included will be the three other stories Laumer wrote which featured the Niss aliens who appear in *Earthblood*. Or, I should say, the Niss. As a rule, Laumer was never very concerned with matters of continuity from one story to the next, and the Niss who appear in *Earthblood* are different in many respects from the ones who appear in the other stories. Nonetheless, those three stories are very good in their own right and deserve to be reissued. They are:

> "The Long Remembered Thunder"
> "The Other Sky"
> "The Soul Buyer"

I'm also taking the opportunity—very dear to my heart—to reissue half a dozen of Rosel George Brown's stories. Hopefully, that will remind a science fiction audience that has almost completely forgotten her what a superb writer she was.

Brown is one of the tragedies of science fiction. She emerged as a writer in the late 1950s, and by 1962 was well on her way to becoming established as one of SF's leading female authors—of which there were precious few, at the time. Her stories were published in most of the premier SF magazines of the day: *The Magazine of Fantasy & Science Fiction, Galaxy, If, Fantastic*.

She then wrote *Earthblood* with Keith Laumer, which was serialized in *If* magazine and published as a novel in 1966. The long gap between her stories and the novel was due to her fight against cancer, which she'd contracted sometime early in the '60s. Her solo novel *Sybil Sue Blue* also came out in 1966. The sequel, *The Waters of Centaurus*, was published in 1970.

By then, she had been gone for three years. She died in 1967, finally succumbing to the cancer. She was forty-one years old. I can't prove it, of course, but I am quite certain that had she lived a normal lifespan she would be well-known today as one of science fiction's major women writers.

I specify her gender, because hers was a distinctly female voice, and a rather unusual one. She was a housewife, and her stories usually reflected that viewpoint—armed with a ferociously intelligent wit. There is no voice in science fiction quite like Rosel George Brown's. The best way I can describe it is as if Alice Kramden from the classic TV comedy *The Honeymooners* had devoted her spare time to writing science fiction, while her husband Ralph was off driving a bus.

From the more than twenty short stories she wrote, I selected what I thought were the half dozen best, and they are also included in the volume. For those (few, alas) already familiar with her work, they are:

"Fruiting Body"
"Save Your Confederate Money, Boys"
"Flower Arrangement"
"Visiting Professor"
"Car Pool"
"And a Tooth"

Finally, I need to take the opportunity here to thank two people who were very helpful in sorting out the Swedish details of Laumer's novels contained in this volume: Karl-Johan Noren and Ahrvid Engholm.

—Eric Flint
November 2004

Mission of Honor hc • 978-1-4391-3361-3 • $27.00

pb • 978-1-4391-3451-1 • $7.99

The unstoppable juggernaut of the mighty Solarian League is on a collision course with Manticore, and billions of casualties may be just over the horizon. But Manticore's enemies may not have thought of everything—if everything Honor Harrington loves is going down to destruction, it won't be going alone.

A Rising Thunder hc • 978-1-4516-3806-6 • $26.00

The survival of Manticore is at stake as Honor must battle not only the powerful Solarian League, but also the secret puppetmasters who plan to pick up all the pieces after galactic civilization is shattered..

HONORVERSE VOLUMES:

Crown of Slaves (with Eric Flint) pb • 0-7434-9899-2 • $7.99

Torch of Freedom (with Eric Flint) hc • 1-4391-3305-0 • $26.00

pb • 978-1-4391-3408-5 • $8.99

Sent on a mission to keep Erewhon from breaking with Manticore, the Star Kingdom's most able agent and the Queen's niece may not even be able to escape with their lives....

The Shadow of Saganami hc • 0-7434-8852-0 • $26.00

pb • 1-4165-0929-1 • $7.99

Storm from the Shadows hc • 1-4165-9147-8 • $27.00

pb • 1-4391-3354-9 • $8.99

A new generation of officers, trained by Honor Harrington, are ready to hit the front lines as war erupts again.

A Beautiful Friendship hc • 978-1-4516-3747-2 • $18.99

"A stellar introduction to a new YA science-fiction series."
—*Booklist* starred review

OTHER NOVELS:

The Excalibur Alternative   hc • 0-671-31860-8 • $21.00
pb • 0-7434-3584-2 • $7.99

An English knight and an alien dragon join forces to overthrow the alien slavers who captured them. Set in the world of David Drake's *Ranks of Bronze*.

In Fury Born   pb • 1-4165-2131-3 • $7.99

A greatly expanded new version of *Path of the Fury*, with almost twice the original wordage.

1633 with Eric Flint   hc • 0-7434-3542-7 • $26.00
pb • 0-7434-7155-5 • $7.99

1634: The Baltic War with Eric Flint   pb • 1-4165-5588-9 • $7.99

American freedom and justice versus the tyrannies of the 17th century. Set in Flint's *1632* universe.

THE STARFIRE SERIES
WITH STEVE WHITE:

The Stars at War I   hc • 0-7434-8841-5 • $25.00

Rewritten *Insurrection* and *In Death Ground* in one massive volume.

The Stars at War II   hc • 0-7434-9912-3 • $27.00

The Shiva Option and *Crusade* in one massive volume.

PRINCE ROGER NOVELS
WITH JOHN RINGO:

March Upcountry   pb • 0-7434-3538-9 • $7.99

March to the Sea   pb • 0-7434-3580-X • $7.99

March to the Stars   pb • 0-7434-8818-0 • $7.99

We Few   pb • 1-4165-2084-8 • $7.99

"This is as good as military sf gets." —*Booklist*